THE JOSHUA FACTOR

THE

JOSHUA

FACTOR

A NOVEL BY

DONALD D. CLAYTON

★

TexasMonthlyPress

Texas Monthly Press, Inc.
P.O. Box 1569
Austin, Texas 78767

A B C D E F G H

Library of Congress Cataloging-in-Publication Data

Clayton, Donald D.
  The Joshua factor.

  I. Title.
PS3553.L3874J6 1986   813'.54   86-5966
ISBN 0-87719-046-1

Preface

I call this story a "scientific novel" because its plot is based on two of the leading scientific mysteries of our time. As a scientist I have worked on those problems, which I try to reconstruct accurately in the novel. The other scientific issues of the plot are also represented with as much fidelity as seems appropriate for a novel.

There is no correspondence between the characters in this story and actual scientists, although some people may feel they see resemblances. There are a few allusions in the names. The name Fred Cowan is a composite of those of the codiscoverers of the neutrino, Fred Reines and Eugene Cowan, for example, but the name Zweig was chosen more as a Jewish name (also the German word for "branch") than for the Caltech theoretical physicist, George Zweig, who invented quarks.

Some people may see here a pro-Israel story; others may see an anti-Israel story. It is neither. It's just a fantasy offered with an intentional mixture of themes. It is a parable of mankind.

Because the plot does rely heavily on current scientific puzzles, it seems appropriate to acknowledge my appreciation of those scientists whose careers have unwittingly led to key ideas presented in this story. Thanks to William A. Fowler for his lifelong measurements of nuclear reactions in the sun; to John N. Bahcall for his many detailed calculations of the expected emission of neutrinos from the sun; to Raymond Davis, Jr., for his heroic attempt to detect neutrinos from the sun with his chlorine-neutrino-absorber experiment in the Homestake Mine; to Stephen Hawking for his many brilliant papers on black holes; to George Herbig for his persistent study of eruptive phenomena in young stars; to Fred Hoyle for combining modern science with the writing of fiction; to NASA for its thrilling exploration of the solar system.

I am especially grateful to Nancy McBride for her advice on many aspects of the writing.

One

Therefore the Lord God sent him forth from the Garden of Eden, to till the ground from where he was taken.
So he drove out the man; and he placed at the East of the Garden of Eden cherubim, and a flaming sword, which turned every way, to guard the way of the tree of life.

Genesis 3:23–24

The scrawny young white-tailed deer stepped slowly out of the thick brush and moved tentatively toward the small tufts of native grass on an adjacent slope. One hundred and fifty yards away, pale blue eyes blinked as if to be sure after the long wait. Slowly the man rotated the rifle within its mesquite support until its cross hairs found the neck. For a moment the finger went slack at the sight of stunted antlers and visible shoulder blades. Then a resolute squeeze, an explosive crack, and the sudden recoil sent bullet number 174 of the precious supply of 1,000 into the deer's lower neck, just in front of its shoulder. Several of the few surviving owls launched into flight as the deer leaped, buckled, and went down.

Quickly the wiry, tall man in his mid-forties began walking toward his prey. He moved conservatively in the stifling night heat, but there was little time to lose. The coyotes would be there within minutes. Most of the exhausting night had been spent in the hunt, so no more than three hours remained before sunrise. If he could not win his race with the sun, the deer would have to be given up.

The young buck was better than the man had thought. It was probably four years old, and not as severely underfed as most of the whitetails that still roamed the hills. Few lived long in the hellish heat. Most died at birth, as did many of the young does bearing them. Some, born to those mothers with sufficient milk during a forgiving season, lived to thankless adulthood. This young male

1

had a growing rack, short, with three points. After inspecting it, the man removed a light backpack, from which he withdrew a small axe and a hunting knife. For a moment he stared at the instruments, then dropped the axe and kneeled by the head of the deer.

The carefully sharpened knife slit the throat, and the neck was laid low to drain along a sloping stone near the fallen deer. The stone was still somewhat hot from the previous day, when it had been warmed by the sun to 130°F. Because it was large it had remained quite warm throughout the night, so the red trickles flowing from the neck thickened quickly in the drain path down the stone's grooves. He placed a small tin drinking cup at the bottom of the stone to catch some of the flow.

Small and nervous figures now moved in the dark. Growls and howls penetrated the hot stillness. Quickly the man gathered pieces of wood. One drying stick of a dead creosote tree, a piece of paper carried along for the purpose, and a precious match would light a fire without difficulty. With carefully cupped hands he lit the match with a caution conditioned by their great value. No more matches existed beyond those he had saved carefully in a dry container these five long years. The flames licked quickly over the hot, dry wood, igniting it before the piece of paper was even consumed. Satisfied, the man rose wearily, sweating, to seek more wood, because a bigger fire would be needed to restrain the coyotes. Amazingly, they had survived in large numbers. Only the scarcity of food inhibited the growth of their population. Even the small fire revealed them passing in the fringes of darkness. He added another stick and a few larger branches until the fire roared. Only then did the bearded face bend close to the fire to continue the hated butchery. He had experienced as a child almost the same revulsion at the biblical stories of sacrificial lambs. "Like it or not," he thought, "I must drink some of that blood."

A lifetime ago, a world ago, he had learned deer hunting with his uncle in the Hill Country. Even then he had disliked the butchering of the beautiful, well-fed bucks that had graced central Texas. Fortunately, that had mostly been done at the meat lockers in Hondo, near his uncle's ranch, where he had played and worked summers. Small, green plants had been abundant and the deer had been numerous then. The Texas Parks and Wildlife Department had urged their thinning by hunting, and so it had not seemed to the youth of fifteen so grave an insult to life as it now did to the forty-five-year-old, sweating his way through the night's work in a race against morning. The whole head had to come off because it was far too heavy. The three-mile trek home would be exhausting enough without it, the bowels, stomach, and lower legs. They would be left for the scavengers.

The coyotes paced the dark periphery, agitated but afraid, while the man paused to grasp the flask of water at his waist. A now bloody hand raised the precious fluid to his lips. He drank thankfully. There was no way to drink as much as he lost in perspiration; that would have required carrying too great a load. Fortunately, the well at home still pumped, even though the tank and river were dry throughout the summer. Returning promptly to the final gruesome task, his pocket axe drove repeatedly into the exposed neckbone until the head broke free. A renewed rush of crimson drained into the tin cup, and the man quickly swallowed it. It was the only food he had had since sunset. He spat disgustedly on the ground, then took another sip of water to chase the hot sweetness. Finally, the legs were axed away just above the knees.

None too soon was he done, for the fire burned lower and the eastern sky was beginning to lighten. Just two more hours remained until sunrise. The coyotes would be no great problem along the route home because they were a bit cowardly even in these hard times. Besides, they would squabble over the head, legs, and stomach left behind. There were greater fears. Other men were the most dangerous, but rarely encountered. Ever present, however, was the blistering sun. The three-mile hike with sixty pounds of carcass would have to be done in haste, and haste in the heat had become one of the greatest killers. But it would be impossible to leave a carcass and return in the evening. Even if it were buried against sun and vultures, the coyotes would dig it up. Food was precious. All that lived clamored and fought for what there was. Man was in this regard the most savage, but he hoped that in this desolate spot, none had been near enough to see the fire. Just in case, the loaded Remington, so well maintained during the five years, hung ready on his shoulder. Generosity had vanished, and the thin man always felt a heavy twinge of regret when he remembered how his humanity had been replaced by vigilant self-defense. He remembered Macbeth as he thought of the blood on his own hands, blood that would never wash away. Then smiling at the irony of a condemned savage recalling Shakespeare, a fragment from the world before, he roped behind the forelegs and began dragging the carcass down the hill toward the riverbed, where the smooth, dry surface would enable him to drag it most of the way home.

A slender, black-haired woman was returning from the well outside the house when the man appeared. He was struggling, sweating, stumbling up the slope from the riverbank. He carried the deer carcass on his shoulder because, for the uphill climb, that was easier than dragging. Quickly, the woman left her water jug by the house door and walked to the weary man. After exchanging a few words, she helped him lay the carcass down. Together they dragged it to an opening in the ground beside an old barn. The man walked slowly to the house and the woman lit a fire in the hole. The fiery sun had just risen over the hills beyond the east bank of the Llano River bed, and to escape its fierce heat the man slumped in the shade on the step of the west porch. He poured water into his cup and drank. Then he poured more water on a rag and wiped his sweaty face and his arms and hands. Sunrise brought as momentary consolation a small southerly breeze, the same breeze that used to make summer life so pleasant in the Hill Country.

For the first time in hours the man's racing heart slowed. He breathed long, relaxed breaths, and the water evaporating from his brow and arms felt almost cool. He thought of the 540 calories per gram needed to evaporate water and how important that little piece of physics had always been to his survival in these severe conditions. He watched the morning sun flash from the stone cliffs along the Llano to the west, and he thought again how light gray the stones looked. They had seemed more reddish brown at sunrise years ago. He knew, without looking, that the sun was brighter yellow now, almost white by contrast to the beautiful orange it had once been. He recalled Max Planck's arguments relating the newborn quantum theory of color to the temperature. The wonder and the magic of it all settled, consolingly, on him, and even as he shifted a cramped leg, life again seemed worth living. He wondered for the thousandth time that his satisfaction in living came from a psychic joy rather than from physical comfort. As a child he had discovered that understanding nature was his passion. He had once read in Einstein's own words how the constructed world of thought had become more important for him than the real world. To understand nature was to render it friendly. Even the harshest sun could not be ominous to one who marveled at the miraculous machine at its center.

The cries of a baby interrupted the peaceful flow of his thoughts, and the man was conscious of the special love he felt for that child, his second. How he hated its discomfort, but there was little he could do and he was too tired now even to move. Slowly he lay back on the wooden porch and gazed at the ceiling. Another wipe across his face brought some relief from the 105°F temperature of the morning air. A slight chill shuddered through his body, and he knew that he was near total exhaustion. He had first known that chill as a Texas teenager after hours of hard play in a summer afternoon's tennis match. It meant that the body was

4

too hot and too dehydrated. Wearily he sat up and drank another cup of water, then cursed as his left calf cramped again. Salt would help, but they no longer had any. Glad now that he had forced himself to down the deer's blood, the man wet his finger, dragged it over his neck and collarbone, licked the salty perspiration, then drank another cup of water. He stretched his aching arms forward to touch his toes and held the position. It was better to stretch the fatigued hamstring muscles than to risk cramps there. It was a simple stretching exercise left over from an athletic youth. His first child, three-year-old Jakob, left his play to sit with his father and to ask him about the hunt.

The woman had placed newly cut logs on the fire in the pit. Already they had begun to smoke and she knew that in five minutes more they would be burning sufficiently to be self-sustaining. The short flames licked the thin logs and smoke rose in the bright morning light. The woman wiped sweat from her brow and hoped that the chore could be finished before sunrise. This fifty pounds of smoked deer would suffice until the late-summer rains began. She lowered the iron grill into the pit, then placed the carcass on it.

She fetched a small pail of water and poured it slowly onto a wooden door lying on the ground, letting the water soak into the wood. Abruptly, she turned the door over and fit it snugly over the top of the pit. She knew the fire would last only a few seconds without air. When it was out, she opened a small window in the door, letting the smoke billow out and letting in just enough oxygen to keep the logs smouldering. She would leave the deer to smoke all through the insufferable day.

As she finished her task, she marveled at how well the process worked and recalled the two awful weeks that had been required to construct the pit. Their first attempt at building it had been too hurried and too simple, and it had been with a sense of deep discouragement that they had sought the inner resources to begin construction on the present pit. This was the fourth deer they had smoked on this pit, and she knew that its success had been a turning point in their lives. They were now much stronger than during the first three years.

Every living thing now sought shelter. Insects, rodents, snakes, and man, the weakest and yet the strongest, avoided the sun's rays. The white heat would raise the ground temperature to 130°F, and exposed dark stones would reach 150°F by noon. An exposed person would live only a few hours. Only the small creosote trees dared to lift their twisted green arms skyward.

The man and the woman went into their small ranch house, built originally in the 1930s as a lodge for a range worker and his

5

wife. Its three rooms had been home for the past five years. Three years ago the man had found some white paint in an abandoned hardware store in the town of Llano during a reckless trip there in his automobile. It was the last trip he ever made in the car, and he had been lucky to make it home alive. Nonetheless, the heavy white paint on roof and walls had rendered the house noticeably cooler during the blistering summer days.

Inside they fell onto the bed and prepared to rest. It was necessary to sleep during the day, because only the night was cool enough for work. In a sprinkler can they kept water with which to wet down towels for cooling their bodies. It was better than sweating so much. They could sleep for two or three hours at a time without heavy perspiration. Fortunately, the groundwater supply in the old well outside held good. Without it they could not have survived. The man fell onto the bed and stretched the muscles still exhausted from the work and heat. The morning air felt deceptively cool, and his head spun into sleep within minutes.

Now at last the woman could turn her attention to the six-week-old infant crying on the bed. Her cries were weak, and, as the woman looked down at her, sadness engulfed her. Even as she wiped her daughter's hot skin with the cool damp towel, the woman cursed her fate as a mother, to give love and hope in a world with no apparent hope. She could dwell on the memory of a better climate and hope that it would someday return, but what could a distressed baby know of hope. The infant could find no reserves of courage in remembering Eden. Even less could she find solace in intellectual understanding, which disarmed nature's terrors by comprehending their causes. The woman felt her own hot tears at the sight of this helpless, suffering reincarnation before her. This was the flesh of her flesh, blood of her blood, her own daughter. She despaired. She wanted to scream out, but from whom could she extract revenge for her daughter's suffering? From the sun? There was no one to blame for this misery. She could only live in it, or die in it.

Her son, Jakob, came and stood beside her. Without thinking she wiped his hot face and arms with the cool cloths and felt renewed resolve. She bathed her baby daughter again, as she would every two hours during the hot day. Then the woman lay with the child and placed her breast to its mouth. It was for this, not for hunger or thirst, that the woman regularly drank and ate all she could. The constant heat lowered her appetite, but the baby needed her milk. The baby sucked eagerly, for which the woman was grateful. Her instincts strengthened her own. She wiped the baby's face to keep it cool while it nursed. Beads of sweat dotted her tiny nose. She called Jakob onto the bed with them. They must

6

all sleep as the heat of day was rising. She made him drink a glass of water and lie by the open south window where the breeze would blow through. The woman, too, still felt a thrill at understanding how a wind hotter than the body could nonetheless cool it. She listened reassuredly to her husband's deep breathing, and she slept, but only briefly. Soon she must get up and bathe each member of her family again.

The man slept a full four hours before he awoke in a dead sweat. It was midday and he was soaked in perspiration. His mouth felt like cotton as he reached for the glass of water that his wife had left for him beside the bed. She lay, sweating, beside him. The children were also asleep, and the world seemed deathly quiet. His drowsy imagination was free to wander without distraction. Through the window beyond the flapping shade he saw the bleached white of the day. It was too bright to look at long. He thought of Stefan's Law, $H = \sigma T^4$, and reasoned that the sun's temperature must be at least 50 percent hotter than before. He searched again in his mind through the reasons for it all. As he did, his leg and one arm jerked in involuntary muscle spasms. His wife sat up abruptly.

"I'm sorry," he said. "I was trying to hit an overhead."

Two

It was late in the afternoon as Fred Cowan's Land Rover headed south from Terlingua. The end-of-winter sun was still setting barely north of due west, and out the left window of the vehicle the Christmas Mountains reflected its reddening rays. The first flowers come before spring in the Big Bend, and some scented and colored the scene even now. The Chisos Bluebonnet, a different species than the Texas Bluebonnet, was one of them. But it was the many cacti that made the Big Bend a splendor in early spring.

The road curved left for its passage over Rough Run and Dawson Creek, both of which had ample water flowing on south to join Terlingua Creek. The floodplains of the Big Bend were full of these seasonal rivers. They rushed and flooded with the spring rains, but were dry as bone in summer. Through the front windshield, Cowan noticed a black cloud hovering above Emory Peak, the highest point in the Chisos Mountains. More rain was possible, but the road into the mine was good enough that he could use it in all seasons. Not all roads in the area were so luxuriously consistent. Cowan had discovered that the long hike back from a stranded automobile was no fun, and he admired the rabbits and deer that could vanish so gracefully across the coarse rock and stubble of the desert hills.

Cowan drove slowly. The scene was so familiar that he could almost name the roadside rocks. But always spectacular were the power and ferocity of the weather changes, the crazy fragmented shadows of the brutal hills, and the fantastic evening colors splayed across the dusty horizon. Even in this critical time he made his way unhurriedly to the lab.

Dr. Fred Cowan had been employed by the Argonne National Laboratory in Illinois since 1957, as a nuclear physicist. His career had begun in 1941 with a B.S. from Utah State University. In 1946 he had received a Ph.D. from the University of California at Berkeley, and from there had joined the staff of the Los Alamos Scientific Labs. He had worked on a variety of scientific problems and on problems of the chemistry of radioactive substances. It was, in fact, during his years at Los Alamos that he had done his single most important piece of scientific research. Fred Cowan had detected the neutrino.

The neutrino is an elementary particle, which means that it cannot be broken down into other particles. It is without mass, so that it moves at the speed of light. It is also without electric charge, so that it passes easily through the mostly empty spaces of the atoms of normal matter. Only electrically neutral particles can do that. Its existence had been proposed by the Austrian physicist Pauli, who had suggested that one neutrino would be emitted invisibly along with an electron in a form of nuclear radioactivity called "beta decay." No one before Cowan had ever detected a neutrino, however. Pauli's hunch had been based on a desire to explain the unbalanced momentum observed when the nucleus of an atom decays. It recoils as if it had sent out an invisible bullet carrying energy and momentum, but without mass or charge. In the years following Pauli's theory, scientists had assumed they were seeing the effects of the neutrino even though it could not be detected. Although two decades of research had made the existence of this particle more plausible, it had remained a wishful figment of Pauli's intellect until Fred Cowan finally measured its presence.

What Cowan had done in 1954 was to set up a large shielded tank of hydrogen outside the Savannah River nuclear reactor. Beta decays occurred copiously within the reactor due to the radioactive decay there of the fission fragments of uranium nuclei. As a result, the nuclear reactor radiated anti-neutrinos, the antiparticle of the neutrino. Because they interacted so weakly with matter, they passed with very high probability through the walls of the reactor, through the giant slabs of concrete shielding, through the water that surrounded Cowan's tank of hydrogen, and into that tank. There, with small but detectable probability, they could be absorbed into the nucleus of the hydrogen atom, changing that atom's proton into a neutron. After an average wait of twelve minutes the neutron in turn decayed into a proton. But

10

that process was easily detected by Cowan's radioactivity counters. By careful experiments, Cowan had shown that the anti-neutrino actually existed, and that it could change a proton into a neutron, as expected. The experiment had been duly celebrated by the scientific world for its verification of one of the underpinnings of the structure of elementary particles.

Fred Cowan knew the rumors that he had been high on the lists of the Nobel Prize committee for the past five years, and it was widely expected that he would receive the prize within the next few years. Driving with the late afternoon sun blazing in his rear-view mirror, he smiled at the irony that he was now making a discovery of far wider importance. He had begun to use neutrinos to measure things in the universe that could not be seen in any other way known to physics.

As the Land Rover passed Basin Junction, where the road to the Chisos Basin took off to the south, the top of Lost Mine Peak came into view. Reaching almost seventy-six hundred feet above sea level, it was flanked by splendid foothills. At least a dozen mule deer could be seen grazing. They were always most visible just before sunset. Cowan loved this part of Texas, just as he loved all of the western states. The highland deserts played out to him the ritual of life's cycle, of sunlight and rain, powered by the rising and setting of the sun. He felt an almost religious affection for the desert sun. He was pursuing his clues like the Apache pursuing his God.

The sun now occupied Cowan's thoughts daily. He knew that his ten-year effort to detect neutrinos coming from the center of the sun would be the last great task of his scientific career. It was an immense task, like looking for invisible needles in an infinite haystack. Cowan joked about the tedious and painstaking aspects of the search. Given a few beers he could eulogize what he laughingly called "that great reactor in the sky." "Who else," he would ask, "would fry like a tortilla for five summers in a mobile home in Terlingua in search of something invisible moving at the speed of light?" The experiment occupied the abandoned copper mine on the east side of the Lost Mine Peak. The construction phase had been difficult and expensive, but for the past three years the experiment had functioned smoothly with only Cowan and a resident engineer to monitor its progress.

Cowan slowed the Land Rover as he saw the Panther Junction Ranger Station approaching on the right. Shifting into second gear, he pulled into the parking lot and eased the vehicle to a stop. Stretching with satisfaction, he stepped out and headed for the Ranger Station for his routine coffee with Tom Williams, just as he had done almost every evening for the past two years.

11

Tom Williams was a U.S. Park Ranger. Except for tours of duty in other U.S. parks, he had lived all his life in the area. He had been born on the Williams ranch on the Castolon road. In those years, the 1930s, hardy souls had still tried to prosper from the land. His grandfather had been involved in the silver and copper prospecting that had resulted in the copper mine behind what was now known as Lost Mine Peak. In that abandoned mine Cowan now hid his experiment twenty-seven hundred feet underground, safe from all cosmic rays save the ubiquitous neutrinos. From that deep and shielded hole, his newly conceived neutrino eyes gazed outward to the universe, looking for new understanding.

Tom put on a pot of coffee about an hour before leaving for his dinner, and Cowan regularly stopped to share it before the trip on to the mine. Tom was already pouring two cups when Cowan came in the door.

"'Evenin', Fred," he said without looking. "Will you see some neutrinos tonight, or is it too cloudy?"

Cowan smiled at the absurd remark, pouring his cream without speaking. His folks, who were Mormons from Utah, had taught him never to respond to a brilliant question with a mediocre answer.

"According to my calendar," Tom went on, "you must be about through bubbling out the argon." He had talked with Cowan enough to know that this happened monthly.

"Oh, yeah. We finish that tonight," Fred replied, referring to his painfully developed procedure for collecting the evidence of neutrinos from the sun. When absorbed by the chlorine atoms in the tank, they transmuted the chlorine atoms to atoms of radioactive argon. These he extracted by bubbling helium through the tank. The helium had the property of scouring out the argon gas and taking it along. Later, Cowan would analyze the argon gas for the telltale radioactivity that was the sign of neutrinos from the sun. It took a month for the radioactivity to build up to its maximum, so he repeated the entire process monthly.

"Where'd you get all that cleaning fluid, anyhow?" Tom asked. Cowan's tank had had to be made large enough to hold one hundred thousand gallons of perchlorethylene, or else it would not have contained enough chlorine atoms to result in a sufficiently high capture rate for the neutrinos from the sun. The equipment would be useless unless he could expect to produce enough radioactive argon atoms each month to be able to count them well. When anything happens randomly, it must be counted many times to estimate the rate of occurrence reliably.

"We bought it from Dupont. They make tons of the stuff daily," Fred responded. "The hardest part wasn't buying the hundred thousand gallons, but getting it up that old road and then down into the mine. That was in 1966. You weren't here then, so you didn't have the pleasure of helping. In Yosemite. . . ?"

"I was working in Grand Teton in 1966."

"Well, you missed the fun of getting those little lift cars running on the old wooden rails. We ended up getting some free advice from the U.S. Corps of Engineers concerning the ability of the tracks to safely carry the five-hundred-pound aluminum kegs that the chemical is stored in. The mine would have been unsafe for quite a while if one had broken away and crashed, but we didn't want to repour it into smaller containers."

Cowan had hated those years of the project. As a scientist he wanted only to get the answers and, understandably, to get them quickly, if possible. It had seemed to him as if there were interminable delays caused by funding and engineering problems. It was only now, in retrospect, that he could remember those frustrations with good humor and even a trace of nostalgia. The nostalgia came not from recalling the difficulties, but from the fact that they had been a part of a project so imaginatively conceived that it seemed to make everything in his life more meaningful.

"But has it been worth it," Tom asked, "considering that you haven't found any neutrinos? At least, if I understand you right, you say you haven't found any. It seems to me that all you've done is upset the pretty predictions of a lot of brainy astrophysicists who said it would be a cinch."

"Well, that's pretty much the case," Fred responded, quickly suppressing an urge to tell all he knew. "We had originally expected to produce about ten radioactive argon atoms daily in the tank. That would have given us about three hundred each month. We did set the theorists jumping when we couldn't find any. What we have actually been able to do is show that if there are any neutrinos from the sun, they're at least twenty times rarer than what they told us to expect when we began."

"They lowered their expectations when they knew there weren't any," Tom chided. "I read in the *Newsweek* account that they've lowered their predictions to only six times your limit. Damned practical of 'em. So that's the way you scientists work."

"Well, you've got to be fair, Tom," Fred laughed. "When they knew there were less than they expected, they took a critical look at the calculations and found that they needed a few revisions. Some of the factors entering the calculations had to be changed. What my experiment did was force them to examine the numerical calculations more closely."

"Yeah, but you told me already that each improvement of the theory just happened to be in the direction of lowering the ex-

13

pected number. Sounds fishy, if you ask me," said Tom, grinning as he imagined a roomful of bespectacled theoretical physicists squirming uncomfortably in the face of the facts. "More coffee?"

"No thanks, Tom," Cowan replied. "I really want to get up to the mine early. We'll have the data on last month's run ready, so I can begin my semiannual summary. I'll probably have the usual visitor or two for the occasion tomorrow. I never know in advance, because they just check in at the Basin and show up after lunch. Anyhow, I've got to get going. We'll see you and Betty on Saturday night."

"Saturday night for sure, but without the margaritas, please."

"But I've changed the recipe."

"Good idea!"

Fred waved as he backed the Land Rover out of its parking place. He enjoyed these coffee stops. Tom had always been interested in the work at the lab, and he liked to stop at the mine whenever he was in that part of the park. Fred looked forward to explaining the news to him, maybe Saturday night over margaritas, but for the moment his mind raced to the hours ahead.

After turning east, then south toward Boquillas, he planned each step of the evening's routine. He must be sure of making no mistake now. For seven years he and the world had been puzzling over his lack of detection of solar neutrinos. This semiannual public report would certainly intensify the puzzle. He was, in fact, so eager to release the item to the news media that he had already prepared the first draft of a bulletin. It had been lying on his desk now for three days while he waited for the results of the final month's counting of the six-month interval.

The Land Rover slowed as the entrance to the Pine Canyon Road approached on the right. The one-lane gravel and sand road was used by park rangers, by the more adventurous park visitors, and by Cowan on his frequent trips to the old mine. From the road, now heading west again, the hulks of the South Rim and the East Rim rose like dark giants in the blue-black twilight. Here, twenty million years ago, they had burst forth in the violence of a huge volcano. Cowan liked to think of the violence that must have enveloped the area at that time, because he found a poetic link to the violence of the solar center that he had for years been attempting to measure in the Solar Neutrino Observatory.

Cogent physical arguments imply that the solar center is hotter than the most intense heat ever produced by man—the fleeting second of heat at the center of a thermonuclear bomb. It had been reliably estimated that the heat content in a single cubic centimeter of matter at the solar center is adequate to bring several tons of water to the boiling point. It was Cowan's dream to mea-

14

sure the source of power that could keep the solar center so hot, even in the face of the cooling resulting from the loss of heat from the solar surface . . . that same heat that had made a Garden of Eden of cold planet Earth.

After twenty minutes of driving at twenty mph over the rough road, Cowan pulled the Land Rover to a halt beside the gate blocking the small track heading off toward the right and up the east side of Lost Mine Peak. A simple sign across the gate read "Argonne Solar Neutrino Observatory. Closed to Traffic." As he swung the gate open, Cowan puzzled that the gate latch was incorrectly closed.

He noticed fresh automobile tire tracks in the dust, and assumed the usual, that a curious park tourist had again been tempted to travel this private road. The road was passable, but not really fit for a conventional automobile. The park rangers had on more than one occasion had to free a stuck automobile. The Land Rover bounced effortlessly up the steep trail, round the several rough turns marking the final mile to the mine entrance. Parked there was a new Ford, a rental car.

Cowan thought little of it as he entered the mine door. There had been frequent visitors to the project over the years, the funding agents, the Corps of Engineers, visiting scientists. He stepped into the small electrically operated elevator and pressed the button that initiated the seven-hundred-foot descent to the control panel area. His heart raced a little as he thought of the press release, and he went immediately to his desk. The typed draft of his report was not on it. He was stunned. As he began to search through his papers, he didn't notice the trembling figure behind him. The man's hands shook as they clutched an iron crowbar so tightly that his knuckles were white. His hands rose slowly, wavered, and then slammed the crowbar into Cowan's skull, killing him instantly.

The bar fell to the floor beside the body with a loud crash. The trembling assassin fell to his knees and gasped, trying to maintain consciousness. He heaved to and fro, sick with an inner pain. Slow, deep sobs racked his body.

Stumbling and dazed, he made his way up the elevator and out into the night. Laboriously he retraced the route to the Panther Junction Ranger Station, where he turned right toward Marathon. When he reached the Persimmon Gap Ranger Station thirty miles to the north, he pulled off to the pay telephone and extracted a coin purse. Shortly after he dialed a number, a woman answered.

"Mrs. Cowan," the man replied, "this is Davidson, a new ranger at Panther Junction. Your husband just called down on the radio. He asked me to tell you that he's having some trouble with

15

the counters, so he'll spend the night on the cot in the lab and he'll be back tomorrow night . . . Yes, Mrs. Cowan, I can call him back and tell him that . . . Sure . . . Good night, Mrs. Cowan."

After hanging up, he made another call, dialing 1, the New York area code, then an apartment on the upper East Side.

"Leon, this is Davidson calling. I had a very difficult job to do, but it is done. Cowan is no longer on the job. I unexpectedly had to remove him. Your organization should immediately liquidate the other company's assets. Everything! Immediately! I will be gone tonight."

"We understand," the voice replied. "It will be done before morning by our El Paso subsidiary. Have a good trip east. Good night."

Silently the receiver was replaced, and the Ford raced north into the darkness.

Three

CIA double-agent Benjamin Wolf usually had very little opportunity within Israeli Intelligence to come across information from high-ranking sources. So when he saw the door to General Sharim's office open he walked down the hallway to the water fountain. He recognized at once the voice of Elias Hirschberg.

"Zweig says that the Joshua Factor will be operative in late August."

"Why in hell do you guys always call this thing of Zweig's the Joshua Factor, even if it does exist?" General Sharim asked.

Hirschberg explained, "Because, you yourself know, Yuval, when Joshua blew the trumpets, the walls of Jericho came down, and the sun stood still."

Both men laughed, and as the footsteps of another military officer turned into the same hallway, Benjamin Wolf stooped to drink at the fountain, then walked nonchalantly away. It wasn't much, but he would report it.

Reading that report in his office in Washington, James Fitzgerald III puzzled over the names. General Sharim and Elias Hirschberg he knew well. Of Zweig he was less sure, although convinced that he knew the name. Probably Jewish, but of any nationality. He turned his desk chair around to face the computer console and screen behind his desk. He typed in a code to access names relevant to Israeli Intelligence, of which he himself was chief Washington monitor, and then the name Zweig. As capsule identifications sprang one by one onto the screen, he searched them for a lead that was not long in coming. "Zweig, David . . . age 39 . . . Professor of Theoretical Physics, Harvard U. . . . Postdoctoral position with Elias Hirschberg at Weizmann Institute, 1967–1969 . . . " So there was even a Zweig connected with Hirschberg

17

in the CIA files. The words physics and Harvard reminded Fitzgerald that he had once engaged that same Zweig in conversation. It had been at the Harvard Club, at least fifteen years ago, just after Fitzgerald's MBA at the Harvard Business School, where his shrewd and calculating personality had made him the outstanding graduate.

James Fitzgerald III was the son of a wealthy Boston banker, but it had been his fascination with international intrigue that had led him to the CIA rather than to any of the dozens of corporations within which he could have quietly and conventionally amassed a fortune.

He loosened his necktie and the collar of his shirt, removed his wire-frame glasses, and recalled his conversation with Zweig. He had been seated by chance in a comfortable armchair next to David Zweig's. It had not been by chance that both had been reading the story of the week—Fitzgerald in the *Wall Street Journal* and Zweig in the *New York Times*—the story of the selective cutback by the Arab oil-producing states of their exports to the United States. Though both were reserved by temperament, they had somehow begun to converse. Each feared that the full implications of the export cutback were appreciated neither by the government nor by the news media.

Fitzgerald, who had specialized in economic game theory for his MBA, had described loosely a scenario for the economic ruin of the United States. Briefly, the cutback would lead to increased oil prices in the U.S. and thereby to increased revenues for the Arab states when the oil flow was later resumed. An organization of petroleum-producing states would be formed to control international prices so that competition would not needlessly lower them. The objective would be to alter greatly the balance of trade, all the time keeping the oil flowing so that the United States would not develop self-sufficiency, but holding the price up to the maximum level that the U.S. would pay.

A second cutback would be instituted when the United States balked at a price increase. The citizenry would so squawk at the gasoline rationing, the long lines at gasoline pumps, and the need for car pools, that the government would succumb to consumer pressure and sell a huge amount of wheat at cut-rate international prices to offset the extra import costs. Spiraling U.S. inflation would be continuously fueled thereby. Fitzgerald had seen these as results maneuvered by the Soviet Union. According to him, the Arab states, in complicity with the Soviets, would be gambling that U.S. leaders would always be forced politically to accept inflation and oil dependence instead of unemployment and oil independence. With their huge revenues, the Arab states would build their military might and their influence with oil-importing states while at the same time not driving oil prices so high that the U.S. would refuse to buy. It was crucial, according to strategists he imagined to be pushing this plan in the Kremlin, that the United States not develop alternate energy policies, but instead maintain and even increase its dependence on oil. The current U.S. administration had been, according to Fitzgerald, complying like a lamb, being more concerned about the coming elections than the need to recognize the true economic value of energy and the need to develop alternate resources and conservation plans. In the name of "stabilizing prices and profits," it had refused to let oil prices rise to their true level.

Zweig had listened intently. His orientation had been quite different, envisioning the embargo to be primarily a plot to eliminate Israel. He had anticipated that pro-Israel Europe would turn its back when threatened with an oil embargo. The delicate balance of arms and international sympathy for Israel would be systematically destroyed by Europe's dependence. Lacking expensive oil, it would be essentially impossible for Israel to maintain even military parity with the Arab states. Its circuitous dependence on Arab oil, even if via the U.S., had made it vulnerable. Zweig had seen it as essential that Israel somehow gain a share of oil production. Certainly the Abu Rudeis oil fields captured in the Sinai in 1967 were insufficient. Fitzgerald had concurred sympathetically, but had not seen how major new oil holdings could be created.

What Fitzgerald now remembered was their agreeing that the fates of both the United States and Israel would be very much improved if Israel had major oil-producing lands. Both had regarded the matter as crucial enough to consider elaborate international intrigues, and perhaps even minor wars. As Zweig himself had said, Israel had known so many wars that another one would in itself mean little. It would be the outcome in the world's balance of power that would give another war its ultimate meaning.

Fitzgerald had gone on to learn from their conversation that the youthful Zweig was a professor of theoretical physics at Harvard. He had then recalled reading in the *Crimson* of Zweig's appointment in 1969 as the youngest full professor in Harvard's history. As he recalled, the article had appeared to celebrate a subsequent discovery of some kind of subatomic particle that Zweig had predicted . . . *quarks* he thought it was. Impressed by intellectual strength, Fitzgerald had managed to engage Zweig in a subsequent half hour of conversation.

"So that's Zweig," Fitzgerald thought to himself as he looked again at the brief exchange reported by agent Wolf. The biblical allusions to Joshua and the Battle of Jericho also caught Fitzgerald's attention. An often repeated code name in recent CIA reports had been *Jericho*, which seemed to stand either for an intelligence organization or a plan. Nothing was known about it, and Fitzgerald would have dismissed it as an irrelevant coincidence except for the allegorically related "Joshua Factor," which was attributed to Zweig in Wolf's report as being something "operative in late August."

Glancing again at the screen, Fitzgerald read another interesting entry under Zweig's name: "Consultant: U.S. Air Force (Test Monitoring: General Hughes)." Zweig seemed to be an Air Force consultant in the area of detecting nuclear tests. Fitzgerald buzzed his secretary and asked her to locate and call a General Hughes in the Pentagon. After identifying himself to Hughes, Fitzgerald moved to the point.

"Do you retain David Zweig, a Harvard professor, as one of your consultants?"

"Yes, we do," General Hughes replied.

"Well, this is a matter that I would categorize as sensitive," Fitzgerald continued. "Do you know that our intelligence files indicate suspicion that Zweig acts in a secret capacity with Israeli Intelligence?"

"I had no such idea at all," Hughes replied. "Zweig has been cleared. **Top Secret**. Only two years ago."

"Is he working on a top-secret area?" Fitzgerald asked.

"Yes. That's right. Maybe we had better get our investigators to review this classification," Hughes said. "Can I send someone to your office to check your information on Zweig?"

"Sure, our files on that point are open to security investigators," Fitzgerald responded. "Give me a ring before you send someone over."

"O.K. And thanks for the warning," Hughes signed off.

Fitzgerald sensed something curious in the situation. Israeli strategists apparently expected something significant to become operative in late August, possibly associated with an Air Force division monitoring nuclear tests. Exposing skulduggery here could be a big opportunity for Fitzgerald. He looked to just such opportunities. His rise in the CIA to program director for Israeli intelligence had already been swift, because Fitzgerald had both brains and perseverance to accompany his ambitions. If something was found in the situation, Fitzgerald would have something to take directly to the CIA director himself. That's what made it more fun than business.

Whistling absentmindedly, he turned from his window and reached again for his telephone, dialing a number himself.

"Laura, this is Jim! Let's go out to dinner and celebrate."
"Celebrate? Celebrate what?"
"Oh, just how well work is going."

Four

The next day in Austin was the kind on which people stay inside with difficulty. An early March cold snap had ended, and a gentle southeasterly breeze carried the warmer tropical air over cloudless central Texas. At the Austin Hills Tennis Club enthusiasts lounged on the sunlit bleachers around the three central courts, where a quarterfinal match was still in progress.

A sharply stroked ball whistled past a player lunging hopelessly to his right in an attempt to cut it off. It landed a full foot within the sideline.

"15–40," said the umpire.

Slowly George Reynolds turned and walked back from the net toward the service line. The yellow sweatbands around his forehead and wrists were dripping, and his yellow shirt stuck to his skin. "Well, this could be it," he thought to himself as he picked up a second ball. The young fellow, Tony Hernández, was just too fast to be beaten by wide balls that were not hit with more authority than the last one. The best serve now would be a high kicker that would bounce up and into him. It wouldn't be spectacular, but it would give the best odds. Reynolds was a great believer in the odds. He bounced the ball twice, looked, then bounced it a third time before tossing it farther behind his head than usual. His slightly exaggerated swing contacted the ball while the racket still traveled upward, producing a heavily topspinned serve. Hernández picked up the spin a bit late, and the high bounce caught him a little unprepared. His return was soft and too high, though angled toward the sideline. With a quick pounce Reynolds easily cut it off with a sharply angled backhand volley, a clean winner.

"30–40," the umpire droned.

"One more like that and I'm still in the match," thought Reynolds as he returned slowly to the service line. On the other side, Hernández, the number-two player on the University of Texas team, jumped gently up and down, keeping himself loose for the kill. Reynolds, trying to ignore his opponent's confidence, glanced up at the blistering Texas sun.

"Damn neutrinos," he thought, smiling to himself at the fleeting reflection. Another good serve, and Reynolds bounced cautiously in behind it and volleyed the moderately good return straight down the middle of the court. Hernández feigned a passing shot, but instead hit yet another top spin lob—another good one. Reynolds leaped back as quickly as he could and barely managed to hit the rapidly sinking shot. The overhead was defensive, too weak, and Hernández, who had ambitiously raced to the net behind his lob, easily dropped it over the net for a winner.

"Game, set, and match to Mr. Hernández. 3–6, 6–4, 6–4. Mr. Hernández advances to the semifinal round."

George Reynolds was not surprised. He had often worked out with Hernández on the University of Texas tennis courts. It was a privilege for a professor to work out with the university tennis team, but George Reynolds had earned it with twenty-four years of competitive tennis. Now, at age forty, he could still take an occasional match from the best of the local players. But not today, not in a quarterfinal match in the Central Texas Spring Championships. As he toweled the sweat from his face, neck, and arms, Reynolds was satisfied just to have made it this far, especially since the remainder of the field of eight consisted of six college tennis stars and the Men's-35 Singles Champion from Houston.

"Don't take it so hard, George," said Rebecca teasingly, as she walked up to greet him. She made a pouting expression and reached out for Reynolds.

He took her outstretched hand and gave it a squeeze. "Hell, he got all the breaks," George said, grinning ear to ear.

Rebecca laughed, already understanding the nuances of the tennis culture after only half a year in the United States. "He also seemed to run a little faster at the end," she responded, mischievously hitting below the belt. George couldn't have cared less. He was content. He knew himself, his abilities, his limitations. He patted her bottom gently, applying a lingering rub, as they walked away amid good-natured condolences from many tennis-playing acquaintances. They were a part of George Reynolds's social world.

More than half the eyes were on Rebecca Yahil. Her dark complexion, pitch-black hair, and astonishingly beautiful figure drew stares. She appeared made for colorful leotards and dancing

24

shoes, rather than for the white overcoats of science labs, or the impersonal solitude of computer terminals. She wore her hair brushed back behind her ears, most often falling straight down her back to her waist. Occasionally, she wore it braided, pinned close to her head in a complicated series of rings, like Mid-Eastern traceries.

Her dress was simple, in contrast to the strength of her features. She usually wore no makeup, and others agreed that it would have been superfluous. She was a creature of extraordinary athletic sensuality, especially uncommon in the rarefied atmosphere of scientific research. She had come to the University of Texas about seven months earlier as a postdoctoral fellow in astrophysics. Her Ph.D. research had been done at the Hebrew University, Jerusalem, and she had come strongly recommended not only by scientists there but also by Harvard's David Zweig. As if that were not enough, her salary was completely paid by an Israeli Fellowship, a rather unusual honor in a time when Israel's negative balance of payments normally forbade external accounts.

Within only a few weeks of her arrival in Austin, Rebecca Yahil and George Reynolds had become lovers. This was in itself not so remarkable, considering the ready-made romance of their individual situations, their professional relationship, their characters, and the way in which fate had flung them together. They were not themselves unaware of the movie script elements of their liaison, for both were by nature skeptical of wish fulfillment. If truth be told, each, out of propriety and professional concerns, inwardly had resisted the first temptation. Both had so many other goals that they were not easily seduced by dreams of a greater happiness. What was remarkable was that the chance of love had asserted itself in the face of skepticism and of those other purposes, that it had spoken daily by way of their eyes' lingering recognition of one another. So it mattered little that others regarded them as a perfect couple in Austin's social scene. And if it was widely recognized that they were now bound to one another, only a few purposeful souls could comprehend the clarity of their fixation.

"Dr. Reynolds," a man in a gray suit asked as they walked toward the parking lot, "could I talk to you for a moment?"

"About what?"

"It's a confidential matter," he went on, "that I would rather discuss with you alone."

"Well, this is not a very convenient time for confidences," Reynolds responded, a little annoyed. "I'm tired, and I have a friend with me. And I've just lost a tennis match. My world is falling apart. So perhaps if you could call my office on Monday, we could see what it's about."

The man stepped deftly between them and pulled his wallet from his coat, opening it to a plastic ID card. "I'm Ed Corrigan of the FBI, and I'm afraid it won't wait."

Reynolds read the badge. Edward G. Corrigan, Special Agent, Federal Bureau of Investigation. "All right," he said, "how long will it take?"

"Don't know. I'd say thirty minutes."

Reynolds turned to Rebecca. "Would you rather wait here or at home? I must talk to Mr. Corrigan. Mr. Corrigan, this is Dr. Rebecca Yahil of the Astronomy Department."

"Glad to meet you, Dr. Yahil, and I'm sorry to interrupt your day," the FBI man answered. Corrigan's eyes dipped furtively.

Rebecca, not knowing what was happening, was uncertain. It was unlike George to leave her dangling. But his eyes conveyed no message of his preference, so she said, "I think I'll just go home. Tony's going that way now, so I can go with him. We can meet there when you're through." With that she walked away. Corrigan's eyes followed her for a moment. Then, somewhat embarrassed, he turned back toward Reynolds.

"Your friend is very attractive."

Reynolds only smiled. That Rebecca drew admiring looks from men and women alike was an annoyance only on rare occasions.

"Could we just sit over here on the bleachers?" Reynolds asked.

Corrigan nodded and followed his lead to an open area in the south stands. There Reynolds laid his two rackets down and drank from the bottle of water that he had carried off the court. He capped the jar, placed it beside the rackets and pulled on a white sweater.

"It's amazing how quickly you can feel a chill after a tennis match," Reynolds said, a little nervous about his first interview with an FBI investigator. "Would you like to have a Coke or something? There's a machine under the west bleachers."

"No thanks, Dr. Reynolds," Corrigan replied, seating himself.

"Well, I guess I might as well ask why you've sought me out here," Reynolds said.

"Is it true you know Fred Cowan?" Corrigan asked.

"Sure. He and I are quite good friends. He spends a lot of time in Texas, and we share a professional interest," Reynolds replied.

"What professional interest?"

"An astrophysical problem concerning neutrinos from the sun. He's trying to detect the neutrinos, and I've calculated a lot of numerical models of the sun in an attempt to understand why he can't find any," Reynolds replied.

26

"Have you been to his Neutrino Observatory?" Corrigan asked.

"Yes, lots of times. Why these questions?" Reynolds asked.

"Cowan is dead," Corrigan replied. "He was murdered in his lab. We don't know if it was a terrorist act or if there was a personal motive."

"For God's sake, tell me you're kidding!" Reynolds said, stunned.

"I'm afraid not. We've turned to you because a National Academy of Sciences source told us you were well informed and often went there. You might even be a suspect, except that we know you were playing tennis here yesterday afternoon about the time he was murdered. When was the last time you saw him?"

Reynolds sat blankly, not saying a word. In part he was considering the answer to the question, and in part he was picturing the gentle face of his dead friend and colleague. Eventually he responded, "I last saw Fred six months ago, when I visited his observatory. It was the time of his last six-month summary report; but I talked to him on the phone about a week ago."

"I understand it was time for him to release another six-month report," Corrigan said, half questioningly.

"That's right. That's what he called me about. He wanted me to come down this time, too. He said there was something interesting in his data. I thanked him for alerting me and told him that I would come, unless by good luck I was still in the tournament. Well, you know how that turned out. I was planning to drive down tonight." Reynolds stopped short.

Corrigan made a couple of notes on a pad. "Was there any important reason to go down there this time?"

"Well, the experiment is quite important to our understanding of the sun," Reynolds replied, "but Cowan had been making public reports every six months for the last five years, and this report was not expected to be much different from the others."

"Excuse me for harping on this point, Dr. Reynolds, but we're still trying to get some quick idea of whether this was a murder with a motive or an act of terrorism," Corrigan explained. "Was there any result of Cowan's experiment that could have aroused great envy or anger within the scientific world? I've heard that scientists can be quite jealous."

"They can be," Reynolds answered, "but not in this case. I've never seen a single expression of ill will toward Cowan. He was lovable and friendly. He was a dedicated scientist. He was the only scientist actually conducting experiments in neutrino astronomy, so there was no jealousy. In fact, the entire world of physics and astronomy was grateful to him. It's such a grand project."

"But I heard that he had embarrassed a lot of scientists who had claimed he would see these things easily . . . these . . ."

"Neutrinos," Reynolds offered. "I wouldn't say *embarrassment*. Very few theorists take their predictions so seriously that they are embarrassed when shown to be wrong. *Humbled* is a better word. But, in fact, the theorist doesn't usually expect to be right in a prediction. He offers a prediction derived from a specific model of what's going on, the answer that one would expect if the model were right. But he realizes that it is the model itself being tested, not the theory. A model is never totally right. Some are just better approximations than others, and we try to find the model that is the best approximation of nature." Reynolds drank again from his water jar.

Corrigan looked him straight in the eye and asked, "Did it never irk you that his experiment showed fewer neutrinos than your models predicted?"

"Not at all, Mr. Corrigan. For me, his experiment was thrilling. It's inspiring that nature is doing something mysterious, that is to say, something we don't understand." Reynolds paused long enough to choose the right words before continuing. "We all feel that the sun is telling us something important. And Cowan's experiment was the means of communicating with the sun's center. There is always a sense of gratitude when a new truth is being revealed. It's almost spiritual. It's as if Cowan were a prophet, going to the mountain wilderness in search of a message from God. And the message came from this god, the sun, and said 'You do not understand me.' But the scientific community has nothing but love and respect for Cowan."

"I was told that that's what I'd hear," Corrigan said, closing his notepad. "I think that's all I need now, but I wonder if I could visit your office Monday. I'd like to delve deeper into the importance of his experiment. I will need to understand that better if I'm going to make any headway."

"All right. Could you make it 10:00 A.M.?"

"Fine. Thanks. Dr. Reynolds, it's been good to meet you, although I'm sorry I came with shocking news," Corrigan said, extending his hand and standing.

"It is shocking news," Reynolds replied solemnly, almost to himself, but accepting Corrigan's hand. "We'll discuss it more Monday. You can't miss the new physics and astronomy building. Sticks out like a sore thumb—twenty stories high."

It seemed as if the conversation had ended, and both men started to move when Reynolds's curiosity got the better of him.

"Is there any evidence within the lab showing what kind of person would do a thing like this?" he asked.

"Well, yes, there is something," Corrigan replied, seating him-

28

self again. "The inside was gutted by fire, obviously arson. Explosives were attached to the huge tank, and when they detonated, it ruptured, making the fire even worse until it smothered itself from lack of oxygen. It was damned tough to get in there, because there was still a lot of fluid from the tank all over the place. Dr. Cowan was pretty hard to recognize when we got the body up to the top."

"For God's sake!" Reynolds exclaimed.

They sat silent for a moment before Corrigan continued. "What it shows is that the thing was done by some very peculiar people. It looks planned, with the dynamite and all; but there's something funny about that idea, too."

"What's that?"

"The autopsy showed that Cowan died from a primitive and violent blow to his skull, primitive in comparison with the efficient destruction that followed," Corrigan replied. "It's as if the murder weren't planned but the destruction was. We don't know what to make of that. It's the sabotage of government property that actually brings us into this case."

"So you have no idea who did it?" Reynolds asked.

"No, Dr. Reynolds, I don't, but maybe you can help me develop a few ideas," Corrigan replied.

The two men sat and talked for another quarter hour. Their incongruence somehow alerted Reynolds's acquaintances to pass with only a smile or wave. No one stopped to interrupt them as Corrigan looked mostly at Reynolds, who in turn looked mostly at his own feet. After Corrigan left, Reynolds remained seated a few minutes. The bright sun, still hot, was now low in the evening sky. Reynolds glanced at it, almost questioningly. It shined for him as it had for all men since the beginning of human time. It had, on good scientific evidence, been shining for forty-six hundred million years, predating all life on Earth. Reynolds wiped the salt from his face and neck and walked slowly to his car. That same sun over which he had puzzled so long with his computer models seemed more mysterious, and its power, which science did not yet totally understand, seemed somehow less friendly.

Reynolds angrily slammed his Porsche 911 into second gear as he spun out of the club and headed south toward the campus area where he lived. Not only was a fine and gentle man gone, not only was a friend lost, but also the dream of understanding that he had pursued; and that dream had also occupied a decade of Reynolds's own conscious thoughts.

Shifting into third, Reynolds relaxed his unusually rigid grip on the wheel. His personality thrived on the repetition of worthwhile things. His right arm had served one and a half million times in twenty-four years of afternoon tennis, and in the evenings his computer programs of the sun made a million calculations in twelve seconds, repeating them hundreds of thousands of times over the years. And now, the Porsche that he had purchased while on sabbatical leave at the Max Planck Institute in Munich just to be able to repeat daily the joy of manually handling a fine car helped him back to even keel.

It was the love of repeating all that seems good that had led him to the Ph.D. in physics at Caltech, so that he could repeat throughout life the joy of those first childhood attempts at making the chaotic understandable. Just as the child focuses his eyes again and again, then comprehends, so the man focuses his mental vitality again and again, thereby creating new comprehension. It is the lifeblood of the scientist. It is, in fact, the evolution of life itself, repeating and repeating, and slowly changing to new forms.

Five

The turbines of the El Al Boeing 747 were throttled back as its captain began the descent into the Tel Aviv approach patterns. In a first-class seat David Zweig looked blankly out the window into the blue Mediterranean Sea. His dark eyes fixed for long periods without blinking on whatever view presented itself. The brilliant afternoon sunlight was scattered primarily in the blue range of colors. This phenomenon of color, Rayleigh scattering, gives the sky and horizon its brilliant hue and is also a quantum mechanical problem that David Zweig had solved at age fifteen, while a precocious student at Beth Zion School, a private high school just north of New Orleans. But it had not been his instructors there who taught him such advanced physics. They had been no match for his sharp intellect. It was instead his father, Jakob Zweig, professor of metallurgy at Tulane in New Orleans, who had patiently led him into the abstract world of theoretical physics.

David Zweig's relationship to his father had been, indeed, still was, a consuming one. It absorbed his emotional energy. It had made of him a solitary child with few friends. The other young people at Beth Zion School had also been Jewish, but they had seemed at home in Louisiana, whereas David had felt misplaced, out of joint in space and time although it had been his only home. Such friends as he had had could not drag him to a high school football game or through the Mardi Gras frenzy of New Orleans. The inner world that David Zweig inhabited as a child had contained little room for teenage occupations. He had been a brilliant and serious boy. His passions had been two—to understand the world of physics and to understand the world of his father. Somehow the two passions were the same, but neither father nor son fully guessed their confluence. The vortex swirled about them,

31

weighted down by some sadness, some loss that emanated from the father. Indeed, David Zweig's childhood had been eclipsed by a pathos cast by his father.

Daily life in his childhood home had been presided over in a much more practical way by his mother. Their spacious old house near Tulane University was spic and span, cleaned and polished daily. She especially loved the leaded-glass door panes typical of the old homes in their neighborhood. Even in summer she threw open the upstairs windows to the breezes from the Gulf, and she marveled at their attic fan which drew air in on the still days and expelled it from the attic. To her, New Orleans was not so bad; but David daily saw his father's skepticism. To her the supermarket was no match for the old Marktplatz, but she took it in her stride. It was hard to be completely kosher, but maybe that wasn't too important. At least they could get on with their family life. She was happy with the European flavors of New Orleans, reminders of her childhood home in Hamburg. It would do.

It was not so for the elder Zweig, who had been born in Dresden. He had left to attend university in Berlin, and on completing his *Doktorarbeit* had moved to Leipzig to assume a professorship there. It had been within the small triangle of Dresden, Berlin, and Leipzig that Jakob Zweig had gathered his most important experience of the world. But, years later, no reminder of Europe, or of his life there, would bring him anything but misery. Jakob Zweig's experience of the world had been one of blossoming hope, prosperity, and success, shattered suddenly, inexplicably, and completely, by madness.

Jakob Zweig had entered the university in 1921. What a place Berlin had been for such a talented and ambitious young man. While still reeling from the initial stimulation of the city, the university, his new friends, and his proud new purpose, he had become aware of something else. There in Germany, in Berlin, in the early 1920s he was witnessing an incredible Renaissance in physics. He was part of it, attending lectures by Einstein, Planck, Heisenberg, and a host of lesser lights. What could compare with the fabulous pulse of living through a scientific revolution? Zweig and his student friends had owned the moment, and he had loved Berlin.

For Zweig, nothing could have bettered the events that followed his student years. He had not been eager to leave the energetic intellectual climate of Berlin, but the offer of a professorship at the University of Leipzig had come just after he had married Anna. Certainly, Leipzig would be the beginning of a brilliant career, and a wonderful family life. So, on the evening of his departure, Jakob and his many friends had met to celebrate his good fortune. Jakob had promised in his parting enthusiasm to carry the magic moment of German physics to Leipzig. In the morning, he and Anna had been sent off with many farewell embraces and hopes for the future.

For a while Jakob had tried to live his promise. Longer than most Jews, he had refused to believe that the anti-Semitism that gripped Germany could last. He had insisted that he and Anna cling to their life and home through all, and surely Germany would grow well again. Jakob's life revolved blindly around physics, not politics. What harm could there be for a man whose life dream had been the advancement of Germany through science? In 1937 he had been awakened to reality by the news that his brother's store in Dresden had been destroyed by anti-Semitic mobs. Eventually, his two sisters were reported missing.

When Jakob and Anna fled Leipzig, there had been no farewell party, and no well-wishers at the train station. They were smuggled onto a freighter in Rostock. Zweig carried with him one small case, nothing more; no dreams, no ambitions, no hopes, no happiness. In three weeks, the freighter docked in New Orleans. Louisiana was strange and cruel in its own way, but it was safe.

David Zweig was born six years later in New Orleans. He was a gentle child and it soon became clear that he was special. He studied Hebrew, which pleased his father, and he showed great powers in those areas, mathematics, music, and chess, where prodigy often asserts itself. By age fourteen he skillfully played all the Beethoven sonatas, and at age sixteen he was chess champion of New Orleans. The next year he finished a strong third in the Louisiana Open Championships. His own line of the Sicilian Defense was later discovered and made famous by Bobby Fischer. Again and again his formative influence had been old Jakob Zweig, who had played Alekhine to a draw in a game in the 1929 tournament in Leipzig. In no way had David been a typical Louisiana boy. Throughout childhood, he could escape neither the quiet desperation of his father's life nor the black history that he had had to learn from books. He learned it with horror and with anger.

The sense of despair in his household caused even the joyous and the triumphant to take on the flavor of vindication. One of his prized possessions during his early childhood had been a copy of Hurlbut's *Story of the Bible*, given to him by his mother to help them learn together, in written English, those great stories. He often stared at its colorful full-page frontispiece entitled "David Meeting Goliath." It showed the young David standing barefoot in a brook, stone held ready in his leather sling, while the huge, gold-vested Goliath advanced menacingly, spear in hand. Had this

33

boy really defeated and killed a giant? The miracle of his success had thrilled the young David Zweig to tears.

He was thrilled, too, by the drawing of the priests blowing on ram's-horn trumpets as Joshua led them in their march around the enemy city of Jericho. By following God's mystic rules for six days, the walls of the city had crumbled and fallen on the seventh day. God so loved his stout people.

These were miracles that had somehow failed his father's family, carted away to concentration camps as part of the ultimate solution.

David lived such heroic fantasies as he, a brilliant, frail, fifteen-year-old, demolished men of all ages across the chess board. He noticed, too, that the incapacitating, unremitting grief of his father seemed soothed by his accomplishments. In those moments of pride old Jakob held his head high. When David was little, his father used to take him onto his lap saying, "David, David, my bright little boy, God has given you to me to heal my pain." And David, with his great natural talents, turned all of his attention toward scaling the mountain of his father's sorrow.

David Zweig graduated at age nineteen with highest honors in physics and mathematics from LSU. From there he went to graduate school at the famed California Institute of Technology. He was the youngest entering graduate student, but he nonetheless placed out of all of the basic required physics courses for graduate students. He simply understood all of physics far too well.

Who could say what gave his brilliant mind such power. One factor had certainly been his lifelong training in mathematics, again under the guidance of Jakob Zweig, who had never forced his son to study mathematics but who had always used mathematics in serious discourse with him. Thus in dealing with physical ideas, David Zweig was never slowed by their mathematical language. To the contrary, his fluency with mathematical concepts allowed him to formulate and understand physical ideas more economically and more thoroughly. Mathematics brought speed and meaning to his physical thought just as language brings speed and meaning to ideas in general. In addition to his propitious upbringing, there were David Zweig's own astonishing mental patterns.

Neurologists cannot explain such precocity. What made Moment with its early computer programs? Some infants apparently write the logic of mental subroutines better than others do, perhaps finding the secrets of using more of the brain's circuits simultaneously. Maybe it's a lucky chance of those first firings of the neurons; or maybe it's inherited, decided by the toss of genetic dice. The great mystery defies easy explanation. But David Zweig must have made some special early discoveries that rendered his brain an especially powerful tool, just as mankind itself had done when it left forever the world of the apes.

If the courses at Caltech held little for Zweig, the professors there did. Their passion was the discovery of new knowledge, and at this they were the best in the world. That faculty counted nine Nobel Prize winners. Zweig quickly became a research student of Morris Feinberg, who was to receive the Nobel Prize just two years later for his discovery of an esoteric group-theoretic property of elementary particles. This property, called "strangeness," had explained in an elegant way the puzzling patterns of the reactions and decays of elementary particles. Feinberg's success had raised the hope of interpreting the growing world of elementary particles in terms of the mathematical language of group theory. David Zweig was much attracted to such a challenge and at age twenty he became the apprentice of one of the world's most important physicists. Feinberg was quick to appreciate Zweig's gifts, regarding his young student with a mixture of awe and excitement.

Zweig did not disappoint him. After two years of imaginative but not very productive research into the dispersion relations of quantum field theory, Zweig returned to the group properties of the known particles. Within six months he and Feinberg together saw a wholly new way of viewing the world of elementary particles. It was as if each particle were composed either of three unknown particles, called quarks, or of a quark and an anti-quark. Their paper on this discovery gave structure to the imagined world of elementary particles. Overnight it became a sensation in theoretical physics, and experimenters around the world turned their attention to the challenge of trying to find one of these quarks. Though none had been isolated, their existence was increasingly implied by the many other subatomic properties that they successfully explain.

While Zweig was writing this Ph.D. thesis, he extended the discovery to include yet another quantum property of particles, a property he called "charm." There should exist, he had maintained, both charmed quarks and uncharmed quarks. Additional subtleties of the weak decays of the particles were thereby explained. In addition, charmed particles many times more massive than a normal nucleon, but that could nonetheless change only slowly into a normal nucleon, had been predicted. It would be nine years before the next generation of high-energy accelerators would find these new particles by performing experiments at higher energies than in the past. The 1976 Nobel Prize in physics would be promptly awarded to the scientists who discovered them in laboratory experiments. Zweig's Ph.D. thesis predicting it all was destined to become one of the landmarks of physics, and it immediately earned him the position of professor of theoretical physics at Harvard University in 1967.

Sitting next to the window of the 747 approaching Lod Airport, David Zweig felt as if he were returning home. His life had been changed in 1967 by the Six-Day War. Because of it he had postponed the professorship at Harvard, although he now held that position. The Six-Day War had placed Zweig in terrible anxiety. It had been too difficult to ascertain what was happening during that war. His Jewish friends had confidently claimed that the Israeli troops were well equipped and well trained. But would that be enough? Or would his people be debased by defeat and yet another captivity, the condition from which Moses had led them over three thousand years ago?

During this period, David Zweig had envisioned daily his parents' terror, his uncle's inhuman extinction at Buchenwald, and the void of two missing aunts. He had taken to rereading the Scriptures during the five nights of waiting for news. He read of and relived the hope of the passengers of the Exodus returning to the Promised Land. He had been too distressed to accept the Harvard professorship. Years ago, his father had accepted the Leipzig professorship while the Nazis were preparing to introduce the ultimate solution. David would not sit still to watch history repeat itself in his own life. He would not blind himself to the precarious state of affairs for world Jewry. He would postpone Harvard and go instead to Israel. This time he would fight back, for Israel and for Jakob. He prayed to Yahweh, a God who gave his people freedom by victory in war. He consecrated himself, even though war and violence were abhorrent to him. In return for victory for his people, he would promise his soul to Zionism.

Then miraculously it was over! The preemptive Israeli strikes at key Arab targets had ended the war with swift precision when it seemed it had just begun. Zweig had been engulfed in a wave of spiritual dedication and national pride. The people of Israel were his people, his father's people, his God's people.

Zweig took a postdoctoral position in 1967 at the Weizmann Institute, already world famous for its scientific research. He began research with Elias Hirschberg on general relativity. Hirschberg had just returned from military duty, where he had been a top-level military strategist, in addition to being Israel's leading theoretical physicist. In him Zweig saw a mind attuned both to the intricacies of nature and to the survival of his young country.

It had been a thrilling time for Zweig. He had found a people united, dedicated, hardworking, and selfless. He had found a friendly optimism springing from zeal for a common good. Everywhere he had found an unspoken determination to end forever the terror and suppression of the Jewish people.

With Hirschberg, he had constructed a theory that quasi-stellar objects (called QSO's), with their big red-shifts, were parts of the universe just now emerging into view from a fantastic condensed state, similar to the Big Bang that cosmologists envisioned for the entire universe. They had described QSO's as parts of the universe lagging behind in their emergence from its dense hot past. During that time Zweig had quickly established himself as an international authority on black holes and had published many theorems concerning their properties. He would remember these as the happiest years of his life.

Now, as the wing flaps were lowered for the final approach, Zweig's blank eyes did not shine as they had on the many occasions that had brought him to this airport in recent years. His mind was preoccupied with a dim and desperate plan for the survival of his people. He chewed mindlessly on a fingernail, sick with guilt.

Zweig took a last glance at the copy of the *New York Times* that he had been reading on the flight. As usual, the news was violent, confused, and chaotic. He read about the growing wave of anti-Israeli sentiment in the aftermath of the massacre of Palestinians in Lebanon. The UN had passed a resolution censuring Israel, receiving vociferous support from the Third World nations. Yasser Arafat was making demands from Algeria, and U.S. AWACS planes were being sent to Egypt. Terrorist attacks against the northern Israeli settlements of Yuval and Metulla had resumed, leaving twenty dead.

Quickly Zweig decided he had seen enough of the newspaper. The ominous portents of these events for the future of his people momentarily steeled his resolve. He was confident that his plan, no matter how bizarre, must be acted upon, for only Yahweh could have produced the present miracle in Israel's hour of need.

Six

Home for Rebecca Yahil was with George Reynolds. It had become so within two months of her arrival in Austin. She had adapted so quickly to life in Austin and to life with Reynolds that he often forgot that she was essentially a stranger to the United States. She comfortably adjusted her habits to her new circumstances, only occasionally mentioning that she missed the scenery, or the climate, or perhaps some Middle Eastern spices that she could buy more easily in a Jerusalem marketplace than along Guadalupe Street. Rebecca brought very little with her from Israel, beyond her clothing. She bought a bicycle as soon as she was moderately familiar with the layout of Austin. When she moved in with Reynolds, she had just these few things. She rearranged hardly any of the furnishings in his home, but she did rearrange his feelings about it.

The transition from bachelor to nearly married man was easy for him, too. He couldn't remember ever being so attached to the townhouse on the wooded hillside near the university. He now looked forward to going home at the end of the day. He loved their evening meals, which they took turns in preparing, and he seldom wanted to return to the office in the evening.

She had been living in the house for six months, and Reynolds could hardly remember what it had been like without her. There had been a few awkward moments after she moved in, such as phone calls from old girlfriends. Rebecca was spirited, though, with a lively sense of humor. She teased him about such things, saying, "If you were to move into my apartment in Tel Aviv, we'd have to change the phone number." Reynolds didn't doubt it for a minute.

As he sat in his office on Monday morning, waiting for Corrigan, he couldn't help thinking about her reaction to the news of Cowan's murder. She was in so many ways unflinching that her reaction surprised him. Reynolds was deeply disturbed by the murder, but Rebecca was distracted by it. He had tried to cheer her up on Sunday morning, setting the breakfast table on the balcony in the spring sunlight. He had cut some early roses from the bushes at the front of the house and cooked pancakes and bacon for a real Texas brunch; but she hardly noticed his effort and ate very little. And she said things that made Reynolds feel that they were distanced in ways he hadn't suspected—by her history. It worried him. She talked quite a while, saying such things as, "I lost many friends and family members during the Six-Day War, and I lost my father in the 1973 war. In Israel we are very accustomed to death. We are almost in a constant state of mourning for someone. You can't possibly understand this. We mourn the soldiers who are killed in war and those who are just bystanders to it. Perhaps we all expect, and even want, to die for Israel. I expect to die for Israel; but Cowan was an innocent victim. What did he die for? How do you understand death when it is so unreasonable? Suppose he had to die for something he knew nothing about?" When she left the table suddenly, in tears, Reynolds had followed her into the bedroom, but she had pushed him away.

She had been calmer that evening, but she had asked him question after question about Corrigan. "Why you, George?" she had demanded, even though his connection to the mystery was not really mysterious. She had even suggested that he avoid speaking to Corrigan again. "I don't trust him. Just tell him that you were here, in the tournament when it happened. Tell him that you don't know anything important. Tell him that you're too busy to help out with an investigation."

Reynolds supposed that Rebecca's distress followed from Cowan's having witnessed the flowering of their love. After all, their previous visit to Cowan in the Big Bend had been wonderfully romantic. She would think less about it soon. But today she hadn't come with him to the department, saying she wanted instead to work at home.

It had been natural for the FBI to contact Reynolds. Rebecca understood that. As an unofficial watchdog for the National Science Foundation, attached to the neutrino experiment, he had followed Cowan's work closely from the beginning. He calculated neutrino emissions from the sun as a part of his research at the university, so he knew as much as anyone about the implications of the project.

Six months ago, Reynolds had taken Rebecca to the Big Bend to visit the Solar Neutrino Observatory. It had been at the time of the October six-month summary report. Reynolds tried to be there for those occasions, even though Cowan's results always showed the same dearth of neutrinos. Reynolds was conscientious about reporting to the National Science Foundation, which was increasingly sensitive about public opinion. He could envision some hotshot congressman making headlines by exposing the two-million-dollar search for "the little neutrino that wasn't there." But Cowan's negative results were terribly important, and Reynolds was always adamant in defending the project.

Just the week before, he had received an annoying phone call from a reporter with the *Washington Post,* asking, "Don't you find the results a little embarrassing?" The reporter had been pushy and asked demanding questions as though he were investigating the experiment instead of reporting on it. The amount of technical expertise the man had shown in his questioning was also surprising. It made Reynolds uneasy. Thinking back on it, the call seemed suspicious. He wondered why the reporter had bothered calling him at all, with the six-month report still a week away from release. There was not much story in it. Reynolds had said as much, suggesting that he wait a week, or speak to Cowan directly. The reporter had then cut the conversation off saying, "Thank you, Dr. Reynolds, I think I have enough information." Reynolds decided to tell Corrigan about it—just in case.

George Reynolds had been born and raised in Wichita Falls, Texas, where the Southern Belle mentality was well entrenched. He had never thought much of his chances of finding such a fusion of intelligence and good looks as he now saw in Rebecca. "Are all women in Israel like you?" he had once asked her. She always listened intently, concentrating on every word, but following with a warm smile as she relaxed and understood. She had answered, "I think, Dr. Reynolds, that you find *all* women the same everywhere. You ought to open your eyes." Her accent charmed him. She was so exotic, and she liked to parry with him, keeping him at a distance. That he found her irresistible soon became obvious. He tried to be charming and to impress her with his wide-ranging knowledge. He even began attending department social functions just to be included in conversations with her. His behavior was transparent to all those around him, but she at first gave very little indication of the presence he was assuming in her thoughts.

Reynolds had had ample opportunity to pursue his interest in Rebecca. They worked together. Her thesis at the Racah Institute had been on an aspect of stellar structure that could prove to have some bearing on the solar neutrino experiment. Reynolds's group at the University of Texas was the recognized leader in the study of the interior structure of stars, and Rebecca had come specifically to work with them. In fact, the Israeli government provided her with a rare fellowship to enable her to do so.

Rebecca had known a lot about Reynolds already. She had read many of his papers while writing her thesis. It had actually been thrilling to meet him, since he was something of a scientific celebrity. It was a reputation he enjoyed and did his best to cultivate. Not many of his scientific friends knew that his vital statistics were also a topic of campus gossip. He was in this sense admired for his good looks, his single status, his tennis skills, and even for his Porsche. At age thirty-two he had become the youngest full professor in Austin, and at age thirty-eight had been elected to the National Academy of Sciences as the youngest member save one, David Zweig.

What could be more natural, Reynolds had rationalized, than to invite Rebecca to accompany him to the Big Bend for the fall report. Actually, he had seldom searched so hard for a strategy. At tea break one afternoon he had begun a lively conversation with Rebecca and Ralph Polkinghorn, another postdoc, about a problem concerning neutrino emission from stars more massive than the sun. "Cowan's solar neutrino experiment in the Big Bend is still not recording any neutrinos. I have some thoughts about how to lower the calculated expectation. I'd like to describe them to both of you. I have to get ready for the astrophysics seminar this afternoon, but we could meet for a beer afterwards and discuss it."

"Sounds interesting. I could make it for a while," said Polkinghorn. Reynolds knew that Polkinghorn was married and usually liked to be home by 7:00.

"That would be very nice for me, too," said Rebecca.

Reynolds left the department that afternoon in time to see Rebecca unlocking her bicycle, about to ride to the small beer patio a few blocks west of the campus where they had arranged to meet. He ran to catch up with her and walked with her, asking a lot of questions about her impressions of Texas: had she done any traveling, did she like the food, was the weather similar in Israel? It was a hot afternoon, typical of the early Texas fall. Rebecca was wearing sandals and shorts, as she often did. "Do all students dress this way in Israel?" Reynolds wanted to know, continuing the barrage of questions. On any warm afternoon there might be five thousand coeds milling around the UT campus and along Guadalupe Street in shorts, but Reynolds had radar for Rebecca. She was different. Laughing at the question, she told him that she had worn those same khakis during military exercises. "That explains it," Reynolds joked cryptically, "there is not another pair of military shorts anywhere on campus." There was nothing militaristic about her athletic gracefulness. Still, he admired the story, amazed at the way in which the details of Rebecca's life were prejudicing him one by one into deeper fascination.

They spent a pleasant hour at the small beer patio, where Polkinghorn was already waiting for them. They deliberated on the solar neutrino experiment, watching the lights of Austin turn on, one by one, against the orange sky. As if on cue, Polkinghorn excused himself first, to get home to dinner with his wife and one-year-old. Reynolds moved his chair closer to Rebecca.

"While you're here in Texas," he continued, "you really must see the Big Bend, where Cowan's experiment is located. It is geologically quite different from the Texas one sees between Austin, Houston, and Dallas."

"Oh, I'd like to!" Rebecca answered enthusiastically. "Perhaps the mountains there are somewhat like ours in the Sinai."

"I couldn't say, since I haven't been there, but I'd like to hear your impression." Reynolds smiled and leaned closer, almost touching her. "How would you like to visit the Big Bend with me next week when I have to make the trip? Fred Cowan will be there and will have his latest six-month report, so you can meet him, too."

"That sounds like an excellent opportunity for me," Rebecca replied formally.

"To tell the truth," Reynolds said, launching a trial balloon, "it's a good chance for me, too, because I'd like to get to know you better." He looked straight at her, to be sure the message was clear.

She hesitated, answering finally, "Let me think about it."

"Let's talk about it over dinner," Reynolds offered.

She stood up a little abruptly, looking at her watch. "I'm sorry," she said, "I've let the time get away from me. I'm meeting friends to go to the theater tonight. I'll see you tomorrow, Dr. Reynolds."

Rebecca rode her bicycle straight home. She had no tickets to the theater. She lived in the second-floor apartment of a brick duplex with a U.T. graduate student. They scarcely knew each other. Rebecca spent very little time at home, often working evenings at the astronomy building, so her roommate, Jean, was surprised to see her. "Do you have the night off?" she asked.

Rebecca threw her satchel onto the sofa and kicked her sandals off. She was frowning.

"Is something wrong, Rebecca?" Jean asked.

"I'm not sure," she said, hesitatingly. "I have a problem with Dr. Reynolds. He seems to be . . . romantically interested."

"And you're not," said Jean helpfully.

"I'm not sure. Yes, I am; well, he's very attractive," Rebecca sputtered uncertainly.

"That's a problem?" laughed Jean. "I've heard things about Dr. Reynolds, Rebecca, and I know at least a dozen women who would be happy to have such a problem! He usually dates tennis players. God knows why. But you know how athletic he is. I've seen him in the gym a few times working out on weights." Jean flexed her biceps. They both laughed. It made Rebecca feel more comfortable talking about Reynolds, and the two gossiped together. Jean told Rebecca all she knew, asking finally, "Why don't you want to go out with him?"

Rebecca looked serious again. "He is very attractive, and I have never known such a lighthearted man. I like to be around him. He treats his work like play. I enjoy him very much, but there are complications. We are colleagues . . ."

"Does that have to be a problem?" Jean interrupted.

Rebecca sighed, flustered. "I guess you could say that I have a commitment in Israel," she said, her voice trailing off.

"Oh," said Jean flatly, "that's different. You mean that you'd like to go out with him but you feel that you can't."

The telephone rang, as if Rebecca's words had sent a psychic S.O.S. across Austin searching for the answer to her quandary. It was Reynolds.

"Rebecca, I've called to apologize. I walked by Hogg Auditorium on the way to my car and noticed there isn't a play tonight. I'm afraid I offended you."

"Oh, Dr. Reynolds," Rebecca paused, thinking. She held the telephone as though she would squeeze it in two, leaving half for the message from her brain and half for her impetuousness. Suddenly, unexpectedly, her voice was calm. She answered confidently, "I feel so silly. I was confused about the date. You didn't offend me, I had a lovely time this evening. In fact, I've decided definitely to go to the Big Bend."

Following the conversation Rebecca turned to find Jean eyeing her quizzically. Rebecca shrugged.

"Well, I guess that settles that!" Jean observed.

Reynolds put a few more things into the trunk and polished one last resistant spot on the fender of the gleaming Porsche. At 8:00 A.M. he pulled up in front of her apartment building. She was waiting at the door, brilliant too, in a yellow sundress. She had an overnight bag and a mystery basket with a wine bottle peeking from one end. "I brought lunch," she said, excited.

The drive west was thrilling. She found the scenery spectacular, and the car fascinated her. "I don't even know how to drive," she said. "In Israel I went everywhere by bus." Reynolds

44

was amazed; it hadn't occurred to him. Every so often she would stretch, exclaiming again, "Oh, how comfortable." They laughed a lot, and exchanged life stories. Reynolds promised to give Rebecca a driving lesson: "If I teach you something new, you'll remember me forever," he teased.

The trip was unhurried. It had to be, because they stopped whenever Rebecca saw something exciting. In Fredericksburg they sat in a cafe on the town square where cowboys, and farmers in coveralls spoke in German. "Anachronistic, isn't it?" said George; but Rebecca was intrigued, telling him what it was like living in a country with such a mixed and active cultural history as Israel's. She liked the town very much, reading many of the German signs aloud. "I learned some German as a little girl, from my mother," she told him.

They stopped somewhere between Fredericksburg and Del Rio for a late lunch. Reynolds chose a hilltop spot with a good view in all directions. There was a slight breeze, and the road was almost without traffic. Rebecca surprised him with a wonderful picnic of Israeli specialties. She had fish and hummus and pita bread and cheese. She called it her "bus-trip special." They drank a bottle of Israeli wine that she had hand carried to Austin. "It is not good wine," she explained, "but it is unique. You have probably never seen Israeli wine before. I brought a few bottles from home, for special occasions."

It was quiet. It occurred to both of them, lying on a blanket in the sun overlooking the vastness, that they were alone. It was not like a man and woman alone in a room, in a building, on a busy street, in a frantic city. The whole countryside spread empty around them. Rebecca's eyes closed, and she fell asleep briefly. As Reynolds watched her, he wanted to enfold her.

The Pecos River and the Rio Grande join in a spectacular canyon east of Langtry. After the day of leisurely sightseeing, George and Rebecca arrived at the Pecos River overlook at dusk. At the overlook they could just see the point to the south where the two rivers joined. Rebecca leaned over the rail for a better look. "It's so beautiful," she exclaimed.

"You're so beautiful," Reynolds responded, sliding his arm around her waist. She turned and took his hand, and after squeezing it gently walked back to the car.

They arrived at Langtry about an hour later. After dinner Reynolds offered to take Rebecca on a walking tour of the town. "I know that one hundred years of history isn't impressively long, but the town does have a colorful past." But Rebecca begged off, saying that it had been a wonderful but exhausting day, and left Reynolds watching her as she walked to her room.

They drove directly to the Big Bend the next day. Cowan would be meeting them in the afternoon. They would go over some data and see some of the park together before dark. When they arrived at the Stone Cottages, Reynolds showed surprise that only a curtain separated the bedrooms. He could find them another place to stay, he suggested weakly. Rebecca assured him that she was accustomed to much less spacious accommodations, and that the privacy was adequate.

They spent an exciting afternoon with Cowan. He gave them an insider's tour of the park, referring to a map of the private ranger roads that Tom Williams had given him. They were bounced and jostled against one another along the rocky, rutted paths to some of the park's more scenic overlooks. "Romantic, isn't it," Cowan suggested, looking at Reynolds and Rebecca.

Later, in the Chisos Mountain Lodge they all dined together. The food was simple but good, considering the remoteness of the place. The view of the mountains and the wild sunset in "the window," a mountain ravine opening the basin to the desert lands below, made a gorgeous setting for their budding friendship.

Afterwards they sat in rustic Stone Cottage 101 sharing a bottle of Old Grand-Dad that Cowan had brought along and looking forward to the visit next day to the Solar Neutrino Observatory. They talked about the lack of neutrino emission and about the six-month summary report. More frequently Reynolds joked with Rebecca, touching her hand. In one exuberant moment he slipped his arms around her, and led her around the room in an Indian dance. It didn't matter that the Indians had never danced like that. Fred Cowan, though older and less limber, was not to be outdone, stealing Rebecca away from George to show off his own version of the ritual. They laughed endlessly. It was late when Cowan walked back to the motel units where he stayed in hot weather. He preferred the air-conditioned room to the hot cot in his lab, and Mrs. Cowan would be able to join him there the following afternoon.

Reynolds walked part of the way with Cowan, allowing Rebecca time to shower and get into her bed behind the curtain. When he returned, he, too, showered, and then, turning off the light, he slid into bed beside her.

"What are you doing!" she exclaimed, pushing him away, but gently.

"Looking for solar neutrinos," Reynolds whispered, kissing her neck.

Rebecca laughed, pushing him away even more gently. She could sense his nudity. She felt his breath against her lips. She could not escape the sense of energy in George's relaxed, muscled body. She felt him pausing, waiting for some sign from her. She had been confused when she had imagined this happening. So many conflicting purposes. Now her heart pounded in anticipation. In one last anxious moment she sought the will to resist. Their lips touched briefly, electrically, and her choices abandoned her. She turned toward George, her hair falling across his bare chest. She kissed him again, deeply, running her hand down his side, and taking his hand, drew his arms around her body.

That had been six months ago. Today Reynolds drove alone to the campus. He did not know that Rebecca had left the house after him and walked quickly to the corner store. After buying a magazine for some change, she looked cautiously about, stepped into the phone booth, dialed one, followed by the Manhattan area code, and the number of an apartment on the Upper East Side.

"This is Yahil calling. Let me speak to Leon."

Seven

"I want to relate something before I ask you about neutrinos," Corrigan was saying while admiring the view from Reynolds's nineteenth-floor office window. "On the night of the murder Mrs. Cowan received a telephone call from a man who claimed to be a park ranger. He wasn't. Said his name was Davidson, a name Mrs. Cowan didn't know. She thought nothing of it because park rangers are rotated frequently by the National Park Service. This guy called to say that Dr. Cowan could not come home for the night— that he had to work on the counters."

"And there is no ranger named Davidson," Reynolds mused.

"We checked that right away," Corrigan replied. "There is no such ranger, in Big Bend or elsewhere in the Park Service. But he was someone who knew about Mrs. Cowan, and even knew their telephone number."

Reynolds frowned. "But there's no telephone in the lab."

"That's right," Corrigan acknowledged. "He told Mrs. Cowan that Dr. Cowan had radioed down the message. So this was a planned murder rather than random terrorism. There ought to be a big motive."

"Whoever it was knew Cowan's telephone number and that Cowan had no telephone in the Observatory itself," Reynolds observed. "Cowan did have a radio that he used to communicate with the ranger station, and he did sometimes ask them to telephone Mrs. Cowan in Terlingua."

"Exactly," Corrigan agreed. "A ranger named Tom Williams told us the same thing. So you can see that we have a very funny set of clues. Our investigation shows that Cowan is not suspected of criminal connections. He didn't fool around. He loved his family, and he loved physics, which leaves us little to go on for such an

49

elaborate crime. Only people who had visited the mine, the Cowans, or the Rangers could have known that Cowan sometimes radioed the Rangers. You knew about it, for example. If I'm going to get anywhere with this case, I probably need to understand the importance of this experiment. That's where I need your help."

Reynolds sipped at a coffee and nodded. "As far as I know, the experiment has no immediate practical value. It was an attempt to learn something fundamental and new about the center of our sun. The Energy Research and Development Administration is supporting a variety of studies concerned with the outer layers of the sun, with an eye to the chances of developing solar energy. But Cowan's experiment was designed to measure something about the center of the sun, a region so hot and remote that it is of no known practical value. Do you want me to explain the basic idea?"

"Exactly," Corrigan replied. "I want to understand, without getting too involved in technicalities like neutrinos and chlorine and stuff, just exactly what he hoped to learn and what the experiment had demonstrated over these few years."

"Well, it will be hard to avoid talking about neutrinos," Reynolds chuckled, "since they're the particles that Cowan was trying to detect. They're ejected in large numbers from the sun, but they're invisible. A neutrino has no mass and it has no electric charge."

"Hold it a minute. What does it have?" Corrigan wanted to know.

"Good question. It moves with energy and momentum, just like light moves with energy and momentum, even though it also has no mass or charge. Perhaps you've seen one of those little enclosed windmills that can be made to rotate by shining a light on it. The real difference between photons and neutrinos is how these particles react with other particles. Light rays are generated by electric and magnetic forces—as are radio waves, X-rays, and all other types of radiation that we call electromagnetic. Since these waves are caused by the motion of charged particles, they can, in turn, cause other charged particles to move. Because the electric force is so strong, and since all matter is assembled out of small charged particles, an electromagnetic wave can't travel very far unless it has almost empty space to move through."

"Like from the sun to the Earth," Corrigan guessed.

"Right! But light can't get out from the *inside* of the sun. There are just too many particles above it, and they impede the flow of the light waves," Reynolds replied. "Even on the brightest day, you can make a room in your house dark just by taping black paper to the windows—paper that's only 1/16th of an inch thick."

"Yeah, but radio waves come through," Corrigan retorted.

"Even so, many radio frequencies cannot penetrate the Earth's ionosphere—a very thin region of free electrons that wiggle so violently when the radio waves try to pass that they simply stop them. No type of electromagnetic wave could travel more than a quarter of an inch at the sun's center. All the light we get from the sun comes from the top layers, from its skin, just as it does from a steel bowling ball heated until it is red hot."

"OK. I got that," Corrigan said. "What about the neutrinos? I guess I'm ready for them."

"We know of neutrinos from only one source," Reynolds replied, grinning at Corrigan's modesty. "They are created by an incredibly weak force that causes a type of radioactivity called nuclear beta decay."

"I thought nuclear forces were very powerful," Corrigan interjected.

"The force that holds nuclei together is very powerful," Reynolds acknowledged. "It is also the source of nuclear energy—in reactors, in nuclear weapons, and even in the sun's center; or so we think. We call that the strong force. But there is a second nuclear force—the so-called weak force—which creates neutrinos during nuclear beta decay. This force is so weak that it changes the nucleus a million million million million times more slowly than the strong force does. Because this force is so weak, a neutrino also passes through matter very easily. There is only a very weak chance that a neutrino can cause another nucleus to react with it. But that's the way it's absorbed. So all matter is incredibly transparent to neutrinos. They come directly out of the center of the sun. Even the crust of the earth can't stop them, so they should be whizzing by just as frequently in Cowan's lab in the mine as they do on the surface of the earth."

"Why did he use a mine, then?" Corrigan wondered.

"The depth was a shield against other kinds of cosmic rays. They get stopped in the ground because they have electric charge. Only neutrinos can get through. That's why the radioactive atoms produced in the mine are due only to neutrinos, not to cosmic rays. Do you get the picture?"

"Yeah, but I never really understood it until now. So thanks. The earth stops all radiation but the neutrino, so the radioactive nuclei made in the mine are due to neutrinos."

"Right," Reynolds continued, trying to avoid the impression of tutoring a student. "The sun should make more neutrinos than any other source of neutrinos—that is, if we understand correctly what its power is due to. The sun would have gone dim in the first 1/50th of its present age if it didn't have a powerful source of heat at its center. The source of that heat was one of the major scientific puzzles of this century. We've believed for some years now that the answer is known; namely, that the sun is a giant thermonuclear reactor, much like the plasma fusion reactors that we hope to construct for clean power on Earth. Hans Bethe won the Nobel Prize for figuring out which nuclear reactions should be happening at the sun's center to provide that heat. And at Caltech, where I was a graduate student, Professor Fowler's team effort in the nuclear lab measured almost all of the reaction strengths. A little over five years ago we thought we knew all of the details of the sun's central thermonuclear reactor. Cowan's experiment changed all that."

"In what way exactly?" Corrigan asked.

"Cowan's experiment concerns the small number of neutrinos captured by other atoms. If our ideas are right, the chlorine atoms in Cowan's tank should be numerous enough to absorb one neutrino a day. Of course, he needed a very large tank to catch any at all. The argument seems to have no loopholes. We know the rate of energy output of the sun. We know which nuclear reactions provide that power, and we know how frequently these reactions emit neutrinos. Knowing the distance to the sun we therefore also know the number and energy of neutrinos reaching each square centimeter of Earth's surface in every second. We know how often a neutrino will react with an atom of chlorine, changing it into an atom of radioactive argon. We therefore know that we will expect one chlorine atom daily to change into radioactive argon in Cowan's tank. The argument is airtight. It's the same way that we correctly tested the rate at which neutrinos emerge from a nuclear reactor here on Earth. Cowan had already done that by setting up an experiment alongside a nuclear reactor to prove that neutrinos do exist. So his technique is known to work. This argument was so convincing to scientists that many believed that Cowan's attempt to find neutrinos from the sun could not fail—that he would only confirm the correctness of our understanding." Reynolds paused and leaned back in his chair, allowing Corrigan to digest the flow of information.

"I've got two questions," Corrigan eventually said. "Do you mean to tell me he could expect to find only one atom a day?"

"That's about right. Actually, he counts them each month, so he is really looking for about thirty atoms of radioactive argon each month," Reynolds replied. "I admit, that's still pretty fantastic, but Cowan conducted a number of sensitive tests that proved he could find such a small number of radioactive argon atoms in his tank. What's the second question?"

"Why does he count them each month? Wouldn't it be easier

to find 360 atoms after a year?"

"It doesn't work that way," Reynolds replied. "The radioactive argon has a life span of thirty-five days. After that, the argon is disappearing in the tank by radioactive decay just as fast as it's being produced by the solar neutrinos. So you don't get more by waiting longer."

"Oh, yeah. I get it. How does he count the radioactive argons?"

"He bubbles helium gas through the tank. That bubbling picks up the argon atoms, like catching them with a filter. By such bubbling he has shown he can get at least 90 percent of the argon atoms out of the tank. Then he simply counts them. Because they're radioactive, the argon atoms in the extracted gas will decay back to chlorine—with a thirty-five-day lifetime—and he can recognize and count each atom as it decays."

"And it really works?"

"It really works. At least the experiment really works. The argon recovery and counting really works. But something else does not work. As you know, Fred Cowan was never able to find any positive evidence of solar neutrinos. All he was able to show was that the solar neutrinos were producing less than three argon atoms per month—fully ten times less than had been expected. This was a shock."

"Why was it a shock?"

"Because we were so *wrong*. Because it has shaken our faith that we understand how stars function. Today we have an elaborate theory of the evolution of different types of stars—how they're created, how they age, and how they die. An important part of that theory, and I would say even the cornerstone of the theory, is that the stars obtain their power from the thermonuclear fusion reactions at their center, and that these same reactions cause the star to age by burning up its nuclear fuel and changing its chemical composition. It's a beautiful theory."

"I understand that you and your colleagues here at the university have been a key group in the development of that theory," Corrigan said.

"We've been active," Reynolds answered. "But the real point is that the solar neutrino experiment was a chance to test the cornerstone of that theory. The sun is supposed to be a simple star. By confirming the nuclear power in our own sun, we would at least have an experimental basis for this whole theoretical structure. We even talked optimistically of measuring the temperature of the solar center by counting neutrinos, because their production rate depends strongly on that temperature. The counts could tell us whether the solar center is at fourteen million degrees, as we expect, or perhaps at thirteen or fifteen million degrees instead. We hoped the experiment would simultaneously confirm our basic understanding and measure new facts about the sun."

"And it didn't work out."

"It sure as hell didn't!" Reynolds exclaimed. "The neutrino flux is so much smaller than we expected that it's challenging our basic belief that thermonuclear energy is the source of the sun's power."

"So what does this mean—philosophically?"

"Well . . . ," Reynolds paused. "I'd say this. If we don't understand the sun, which is in theory the simplest star in the sky, then we must not understand any star. Since the sun is so important to life on Earth, we may make a terrible picture of something fundamental to our existence. New knowledge always extends old knowledge, but here we have a demonstration that our understanding is just plain wrong. It's pretty shaky to extend that kind of knowledge."

"Doesn't it damage your career that you've spent so much time building a theory that gives the wrong answers?"

"I really don't think so at all," Reynolds replied. "Science just doesn't work quite like that. I would even say that my own career has been accelerated by Cowan's negative result. In science we judge the merit of a theoretical idea in terms of its effectiveness at stimulating new and deeper understanding—not just in terms of whether the idea turns out to be right or not. Let me give you an example. Newton's theory of gravity is one of the jewels of our culture, even though it has turned out not to be the correct theory of gravity. But it is still an excellent approximation of the truth— good enough to have gotten Neil Armstrong to the moon—and, equally important, it stimulated a revolution in mankind's capability for interpreting the cosmos."

"But why do you say it isn't correct?" Corrigan interrupted.

"Because it explains only limited situations. It doesn't give the curvature of light from a distant star as it passes near the sun; it predicts that the orbit of Mercury should exactly repeat its elliptic path rather than slowly change, as it does; it doesn't explain why a radar echo from a planet arrives somewhat tardily when that planet is passing behind the sun; it doesn't give the gravitational redshift that we see in the light from dense stars, and even in terrestrial laboratories; it doesn't predict black holes; it doesn't. . ."

"Stop! Enough's enough," Corrigan surrendered. "Just clarify how it is that your getting the wrong answer for Cowan's experiment has helped your career?"

Reynolds laughed at the question, then responded, "It's really simple. I've had the good luck to invent a good numerical routine for constructing models of stars on computers. I worked very hard, as have my students and postdocs, at putting the most advanced and careful physics into these models. Others have followed and repeated these calculations, but they all get essentially the same answer I do. So it's natural in the scientific world to compare Cowan's surprising negative result with my computer models. My models have come to symbolically represent a philosophy of thinking about the sun. In that sense, my answers represent a laboriously constructed viewpoint, whether right or wrong, and the viewpoint is an intelligent viewpoint. As a formulator of this viewpoint, my career has definitely been helped—all the more so since Cowan's results have focused attention on this viewpoint and called it into question. Lurking behind all this is our awe of the sun. It makes life possible. It is a bit frightening to admit that we don't understand it after all. Cowan's result has caused this unease, and has suggested that this esoteric and impractical science, stellar evolution, might be more relevant to a wider range of big issues than we had previously suspected."

Corrigan sat back thinking it over, for he had just heard many things he had never thought of before. Glancing at his notes, he asked another question: "Is it true that Cowan was the only scientist attempting such an observation? Was there no one else who wanted to do the same experiment?"

"Many scientists would have liked the chance to try such an experiment," Reynolds answered, "but Cowan's is the only such experiment in operation. The trouble is that it is very difficult and expensive to set up such an experiment. A University of Pennsylvania group has another neutrino observatory, but their detection technique is sensitive only to bursts of high-energy neutrinos, quite unlike those from the sun. Basically they are hoping to find evidence for the collapse of the centers of stars much bigger than the sun. So their experiment is not really in competition. There was another attempt started about five years ago in Israel, in the Negev. When I saw Elias Hirschberg at the Texas Symposium on Relativistic Astrophysics four years ago, he told me their hopes. The experiment was planned to be similar in philosophy to the Cowan experiment, but it would use a gallium absorber rather than a chlorine absorber. The experiment was to be conducted by Jamil Koren, professor of physics at Ben Gurion University in Beersheba. I wrote Koren for a couple of years, and the preliminary studies of the experiment looked difficult but feasible. Then two years ago they shelved it because it was too costly to obtain the gallium—they would have needed almost fifty tons of the stuff. Now Till Kirsten in Germany is trying to gather support for a European experiment. There is also some indication that a U.S.S.R. group is very interested in trying an experiment, but we can't find out if they're actually building something, and, if so, what. But Cowan's was the only operating experiment and his ran about seven years. So any thought of competitive scientific envy seems out of the question to me."

Through all of this Corrigan's interest had perked up. His expertise was in the field of motivation for murder. That was why he had been assigned to this case. And although Reynolds could see no connection, Corrigan's instincts and a knowledge of a few extra facts quickly led him to think that they were now in the right ballpark.

"Does David Zweig sometimes go to the Neutrino Observatory at report times?" Corrigan asked in an abrupt change of direction.

"Yes," Reynolds answered. "He's one of the frequent visitors, because he's one of the scientists who played a big role in getting the experiment going."

"What role?" Corrigan asked.

"Well, let's see, it was 1965, I think. He was a graduate student at Caltech at the time, and it was he who realized that the mass-37 isotope of chlorine was an ideal absorber for solar neutrinos. He was working on the theory of the weak nuclear force, and he realized that a fraction of the solar neutrinos had enough energy to be absorbed when they struck the chlorine nucleus. It made everyone more optimistic about a chlorine detector. He worked on the physics of that for a while and has maintained a keen interest in the experiment ever since," Reynolds concluded.

"I know that," Corrigan said. "We were given both of your names by the National Academy of Sciences as pundits on this experiment. Can I ask you for your confidence in discussing Zweig?"

"Yes. I can't promise to tell you anything, but I can promise not to reveal anything we talk about," Reynolds answered.

Corrigan put down his notes and looked gravely at Reynolds. "When we called his secretary at Harvard on the day after the crime, she said that Zweig had left the day before for Texas and the semiannual report. His airline route was Boston–New York–Dallas–Midland. She said he usually rents a car in Midland. The car rentals there did not show anything, but Avis rented a car to a man named Davidson, who took it out at 1:30 P.M., just fifteen minutes after Zweig's flight would have arrived in Midland; what's more, the car was returned sometime that night, because it was found at the airport the next morning."

"That's no reason to suspect Zweig. In fact, it's preposterous," Reynolds said. "He wouldn't harm a fly."

"You forget that the man who called Mrs. Cowan claimed to be a Ranger named Davidson," Corrigan stated, "and you also don't know that the next day a man named Davidson bought a cash ticket from Midland to New York, where we lost him completely. You also don't know that Zweig has disappeared! The FBI can't find him anywhere. On top of that, the Avis agent in Midland identified a photograph of Zweig as the man who rented the car."

Reynolds whistled, then responded, "But this was an elaborate destruction—an explosion, arson, destruction of the counters and the electronics, and . . ."

Suddenly Reynolds stopped and bolted upright in his chair.

"Did they destroy the white steel box about fifty yards above the mine entrance?" he asked.

"What box?" Corrigan asked, puzzled.

"There's a white steel box, about four feet on a side, like a small closet, located fifty yards up the hill above the entrance to the mine. That's where an air pipe comes through to vent the mine below. Cowan ran electric cables up through it so that he could house an auxiliary recorder above ground."

"We never saw this box," Corrigan said, somewhat excited. "What do you mean by a recorder?"

"Cowan kept electronics and a magnetic-tape record system in the box. It keeps a digital account of the record of every count of radioactive argon for the past year— its date, its pulse characteristics, etc.— so that he would have a full external record if he had to abandon the mine temporarily for safety reasons," Reynolds said.

"What do you mean, safety reasons?"

"Well, I don't know exactly, but a leak in the perchlorethylene would be a bad threat. Fire, gas, or maybe even structural danger due to earthquake or heavy rains. I can't say why he would have had to evacuate. But I do know there is a tape recording there of his counts! Was it destroyed?"

"I flat don't know," Corrigan said. "We never noticed it."

"Well, I think we ought to look," Reynolds said, obviously excited. "Maybe there's a clue there to what happened."

"Could you go there with me?"

"Sure. This is important to me. There isn't a flight to Midland until 5:00 P.M., so why don't we leave now in my car? It's a long drive, but we'll be there by 9:00 tonight."

"We can take my rental car," Corrigan replied. "This is FBI business."

"I'd rather drive my car," Reynolds said.

"OK. When can we go?"

"Now," Reynolds answered. "Just let me call Rebecca to tell her where we're going."

He quickly dialed the number of his apartment. No one answered. He dialed the department office, and when he was told that Dr. Yahil had not been in, he left a brief message. Then he stood up saying, "Let's go. I'll just get the lantern and some extra tools from the lab."

Within fifteen minutes, the Porsche was rolling west toward Fredericksburg; from there it would drop down to Highway 41. The road to Rocksprings and on to Del Rio bears little traffic, and they covered it at 85 mph in an attempt to reach Panther Junction before dark.

"Will your FBI badge defend us against a speeding ticket?" Reynolds joked.

They pulled into a gas station north of Del Rio in record time—even for Reynolds, who admitted to a slight weakness for fast driving. The Porsche cried to be driven, a mismatch to Texas's wide straight freeways and 55 mph speed limit, so that Reynolds sometimes yielded on the remote smaller roads of the Hill Country and on west. This was so characteristic of him, who strove in all things to utilize capabilities fully. It was, for example, a curious part of his passion for tennis. He possessed an accurate topspin backhand that was the envy of many highly ranked players, and it was this skill that almost compelled him to continue his matches with the rising young experts of tennis, for it was only by extending himself in high-level competition that the stroke could be fully utilized. And it was a similar striving that had caused him to utilize the computer so excellently in his numerical models of stars. The computer was a superb tool, and the star was a sublime problem; so he had wedded the two with sympathetic understanding.

On the road again, a right turn joined U.S. Highway 90 just north of the Del Rio city limits, and he headed due west, past the high Amistad Reservoir and Dam, over the magnificent bridges spanning the east end of Amistad and the flooded canyons of the Pecos River near the west end of Amistad, past Langtry where Judge Roy Bean had declared himself the only law west of the Pecos, and over the rising desert lands toward Sanderson. It was a long drive, and the conversation between the two men periodically paused and then started again. They discussed Cowan's tape record, then cars, then tennis, then the FBI, then the University of Texas, then back to the tape record. As he explained it to Corrigan, Reynolds was striving to reconstruct the nature of the information on the magnetic tape. He remembered that Cowan counted the pulses in the bubbled-out gas, and that the time of each electronic pulse was recorded. There also was a record of the characteristics of each pulse—its rise time and energy—so that the pulse from ^{37}Ar decay could be distinguished from pulses from other sources. What he was unsure of, and tried to explain to Corrigan, was just how this information was digitally coded onto the magnetic tape. He simply did not know. Finally, both men agreed that that bridge could be crossed when and if they came to it. First they had to find out if the recorder box was destroyed. It was on this point that Corrigan was optimistic, for he had himself inspected the crime scene but had not even seen such a box.

The sun was setting before their eyes behind the Davis Mountains when the Porsche pulled into the Texaco station in Marathon, just eighty miles north of their final destination. A tank of gas would be more than sufficient to drive into the Chisos Mountains and back out again. They would be able to cover the curving road in the gray light of early evening.

Eight

The sky was just turning black when they pulled into the Ranger Station at Panther Junction. The Visitor Entrance was closed at sunset, but Corrigan, who had been in close contact with the rangers during the crime inspection, asked Reynolds to pull to the back, where there was a small office attended by a single ranger until 10:00 P.M. It was, in fact, Tom Williams who answered their knock.

"Well, hello, Mr. Corrigan," Williams said with almost immediate recognition. "What brings you back—especially at this late hour?"

"We've got a new idea about the crime, Mr. Williams," Corrigan replied, "and we want to check it out."

"Well, you already know that you can have all the help I can give. The bastards who did this don't belong on this earth," said Williams, glancing at Reynolds.

"This is Dr. George Reynolds, from the university in Austin," Corrigan explained. "And this is Tom Williams, Dr. Reynolds. Tom was a lot of help in our investigation. Now I need the help of both of you."

"Well, don't stand out there with the mosquitoes. Come on in and have a cup of coffee," Williams offered, leading them into the small office, where he waved without comment toward two chairs next to the plaster wall.

"Thanks," Reynolds said. "We can both use a cup of coffee. We haven't had a thing since Sanderson."

Williams had barely two more cups in his pot and he offered them to Reynolds and Corrigan. Then looking at Reynolds, he asked, "Did you know Fred?"

"I'm a scientific colleague. Also a friend. But the point of the

61

moment is that we have come to check out something we overlooked," Reynolds said, glancing questioningly at Corrigan.

"Go ahead. Ask Williams about it," Corrigan urged.

"Do you know about the small white metal storage closet about fifty yards above the opening of the mine?" Reynolds asked. "It sits on a large level rock beside the air shaft into the mine."

"Can't say that I do," Williams responded, obviously interested. "Are you sure there is such a thing?"

"Yes, I've seen it. It contains electronic recording equipment of Cowan's," Reynolds replied.

"We wondered if it was also destroyed," Corrigan interjected. "When we were examining the damage, I'm sure we never looked at it."

"I never even knew about it," Williams repeated, "but I wasn't working here when Fred set up his lab. I've got an idea, though. Our file cabinet has a drawing of the entire installation. Let's look at it."

Williams yanked a manila folder marked "Argonne Neutrino Observatory" from a gray metal file cabinet. The three men leaned over the desk to examine the line drawing of the observatory facility. It didn't take long to find it. The vertical section showed clearly the wires running upward through a tube from the central console below and terminating on the 4' x 4' x 3' box marked simply "steel cabinet."

"Yeah, there it is all right," Williams admitted, "but I'll be damned if I ever saw it."

"The point is," Corrigan explained, "that the box contains a record of Cowan's experiment. Reynolds remembered its existence and wondered if it had been destroyed, too. We had no idea from our investigation. So we came to have a look at it on the chance it might contain some clue."

"Well, I sure hope so," Williams said. "You can't very well go up there tonight, though. The Pine Canyon Road is too rough to drive at night, unless I go with you in the Rover. And it's very hard to see on these black nights."

"No, we'll get some sleep and go up there first thing in the morning. Right now we'd better go get a room," Corrigan replied. Inwardly he cursed, recognizing a professional mistake. He had no control over Tom Williams. Should he ask Williams to not disclose their presence or that of the cabinet, or should he trust his sincerity and good sense?

"OK. But you can stay in the ranger bunks if you want to. We have three extra beds at the moment. Why don't you do that and have breakfast with me?" Williams offered.

"Good enough," Corrigan replied. He relaxed somewhat.

The three went back to a large room containing four beds. Tired, they washed up quickly in the hand basin. Thinking it over, Corrigan decided that any destruction to the cabinet tonight could probably be recognized by expert attention as not having occurred four nights ago. Williams joined them twenty minutes later, after locking up the office. It was quiet, dark, and cool, and all three men slept in the calm of the wilderness.

Williams himself fried eggs on a small grill at 7:00 the next morning. Over the simple breakfast, they resumed the conversation, going over all points again. Williams pointed out that they had locked the gate to the Observatory while the crime was still being investigated, and he gave them the single key to its padlock. Thanking him, the two men walked out toward Reynolds's car. When Williams saw the Porsche he advised against driving it all the way to the Observatory because of the roughness of the final part of the road, suggesting instead that they park on the flat about one-quarter mile above the gate and walk the remaining few hundred yards.

The Porsche covered the road they both had now traveled many times, Reynolds over the last few years, and Corrigan over the last week. The sun was just peeking over the mountains on the Mexican side of the Rio Grande as they followed the curve southeast toward Boquillas. Within ten minutes they left the paved road, making the right turn into the Pine Canyon Road. Reynolds drove well, but even with caution the Porsche occasionally scraped bottom passing through the many dips and potholes that pitted the gravel-covered park road. Reynolds decided not to exceed twenty mph, so the seven-mile trip was a bit tedious.

"There's another car coming about a mile behind us," Reynolds said, glancing into the rearview mirror. "I've noticed a dust cloud a couple of times already, and judging from the size of it, it's moving faster than we are. Probably hikers coming into Pine Canyon or continuing on to Mariscal Canyon. That's a beauty— Mariscal Canyon—if you ever get the chance to see it, take it."

"It's a police car," Corrigan finally said from the half-turned position from which he had watched for it. "That's actually quite unusual," he continued, "because the Highway Patrol doesn't normally get off onto the unpaved roads, and we've already concluded the routine investigation of the site."

"Well, I can see the Observatory gate about three-fourths of a mile ahead now," Reynolds said, "so we'll see there what's going on."

Corrigan kept watching as the trailing car drew nearer. There were the unmistakable lights atop the Ford sedan of the Texas Highway Patrol. As the Porsche pulled off the road to the right, stopping just in front of the Observatory gate, he turned to Rey nolds and said, "Let me do the talking to this car, if you don't mind."

"Of course I don't mind," Reynolds said, shooting a quizzical look at Corrigan.

"Well, it just seems strange to me," Corrigan replied, more to Reynolds's look than to his words.

The two unlocked the gate, a simple Yale padlock, and swung the gate open just as the trailing auto pulled up beside them. The black and white Ford had Texas Highway Patrol emblazoned on the side, and contained two men. The one in the passenger seat got out, and walked up to them.

"Hello. I'm Officer Samuelson of the Highway Patrol," he said, glancing at the open gate. "How did you open the gate? The road is closed."

"We got the key from the Panther Junction Ranger Station," Corrigan replied.

"Well, I'm surprised they gave it to you, because the road is closed to the public," Officer Samuelson continued. His eyes were attracted by the University of Texas parking sticker on the rear window. "Is this your car?" he asked Reynolds, who had clearly been the driver.

"Yes, it is," Reynolds replied.

"What are you doing up here, that you have a key for?" Samuelson pressed on, then added, "And aren't you from the University of Texas?"

"Yes, we are," Corrigan interjected. "I'm Professor Fisher, and this Dr. Jones. We're from the Geology Department, and our purpose is a research program to study how veins of copper could have formed in this volcanic area. We have the key because the National Park Service has approved this scientific research program, and the richest copper veins are near the old mine, on the east slopes of Lost Mine Peak."

Reynolds was dumbfounded, but managed not to show it. Wondering what madness he had become involved in, he added, "There really isn't another good route to the mine. It's just beyond that hill."

Pointing toward the hill, his heart practically fluttered, because, although the mine could not be seen because of the intervening slope, his sharp eyes fell immediately on the white box, which was barely in view. It was still there, but he couldn't tell if it was damaged.

"I'm afraid I'll have to ask you to go back," Samuelson said slowly, noting again the sticker number on the Porsche. "You may not know it, but there was a murder at the mine, and no one is allowed there while the investigation continues. Maybe by the end of the week . . ."

"Well, it's a considerable inconvenience, but I suppose we can return next week," Corrigan said firmly, as much to Reynolds as to the officer. "We have not been told of any crime investigation, but we obtained this key just today, along with a note that a lock had been placed on the gate, so there is a communication breakdown somewhere. But we don't want to interfere with a criminal investigation. Come on, George, let's go."

Corrigan sat abruptly in the Porsche and closed the door. Sensing that he was being led, Reynolds did the same. The officers looked uncertain, and both stared at Reynolds.

"Just start the car and go," Corrigan said softly.

Reynolds backed around the Ford at one of the few places where there was space on that road for such a maneuver, and drove quickly away. The two officers got in their car, eventually turned it around, and slowly followed. The driving officer turned to the other one and said, "Perhaps it is Reynolds. The athletic-looking one fits the verbal description that we have of him. We just don't have a photograph. That's stupid, don't you agree, Amos?"

"We'll soon find out," said the other, picking up the car radio. "Jamil, come in Jamil, this is Amos, Jamil, this is Amos." He relaxed the call button.

"Yes, Jamil here," came the reply. "What do you need?"

"Find out the owner of University of Texas parking sticker 1193, it's purple, and radio us back when you can."

"Right. Purple sticker, number 1193, we'll get it easily," came the reply. Nothing more was said.

Corrigan was saying to Reynolds in the other car, "I'm glad they didn't ask for your driver's license. They are not highway patrolmen. Drive a little faster; I'll buy a new muffler if you need it."

"Why do you say they aren't?" Reynolds said, now concentrating on the pockmarked road.

"It's all too strange," Corrigan replied. "The Highway Patrol never patrols the park roads. We didn't use them at all in the investigation. Never even contacted them. We used only FBI men and the staff of Park Rangers. Besides, the Highway Patrol only drives one officer per car; in these wide open spaces, they can't afford two men per car. But the clincher is the license plate. It's wrong."

Reynolds had nothing but admiration for Corrigan's powers of observation, but that admiration did not relieve a slowly growing sense of fear. Was he in fact involved in something dangerous for him, as it obviously had been for Cowan? What possible connection could there be? Corrigan was, of course, asking himself exactly the same questions. Accelerating now over each smooth strip of gravel and braking just before coasting through the many rutted holes, they covered the return route at about thirty-five mph, and could have done so faster if the alleged police car were gaining on them. In fact, it was out of sight, so great was their lead, although Corrigan soon noticed their dust cloud a mile or so behind them.

"By the way, I saw the steel cabinet," Reynolds said, "among the rocks on the side of the mountains, but I couldn't tell if it was damaged or not."

"Well, at least we know it's still there," Corrigan replied. "We've got to have a look at it. What worries me is that these fake policemen are keeping surveillance over the mine. If so, they are almost surely connected with the crime, and they must be apprehended, but we'll want to call in help for that. That will take a little time, because I'll want to fly in some of our men from El Paso. We'll do that at the ranger station."

"It worries me that they somehow know who we are and that we're looking for something at the scene. If they have ways of checking our identity, for example, my license plate, they may return to the mine for a look around. If they do, they may easily see the steel cabinet," Reynolds speculated.

"That's true, and they do seem to have stopped," Corrigan said, looking out the rear window. "Why don't we wait a minute here until we see if they're coming?"

Reynolds agreed and pulled the Porsche to a halt while Corrigan continued watching. No more dust cloud could be seen, a sure sign that their car had stopped or reversed. In the meantime the car radio in the fake police car was calling urgently.

"Amos. Amos. Jamil calling. Come in."

The man in the passenger seat picked up the microphone and replied: "Yes, this is Amos, what is it?"

"The auto belongs to George Reynolds. Our men called as Highway Patrol and easily got the identification from Parking and Traffic at the University of Texas. We checked with Leon. He says that Reynolds has obviously come to look for something. You are to keep him under surveillance at least and, if possible, simply eliminate him, because this wilderness would be a good place to be rid of him. Leon authorizes this because Reynolds is perhaps the only man capable of exposing the scientific thread. It is important, Leon urges, so do what you can."

"Will do, Jamil. We will now try to follow them."

Within seconds, Corrigan noted the large cloud of dust, less than two miles behind, moving toward them at a high speed for the road.

"They're coming fast," he said to Reynolds. "Let's get going."

Immediately Reynolds restarted the car and moved it ahead as fast as he safely could. Their lead was in any case great, and they were now only two miles from the paved road.

"They're really trying to keep us in sight now," Corrigan observed. "They can easily see our dust trail, so they know where we are. Just keep driving at only moderate speed unless I tell you to go faster. I don't want them to know we're running from them. It makes me doubly glad that we stopped. But when we get to the paved road, drive to Panther Junction as fast as you can. We can get there and out of sight before they realize how fast we're going. When we get to the Ranger Station, pull on to the back and into the double garage where the Land Rovers are kept. Then I'll close the door and they'll never know we're there."

"OK," Reynolds replied, then added, "I know how we could check the tape record without waiting for help to come from El Paso. We can go up to the Lost Mine Trail on the west side of the mountain, over the top, and down a few hundred feet to the cabinet."

"Sounds risky," Corrigan replied. "They'd know we were going up there by seeing our car parked at the trailhead.

"I know, but that will even help," Reynolds countered, "because it's actually a difficult climb, and without intimate knowledge of the peculiarities of this mountain, and without proper hiking boots, they couldn't follow me. The trouble is, neither could you."

"Take it easy, jock," Corrigan said, smiling, and looking at his plain calfskin shoes. "How would we solve that?"

"Easy," Reynolds continued. "When we see them start up the trail behind us, you go back and say that I want to take a little hike up the trail but you're out of shape and prefer to wait in the car. They'll follow me if they really do want to intercept us, or one will, but he'll never catch up with me—I can guarantee that. One of my other interests is mountain climbing, and I know exactly what we get into on this mountain. Those guys will either not make it or it will take them at least an hour longer than it takes me to get to the mine. I'll let them see me just enough so that they continue following, but I'll decoy them into the worst routes. It'll work."

Reynolds now made a left turn onto the paved park road while Corrigan considered the merits of his plan. Reynolds obviously knew what he was talking about, and Corrigan had been worried about having to wait a full day before checking the tape box. Reynolds pushed the Porsche quickly to forty mph before shifting into third gear, then accelerated abruptly to seventy mph before shifting into fourth. Several seconds later they were at ninety mph, which brought them to the Ranger Station in five minutes. Reynolds knew that at that speed on that road, they would never see the trailing car, which would realize too late that they must be driving very fast. They turned sharply left into the visitor parking lot, drove through to the rear and into the two-vehicle garage. Within seconds they had the garage doors down, after first slipping out so that they could discreetly watch for the passing car.

Three minutes later it came, slowed down at the roadside and surveyed the parking lot, then accelerated onward to the road upward into the Chisos Basin. It was sensible to assume that Reynolds had gone into the Basin, because it contained the only civilization around. But it would take a half-hour search for them to discover that he was elsewhere.

Quickly they explained the situation to the Park Ranger, and Corrigan called the FBI in El Paso. Just as quickly, Reynolds explained the plan to check the steel cabinet at once, before the others could return and perhaps find it. Tom Williams understood the plan and the routes well and agreed with Reynolds that he could certainly safely make it to the mine before the others could react. After they agreed on the positioning of the cars, they returned to the Porsche. Reynolds extracted his heavy leather climbing boots from the trunk where he kept them in a backpack. Into the pack he put screwdriver, pliers, and hacksaw, along with a quart of water. Then, with Corrigan driving so that Reynolds could get his boots laced, they also raced toward the Chisos Basin. Before getting there, they pulled the Porsche into the small parking lot at the head of the Lost Mine Trail, quickly got out, locked the car, and started up the trail. Corrigan kept the ignition key. Tom Williams followed leisurely along the road in a Park Service Land Rover, from which he would monitor developments. When he parked it at a wide spot on the road about two hundred yards beyond the trailhead, Reynolds and Corrigan were already one hundred yards up the trail. He waited there only seven minutes before he saw the police car coming back up the winding road from the Basin. He was studying a map when the two passed him in the police car, and he noticed that they gave him only a casual glance. In the rearview mirror, Williams also noticed that the license of the car was incorrect, and he could easily see that they pulled the car into the small parking area and stopped it beside Reynolds's Porsche. They got out, examined the empty Porsche, and looked up the trail.

The Lost Mine Trail was wide and easy, even paved for the first one hundred yards, and smooth and easy walking beyond. They had a brief discussion, looking periodically up the trail, then finally, as if making some decision, left the police car and started up the trail after Reynolds and Corrigan. Williams then started the Land Rover and moved it back up the hill and parked it beside the false police car. He walked around it to the driver's side, bent down and unscrewed the cap on the rear tire and with his ignition key quickly let out the air. Finding the door unlocked, he released the hood and removed the wire to the distributor cap and re-closed the hood. He then returned to the Land Rover and pulled it a quarter of a mile back down the road toward Panther Junction, from where he could watch the Lost Mine Trail through his binoculars. Except for a few sections, he could see the first half mile of the trail, up to the flat between the eastern decline of Casa Grande and the western slopes of Lost Mine Peak.

From about a quarter-mile up the trail, George Reynolds and Ed Corrigan had watched the little drama in the parking lot be-low. After the two officers left their car and started up the trail, they passed out of sight. Then Corrigan turned to Reynolds and said, "OK. Here they come. They obviously want to catch us, which leads me to believe that they have identified you. They could not really be interested in me, and I suspect that it's your relationship to Cowan's experiment that interests them. So you go on, but keep a very good lead and don't take any more chances. They must be dangerous. I'll return to the car and on the way I'll tell them you're just taking a hike. So, good luck. I'll be waiting for you on the slopes down toward Panther Junction, as planned."

"Right," Reynolds said, extending his hand for good luck. "Don't worry. I'll keep ahead of them."

"Be sure you do," said Corrigan, beginning the descent down the trail. "If one of them returns to the car, he may try to get around to the mine road if he guesses that that's what you're doing. Let's hope that Tom has successfully deactivated their car."

Within four minutes after beginning his return, Corrigan could see the two officers approaching up the trail. They instantly recognized each other. Corrigan retained his professional calm.

"Hello, Officer Samuelson," he said as they approached. "Out for your morning stroll?"

"Well, hello to you, Professor Fisher," said the one called Samuelson. "We thought we recognized your car, and we wanted only to explain that Police Headquarters has confirmed that you can go to the mine after all. Where is Dr. Jones?"

"Oh, he wanted a little hike, so he's gone up the trail a ways. He wants to go to the top of the trail, on a scenic overlook between the main peak and Pine Canyon. But it's an hour's hike, and I'm in no condition for it, so I decided to wait in the car. Might even take a little nap," said Corrigan, relaxed and good-natured.

"Well, we'll walk on after him and perhaps we can let him know that you can go to the mine," said one of them.

"Fine, I'd appreciate that," said Corrigan. "If you do let him know, wake me up when you come back."

Smiling, the two continued on up the trail while Corrigan began an unhurried walk back to the car. When they were well separated, the two officers began to discuss their opportunity.

"This is really fine," said one. "When we overtake Reynolds high up this trail, we'll simply get rid of him there. If we hide him, it will take a long time to find him. Then we can decide what to do with the fat one below in the parking lot. I think we can just leave him waiting for Reynolds."

"I wonder who he is," said the other.

"I would guess that he is someone related to the investigation," said the first. "Leon said that we should not be concerned by nonscientist investigators."

For five minutes they hiked on in pursuit of Reynolds, whose back they had briefly seen turning a corner about a quarter-mile ahead. Then suddenly they heard the unmistakable sound of the Porsche exhaust as Corrigan wound it up in first gear. The curving road below toward Panther Junction was visible in several places, so they stopped and watched. Finally, they clearly saw the silver-gray Porsche moving toward the junction. They gave each other puzzled looks, as if trying to decide if this development had any implications for their orders to watch the mine. They both immediately realized that they might have been tricked.

"Amos, I think he may be going to the mine!" said one.

"Yes. They are looking for something there. I don't know what it is, but we must keep them both in sight. I think you had better go back to the car. Try to follow their car if you can find it, but if you do not see it anywhere, just return to the mine so that you can watch it," Amos instructed. "I'll make the hike up this trail with Reynolds, where I will, regrettably, leave him for the vultures. Go quickly!"

From his vantage point below, Tom Williams watched most of this. He saw the one officer turn around to return to their car. He soon saw the Porsche approaching him down the hill toward the flatlands below, and he gave Corrigan a discreet little wave as he passed by. After watching for five minutes, Williams started the Rover and followed Corrigan back to the Ranger Station at Panther Junction, where the latter would have again parked the Porsche out of sight in the garage at the back. Before doing so he watched Reynolds disappear over the flat plateau between Casa Grande and the Lost Mine Peak. From there the trail turned to the left, mostly out of sight, as it began its ascent of the outlying slopes of Lost Mine Peak. He also saw the one called Amos a quarter-mile behind, walking hurriedly up the trail, which was deceptively easy going at that point. He hoped Reynolds was as strong and fast on the mountains as he had implied by his calm assurance that he could not be caught. Clearly, Reynolds knew the mountain well, and his boots were right for the tortuous walking that would follow the trail's end, so Williams could not help but share his confidence. He could not imagine scaling Lost Mine Peak in street shoes. He returned to the station, trying to imagine the consternation the one descending must feel as he tried to start his car.

The second officer was looking for his car keys when his eyes fell on the flat rear tire. Cursing silently, he opened the trunk and began feverishly to extract the jack and spare. Twenty minutes later, the car would not start, confirming his suspicion that the one called Professor Fisher, who certainly could not be a professor, had probably let the air out of the tire before taking off in the Porsche. A check under the hood soon revealed the missing part. The police car could not be driven, and it would take him hours to get help from the service station in the Chisos Basin. He saw no point in chasing Amos, whose deadly mission now seemed more advisable, considering the obvious purposefulness of the opposition. Deciding what must be done, he sat in the front seat and picked up the two-way car radio.

"Jamil, come in, Jamil. This is Joseph calling. Come in Jamil," he called, then relaxed the call button.

It was a full fifteen seconds before the call was returned, from a transmitter atop a mobile caravan in a campsite in the Terlingua Flats about ten miles to the north.

"Yes, Joseph. This is Jamil here. What do you need?"

Quickly Joseph explained all that had happened. Then he suggested the logical course of action.

"What you must do, Jamil, is to drive the camper around to the mine," he said. "The fat one in the Porsche is almost certainly going to the mine for whatever it is they seek there. He has a head start and will already be to Panther Junction. But there is no other road out of Pine Canyon. So if you follow him in there, he will be trapped. Search him; interrogate him; then leave him there—forever."

"I agree, Joseph," replied Jamil. "I will first let Leon know what has happened. I think we can assure him that both adversaries are as good as dead. 10–4."

Joseph turned off the radio and began the two-mile hike on into Chisos Basin, where he hoped the station attendant would not find it too surprising that a Texas highway patrolman sought help from a service station, rather than from Highway Patrol maintenance. He was sure he could handle it, but it would take a few hours.

Amos had reached the flat at the top of the smooth wide part of the trail, just at the point where it turned into a stony footpath to the left up the Lost Mine Peak. Catching his breath he scanned the trail ahead, until finally he saw the bright red backpack on Reynolds's back. Unfortunately, he was still more than a quarter-mile ahead, and moving on steadily. Seeing that he would not catch up to him before the top of the trail, Amos decided to shout. Reynolds would probably recognize him, and since he suspected nothing, perhaps he would return to the waving officer. Reynolds trudged on, preferring that the other man think that he could not be heard at that distance. Annoyed, Amos continued his pursuit, philosophizing that it might even be preferable to catch Reynolds at the top of the trail.

Corrigan did not drive to the Pine Canyon Road. Instead, he made a sharp right turn into the Ranger Station and drove directly into the garage at the rear. There he would wait until later, when Reynolds was expected to arrive via a long but little-used deer trail from the Lost Mine Peak. While there he would also telephone the FBI offices in El Paso once more, leaving additional information and instructions concerning the two men he hoped to apprehend.

Reynolds heard the faint shout behind him for the second time as he neared the end of the switchbacks at the top of the Lost Mine Trail. Pretending to not hear, he nonetheless paused to look out into Pine Canyon, as any hiker would, while from the corner of his eye he located the climbing officer below, still about a quarter-mile back. Now came the important time-gaining maneuver. Reynolds pretended to follow the right-hand trail to the top, where it led several hundred yards out onto a stony overlook, but out of sight he turned around abruptly and headed in the opposite direction onto a wild and wooded ridge connecting with the Lost Mine Peak. Pressing on through the rough stones and cactus, Reynolds picked up his pace noticeably over a mountain route he knew well. This ridge was the only good route to Lost Mine Peak, because the direct route contained very rugged canyons, not apparent to the distant eye, through which a man in street clothes could hardly pass at all. Reynolds covered the rough half-mile in only twenty minutes, about the time it would take his pursuer to make it out onto the lookout point far to the south. Out of the dense brush, he emerged into the open on a stony escarpment on the slopes of Lost Mine Peak. The rough canyons now lay between him and Amos, who was by straight line only about four hundred yards away. Reynolds saw him at once, walking carefully out onto the stony overlook. Clearly, Amos was looking for him and would be increasingly puzzled that he was not there. Reynolds continued up the now uninterrupted slopes of the mountain, through rough rock and cactus that chewed harmlessly at his tough leather boots.

Reynolds repeatedly turned to look at Amos. The plan had worked so far, and Amos must now either take another ninety minutes or so to return to the car park or, if he saw Reynolds, attempt pursuit on the rough mountain.

Reynolds had prepared for the chase. When Amos saw him straining upwards on the wild slopes, he realized at once that he was heading for the mine, that he could go over the peak ridge and somehow descend from there. Reynolds knew he had been seen when Amos began a half run back toward the north, to the top of the trail. This rapid pace surprised him, and he again felt fear at the realization that the man wanted very badly indeed to catch him. Reynolds climbed with strength and endurance, so that he was several hundred yards above Amos when he paused at the top of the trail and realized that he had been tricked. Without hesitation Amos started for Reynolds as the crow flies. Reynolds saw with astonishment, and not a little satisfaction, that his pursuer was beginning the descent into the shallow-looking canyons between them. The plan had worked perfectly, and Reynolds knew that it would take at least an hour for him to emerge, because the canyons were much deeper and much rougher than they looked. His overall lead was probably two hours. He kept his steady pace upwards with calm assurance, while Amos's ankles were already bloody from his hectic and self-defeating pace downward through the thickening cacti and stones.

When Reynolds had made it to the crest ridge of the mountain, he stopped and looked around. His pursuer was nowhere in sight, still struggling in the canyons. To the southeast Reynolds could see the deserted road coming into Pine Canyon. Looking downward toward the east, he saw a good route toward the mine. To avoid more small stony canyons, he first walked two hundred yards south before descending a gentle slope. It was easy, and within fifteen minutes he could see the white steel box looming before him on a large rocky flat below. He saw the closed gate where they had turned around this morning. No cars were in sight.

The steel box revealed no damage at all, although its hinges were now slightly weathered. Obviously, the saboteurs had overlooked it. Its door was secured with a small padlock. Reynolds extracted from his pack the hacksaw he had brought for the purpose, took a long drink of water from his flask, and sawed through the loop in the padlock. Inside was another unlocked door with weatherstripping, which swung open easily to reveal the computer tape deck and reels. It was immediately obvious that the tape deck now was without electric power. Rewind seemed in any case unnecessary, so Reynolds cut the magnetic tape just before the recording head, pulled it through the head, and removed the take-up spools. Carefully he put the tools and tape into his pack and re-closed the doors.

Glancing around he saw for the first time the trail of dust to the southeast from a large white vehicle coming up the Pine Canyon Road. It clearly was neither Corrigan nor a Park Ranger, and Reynolds was not at all inclined to find out who it was. Quickly he located the northerly direction that he would follow along the east side of the mountain. It was rough going, crossing several slopes of falling rock, but it quickly took him out of sight of the impending visitors, who were at last visible, parked at the locked gate down the mine road. Pressing on to the north, Reynolds worked his way between the Lost Mine Peak and the subsidiary peak to its east, and within half an hour found the deer trail leading down the northeast slopes of Lost Mine Peak toward the Panther Junction Ranger Station. It was an hour and a half away, even at a strong pace.

It was 3:00 P.M. when Reynolds walked out of the wilderness and into the ranger hut behind the station.

"I've got the tape," he said to Corrigan, who had been dozing. "Let's get out of here. A white truck was coming up the Pine Canyon Road when I left. They could get back here anytime if they're looking for us." Reynolds took a long drink of water and accepted without comment the Milky Way that Corrigan tossed to him.

Corrigan left briefly to ask Tom Williams's help. Would he stand at the road and raise his arm if a vehicle approached from either direction? Only when it was clear would they race off in the Porsche. One car passed and one group of tourists pulled into the Ranger Station while Reynolds idled the Porsche. He waited in the car and Corrigan watched Williams's signals as the tourists got out to enter the Visitor Information Center. After another thirty seconds, Corrigan hopped into the car. They pulled up to Williams, gave a brief wave, and they sped away, across the road and down-hill toward the north.

"How long will it take to see what's on the tape?" Corrigan wanted to know immediately.

"We'll play it at the university's Computation Center," Reynolds responded, "but I can't promise how long it will take me to get the format of the information. Do you really think there can be anything in the record of a scientific experiment to reveal the motives of murderers? I wouldn't be very optimistic about that."

"It's all we have to go on. All evidence suggests that it was the experiment that motivated the destruction rather than Cowan himself," Corrigan continued. "And after this episode with the fake police, I'm even more optimistic. They seem to play a serious game. Tell me your impression of events on the mountain."

74

Reynolds did, more and more agreeing with Corrigan's analysis. After filling up in Marathon, Reynolds suggested a steak dinner in Sanderson, to be followed by a motel in Del Rio.

Nine

Rebecca Yahil was returning home while the gray Porsche was streaking out of Sanderson on its way back to Del Rio. She had worked fitfully during the day at the Astronomy Department, just as she had slept fitfully the night before, alone. Pedaling effortlessly over Austin's hills, she wondered again that Reynolds had not come home at all last night. She shivered at the thought of his safety. But he would in his enthusiasm take off suddenly from time to time. His self-confessed boyish impetuousness no doubt accounted for his unmarried status, and Rebecca was not the type to want him otherwise. Normally, it would have been a quick trip to Corpus Christi to sail with a friend, or to West Texas to climb in the Guadalupe Mountains or Big Bend, or to Fort Worth or Dallas for a sectional bridge tournament. Even after asking Rebecca to live with him, Reynolds remained playfully unpredictable. His notes to her over his sudden escapades nonetheless showed the sure stamp of his affection. But the message he left this time with his secretary had said only "Back tomorrow."

As she turned into their garage, a glance at the windows, still closed on such a beautiful afternoon, told her at once that he was still not home. As she eased her bicycle into its parking slot beside piles of Reynolds's junk, she paused again to survey the evidence of the man: tool boxes, an inflatable rubber raft, a kayak, garden equipment, skis, two tents, a junked computer console, boxes of books, a rolled Persian carpet, antique odds and ends, three rolled sleeping bags, outdoor cooking gear, band saw, woodworking bench, portable homemade eight-inch telescope, cans of paint and turpentine, three old tennis rackets, and deeper, unrecognizable layers of stuff. Rebecca smiled briefly at the portrait of the man, then turned and stared blankly for a while down the driveway toward the street. She sensed that Reynolds was not away pursuing one of his hobbies or on a sudden retreat from his complex life. The reason for her having been sent to Austin was involved in whatever was now happening. All she had been able to ascertain was that Corrigan had visited Reynolds in his office yesterday morning, as confirmed by Reynolds's secretary, and that both had suddenly left and had not been heard from since. Tentatively at first, she admitted the fear that she would never see him again. Jericho had certainly dispatched Fred Cowan violently, and for reasons that she was not fully privy to. Taking a deep breath, she entered the townhouse to confirm that Reynolds had not been home.

Rebecca walked to the bar and poured herself a white rum and tonic. Her anxiety lay in the thought that she could be an accomplice to a deadly danger to Reynolds. She loved him. She loved him in a way that exposed new aspects of herself. She loved him for his sense of identity, not for anything he represented. Rebecca had heretofore embraced largely images, causes, symbols, and militant action. She had shared with the men in her life the comaraderie of Israel's intense struggle for freedom and survival. She had matured with a keen sense of outrage at injustice and the determination to secure a better world. Now, quite suddenly, within the last few months, she longed for a quiet life in Austin, with only emotional and intellectual fulfillment as her causes. She loved Reynolds, astrophysics, the university, and even tennis, which she was learning with athletic speed. She had glimpsed for the first time what life is to those previously mysterious souls who live in daily contentment.

Austin was the end of the rainbow, the kind of simple paradise that she wanted for Israel. She felt traitorous for being in love with it, her destiny having been bartered away in childhood as she was sucked year after year deeper into the fray of her homeland. Her father, a major in the army, had been killed during the 1973 War with Egypt. His death smeared the boundaries between her personal struggle and her country's struggle. She had come from noisy, bickering Jerusalem, with its layers and layers of conflict mirroring each mammoth stone laboriously piled on top of the last, to Austin, quiet, young, energetic, unblemished, and uncomplicated Austin.

Rebecca had been placed with Reynolds because of her outstanding record in Israeli military and security matters. She had been sixteen years old when her father died. She was then already an active leader in youth training groups. During her university years she had become the leader of a select group of young women intensively training for special security assignments. She had even become the lover of a fiery young security strategist. Her first promotion had followed the clever and successful detection of a terrorist plot to detonate a bomb at Lod Airport. She had become suspicious during a conversation between a young female Palestinian student at the university and a Japanese student and had carefully cultivated them enough to find a chance to search the girl's apartment, where she had found hand weapons and an airport map of the area for passengers in transit. Rebecca had then instructed one of her young colleagues to trail the Japanese student. Clues were gathered quickly, with the result that the police were well briefed before the day on which the girl terrorist had traveled to the airport with a bomb-laden 16mm movie camera. The bomb and both terrorists had been easily and safely apprehended. The promotion had provided more opportunities for using Rebecca's talents, and she established herself as a tough and cool thinker who seldom made a mistake.

Graduate school in astrophysics had distanced Rebecca from security assignments, so the phone call from Elias Hirschberg had come as an exhilarating surprise. He had even been in her home in Jerusalem once, before her father's death. His request had been simple, resurrecting at once her dormant interest. The Israeli government, considering her background and expertise in stellar astrophysics, wanted to send her to the University of Texas to monitor the interpretation of results from the solar neutrino experiment in the Big Bend. It was a matter of Israeli security, not scientific espionage, Hirschberg had insisted. It would probably amount to nothing. She would be a legitimate postdoc with Dr. George Reynolds and report only unexpected findings. It was such a benign request, attached to such an unusual opportunity, that she had accepted eagerly, but after six months in Austin, Rebecca was acutely aware of the double edge to her simple assignment.

When the telephone rang, Rebecca rushed to answer and heard with mounting concern the voice of the unknown Leon from New York. With the usual care, he first established identity and second her freedom to talk.

"Yes, I can talk freely," Rebecca said. "I am alone."

"Good. You must act with decisiveness. Reynolds has been at the mine. We believe he was searching for something, but we failed in our attempts to apprehend him," Leon said calmly.

"Where is he now?" Rebecca answered slowly, trying not to betray her nervousness.

"We are not sure, but we believe he has left the Big Bend and is probably on his way back to Austin. A heavy middle-aged man is with him. Do you know who he is?" Leon asked.

"I presume it is Mr. Corrigan of the FBI, since they were to gether yesterday morning before Reynolds disappeared. He was questioning Reynolds about the—about the crime at the mine," Rebecca answered.

"Good. The FBI is of no concern to us. They will be content to investigate an apparent murder and are unlikely to suspect anything else. Reynolds is more of a risk because of his preoccupation with solar neutrinos. You must discover what he has found out."

"What can he possibly have found out? I am not fully briefed on the Joshua Factor. As you know, my instructions are to report to you any exciting scientific news about the sun. But I myself was told only that developments in the sun, developments that are unknown to me in detail, are of considerable importance to Israeli security. You know what a great surprise Cowan's murder was to me, so if I am to help, I should know a little more," Rebecca insisted.

"You are right, of course," Leon said, quickly making decision, but one that he had already discussed the possibility of with Hirschberg. "Top-secret state plans will proceed more smoothly if the world calmly regards the sun as uneventful. Any evidence to the contrary from recent solar neutrino counts must be quickly suppressed if possible. Determine whether Reynolds has discovered anything unusual about the counts. If there is evidence, destroy it if you can."

"But what about Reynolds? He would know of any such evidence, at least if he discovered any," Rebecca asked with growing alarm.

"Suppress the evidence. We have agents coming to Austin. They can be reached at 516-2239, room 44. Call them the minute you discover anything. They will prevent Reynolds from disclosing it," Leon continued.

"You mean he will be silenced?"

"Yahil, you should not ask. You have undergone the full training of our organization. You know that our situation in the world is desperate. Ask only what you need to know. If there is danger that he may reveal a new discovery, we will decide what must be done. I cannot, because of security, tell you what the discovery would be, but I can assure you that, if he has made it, it will be very obvious to you, with your scientific expertise. Don't fail. Millions of countrymen depend unknowingly upon your resoluteness. Israel cannot survive another five years without a new strategy, which we now possess. This is all you need to know. Is it clear?"

"Yes, it's clear," Rebecca replied, only half truthfully, twisting the telephone cord nervously.

"Don't leave the Austin telephone number lying about," Leon cautioned. "Call it instead of me if you hear anything from Reynolds. Any questions?"

Rebecca hesitated, hardly daring to ask: "If I am uncertain what he has found, but can see only that it is something exciting, should I simply silence him?"

"It would be for the best," came the cold, clear reply, "but our experts there will do it if you call them. Goodbye for now. We expect to hear from you."

"Goodbye," Rebecca said, slowly placing the receiver in its cradle. For several minutes she sat still, trying desperately to form a plan.

It suddenly occurred to her that she was not prepared to face the split-second decisions she might have to make whenever Reynolds returned. She stood and looked out the window. Relieved that Reynolds and Corrigan were not arriving, she turned away in such haste that she bumped into the side table, spilling the remainder of her drink. With a curse she set the glass upright, grabbed her purse, keys, and sweater. She walked briskly down the single flight of stairs, paused at the door again to be sure that Reynolds was not approaching, and walked out and down the street to the drive-in grocery. She pushed her way past two men talking at the checkout counter and bought a pack of Marlboros. She had smoked that brand during her university years, when she had felt so tough learning terrorist countermeasures. American cigarettes had been considered synonymous with toughness even though local cigarettes were stronger. She had given up the habit in graduate school, when astrophysics became more interesting than espionage. She had also taken up gymnastics, then running, and then swimming, all with endurance and enthusiasm. She had become very good on parallel bars, at least for a twenty-two-year-old. That had been part of an altered Rebecca. Increased endurance and a slenderer, more muscled body seemed to be part of her new dedication. But now, as if to re-create the milieu of crisis decisions, she needed that smoke. Lighting up at once, she crossed the street and sat in the schoolyard, half-watching the kids playing softball. Her fingers trembled as she lit up again and took a deep drag. A helpless smile crossed her face.

"God, what a wreck I am," she said to herself.

Ten

Jericho was a secret organization. Its purpose was to develop a careful plan for Israel's dominance of the antagonistic portion of the Arab world. It had formed around a single idea, to cooperate with an "act of God" in shifting the balance of power in the Near East. The act of God was called, within Jericho, the "Joshua Factor," and was the most closely guarded secret in an organization with many secrets. The membership of Jericho included the prime minister, the minister of defense, a few top military men, members of Israeli Intelligence (whose organization was indispensable to implementation of the plan), the scientists responsible for the Joshua Factor concept, and assorted experts from various endeavours that were essential to its success. Jericho served as a think tank for the special scientific problems of the plan and, as it was being formulated, as a strategic planning center. The unlikely strategy surrounding the Joshua Factor daily became more viable as the mechanism of Jericho gained momentum.

One meeting place for Jericho was in a highly secured suite of offices in a modern Tel Aviv office building belonging to the Ministry of Defense. There David Zweig was talking to two members of Jericho. Sitting in a leather-covered armchair was Elias Hirschberg, the world-renowned theoretical physicist who had been Zweig's postdoctoral supervisor at the Weizmann Institute. Hirschberg had been a scientific consultant to the military for over twenty years and had grown personally close to the minister of defense following the 1973 war. It was his unique blend of scientific and strategic brilliance that made him Jericho's most influential member. It was he who first formulated the strategic implications of the "act of God," following its scientific discovery by David Zweig.

The other man in the room was Aaron Rabin, a rabbi and a

trained psychologist. He was the member of Jericho concerned with the psychological aspects of the Joshua Factor. Mass hysteria would be an important aspect of the plan, one that would have to be minimized among the Israeli citizenry and optimized in the Arab world. His task was to analyze this potential hysteria, to conceive a plan for preparing the Israeli people without revealing impending events to them, and to conceive plans simultaneously for amplifying the Arab hysteria in ways that would aid the success of the overall plan. At age fifty-seven he was the third-oldest member. As a rabbi he attended the religion of his people in Jerusalem, where he lived in Mea Shearim. He was a politically important personality whose reputation had been established during the reorganization of Jerusalem after the 1967 war. He had been instrumental in obtaining prayer rights for Jews in Hebron in the Mosque of Abraham, alongside the Arabs who also saw Abraham as their forefather. Rabin was also a survivor of Dachau.

David Zweig had done nothing but recuperate since arriving in Tel Aviv. He had quickly communicated the basic facts to Hirschberg—his discovery and destruction of Cowan's impending semiannual report, his murder of Cowan, and his hasty flight from the United States. Hirschberg knew the rest, having personally outlined Agent Leon's task of subsequent surveillance, of which he was continually informed. Zweig's rest had been as much for nerves as for the overwhelming fatigue that accompanied him to Tel Aviv. He had, in fact, been under sedation for several days. Poor sleep, depression, and nightmares had plagued him, and he was feared to be on the verge of a nervous breakdown.

"I really was not prepared to kill him," Zweig was saying in obvious anguish. "I had let myself into the mine with a key I had obtained on a previous visit there. It was just twilight and I had not expected Fred Cowan to appear at that time. I wanted only to check the upcoming report in advance. Those were my instructions."

"You certainly did the right thing, David," Hirschberg interjected. It was at least the fourth or fifth time that Zweig had obsessively returned to the same point. "Israel was depending on you to maintain watch over that experiment. It was essential that we learn what he was finding."

"But I didn't plan to kill him!" Zweig burst out. "When I read his report I knew at once that Jericho would have to destroy the experiment; but then he surprised me by coming in, and . . . But I didn't want to kill him!"

"Of course you didn't, David," said Rabin. "Don't think of yourself as a murderer. You simply had no choice."

"I did have a choice! I could have simply reacted normally. He would have been surprised to see me there, but he knew I had a

84

key and he knew I was returning for the semiannual progress report." Zweig wrung his hands.

"You could see what had to be done," Hirschberg countered. "You read Cowan's report, and you understood better than anyone in this world that it must not be released."

"Actually, it wasn't as vital as all that," Zweig worried. "Even if the report had been made public, it would probably have taken much too long to figure out what was happening."

"But *you* were able to figure it out," Hirschberg countered. "And Cowan's results confirm beyond doubt that your analysis was correct. Koren's experiment continues to show the rise in neutrino flux. We repeated all the calculations yesterday. So if you could figure it out, there is a chance that someone else could, too. Cowan and Reynolds together, for example. The atomic bomb and the hydrogen bomb proved that secrets cannot long belong to any single country. No, you did only what was necessary."

"But murder is wrong! We know it. Laws forbid it, our laws and the Old Testament laws as well," Zweig went on, as if only condemnation could lift his burden of guilt.

"Yes, murder *is* wrong," Rabin suggested quietly, "but what you did was not technically a murder. It was an act of war. Death in war is not murder. You were acting for your people, that they might assume a better position in the world."

"To take a life is murder," Zweig said.

"But David slew Goliath," Rabin went on, "and he did it with Yahweh's blessing. It was for His people. Joshua killed the inhabitants of Jericho in order that Israel might find her place in God's plan. Samson pulled down the temple on the Philistines. Our people sing the praises of these men, with reverence that so great a thing as the mission of God's people could be formed through the hands of men. These men were not murderers, any more than you are a murderer, David."

"If you want to see real murder," Hirschberg added, "you need only patrol our borders today. Mothers and children are still killed by mortar shelling from the hills. We try to keep the terrorists away, but their single-minded attempt to slaughter our villagers keeps them coming. Or if you really want to think the unthinkable, you have only to remember the Polish ghettoes and the Nazi extermination camps. There was murder! Your father was lucky to escape, David, as you yourself have insisted, but what of his brother? His sisters? What of six million Jews? Their voices cry out today from their graves!"

"Yes, of course, that was worse," Zweig mused quietly. "But to kill a man with your own hands . . . "

"David cut off Goliath's head with Goliath's own sword while he lay stunned on the ground, and David was chosen by God to found the Kingdom where the Messiah will one day reign," said Rabin.

"Yes, but that was long ago," Zweig replied. "A religious myth."

"Was Auschwitz long ago? Was Birkenau? Riga? Dachau? Was the Yom Kippur attack of 1973 long ago?" Hirschberg retorted with mounting anger at the realities of his time.

"Elias speaks the real truth, David," added Rabin. "Our position in the world is desperate, and God has given us a modern miracle. He gave you to us, that your great mind would see the meaning of what is happening. He has given us a plan, just as He gave our forefathers a plan. He is keeping a promise to His people. You bore no malice to Cowan. You had no murder in your heart. You did what had to be done."

"Strategically, it had to be done," Hirschberg concurred. "Let me put it this way, David. Cowan's blood does not lie on your hands. If you had not silenced him yourself, I would have ordered it. Jericho eliminated not Cowan, but Cowan's knowledge. If you had left the mine and just informed Leon, he would have done the same within hours. You were only part of Jericho. Because of you, the Joshua Factor exists. To use it well requires secrecy. The entire Jericho organization insists on that."

"True," Rabin added, as soothingly as he could. "Divorce your act from David Zweig, the man, and see it as the plan in action— an ugly necessity."

Zweig leaned back and breathed deeply. His eyes moved to the ceiling and then to each man. He thought, then finally said, obviously much relieved of tension, "So be it. Nonetheless, I would like to go to the Temple. I have not prayed since I was a young boy, but I will on this occasion. I will pray for forgiveness. Cowan was an innocent man, a good and gentle man. I will pray for us all."

Rabin nodded in response to a worried glance from Hirschberg. This conversation only confirmed their earlier decision that Zweig would have to be closely watched. His emotional state suggested that he might himself be the greatest danger of a leak. But he was, for his physics, totally indispensable. So Rabin rose saying, "I will go with you, David. And then you might like to sit in the Temple for a while, while I go into my office to tend to a few matters. Then you will come to my house for supper."

"I'd like that," Zweig replied. It was a half-lie. He did not much like Rabin, despite needing his counsel. He seemed to be too morally flexible, too much in compromise with the affairs of men. And Hirschberg seemed suddenly lacking in the devoted brilliance that he had once radiated. Would it now be forever impossible to concentrate on pure physics, of and for itself?

Eleven

In the University of Texas Computation Center the racks of magnetic tapes whirled and spun, humming their coded instructions for the many programs being handled simultaneously by the CDC 6600 computer. Light panels blinked constantly on the many electronic consoles that monitored the performance of the giant brain. Scientists and mathematicians were seated at dozens of keypunch consoles translating their coded instructions onto cards, decks of which were constantly being fed into the machine by the attendant. The giant typewriters never stopped printing out the numerical answers. They typed them a whole line at a time, as fast as the computer printout paper could be processed through their special assemblies of gears and sprockets. The 6600 was simultaneously computing fourteen separate numerical programs, on one of them alone making as many calculations each minute as a person with pencil and paper could have done in three years. Even so, it was a rather slack afternoon and the computer's solid-state-circuit brain had been occupied only 12 percent of the time. Only a very small fraction of that time had been spent on analyzing the data stored on the tape from the Big Bend.

It was now 5:30 P.M., and Reynolds and Corrigan retired for the fifth time to a small adjoining room to study the typewriter printout. They had been at work since noon, following the rapid drive to Austin from Del Rio, a drive that had gone directly to the Comp Center. The playout of the tape had been perfectly straightforward; it had taken the machine just five minutes to type out all of the stored data. The format clearly identified the data as a complete record of the previous nine months of the solar-neutrino counts. Each time the tank had been swept clean of argon by the helium gas, a new series of radioactive counts began. The format showed clearly the date and time of each count, the electronic pulse height of the count indicating its energy, and the rise time of each pulse. Some counts were labeled "reject" and some "accept," according to whether or not the pulse height and rise time had been appropriate to the decay of the sought-for radioactive ^{37}Ar nuclei. Two calibrated test pulses were also printed out with each count as a calibration of the amplifier systems.

Reynolds had just hung up the telephone extension and said to Corrigan, "There's no doubt about it. In the last month alone there were 1,243 ^{37}Ar atoms scoured from the tank. That's two hundred times more than Cowan ever found in a month's run!"

"You keep telling me that," Corrigan said with apparent exasperation, "but what does it mean?"

"I don't know what it means, but I have one last cross-check to make sure we're right. I just asked Rebecca to bring over Cowan's last six-month report. The reports contain the date of each counted ^{37}Ar pulse during the previous six months, and that six-month period overlaps by three months the records that are on our tape. By comparing his last report with the printout of this tape, I can be sure that we are correctly identifying the format of the tape."

"What do you mean?" Corrigan asked.

"Well, I can check the published counts from the previous three months to see if they correspond exactly to the 'accepted' counts on this tape," Reynolds replied, talking much more excitedly than was his custom. "If they agree, we'll know that the counts designated as 'accepted' on our tape are the same counts that Cowan was reporting to the world in his semiannual reports. That's got to be what the format on his tape means, but I want to be sure."

"Suppose the counting rate was two hundred times bigger last month, as you say," Corrigan queried, "what might that have to do with Cowan's murder?"

"I can't say what it would have to do with Cowan's murder," Reynolds replied, "but it wasn't just last month. Look again at this printout. Here, the last line of each month tells the total number of ^{37}Ar counts for that month. It's 1,243 counts in February, and that's about two hundred times the average of 6 counts monthly that Cowan had found over the past five years. But look at January, 237 counts in January; 61 counts in December; 25 counts in November; 13 counts in October. That's not much more than the average he used to report. And in September it was only 9 counts, which would never have been regarded as more than usual, since there is at least a 50 percent uncertainty in the small number of counts he usually got. In fact, he never knew for sure that he had any real ^{37}Ar counts at all."

88

"Why is that?" Corrigan wanted to know. "You said he normally got six counts in a month. Now you say he never was really sure he had any."

"The uncertainty's in the background due to cosmic rays. They're also expected to transmute about three ^{37}Cl atoms monthly into ^{37}Ar atoms. In that sense they have the same effect as solar neutrinos," Reynolds explained. "So the situation is a little dicey. He typically got nine counts monthly, of which about three monthly are expected to be due to cosmic rays. Presumably, neutrinos account for the rest, but since there are so few counts the small difference between two pretty small and uncertain numbers doesn't have much statistical significance."

"I can see that, I guess," Corrigan admitted. "What really gets me is that all you astrophysicists made such a big deal over a very chancy small difference that might not even be real. I've got to hand it to you guys. From the stories I occasionally read in the paper it sounded like you were faced with a very real puzzle, not just a tiny, nearly nonexistent, suggestion of one."

"The small difference was uncertain in magnitude, but it was very certain that the difference was much smaller than the one we had all expected. We figured the solar neutrinos would produce about sixty ^{37}Ar atoms monthly, in which case Cowan could easily have measured an average of sixty-three monthly, and subtracted the three due to cosmic rays to get the answer—and with good statistical significance. Do you see? The puzzle has been real and very certain even though the data were uncertain. The main point was that the counting rate was so damn small!" Reynolds concluded, slamming his hand onto the table.

"OK. I get you, but what has this new finding to do with Cowan's murder?" Corrigan puzzled.

"Damn it, Ed! How should I know what this has to do with Cowan's murder. That's your department. Why don't you tell me!" Reynolds was clearly growing tired of explaining and reexplaining each point of Cowan's experiment. It was the usual difficulty of talking to a nonscientist, amplified in this case by stress. He could not in these circumstances use the specialized words and concepts and ways of thinking that two scientists would share and that would allow them to exchange their ideas quickly and accurately. Reynolds was mindful of the cultural gap and tried daily to bridge it, but now his mind was spinning with the shocking excitement of this new discovery, and he secretly wished he had more solitude just to think about it in peace.

"Take it easy, boy," Corrigan pleaded, "before you blow a fuse on that console. It takes no genius to suspect that this discovery provides the motive for Cowan's murder. Here was a gentle man, without enemies, who searched in vain for seven years for neutrinos from the sun. Then he suddenly found them, getting stronger every month—and boom!—he was murdered and his lab destroyed before he could report his discovery."

"Yeah. It's strange all right," Reynolds acknowledged.

"Why didn't he report it sooner?" Corrigan asked. "From the numbers we just looked at, he had a very positive discovery by the end of November, and even more so at the end of December. Why didn't he announce his finding?"

"That's hard to say for sure, but I believe it was just a desire to be careful," Reynolds said. "Cowan was a conservative man who had set his sights on a great discovery. He was accustomed to patience, and he knew the importance of being sure before announcing anything. He was sensitive about all of the theoretical work that his reports stimulated. He didn't even have any competition, for Christ's sake! He was the only person in the world doing the experiment, so he didn't have to hurry his disclosure. At least, he didn't think he would have to. I would guess he planned to send a paper to *Physical Review Letters* based on the semiannual summary of his data. I know that's what I would have done."

"Well, someone didn't want him to reveal his discovery. The question is *why,*" Corrigan mused. "Perhaps a jealous competitor wanted to deprive him of his big triumph?"

"We went through all that," Reynolds shot back. "I can't imagine anyone who would have wanted to deprive Fred Cowan of his big triumph. It just doesn't make sense. Hey, here comes Rebecca."

Rebecca Yahil was walking through the corridor and saw them through the glass window of the small study. Reynolds opened the door and she came abruptly through, carrying a packet of papers in a manila folder. They were Cowan's report of his individual counts from the previous six-month period. She smiled at Reynolds, who wrapped one arm around her in a vigorous hug.

"What is happening, George?" she asked at once. "Where have you been for the past two days?"

Quickly Reynolds told her the entire story. Her expression was anxious as she listened to the harrowing details of their encounter with the fake police. Corrigan was watching her as she leaned back, half sitting, against the edge of the desk.

"And here's the most exciting thing," Reynolds continued. "The tape shows a rapid increase in the solar neutrino flux beginning about last November! It has increased each month, until in February it was some two hundred times the count rate he usually got in a month."

"Oh my God, no!" Rebecca gasped, her hand rising involuntarily to her mouth. Corrigan was watching every gesture, and both men were a little surprised at Rebecca's reaction. Had Rey nolds told her something terrible?

"Here. Let's look at that last report," Reynolds said, taking up the manila folder. "I want to check the overlapping three months from Cowan's last report with the tape." He opened the report to a table of counts for June, then carefully flipped the computer print-out to the June counts. It was immediately clear that every count agreed, both the "accepted" counts and the "rejected" counts. Reynolds pointed out the agreement to Corrigan and to Rebecca.

"Well, there's no doubt that you understand the tape correctly," Corrigan said. "Good work. At least we've got something to go on now, something that may eventually help."

"We've also got a major scientific mystery on our hands," Reynolds replied. "There was mystery enough when Cowan couldn't find as many counts as we expected, but now he's counting two hundred times more than we ever expected! Something peculiar is happening in the sun!"

"Perhaps it's all a big mistake of some kind," Rebecca insisted, again causing both men to look at her in surprise. "Well, I mean the sun just cannot suddenly emit neutrinos. . . ."

"Well, it seems to be doing so," Reynolds said. "I think there's little more to be done here."

"I'll need to have the printout," Corrigan said. "Can we have a copy made?"

"Yes. But I certainly want my copy," Reynolds answered. "The shortest and easiest thing will be to run the tape through the computer again and let the typewriter reprint it. That'll take about ten minutes. We'll do it now."

"I think I'll go on home to start dinner," Rebecca said. "I bought some calf's liver, but I want to pick up some vegetables. My bike is just outside anyhow, and I don't want to leave it here."

"OK, Rebecca. I should be home within an hour," Reynolds said. "Don't worry about all this excitement," he said, taking her hand, "because Corrigan will have it figured out soon."

Rebecca pedaled quickly away and Reynolds asked the attendant to print out the tape once again. The two men continued their conversation while the tape was being replayed. They were both tired from the excitement and pace of the past two days, but, with nothing to do but wait, they reconstructed the bizarre sequence of events. Their thoughts returned to the baffling encounter with the men disguised as police and to their apparent eagerness to prevent visits to the mine. Corrigan felt sure that they must be connected with the crime, but was puzzled by the fact that they seemed to represent an organization of substantial means rather than a few demented terrorists.

"I certainly hope our men are able to apprehend them without difficulty," Corrigan thought aloud. "Their identity and background will be interesting. Say . . . on another matter . . . didn't your friend Rebecca react somewhat strangely?"

"In what way?" Reynolds asked.

"Well, let me ask you. How would you characterize her reaction to the news about the neutrinos?" Corrigan responded.

"She did seem upset by it, maybe even a little frightened. That's not surprising, considering Cowan's murder and our encounter with those guys out there."

"Right, but did you notice her reaction specifically to the news of the neutrinos?" Corrigan pressed on.

"Yes, I did," Reynolds answered calmly. "It was an unusual reaction. But I wouldn't place any meaning on it. What are you driving at anyhow?"

"Just observing," Corrigan replied.

Twelve

Rebecca Yahil pedaled furiously toward the orange glow spreading across the western horizon. The winds had turned from the north as the last cold air masses of winter flowed like a river across Texas from the Panhandle toward the Gulf. The Canadian highs that give Texas its changeable winter weather had left a string of snow across the Rockies and clear cold air through northern Texas. The day had started warm, however, and Rebecca shivered in her T-shirt and sandals as she swung abruptly into a pay phone on West 24 Street. She dialed the number of a motel along Interstate 35.

"This is Yahil speaking," she said in response to the quiet answer. "This is urgent, so get it straight. Call Leon and tell him that I fear I have blown my cover. I must leave to avoid FBI interrogation. Then come immediately to pick me up at Reynolds's apartment. You know where it is. Be there in less than thirty minutes. Don't be late because Reynolds and Corrigan may arrive within an hour. Arrange quick transportation back to Israel. We may have to drive to Dallas or to Houston if there are no immediate flights from here. I am at a phone booth and must hurry. Do you understand?"

"Yes, Yahil. This is a surprise, but we understand you. We will call Leon and arrange your departure, and then be at Reynolds's apartment in thirty minutes. We will be parked on the street, about thirty yards beyond the apartment, in a white Ford with an Avis sticker in the rear window. Will you need help carrying things?"

"No. I will leave everything," Rebecca answered, "so you can just wait for me in the car. See you then."

"All right. Goodbye," came the anonymous response.

Rebecca pulled out the telephone book and searched through

it briefly. She inserted another quarter and dialed the *Austin American-Statesman*. She asked for the City Desk, expecting it to be the only place she could find an editor of any importance at that hour.

"City Desk. Roberts speaking," came the answer.

"Hello. This is Julia Spencer, secretary in the Astronomy Department at the university. Professor George Reynolds has asked me to call you with a news item of considerable interest. He is too busy at the moment to discuss it himself but suggests a press conference tomorrow at 11:00 A.M. if you want to obtain the full story," Rebecca said.

"OK. I'm the editor in charge at the moment. What's the story about?" Roberts asked.

"Do you remember Saturday's story about Fred Cowan, the scientist who was murdered in the mine in the Big Bend?" Rebecca asked.

"Sure we ran a short story, and it brought out a lot of phone calls from people wondering what the experiment was all about. We put in all we knew, which wasn't much," Roberts replied.

"Well, the current news is this," Rebecca said, her heart pounding as her mind was rapidly but cautiously seeking the only plan likely to leave Reynolds free from harm. "Professor Reynolds and Investigator Corrigan from the FBI just returned from the mine in the Big Bend. You may know that Professor Reynolds was a close collaborator of Cowan's in proposing the experiment. At the mine they found an electronic tape record of the experiment."

"Hold on. Let me get this down," Roberts interrupted.

"Yes, please do," Rebecca responded. "Professor Reynolds thought you might want to run a short story tomorrow, and then follow with the full account after the press conference. It should be quite a coup for you to send this to the wires."

"Yeah. It sure might. Your name is Julia Spencer and you're Professor Reynolds's secretary in the Astronomy Department. Right?" Roberts asked.

"Yes. Professor Reynolds and Investigator Corrigan brought back a tape from the mine that contains a detailed record of Cowan's experiment for the past nine months. They have just played it out at the University Computation Center. It shows an astonishing fact," Rebecca went on.

"OK, got it. What new facts?" Roberts wanted to know.

"The tape shows that in the past four months the counting rate due to neutrinos from the sun has risen steadily to a value at least two hundred times greater than Dr. Cowan ever measured previously. This is at face value a very great discovery and must be related to the murder, since Cowan was at the time preparing his six-month scientific report to release the startling news," Rebecca said.

"Wow!" Roberts exclaimed. "That does sound interesting. These neutrinos come from the sun, right? In which case something must be happening in the sun. Right? What are the extra neutrinos believed to be due to?"

"Professor Reynolds asked me to say that the center of the sun is believed to be a giant thermonuclear reactor, and the neutrinos are due to the radioactivity at the solar center caused by that reactor. He will explain the meaning of all this more clearly at the press conference," Rebecca said.

"Miss Spencer," Roberts said, "you said that 'taken at face value' this represents a great discovery. What do you mean by 'taken at face value'?"

"I'm glad you asked that," Rebecca said, suppressing a smile, "because Professor Reynolds wants to explain his doubts on the reality of the counts. He says, and I now quote from a statement he asked me to read verbatim, so that you could quote him:

> I do not believe that the actual neutrino flux from the sun can have possibly risen by such a huge factor. Our theoretical understanding of stars is good and it has no place for such a dramatic rise. The FBI and I therefore suspect that the tape is a fake, tampered with by someone familiar with the experiment.

"Professor Reynolds has promised to answer questions about this at the press conference."

"That *is* newsworthy," Roberts said, seeing himself with a big scoop. "Did Professor Reynolds comment on the fact that the murderer would have to be quite an expert in order to perpetrate a fraud that would look authentic?"

"Yes." Rebecca replied. "The FBI had asked him the same thing, and he replied that the murderer would have to be an expert on the solar-neutrino experiment, perhaps a jealous colleague."

"Fascinating!" Roberts said. "Can I talk to Professor Reynolds at all?"

"I'm sorry. Not at the moment," Rebecca replied. "You will understand that the FBI has precedence for its investigation. They are now quite busy, but the professor asked me to call with this news release because of his conviction that the media have the right to full knowledge of matters related to publicly supported scientific research. He suggested that you could release a brief story containing these facts and follow with a full feature story after the press conference. He regrets that this is all he can say until 11:00 A.M. tomorrow. You can telephone in the morning to let us know if you want to come to his office for an interview."

"I can tell you now that I'll be there personally," Roberts said. "We'll run a small story tomorrow. Thank you very much for calling, Miss Spencer, and please thank Professor Reynolds for us."

"I will thank him," Rebecca said, suddenly feeling a whirling anguish at the irony of her own words. If only she could. "Goodbye."

Within seconds she was on her bike, riding swiftly again into the darkening west. In just three minutes she turned north for the final one-block drive to the townhouse. She locked the bike she had grown to love in its accustomed place in the garage, hoping to keep it secure despite the belief that she would never see it again. Quickly she was up the stairs and into the dark house. Her watch told her it was now nineteen minutes since her call to the motel. She had eleven minutes. She planned to take nothing, but quickly changed into something more comfortable and inconspicuous for travel, stuffing the clothes she had been wearing into a bag to carry away for disposal. Then she quickly sat down to write the all-important note:

> My darling George,
>   This will be difficult to understand, but you must take my assurance that your life is in danger. Those who murdered Cowan will murder you, too, if they think that you are the only one who can reveal the sudden increase in solar neutrinos. I therefore gave the entire story to the newspaper, saying it was from you via Julia, whom I impersonated. Please don't expose this lie, your life depends on it. Don't reveal that you didn't authorize the call to the newspaper, or my life may also be over— if, in fact, I can find any life at all without you. Forgive me in knowing that I had some part in this awful affair, but please believe that I never knew there would be any violence. I am sick at heart, my darling, and now want only your safety. I arranged a press conference for you at 11:00 A.M. tomorrow in your office. Hold it, and tell everything truly except, please darling, don't disclose this note. I am trying to save you, and my life is forfeit if this note is revealed. One more thing—*express doubt to the press that the tape is genuine.* Express belief that it was the sick act of a murderer who understood the experiment but hated Cowan. Please, darling, with your mind and personality, you will want to make your own decisions. Don't. Please do this my way, or we can never have

a chance again. Your love changed me and my life, and I hope that one day you can forgive me, let me explain, and hold me close again. I will love you forever.

Yours alone,
Rebecca

Rebecca reread the note one time, trying to determine whether she had left out some important detail. She realized that it would take a book to try to explain her relationship to the mysterious situation, and she also realized that additional words would be powerless to convey the sense of loss she now felt. This plan seemed the only way to neutralize the danger. Glancing at her watch, she saw that in only four minutes the car would arrive. She took the note and sealed it in one of her envelopes decorated with bluebonnets. She wrote simply "George" on the outside, and placed it on the small coffee table before the sofa. Then she returned to the bedroom to get the light green suede coat that was one of her few luxuries. As she glanced around the room, pain welled within her. There beside the bed, their bed, was George's Hewlett-Packard 65 hand computer, which he jokingly kept there so he could "compute stars at night." On his desk lay the draft of a new scientific paper he was writing. She walked to the corner and picked up one of his tennis rackets, looking lovingly at the gauze tape wound around the handle to secure his sweaty grip. Sobbing now, she picked up his tennis clothes from the heap atop the basket and buried her face in them. Then, without another look, she pulled a photograph of herself from her purse, wrote "I love you, George" on the back, threw it on the pillow, and quickly fled.

Outside, the first drops of rain began to fall gently. As the cool southward moving high-pressure zone penetrated the warmer moist air from the Gulf of Mexico, huge dark clouds collapsed in turbulent instability. Chill winds blustered, and the rain came harder. Soon the atmosphere could not withstand the millions of volts of potential difference induced by the turbulent front, and brilliant jagged strokes of lightning blitzed the surrounding Hill Country. The animals dashed for cover as they had done throughout millions of forgotten generations. Still the rain came harder. When the dark soil could absorb no more, the water rushed in great washes toward the Hill Country rivers, toward the Llano in the north, the Colorado and Pedernales in the center, and the Guadalupe in the south, from which it flowed full and heavy toward the Gulf from which it had come.

Thirteen

The paper's story publicizing Reynolds's suspicions and his press conference appeared in the sunrise edition the following morning. Reynolds was awakened at 7:00 A.M. by the insistent ringing of the telephone. It was an unwelcome wake-up call. He had been up until four scouring the apartment for clues to any of the mysteries that crowded his brain—Rebecca's departure, Cowan's murder, the phony press conference, and the unexpected neutrino counts. He had gone through everything that Rebecca had left behind, her clothes, her books, her papers, her mail, for some scrap of explanation. There was none. Finally resigning himself to bed, he had struggled even there for an hour or more, in its emptiness, so that it seemed just moments after he had finally found some peace that the phone jolted him. Reynolds jumped for it, hoping for Rebecca.

"Reynolds, you have got some explaining to do. You're in trouble with me." It was Corrigan.

"Corrigan, it's early, and I'm in no condition to face the world or you this morning," said Reynolds, recognizing the voice. "Call me at my office in a couple of hours, OK?" He was ready to hang up, but Corrigan's voice came blasting from the receiver.

"You might as well consider that your time is not your own any more, because I'm placing you under arrest. I'm going to give you the privilege of driving yourself to your office, but you'd better be there in fifteen minutes, or I'll have every police car in Austin out after you."

"Oh, for Christ's sake, Corrigan, you're running on Eastern Standard Time. It's only 7:00 here. What on earth has got you riled up so early this morning?" Reynolds pleaded, glancing through the window at his own copy of the *American-Statesman* lying on the front lawn wrapped in a clear plastic bag.

"I think you know," shouted Corrigan. "Just get the hell over there, right now!" Corrigan hung up abruptly. Reynolds stumbled around the bedroom for a few minutes, concentrating momentarily on the chaos of his nighttime search, stopping finally to pull on a pair of blue jeans and a tennis shirt lying at hand.

He drove almost directly to the office, taking a detour a few blocks before the campus to pull into a diner. There he bought a cup of coffee and a couple of rolls, bagged to go. As he stepped onto the sidewalk, a police car pulled up in front of him. Reynolds sighed in disbelief, as the officer shouted, "Hold it right there, Dr. Reynolds." The police car then escorted him directly to the parking lot of the Astronomy Building, where Corrigan was waiting in his car.

"We found him at the Longhorn Diner, picking up breakfast," explained the policeman, who exchanged a few more words with Corrigan before pulling away. Corrigan's expression lacked friendliness. He escorted Reynolds to the elevator, where the two stood silently, looking away from each other. Corrigan slapped a rolled copy of the newspaper nervously against his thigh as they rode the nineteen stories to Reynolds's floor.

Reynolds sat down at his desk and sheepishly unwrapped the breakfast rolls, offering one to Corrigan.

"You've got a lot of nerve," Corrigan shouted. "I bought a newspaper at the motel on my way to breakfast this morning, and I wasn't two sips into my coffee when I discovered your press release. God damn it." He slammed the newspaper onto the desk. "You're in a lot of trouble if you can't explain it."

There on page one, next to a photo of Reynolds that the *American-Statesman* had run with a story three years ago, was the headline: "UT SCIENTIST CLAIMS NEUTRINO TAPE A FAKE."

"Can't miss it, can you?" Reynolds observed.

"Damn right," said Corrigan, not amused, "and let me point out to you the exact sentences that are responsible for the specific charges that I intend to bring against you." Corrigan read slowly, hammering out the offenses and detailing the possible penalties.

"And you know," he added, "I'm disappointed in my judgment. I'm usually careful to avoid overconfidence in a suspect, but you fooled me completely."

"Now, wait a minute," Reynolds began, but Corrigan wouldn't let up.

"You lied to me about everything, about the jealous colleague business, about the authenticity of the tape, and you even made an unauthorized statement for the FBI! That's serious business "

Reynolds was silent.

"Why?" Corrigan shouted. "It doesn't make sense, Dr. Reynolds. You're a bright man. Why would you do such a thing? You must have imagined that I would submit a disclaimer."

"No, don't do that," Reynolds interrupted, momentarily in mental disarray. His scientific expertise was of no value now.

"Do you seriously think that the FBI can let you pass stories to the press? Claiming that you know what our opinion is? Maybe alerting the guilty party to be cautious? Do you?"

Reynolds mumbled "No, of course not . . ."

"Can you explain to me what you've done?"

"I really can't," Reynolds replied.

"Well, you've promoted yourself to chief suspect. That's one thing you've done. So you'd be better off to explain the whole thing rather carefully, and fast! Then perhaps you'd like to offer your own disclaimer at this crazy press conference that you've arranged!" Corrigan slapped the paper again.

"Corrigan, I can't do that because my life may be endangered by it," Reynolds admitted reluctantly. "I can't tell you anything more."

"You can't?" Corrigan shouted. "You damn well better. You may think that you're playing an intellectual undercover game that you can tell about at university parties, but you're not; and this isn't science, either. If your life is in danger, you may be contributing to it by your stubbornness. I'm not going to do you any favors unless you do me one and tell me what this is all about. You may be endangering others; have you thought of that?"

"The choices aren't so clear, Corrigan. Rebecca is in trouble, too." Reynolds offered, seeking the best way to reveal what clearly he must. "I'll tell you what I know if you'll promise to try to keep it to yourself. I'm convinced that our safety depends on it. Just don't issue that disclaimer. Leave the story as it stands."

"George, I'll help you if I can," Corrigan began. "But you should let experts decide what is the greatest danger."

"I need help, Corrigan, but I think it needs confidentiality," Reynolds insisted sharply.

"OK, I'll be as confidential as the law allows." Corrigan looked at him earnestly, and Reynolds pulled Rebecca's note from his pocket and handed it to him across the desk.

Corrigan looked up from the note, relieved that its contents did not implicate Reynolds, and said dryly, "She's gone, and you didn't expect it. This note looks bad for her." He looked at Reynolds for a moment, concerned, and said finally, "I'm sorry." Then, backing off from his angry stance, "You're not under arrest any longer. But you will understand that I have to make a thorough study of this note, confirm her handwriting, interview the reporter that took her call, and so on."

"It's her handwriting. I can tell you that."

"But we have our own investigative procedures. And part of them will remain focused on you. I hope you can appreciate that."

"Have a roll?" Reynolds asked, pushing his purchase across the desk.

Corrigan grinned, then leaned back against his chair. "What do you make of this note, George?" It had been "Dr. Reynolds" when he had been angry, but now Corrigan returned to the more personal tone that the two had established during their frightening experience in the Big Bend.

"I don't know," Reynolds replied, "but I take it seriously. Rebecca *has* vanished. Last night I searched everywhere. I called all of our friends, and all of hers that I know of. No one has a clue. And after what we've seen, I'm scared."

"I agree. We must be careful with this. But can you explain letting them run this story?" Corrigan slapped the paper again, gently this time.

"Corrigan, I know this will sound fishy, but I forgot. I just found the note last night. I intended to call you, but then I started looking for evidence of Rebecca. The search got bigger in my mind, searching her stuff, calling people, until I forgot about calling you. When I thought of it again, about 2:00 A.M., may I add, I decided to wait until this morning. But you beat me to the phone."

"But when I called you, you didn't exactly say 'Hey, I've been wanting to talk to you!'"

"I know," Reynolds realized. "It was kinda dumb. I was just so scared, so cautious, that I was reluctant to blurt out anything—as if I have to think all the angles through for myself."

"Why don't you relax about that, George. This is not a problem in stellar evolution. It's not a tennis match either. You're an amateur, so don't try to do it yourself. You've got to have help, and I suggest that you level with me and let me judge the safest course."

Reynolds nodded, a little embarrassed at his foolishness.

"But what about this press conference?" Corrigan asked, slapping the paper a fourth time.

"I guess they'll be expecting me at 11:00, judging from the newspaper. What should I do? Expose the lie or pretend I really mean it?"

Corrigan's brow wrinkled. "That's a good question, George. Why don't we go get a real breakfast with hot coffee and think it through. There's still three hours until the press conference."

In the month following Rebecca's disappearance Corrigan and the FBI were totally unable to trace her. Because the newspaper story did not impede his investigation, Corrigan kept the letter secret. Reynolds carried off the press conference. The Israeli agents took great interest in Reynolds' public suspicion of a sick colleague. They watched him closely but left him unharmed. Rebecca's ruse had worked.

It was in that time of confusion that CIA agent James Fitzgerald III appeared in Austin to speak with Reynolds and Corrigan. Fitzgerald in his dark suit and dark glasses made an imposing first impression, more impressive and commanding than his medium height and build should warrant, and his secretive but informed manner was unnerving. It was a carefully constructed appearance. Fitzgerald seemed to know everything about the investigation, about Corrigan, and about Reynolds. He moved back and forth with ease between his store of secrets and the conversation. Gradually, as he put his dark glasses away, folded his suit jacket across a chair back, and sat in shirt sleeves, only his serious expression remained to suggest the dark demeanor with which he had arrived. His young face and blue eyes teetered on the edge of boyishness, and only secrets and his earnest conviction to buttress the original larger-than-life impression of importance kept it from being so. He was a college bright-boy, arrived to give higher purpose to Corrigan's private-eye approach to the murder, and in half an hour's conversation he enlarged and reoriented the entire investigation.

Through routine surveillance of internal FBI reports, the CIA had noted that David Zweig was a suspect in the murder of Cowan. Their own computer files had quickly revealed that Zweig was believed to be a member of an important arm of Israeli Secret Service, largely through his well-documented relationship with Elias Hirschberg. Fitzgerald told how their own attempts to trace Zweig had lost him after the New York to Dallas flight on the day of the murder, and why they suspected that he had returned to New York and departed to Tel Aviv on the day after the murder. A man named Jakob Brenner, bearing a Swiss passport, had purchased a ticket with cash and caught a Swissair flight to Zurich, after which he bought another ticket and transferred to an El Al flight to Tel Aviv; but a computer check showed that no Jakob Brenner had previously entered the U.S. and that there existed no such Swiss passport. Carefully disclosing his reasons, Fitzgerald revealed CIA bewilderment over Zweig's past activities. Slowly he outlined the CIA belief that Zweig was involved with something important to Israel, but Israeli security, which usually voluntarily kept the CIA well briefed on routine security practices, denied any possible role for Zweig in their organization.

Through careful pleading, Fitzgerald persuaded Reynolds to try to help the CIA investigations. His reasoning was interesting, perhaps even novel. What they needed, in Fitzgerald's opinion, was a knowledgeable scientist who would scrutinize Zweig's office papers and correspondence for possible scientific threads that could relate his activities to Israeli secrets and to Cowan's murder. The CIA's fragmentary investigation had revealed nothing overt. Yet, so complicated were Zweig's papers and correspondence that Fitzgerald had decided they needed a "thematic analysis" by someone well versed in the scientific issues. He had finally selected Reynolds because his reputation pointed to him as an able scientist, one already familiar with the astrophysical aspects of Zweig's work. And for the sake of secrecy it had also seemed convenient that Reynolds already held a top-secret Q clearance for his work at Los Alamos on underground nuclear tests.

Reynolds did not like the request at all, but he ultimately agreed for a mixture of good reasons, of which Cowan, Rebecca, and David Zweig were the first tier. The second was his practice of helping the government with every scientific request that did not seem morally objectionable. And in this incomprehensible situation the CIA might, after all, actually have the means to an answer. Fitzgerald's careful delineation of what he meant by a *thematic analysis* was impressive, well thought through. It would have been hard to refuse.

The FBI had already recognized the need for this type of investigation and they had cooperated with the CIA request to the extent of impounding Zweig's papers with a search warrant issued on the grounds that he was the chief suspect in Cowan's murder. Alleging scientific jealousy as a motive, the warrant had called for his scientific notes. The file of correspondence, much of it photocopies of handwritten letters, had been lifted from his locked file cabinet. It had been among these that Fitzgerald found a strange handwritten letter to Major General Harold Hughes of the United States Air Force. Both CIA and FBI files showed that Zweig was a consultant to the Air Force, but neither agency knew why. The Department of Defense had its own reasons for contracting with special consultants and felt not at all obliged to make those reasons known to civilian government agencies. Fitzgerald displayed that letter to persuade Reynolds that he should help with the thematic analysis, but he held a few others in reserve, like trump cards. The letter had been short and puzzling:

Dear General Hughes:

All six locations and times fit an asteroidal orbit. Frequency of bursts suggests asteroidal mass—perhaps a million tons, or perhaps even as massive as the moon. Even though you can't see it, the space probe in asteroid orbit could find it due to its gravitational effects. The bursts suggest a dust cloud of small particles surrounding it in a swarm. In answer to your other question, a rocket could change its orbit, but it would be very slow—too slow to be practical. The rocket would have to float in its gravitational field, occasionally burning fuel to keep from falling toward it. Reaction on object could alter orbit, but not in our lifetime. Please come to Cambridge and I will explain.

Sincerely,
David Zweig

Several unusual features of this letter prompted Reynolds to accept Fitzgerald's invitation.

For Reynolds it was a stressful time, and he felt certain that he was being watched. He requested and received assurance that both the CIA and the FBI would keep his investigation of Zweig a guarded secret and would help him conduct it surreptitiously. Then afterwards he tried to get away from it all for the annual spring Tennis Open in Houston. He was seeded third in his attempt to capture the Men's-35 Singles Championship, but even in the early rounds he found that it wouldn't be easy. Everyone playing in Men's-35 was a serious player, in contrast to the younger duffers that one meets in the early rounds of the open singles. The fast, uneven courts at Memorial Park Tennis Center made Reynolds's powerful topspin drives potent weapons, but they aided even more the agile volleyers among the strong younger men in that age group. Thus each of the first rounds, though he was victorious, was tough for Reynolds. The last two were three-setters, and today he faced big and strong Roy Casserly, a thirty-six-year-old Houston lawyer who had played number one at the University of Houston in his student days. The concentration required for that match had already been disrupted when Reynolds received an urgent telephone call in his room on the previous evening. It had been General Hughes, who needed to see him at once, saying only that he was very concerned about Zweig's disappearance in that he had been an Air Force consultant on a matter of great secrecy. The CIA had also talked to Hughes and had alerted him to the strange implications concerning Zweig. Considering Reynolds's expertise and involvement, Hughes also needed to talk to him. With a resolute sigh Reynolds could only agree to the continuing barrage, and Hughes took a flight the next morning from Washington to Houston.

Reynolds's concentration on court was not up to par. Time after time Casserly's big left-handed service skidded in on the fast, smooth laykold, and time after time Reynolds's return was too late for power, floating over the net to be met by an aggressive sharp volley. Reynolds simply could not break his opponent's service, and in two sets it was over: 3–6, 4–6. Reynolds congratulated the beaming victor and sat back and basked for half an hour in the intensely bright April sunshine, alone and unconcerned for a moment. He glanced at the sun, which seemed unchanged by the fast flow of human events, and was amazed that his interest in an elusive subatomic solar particle had turned him into the monkey in the middle of three simultaneous investigations. For the first time, Reynolds sensed that he was the key figure in a puzzle as bizarre as astrophysics itself.

Exactly at noon the government car pulled into the parking lot at the tennis center. Both the driver, an enlisted man in air force blue, and the passenger, a tall man bearing a general's stars, stepped out of the car. Reynolds had been watching the parking lot and at once recognized his visitors at the predetermined place. Resolutely, he picked up his racket and towel and walked toward them.

"General Hughes," Reynolds said, "I'm George Reynolds. Welcome to the Memorial Park Tennis Center."

General Hughes smiled broadly, extending his hand. "Very pleased to meet you, Dr. Reynolds. Dr. Reynolds, this is First Officer Baker, from Ellington Air Force Base. Well, do you play a match soon, or can we talk?"

"We have lots of time to talk, General Hughes, because I was eliminated in my match this morning," Reynolds replied.

"Sorry to hear it, but, of course, it's just as well from my point of view. What can you recommend, then?" General Hughes asked.

"Probably the best place to talk is at my motel, the La Quinta on the Southwest Freeway. You can follow me there if you like."

"Very good. Do you know the La Quinta, Baker?"

"Yes, I do, sir."

"Good," the General said. "We'll follow you there."

He was not the only person to follow Reynolds to the La Quinta Motor Inn. From the moment Reynolds rose to meet General Hughes in the parking lot, another man sitting in the bleachers watched him intently. While Reynolds talked to Hughes in front of the tennis center, the man quickly inserted his bayonet-mount 135mm lens into his single-lens reflex camera, took a hurried shot of a tennis player and then two more carefully focused shots of Reynolds, Hughes, and Baker standing together. He then moved quickly to his rented Ford, in which he raced off in pursuit of General Hughes's car, which he had carefully watched departing along the park road toward Memorial Drive. He easily identified the car as it pulled onto Loop 610 heading south, and later as it took the turn onto the Southwest Freeway heading toward downtown. He pulled slowly into the La Quinta Motor Inn, parking unobtrusively while the three climbed the stairs directly to Reynolds's second-floor room. The man then reparked the car out of sight of Reynolds's window by another wing of the Inn, past the central swimming pool.

Inside his room, Reynolds picked up the telephone and ordered tea and sandwiches to be brought to the room. After some small talk and a hesitant interchange to establish the confidentiality of the topics to be discussed and the degree of their mutual awareness of events, General Hughes launched into an amazing story.

"Frankly, Reynolds, we in the Air Force need your help," he said. "We need someone to replace Zweig as a specialized consultant, and we also need to establish whether Zweig's disappearance, which I see you know more of than I do, is related to the topic he was helping us with. In this sense you will be sworn to top secret security, which I am empowered to extend to you from the Department of Defense based on our examination of your record and upon your functioning Q-Clearance."

"I understand the security requirements," Reynolds said, "and I agree to abide by them. The first thing I would like to know is what David Zweig was providing to the U.S. Air Force."

"His knowledge of black holes, Dr. Reynolds. You know, of course, what a black hole is much better than I do. That's one reason I have come to you. Zweig was, as you also know, the world's most inventive expert on the theory and behavior of black holes. We needed him because he thinks we have discovered a black hole!"

Reynolds chuckled involuntarily. "You must be joking. What do you mean, you've discovered a black hole?"

"We believe that we have found a black hole orbiting the sun, within the asteroid belt," General Hughes went on, appreciating the incredulous look on Reynolds's face. "Let me describe to you how we found it, and then you can understand much better what the situation is. You are no doubt aware of our Vela Satellites operated by Los Alamos Scientific Laboratory, where you are also a consultant?"

"Yes, I know that program," Reynolds replied. "They made a big discovery for astrophysics—the gamma-ray bursts coming from outside the solar system. I think they've detected about a dozen such over the past two years."

"That's correct," General Hughes went on. "What you probably do not know, because it is still strictly classified, is that those same Vela satellites have detected nine gamma-ray bursts coming from *within* the solar system."

"You're joking!"

"Certainly not," Hughes went on. "Seven of these bursts were recorded by all three satellites, and the other two were recorded by two of the three satellites. The relative times of arrival show a very surprising thing. The duration of bursts of gamma rays is very short—about a millionth of a second, as best we can tell—which makes them much shorter than the ones reported in the scientific literature."

"Yes. Those are spread out over about a second or a tenth of a second," Reynolds interjected. "But the shortness of the bursts would make it even easier to time their arrival at each of the three satellites. That makes it easier to triangulate the direction the bursts come from."

"Exactly so," General Hughes replied. "And that brings up the surprising thing. Each of these nine special bursts came from a different point within our solar system, but all nine lie in the same plane as the planets, in contrast to the longer bursts that come from outside our solar system. Those seem to be found in all directions with equal probability. According to the Vela scientists, this concentration in the ecliptic plane can only mean that the bursts come from an object associated with our solar system."

"I'll buy that," Reynolds said. "It's not proof, but it's the likely conclusion."

"You certainly follow this much more quickly than I did," General Hughes said with a chuckle. "It took those poor blokes half an hour, with diagrams on a chalkboard, to help me see what is very clear to you. Well, to continue, the bursts came from points about midway between the orbit of Earth and the orbit of Jupiter. And here is where the next big surprise comes—when the nine positions of the nine bursts were considered along with the times of their occurrences, which were spread out over almost a two-year period, it seems that each burst came from the same source! It was simply moving in a normal orbit about the Sun. The scientists tell me that those facts do not *prove* that it's an object in orbit in the asteroid belt, but they say that it is too much of a coincidence for any other explanation to be correct."

"You mean the distance and the period of the orbit fit all nine burst locations?" Reynolds asked for clarification.

"That's right," Hughes replied. "They tell me that the only funny thing is that the orbit would have to be somewhat more elliptical than for the normal asteroids."

"If the distances and times fit a Keplerian orbit, then the source is almost certainly a single object in orbit around the sun. This is an astounding discovery!" Reynolds exclaimed. "But what has this to do with black holes, and how did David Zweig get involved with the discovery?"

"I can't blame you for wondering," Hughes replied, "because the discovery has been a well-kept secret. Here's how that happened. Most of us in the military believed we had discovered a special Russian satellite, although it was difficult to contemplate the source of the gamma-ray bursts that could lie within their technological capability. A pulsed electrostatic accelerator, whose pulsed beam was striking a thick target was one idea the scientists came up with—like a big pulsed X-ray machine. My worry is that they have developed a gamma-ray laser. That would put them ahead of us in the Star Wars game. Most of the scientists discounted the Russian satellite idea as being what they jokingly called "military paranoia." They had their own fantasies. They were inclined instead to a viewing station for an advanced galactic civilization. The idea was that the gamma-ray bursts came from the pulses of a plasma fusion reactor that provided their power."

Reynolds was stunned. This was too much.

Hughes smiled and carried on. "Right. It had us all pretty excited. The Los Alamos people said that in certain kinds of plasma devices pulses only a millionth of a second in duration might be possible. However, the numbers didn't work out right. Nine pulses in two years wouldn't provide enough power, considering the modest number of gamma rays from each burst."

"That's a good point," Reynolds agreed. "It also doesn't make sense that a visiting civilization would park within the asteroid belt, where they would run maximum risk of a collision with a solid body."

"Yes, we thought of that problem, too, and when repeated telescope searches didn't reveal anything in the appropriate orbit, we decided that it was not an outstation of another civilization. A bit like science fiction, anyhow. The Vela scientists suggested David Zweig. It was, in fact, Dr. Herbert Kraft who came to me during one of my visits to Los Alamos and told me about Zweig's paper on the X-ray stars. Do you know Herbert Kraft, Dr. Reynolds?"

"Yes. Kraft helped me understand their published data."

"It was Kraft who told me that Zweig's model for X-ray stars consists of a black hole in orbit around a common star," General

Hughes continued, "somewhat like a common pair of close binary stars, I am told, except that one of them is a black hole. Do you know this paper of Zweig's?"

"I sure do," Reynolds answered. "*The Astrophysical Journal* asked me to referee it for them. It did it, but that one paper took me longer to report on than any other I have ever been asked to do. It seemed to be of fundamental importance, if correct, but at the time I wasn't accustomed to thinking of black holes as being something real. I hadn't even thought about them much. I regarded them as a mathematical curiosity of Einstein's equations. It took me some effort to appreciate the possibility of their reality. This hang-up, I guess you might call it, more than Zweig's mathematical treatment, was what made refereeing the paper so difficult for me."

"You're being too modest, Dr. Reynolds," General Hughes said. "That was six years ago, when almost no one regarded black holes seriously. But our scientific advisory panel tells me that no one has better appreciated the possible role of black holes in astrophysics than you have. That's one of the reasons I seek your help."

"Well, I thank your scientific advisers for their high regard," Reynolds replied with a resigned smile, "but it has really been Zweig who led us at every turn into these black hole problems. His work has been very creative and full of power—far ahead of his peers."

"I am told that as well, Dr. Reynolds," General Hughes went on, "and from my layman's study of Zweig, I feel certain that opinion is correct. I have watched him in action on this problem of the very short gamma-ray bursts coming from the orbit in the asteroid belt. We called him to Los Alamos after what we thought was a thorough security check, and within one hour he convinced us that the source could be *neither* a Russian satellite *nor* an external civilization. Within another hour he had us convinced that it was a black hole orbiting the sun in the asteroid belt. We all had the feeling of listening to an extraordinarily inspired intellect."

"Amazing!" Reynolds exclaimed. "But can you remember his explanation of how such a black hole would emit gamma-ray bursts?"

"Yes, but only because I spent so much time listening to his attempts to explain it to us," General Hughes replied, "and also in listening to Dr. Kraft's explanation of Zweig's explanation! The key point seemed to be that the black hole should have enough mass to hold a swarm of dust grains in orbit about it, but not too much mass or it would consume the dust and perturb orbits of other asteroids. Zweig suggests about 1/1000th of the mass of our moon, although he made it clear that this was only his guess and

110

could be off by a fairly large factor. The point was that a black hole that massive would be even smaller in size than the grains of sand orbiting it. That really astounded me."

"Wait a minute! Let me see," Reynolds interrupted, scribbling a few numbers on the notepad by the telephone. "By God, that's right; it would be less than one-millionth of a centimeter in radius if it had a mass about 1/1000th of our moon's mass. That's about one hundred times smaller than typical dust grains. But what significance did Zweig see in the size of the black hole?"

"From time to time—Zweig suggested every couple of months or so—one of the dust grains would hit the black hole," Hughes responded, "but because the black hole is so small it would pass right through the larger dust grain. The shock would shatter the dust grain, and, as it did, would capture some billions of atoms of the grain—atoms that would score a direct hit on the black hole. Zweig estimated that their capture by the black hole would radiate energy in the form of gamma rays and that the whole thing would take less than a billionth of a second while the black hole passes through the grain."

Reynolds was stunned again. His scientific training rendered this scenario even more brilliant to him than it must have seemed to General Hughes. It was a wild scenario, constructed to fit incredible facts, but one that possessed the special beauty of scientific plausibility. Reynolds stirred with the excitement of it, just as he had always done upon hearing of great discoveries. If Zweig was correct, it was a magic moment in the history of intellectual discovery. Obviously, the important thing was to investigate these flashes at close range.

"We should mount a scientific investigation to study the source of these gamma-ray bursts," Reynolds exclaimed. "We can enlist the entire world of astronomy, of space physics, NASA . . ."

General Hughes raised his hand like a policeman halting traffic. "Dr. Reynolds, an open investigation is out of the question at the present time. We are exploring this thing with maximum security, and any leak of this discovery would be prosecuted as a revelation of classified military material. I'm sure you will understand that. Your record of government service shows that you appreciate such security requirements. Let me show you additional classified evidence on grounds of your need to know. You must accept the secured nature of this investigation. I cannot be too emphatic about that."

General Hughes paused, staring Reynolds squarely in the eye. His stare was steely and resolute, though not unsympathetic. Nonetheless, Reynolds did not much care for the situation that was unfolding. General Hughes was treating the discovery like another Manhattan Project.

"As you know, General Hughes, I have been involved for ten years with our nuclear tests in Nevada, and I believe in and respect this security. But none of us believe for a moment that the Russians are not obtaining similar knowledge with their own tests. Facts of nature cannot be long hidden. Of course, I can be trusted to not reveal security secrets. You can be sure of that. However, I can't guarantee to agree with your rationale for placing this matter under security. You know, for example, that I also serve as a consultant on special matters to the Arms Control and Disarmament Agency, which I assist in a small way with disarmament strategy. There is for me no conflict between that role and the role I play with the bomb tests. But you know that many high-ranking military men disagree with disarmament philosophy. If I should ever feel that my own beliefs run counter to our secret activity, I'll discuss it with the secretary of defense. In that way I can feel that I have responsibly reported to the president—and with no security leak."

"That seems perfectly reasonable to me. We could hardly expect more from a civilian consultant," General Hughes said, with a tone of voice suggesting that the subject was closed. He paused, then looked at Reynolds with a faint smile of amusement at what he was about to reveal. "Do you remember the surprised relief of NASA and the scientific community when the Office of Management and Budget approved so suddenly the funds for the Pioneer 10 and 11 flights to Jupiter?"

"I remember it," Reynolds replied. "That was a happy moment, just when it looked like NASA's scientific budget would be heavily cut in an economy measure."

"*We* paid the extra for those flights, Dr. Reynolds, and we had to delay work on our new long-range bomber to do it, too. We agreed with the OMB to take a fifty-million-dollar cut over the following two years so that the Pioneers could go. We insisted only that we choose the launch times and the orbits, so that Pioneer would pass through the asteroid orbit where we wanted it to. We also insisted on having sets of photos transmitted back exclusively for the Air Force. Here, let me show you a few." General Hughes enjoyed Reynolds's incredulous expression as he reached into a briefcase beside him.

"You're not trying to say that you contributed that money in return for TV pictures of the object?"

"That's exactly what we did," General Hughes replied, while handing Reynolds an 8 x 10 black-and-white photograph. "Here is the view of the expected asteroid field taken from an encounter distance of about ten million miles with the 500mm lens. You can see several asteroids of various sizes, including one large one, along the line from lower left to upper right. If you look at it a while, you can also see something else."

"This is a very good TV photograph," Reynolds said as he eyed it appreciatively. "Here's a funny spot—rather fuzzy like a photograph of a globular cluster of stars."

"Yes, that's our target," General Hughes replied calmly. "Here's what it looks like from a half million miles . . . and here's another view from one hundred thousand miles."

"Good heavens! This looks exactly like a globular cluster!" Reynolds exclaimed. "It's a swarm of small asteroids bound together by gravitational attraction—in orbit about something."

"That's right," General Hughes confirmed, "but you should see our movie assembled by computer from the two thousand photographs we gathered of this object on our approach to it. The larger stones you can see in this photograph are moving very rapidly. They are not just suspended there, floating along together. They rapidly orbit some central object."

"Hey, that gives the mass of the central object!" Reynolds blurted out. "From this photograph and the distance to the object, you can get the size of this swarm . . ."

"It's about five hundred miles in radius—out to where the swarm looks as dark as the sky," General Hughes confirmed. "That size and the period of the orbit of the larger rocks in the swarm gives a mass for the central object that is about 1/10,000th of the mass of the Earth. Notice also the spherical white glow of particles too small to be seen—rather like the zodiacal light. It seems to be a five-hundred-mile cloud of dust particles too small to resolve with this camera."

"But it's still very noticeable," Reynolds added. "If one assumes a size distribution for the particles, one could easily compute a mass for the dust swarm from the total amount of sunlight that it's reflecting."

"Zweig suggested that, too, and our men in Air Force Cambridge Research Labs, where we have three scientists studying the discovery, estimated about ten thousand tons of dust. That's only about one-millionth of the total mass of the object," Hughes said.

"Didn't you have to make a midcourse correction after passing this object?" Reynolds asked.

"You think of everything, Dr. Reynolds," General Hughes said with a smile. "Our closest approach was fifty thousand miles with Pioneer 11, and we had to make a substantial burn to get back on course to Jupiter after that. Here's the photograph of that closest approach, and you can see that nothing is visible at the center of the swarm except a finer brighter white glow due to the increased number of dust particles. Those near the center are all too small to be seen individually. But our required midcourse correction confirmed that the mass of the object is 0.87/10,000ths of the mass of the Earth—a number in exact agreement with that obtained from the orbital period of the larger rocks farther out. There can be no doubt that that mass is the mass of the central object, but its value is billions of times greater than the combined mass of all of the objects that can be seen in these photographs!"

"It sounds like a black hole, all right," Reynolds said leaning back in his chair. "And since it's in the direction of the gamma-ray bursts, it surely must be the source of those bursts. By the way, I can tell you that this object is an old one, probably as old as the solar system itself; however, the dust cloud is younger."

"Oh, how is that?" General Hughes asked, raising his eyebrows at an observation he seemed not to have heard before.

"Notice that the larger rocks all have orbits lying very nearly in the ecliptic plane—like a somewhat thickened Saturn's rings. This is just what one expects to happen after a very long time because of the weak gravitational effects from the other objects in the solar system—especially the Sun and Jupiter. A spherical swarm would slowly flatten into the same plane as the rest of the solar system. It might take a billion years, but it would happen. The dust, on the other hand, is almost a spherical swarm around the center. That suggests to me that the dust is being maintained by collisions of larger rocks—collisions that break them apart. Or perhaps larger rocks break up as they move near the black hole. Let me see—a rock weighing one pound on Earth would weigh fifteen tons at a distance of one meter from this black hole! Such forces would break the rocks up into fragments. At any rate, the object is old and the dust cloud much younger. As a guess, I would say that the dust cloud must be replenished every million years or so."

"That's an interesting observation," Hughes offered, "but I presume it affects only the history of the object, and not how it functions today?"

"Well, yes, that's true," Reynolds said, "but a clear understanding of how it functions today has to be consistent with a natural history for the object."

"Can I take it, then, that you will help us with the analysis of this object?" General Hughes asked, redirecting the conversation somewhat toward his own objectives. "We would like you to come to Washington to get a full account of all we know about it."

"You bet I will; but only if you'll tell me why Zweig wrote 'A rocket could change its orbit,'" Reynolds said.

General Hughes was visibly surprised. He stood silently for a

114

moment before answering. "How did you know about that letter?"

"It was found in Zweig's office," Reynolds said.

"Well, I hope you're better with security than Zweig was," Hughes responded with a despairing smile.

"I will be," Reynolds assured, "but I still want to know why you asked him about changing the orbit."

"You've hit on the secret part of this topic, Dr. Reynolds," Hughes admitted.

"But you'll have to share your intentions with me to give me a clear conscience to work with this discovery, no matter how exciting it is," Reynolds stated firmly.

"All right. I can do that right now. We actually have no *plan* as such. We're only examining whether it would be physically possible to move this black hole to a closer location—say in Earth orbit, or in lunar obit. The air force is evaluating a secret plan for its tactical utilization there."

Reynolds had to keep a rein on himself. It seemed to him that the general's idea was crazy; it was also clear that it would not be physically feasible, owing to the very large mass of this black hole—almost one-tenth of the mass of the moon. It worried Reynolds that the general did not appreciate the great instabilities in three-body orbits, and the attendant physical danger in having a large black hole out of control near the Earth. What a nightmare! He worried throughout this lengthy discussion about the popular caricature of the military mentality; but he also found that General Hughes was himself much more skeptical of the idea once he heard of its problems. It was, moreover, exactly the type of situation that called for responsible civilian consultants and, with that in mind, Reynolds agreed to participate.

Reynolds stretched the muscles fatigued from his morning tennis match, rose, stretched again, and strolled idly to the window. Immediately he froze. Outside a man in tennis gear was photographing the rear of General Hughes's car. Glancing up, the man saw Reynolds at the window, and sensing he had been seen photographing the Ellington Air Force Base decal, he walked calmly but quickly toward the central patio and disappeared. Recovering from the shock, Reynolds quickly told Hughes and Baker. Baker raced out to look, going quickly himself across to the patio and through to the other wing. He saw no man in tennis gear, only a Ford pulling away on the side road. Reynolds telephoned Corrigan at the FBI and told him of the strange occurrence. For Reynolds it was all a bit frightening. Corrigan's confession that FBI El Paso had not been able to find the police impersonators made it even more so. Corrigan gave Reynolds a special FBI telephone number in Houston, urging him to call quickly if he seemed to be watched. When Reynolds revealed that he planned to drive to dinner with air force personnel who were with him, Corrigan decided to have an FBI man watch the restaurant and Reynolds's room. It was an act of surveillance that was also to be fruitless.

The three men finally went out to a restaurant on South Main Street, where they ordered badly needed drinks and dinner. There they discussed the peculiarities of Zweig's behavior and the Cowan murder, of which General Hughes was only vaguely aware. Hughes wondered if the stranger had been watching him rather than Reynolds, but the tennis clothes suggested otherwise. He was alarmed that the CIA regarded Zweig as part of a foreign security system. All in all, the evening somewhat aggravated the anxieties of each of them, and on parting it was agreed that Reynolds would come to Washington. They would obtain there a much more realistic view of the possibilities of the situation.

A huge question mark hung over the events surrounding Reynolds. In only a month he had participated as an unwilling witness in two of the most astounding astronomical discoveries of all time. The near coincidence of two discoveries so breathtaking was hard to regard as accidental, yet Reynolds could see no conceivable relationship between them. Nor could he fathom the coincidence that David Zweig, an acquaintance and brilliant colleague, seemed to have been involved in both discoveries. Nor could he ignore the emptiness left by Rebecca's disappearance. That was the most aggravating of the mysteries, the one for which brilliance and perserverance and patience were useless.

Fourteen

David Zweig was making his second trip from Tel Aviv, where he was maintained under the watchful eye of Elias Hirschberg, to Jerusalem. For Zweig it was a symbolic journey, a pilgrimage of sorts. As on the previous occasion, he made the trip with Rabbi Aaron Rabin. Hirschberg wanted Rabin to accompany Zweig because he was concerned about the latter's mental state. He wanted the rabbi, the psychologist, to be on hand to reinforce Zweig's resolve in the face of his frequent waves of remorse. Nightmares of the murder still plagued him, but Rabin had skillfully minimized his guilt. They handled Zweig like an emotionally damaged child, not aware that he comprehended their motives.

Aaron Rabin believed that man's welfare lay in subjugating himself to a higher purpose. But if it be admitted that his conception of higher purpose was much more general than traditional religious belief, it must nonetheless be added that he had witnessed and assimilated the powers of misery, hope, and spiritual fervor. Rabbi Rabin led his temple in prayer without actually believing in God. He believed instead in the value of spirituality and that his long-suffering people were a spiritual arm of mankind, just as the Scriptures said they were. These and other convictions allowed him to be an effective rabbi despite his disbelief in the God to whom he prayed daily. He did share an Old Testament fervor for the Jewish people and for their need to prevail against enemies and persecution. In this he had been hardened by a horrifying nine months in Dachau, where, just northwest of Munich, his photograph with other survivors still hangs in the German memorial to the Jewish victims.

On their first trip to Jerusalem, Rabin had taken Zweig to Hebron to visit the Mosque of Abraham. The mosque had been a

Muslim shrine throughout recent history, until Hebron was captured by Israeli troops in the Six-Day War in 1967. Since that time Jews had also been allowed to pray at the shrine, but only at specific times. This restriction had caused new problems. An extreme group of Israeli zealots from the nearby Jewish settlement of Kiryat Arba had not been satisfied with the privilege. Almost at once they began protest sit-ins at the mosque, claiming that it was actually an Israelite temple, inasmuch as Abraham had purchased the Cave of Machpela for four hundred talents four thousand years ago. This reasoning was not accepted by the Supreme Muslim Council, which pointed out that Abraham was their forefather also and that it was not clear which lineage, Israelite or Muslim, had actually developed the mosque as a religious shrine. The emotions of confrontation ran high, so this ancient dispute had become a major issue.

Rabin had been involved in preparing the appeal to the Israeli government, which had changed the relationship. The Knesset had then decreed that the Muslims would henceforth use only the large hall commemorating Isaac and Rebecca, and the Jews would use the two smaller halls commemorating Abraham and Sarah and Jacob and Leah. Israeli troops stood by when Zweig and Rabin visited, just as they had done since the change had been instituted. The zealous Kiryat Arba community had been persuaded personally by Rabin to accept this compromise, although it had initially demanded a complete Jewish takeover.

Zweig had read about that confrontation during his postdoctoral years at the Weizmann Institute. He remembered that both the leading Israeli newspaper, *Haaretz*, and the Arab newspaper, *Al Quds* of East Jerusalem, had condemned the alteration of the mosque in Hebron. *Haaretz* accused Israeli Defense Minister Shimon Peres of giving in to pressure from the fanatic Kiryat Arba group, and *Al Quds* had stated, from a different point of view, that the new system transformed part of a Muslim mosque into a Jewish synagogue, concluding that seeds of hatred had been sown that would make future coexistence between Arabs and Jews impossible. David Zweig himself felt that the government had made a mistake, although Aaron Rabin, from his vantage point as a daily participant in life in Jerusalem, disagreed, arguing that it was essential that Jewish religious rights be as formally established as were Jewish political rights.

On the present trip Zweig was taken into the heart of Jerusalem, into Mea Shearim—"a hundred gates"—where Rabin lived. It was a hot April day as the two men, wearing sandals and ordinary Western street clothes, walked through one of the stone gates into the historic alleyways. The bright sun blazed in a cloudless blue sky. As they strolled, Rabin asked about something he did not understand.

"What is a black hole, David?"

"It is a form of matter about which we can know nothing, except that we can sense its gravitational attraction," Zweig began in response. "I find it useful to imagine a small, very black sphere so opaque that it reflects no light. I think of a black marble, but without the shiny reflectivity of glass marbles. I see in my mind a small black dot, in which I can see nothing but blackness, as if there were nothing there, but to which all nearby objects are attracted by a gravitational pull. This gravitational pull remains the only detectable feature of the simplest black hole."

"What do you mean by the *simplest* black hole?" Rabin asked, very much interested.

"The black hole could also possess an electric charge," Zweig replied, "in which case there would also be an electric force on charges near it. It could also be spinning, possessing a physical property we call angular momentum."

"How can one say it is spinning if there is nothing that can be seen?"

Zweig smiled. "Your question is a good one, but it presupposes a certain philosophical outlook on knowledge, an outlook that I do not share. I find it perfectly easy to imagine that an object possesses angular momentum without having to be able to see it spinning. Elementary particles have the same property. In fact, the angular momentum of a black hole does have observable features, because the structure of space-time around the black hole differs from the case in which it has no angular momentum. All any black hole does, at least from Einstein's viewpoint, is modify the structure of space-time near it, and it is the effect of those modifications that we seek."

"How?" Rabin asked.

"Have you heard of the gravitational redshift?" Zweig asked.

"Yes, I have read about it. As I understand it, the light waves from the surfaces of stars oscillate more slowly than they do on Earth when they come to us because of the strong gravity at the surface of the star," Rabin replied.

"That's exactly right," Zweig said, "and that shift reflects nothing more than a shift in the relationship between space and time in the strong gravity. The stronger the gravity, the bigger the shift in the frequency of the received light. In a black hole, the shift has become so extreme that nothing seems to us to happen at the black hole. Time seems to us to stand still there."

"Incredible!" Rabin exclaimed. "That must be related to the idea that no information could come out of the hole."

119

"Yes, it is. Another effect of the modification of space-time is that light rays appear to us to follow curved paths near the black hole, in fact, near any massive body. You will have heard of the deflection of light. Near a black hole the deflection is quite large, and, in fact, light rays too near the black hole can never get away at all, so curved is space-time."

Suddenly Zweig stopped and turned to look curiously at two men they had just passed. Even in the heat, they were dressed in long black frock coats. They wore large black hats from which dangled long, black, tightly twisted curls. They had seen many such men on their walk, some bearded, some wearing sunglasses. They were solemn and foreboding. Zweig asked Rabin about them and their peculiar style.

"They are the Neturei Karta," Rabin replied. "They are a very zealous Jewish sect, very orthodox in their religious beliefs and customs, but very much out of tune with today's world. They mostly live here in Mea Shearim."

"In what way out of tune with today?" Zweig asked.

"They regard much of the modern world as wicked," Rabin answered. "They will not attend a cinema or watch television."

"That's not such a bad idea!" Zweig said with a smile.

"A neighbor of mine was totally ostracized from his acquaintances when he dared to buy a TV," Rabin went on.

The men walked on silently while Zweig watched the numerous members of the sect as they moved along the street. He was fascinated by the large hats and the long sidecurls, symbols of the medieval ghetto. He remembered seeing an old photograph of his father's grandfather, a stern-looking man with the same hat and curls. To these darkly dressed fanatics, black had a different meaning from the one with which David Zweig wrestled daily.

Suddenly Zweig stopped again, staring this time at the stone wall before them. There, in broad strokes of black paint, were a swastika, a star of David, and a hammer and sickle, smeared across the wall side by side, three black partners.

"What is the meaning of that?" Zweig asked Rabin, pointing toward the wall.

"That is done by the Neturei Karta," Rabin replied. "Their name means 'guardians of the walls,' and they regard themselves as the watchdogs of the Israelites. The swastika, star of David, and hammer and sickle stand together as a statement that each is believed to be equally evil for Israelites. To them Zionism and the modern state of Israel are as contrary to God's plan for His people as were the genocide and persecution by the Nazis and Soviets."

Twenty feet beyond that implausible mural stood a member of the sect speaking to any of the people who would listen.

"How long shall we live as a part of this blasphemy!" he cried. "I have seen thirty years of counterfeit Israel, of the usurpation and profanation of the sacred name of Israel by a secular socialist state that methodically violates the sanctity of the Jewish people."

"Let's go, David," said Aaron Rabin. "We don't want to listen to this nonsense."

"No. I want to stay. I want to listen," Zweig replied, not moving.

"The three million members of today's state of Israel are transgressors!" the bearded man continued. "It is not in man's power to establish God's kingdom! The Torah says that Israel will not be reborn as a nation until the Messiah comes. For men to attempt to preempt this divine prerogative is the greatest sin. We will pay for this iniquity! God will punish us by causing our nation to fall. We will crumble like the walls of Jericho, and only then will God rebuild his kingdom among the rubble. Pay no more taxes! Refuse, as we do, to serve in the military. Pray God's forgiveness and sin no more."

Rabin was tugging on Zweig's arm, urging them to leave. Zweig turned instead and stared at the star of David painted on the wall between the swastika and hammer and sickle. Were there in fact two sides to the story of the state of Israel? Was he making a mistake in helping to plan the first step toward Israel's domination of the world? Zweig thought of his father's praise of the United States, which had given their family refuge. Despite its faults, he had said, the United States gave freedom and dignity equally to every man. He had in 1954 predicted a great social change in which the American blacks, still at that time living servilely about them in Louisiana, still locked in slavery's attitudes, would soon emerge as socially equal, protected by the Constitution. Jakob had once become tearful under the emotional stress of these issues and his own haunting memories of persecution and had wondered to the young David if the world's hope were not for a United States of the World, a single government in which all individual nations, including the Jews, must disappear. Jakob Zweig was, in that sense, linked philosophically to the Neturei Karta, and David now felt that kinship at least as strongly as the nationalistic one.

Eventually they walked on, resuming their discussion of black holes. Rabin's interest was only in part due to the role black holes were to play in the Joshua Factor. His hunch was that the concept of space and time, invented by Einstein as relativity, might have spiritual relevance.

Meanwhile, sixty kilometers to the northeast, in an office in Tel Aviv, Elias Hirschberg and two officers of Jericho were conversing with Rebecca Yahil. It was, in fact, the official debriefing following her return from Austin. Her earlier explanatory remarks had been precise, but nonetheless difficult to interpret. So important were the details of the solar neutrino experiment that the head of Jericho, Elias Hirchberg, was himself conducting the debriefing. The two officers from security police merely ensured sufficient observational detail. Rebecca's sudden flight had been regarded with some suspicion, so that for a second time, Hirschberg attempted to clarify its circumstances.

"You felt that they could sense that you knew too much about the murder?" Hirschberg asked.

"Well, not necessarily about the murder," Rebecca responded calmly, "but at least that I knew that the contents of the tape were related to the murder. I have to admit that I was not calm enough when they surprised me with the tape. I fear that I gave my excitement away, and I still recall the curious way that Inspector Corrigan was staring at me at that very moment."

Rebecca adhered to the thin but plausible story that she had constructed during her flight from the United States. She had been worried that her story would not be believable because she had been forewarned that some surprising discovery concerning the sun *was* a possibility. Her surprise at the discovery of its true nature would therefore not have been sufficient to have caught a true professional off guard. Rebecca instinctively felt it was better to emphasize her weakness by in part apologizing for it and in part by counteroffensive.

"I just wish you had told me what kind of surprise about the sun I should watch for," she continued. "I know it's my fault; but I would have functioned much more calmly if I had known the nature of the hidden information."

"But what was said that caused you to react in such an emotional way?" Hirschberg pressed on. "Why did you feel a reaction so strong that it caused you to show yourself out of character?"

"As I said before," Rebecca came back, "I think it was because I had had the chance to become personally acquainted with Fred Cowan. He was a dear and lovable man, Dr. Hirschberg, and you yourself would have been much attracted to him. He was infectiously excited about his solar-neutrino experiment, and so good-natured about its many years of negative results. I had come to identify with his effort emotionally, especially since I had myself begun to work on new computer models of the sun in an attempt to learn more of its meaning. The last thing I suspected was that the surprising discovery about the sun would lie in the solar neutrinos themselves. When I was told to watch for any surprising new discoveries, I naturally took that to mean the visible sun—solar flares, or a change in the solar wind, for example. I did not understand why Cowan was murdered, and I felt genuine grief. When I discovered that his experiment had finally succeeded and that the new knowledge was what necessitated his murder, I was shocked. I can't explain it any better, because my whole judgment of events is too subjective." Rebecca paused, confident that she was looking weak but that her story would stand.

"But why would an inappropriate reaction on your part make it necessary for you to flee?" one of the security officers interjected.

Rebecca paused before answering, focusing on her main objective, which was to guard Reynolds's safety: "It seemed from the outset that Reynolds and Corrigan assumed that the murderer must have been a sick scientist who was so familiar with the experiment that he would have been able to falsify a taped record of half a year's counts. I assumed that for us it would be best if Reynolds continued to believe that, and I realized that it would be much worse if the FBI were to investigate me carefully. I did not know how much access they might have to our security system, but it was conceivable to me that through CIA contacts I might be tied to our security. After all, David Zweig is implicated. I could not be sure how I would respond to their questioning techniques, so I thought it would be better if I simply vanished. Then at least I could not be forced to give away anything."

"I think that was well enough done, Rebecca," Hirschberg said. "Of course, I'm sure you also realized that your hasty departure would call even more attention to your possible relationship to the destruction."

"Of course," Rebecca replied promptly. "It was a trade-off. This way they suspect me but can't discover anything by interrogation. The other way they might not suspect me, depending upon how penetrating were their observations of my reactions. I had to decide quickly, and for better or for worse, I decided to flee."

"I agree," Hirschberg said with clear finality. "I think that will close the matter. You can go now, but I must remind you that you must remain inconspicuous in Jerusalem, without contact with the outside world until this plan is concluded."

Rebecca was sure that her story would be regarded with some suspicion and that she would be watched. But she was also sure that if she acted carefully, nothing more would come of it, because her story could equally well have been the whole truth. At least she had accomplished her purpose of helping to spare Reynolds's life. It was still too early for her to face what would be a bigger problem, her own life without him. She loved him, that was certain. She would, if she could, have exchanged her life in Israel for a life with him in Texas, ignorant of Jericho. But she was not ignorant, and she assumed that she must now ignore that love in favor of a loyalty to a people and a country that in total meant far more. But daily she was to confront a loneliness that would not go away.

In the Jericho office, the men debated Rebecca's story. None of them fully believed it, but none could see anything hidden behind it. Because of that, Hirschberg expressed the conclusion that spared Reynolds.

"I think it will make no difference," he said, "assuming that Reynolds does not know why we were involved in the murder. Even if they do not believe that the murder was committed by a sick colleague, I do not think they have enough scientific clues to fathom why it was to our advantage to murder Cowan and to destroy his experiment. One set of old data will not get them very far.

"Rebecca's story is for the most part believable, although not totally accurate. Leon did tell her in a telephone conversation in New York, while Reynolds and Corrigan were at the mine, that the sensitive information concerned the solar neutrinos. It is possible that she forgot that in the excitement. Her preassignment briefing did not tell her that neutrinos were involved. It is a small point, and I may decide to question her again.

"In the meantime, continue surveillance of both Reynolds and Rebecca. If Reynolds does not seem to solve the mystery, just let him be. Getting rid of him now would only accelerate the investigation. We do not want that!"

David Zweig, Rebecca Yahil, and Elias Hirschberg sensed, each in his own way, that time was too short for the flow of events to be reversed. Rebecca was frustrated at seeing the newly identified life she hoped for disappearing like a raft over a waterfall. Only Hirschberg was content with the odds of the coming gamble, offering the chance in his mind of great gain against the likelihood of inescapable disaster. He was not so much flirting with danger as he was calmly evaluating routes that could, in his firm opinion, leave the world changed for the better. David Zweig continued to think about the Neturei Karta and their black predictions of an Israeli state doomed by its premature appearance among the nations of the world. In the world of the religious versus the atheistic, the mystic versus the scientific, the fanatic doomsayer versus the coldly constructive strategist, he felt suddenly naive, and his dominant feeling was an unspecified remorse at his own timid conviction.

Fifteen

Reynolds was impressed by the speed at which the CIA had been able to free him from his other duties so that he could study Zweig's notes intensively. The CIA's Fitzgerald had put it bluntly to the air force: "We want an in-depth thematic analysis of Zweig's recent work and, in your present uncertainty over Zweig as a secure air force consultant, you had better support the same thing." They found a simple ruse for channeling money to Reynolds to support his release from his duties. The Air Force Office of Scientific Research promptly awarded a research grant to the University of Texas, with Professor George Reynolds as principal investigator, entitled "On the practical effects of condensed objects on nearby material systems." Such a title was flexible enough for everyone—the AFOSR itself, the University of Texas Regents, who were routinely nosy about academic affairs, and the U.S. Congress, where a few senators and congressmen had of late become infamous for criticism of the awarding of government research grants. The forty thousand dollars awarded to the University of Texas allowed Reynolds to take leave from his classroom duties during the spring semester, provided a summer salary for continuation of that research during the summer months, and provided a surprisingly large amount of unrestricted travel funds. Reynolds had not even had to write the grant application. Fitzgerald and General Hughes had done it for him.

Reading through Zweig's papers was an exhilirating experience for Reynolds. His 1968 paper, "On the existence of objects having no properties other than strong gravity," was the first to argue that black holes actually exist in nature. He obscurely described them as "collapsed objects at the Schwarzschild space-time singularity." It was not until six months later, at the General Assembly of the International Astronomical Union in Warsaw, that

125

these objects were first referred to as "black holes." The name stuck. Two aspects of Zweig's 1968 paper made it remarkable: its brilliant mathematical analysis which rendered black holes more understandable and, therefore, more plausible, and its double-barreled description of how and when black holes formed. In the mathematical part, his analysis showed that the Schwarzschild singularity, which had been known for decades and was condemned as unphysical by many leading scientists, was only a pathology of the coordinate system rather than an actual physical singularity. His presentation of a new coordinate system, now commonly called "Zweig coordinates," allowed one to time an object falling continuously into a black hole, although that fall could not be seen by someone on the outside. And of course, nothing could come out of a black hole. Not even light.

As to their origin, Zweig had made two innovations that were not digested by the scientific community for several years. He showed that if a collapsing stellar core were too massive, it could not be held up either as a white-dwarf star or as a neutron star, but must instead collapse to the apparent singularity of space-time. The discovery of pulsars one year later by a Cambridge University research student immediately intensified interest in such theoretical arguments because they represented the last step before a black hole. In the same 1968 paper, Zweig also argued that if the universe has expanded from an early dense state, the so-called Big Bang, there should remain countless black holes of widely varying masses left over from that early period. These black holes could fill the universe with invisible gravitating mass points.

When he finished reading this paper, Reynolds leaned back in his desk chair and closed his eyes. The esoteric concepts were difficult, virtually unintelligible to anyone untrained in them, and yet Zweig wrote of them with such a directness and simplicity that they seemed very real. Reynolds ran his hand absentmindedly through the hair on his left temple. After a few minutes he left to get a cup of coffee, which he brought back into his office. Carrying it to the large window, he gazed over the campus. He began to pace the floor. There was something about Zweig's work that thrilled and agitated. The familiar sights of the campus stretching out below seemed momentarily transformed, unique, special, even miraculous. Reynolds remembered having heard older physicists describe the same sensations upon their first readings of Einstein's papers. He put down his coffee, left his office, rode the elevator to the ground floor, and took a long stroll toward the east end of the campus. It was to be a rare hour of idle contemplation for a man on a treadmill.

It was 3:00 P.M. before Reynolds set aside some correspondence, finally ready to continue his mind-searing rush through the works of a contemporary genius. He lifted a photocopy of Zweig's next published work from the stack. In this work, Zweig argued that, since a high percentage of stars existed in pairs in orbit about one another, the transfiguration of one of them into a black hole by collapsing upon itself would leave it still in orbit around the other star. An astronomer would see the star "wobbling," as if it were in orbit about nothing.

Zweig included in that paper an analysis of events that should occur if the visible star of such a pair were subsequently to lose some of its outer atmosphere. The outflowing gas would be gravitationally attracted by the unseen companion black hole. It would then fall toward the black hole, but would largely miss it because the black hole would be too small. Therefore, the matter would be expected to accumulate in a disk around the black hole, similar to Saturn's rings, and only then would that disk slowly spiral into the black hole, like water down a drain. Zweig predicted intense X-ray and gamma-ray emission from such objects, and he predicted that the emission would come in bursts because the black hole's accretion of matter would occur sporadically because of the irregular flow of material in the disk. The argument was terribly complicated and had been ignored for three years by a skeptical scientific community until, quite unexpectedly, the variable X-ray sources and the gamma-ray bursts had been discovered, the latter by General Hughes's satellites designed to detect nuclear tests. Reynolds spent an entire week studying Zweig's analysis of the accretion disk around the black hole and even managed to construct computer models of the disk that had just the features Zweig predicted. Through such efforts he developed a rapidly growing feeling for black holes as physically real objects. They became as real in his mind as the many other species that populate the stellar zoo. It was an intense learning experience.

Zweig's published works showed clearly that by 1971 he had abandoned completely the field of elementary particle theory in which he had won his early fame. His interests had become focused completely on the physics of black holes and their possible occurrence in nature. Even when the new J particles were discovered in 1975, particles whose unusual decays were best explained by Zweig's Ph.D. thesis and its immediate extension to charmed quarks, Zweig published not a single scientific paper on those new particles. To repeated questions he had always replied, "My Ph.D. thesis says all I have to say on the subject," much to the dismay of the rest of the world of particle physicists.

This single-minded concentration on black holes made it all

the more difficult to see any possible relationship between Zweig and the Cowan murder. Indeed, Reynolds could see no connection at all and, despite Fitzgerald's persistent queries for the CIA, he could see even less of a possibility of connecting Zweig's research with an imagined international Israeli intelligence operation. Indeed, were it not for the fact of Zweig's disappearance, Reynolds would have concluded that the CIA was pursuing a thread of speculation and paranoia. But Zweig *did* maintain that interest in the solar neutrino experiment—an interest so keen that he sometimes went to the Big Bend to check its progress. Reynolds had to acknowledge that some connection escaped him. To this Fitzgerald's constant reply was, "Right. Keep trying."

So it was one week later when Fitzgerald again telephoned Reynolds. But this time Fitzgerald had become excited about a few ideas of his own.

"Look, Dr. Reynolds," he implored, "I've got a couple of items I want to talk to you about. I'd like to show them to you."

"You might as well call me George as long as we're going to be frustrating one another," Reynolds shot back.

Fitzgerald chuckled. "And I'd like you to call me James and also to meet me if I fly to Austin tomorrow."

"OK, Jimmy," Reynolds replied a bit devilishly. "What have you got?"

"I'll show you tomorrow. I'll bring them along. I have tickets on American flight 307 arriving at 11:30 A.M. Can we meet after that?"

Reynolds sighed. "Well, I'm not much in the mood for my tennis match tomorrow anyhow. After all, what's a Sunday for? Why don't we meet at Hill's Cafe for lunch?"

"Great! Where is it?" Fitzgerald asked.

"On South Congress. Just take a taxi from the airport. It's not far. I'll show up about noon."

Hill's Cafe was a simple old-fashioned Texas steak house, well known to locals, but not much for international cuisine. The beginning of their lunch was spent in convincing Fitzgerald that he should forget about his usual food habits in favor of broiled T-bone, a baked potato, and Lone Star beer. Having passed that hurdle with some jocularity, the two found themselves increasingly drawn into the puzzle of the Zweig connection. The sharing of it almost made them begin to like one another. Well into the beer and steak, Fitzgerald changed the tone of their review a little.

"How did Zweig initially get interested in a solar neutrino experiment?" he asked.

"Well, the first I know of it happened in 1965," Reynolds replied. "Zweig came to a seminar where Professor Fowler planned to discuss neutrinos from the sun. It was a routine scheduled talk in our nuclear astrophysics series. And I was a graduate student in Fowler's group."

"But why do you think Zweig attended?" Fitzgerald asked.

"We all wondered about that, because we knew of Zweig only as a hotshot graduate student working on the theory of elementary particles," Reynolds replied. "I assumed then, and still do, that he came because he was interested in the theoretical structure of neutrinos. He was working on neutrino theory as a problem in elementary particles. But I don't think he had specific interest in the sun."

"Did anything interesting happen during the seminar? Anything about Zweig that you can recall?" Fitzgerald asked.

"Yeah. Zweig made a comment that Fowler and Cowan have agreed pushed the experiment ahead."

"What was that?" Fitzgerald said impatiently.

"He pointed out that the technique for detecting the neutrinos should be better than everyone was assuming. Cowan and Fowler had been discussing chlorine targets for absorbing the neutrinos, but they had overlooked the most probable way for the absorption to happen. Zweig remarked that the decay of radioactive boron in the sun should emit neutrinos with such high energy that the chlorine nucleus could absorb them much more easily than it could most of the other neutrinos."

"Is there radioactive boron in the sun?" Fitzgerald asked.

"Not much of it. But enough that Zweig was right. Fowler later published a paper showing the full calculation. He had wanted Zweig as a co-author, but Zweig refused."

"Refused! Why refused? What would that mean? Does this guy just specialize in surprises?"

"Well, it was rather self-defeating," Reynolds agreed. "Most of us would have jumped at the chance to publish such a calculation with Professor Fowler. But Zweig seemed uninterested. Fowler told me that later."

"Could that refusal have anything to do with what's happened?"

"Damn it, Jimmy, you know that's the kind of question I can't answer," Reynolds snapped. "I don't know for sure what has happened. And neither do you."

"OK. You're right. But don't jump on me. Let's assume for the sake of conversation that Zweig was part of the Cowan murder. Do you think he might have already been maintaining a low profile on his solar neutrino interest, even then?"

"I really doubt it," Reynolds said. "Zweig was only a graduate student then. He must have only been about twenty. I'm not sure he was shaving yet! We grad students regarded him as some kind of boy-genius. He seemed to know everything. He was busy with Feinberg, his own thesis adviser, and the theory of elementary particles. He probably just attended the solar neutrino seminar out of a general interest in neutrinos."

"Another thing," Reynolds continued. "Zweig didn't maintain what you'd call a low profile as the experiment developed. He came regularly and openly to the briefings and the progress reports. Everyone knew of his interest. He certainly didn't hide it then. So I think it was just his curiosity."

"But does that curiosity really fit the subsequent development of his career?" Fitzgerald asked.

"That actually is a very good question," Reynolds replied. After a moment's thought, he continued, "The funny thing is that Zweig almost gave up his interest in elementary particles after his year in Tel Aviv. He got almost exclusively into black hole ideas. That was the source of a lot of dismayed gossip in the world of elementary particles. The theorists were appalled that a guy who had done so much in that area would just drop it."

"And yet he continued to show interest in the solar neutrino experiment," Fitzgerald interjected.

"Yeah, it's strange, Jimmy," Reynolds conceded.

"Do you really think I look like a 'Jimmy'?"

Reynolds just smiled and took a sip of his longneck. Fitzgerald returned the smile, or half a smile. Then he reached into his attaché case and pulled out a piece of paper, which he handed to Reynolds.

"What's this?" Reynolds asked. "Looks like a letter."

"It is," Fitzgerald said. "One of the few interesting ones that could be found in Zweig's correspondence files at Harvard. It's to Elias Hirschberg, confirming that Zweig planned to spend next year in Tel Aviv, beginning in summer. Read the second paragraph."

> I ran into Rebecca at the Boston meeting of the American Astronomical Society in December. We discussed her work thoroughly. She is doing very well there, although they have discovered nothing of importance.

Reynolds felt a momentary faintness at this unexpected mention of Rebecca. He had sent Rebecca to that Boston meeting, but she had not once mentioned seeing Zweig there. That omission was remarkable. After her return to Austin they had gossiped for hours about the science and about the scientists that Rebecca had met with. But she had not once mentioned a discussion with this very famous colleague. Suddenly it seemed that she had intentionally attempted to downplay her relationship to Zweig. He felt a little heartsick at this discovery, which in fact only confirmed what she had admitted in her departing letter to him. But it was almost more than Reynolds could easily believe, for to him the reality of her was their hunger for one another. Reynolds leaned back and tried to remember her reactions to the murder, the look of shock, the alarmed verbal outbursts, and his heart went out to her. Her own anguish had been evident. She had been an unwitting accomplice to the murder, of that he was sure. But he couldn't say as much to Fitzgerald, remembering Rebecca's warning that he dare not divulge her parting letter. Doing so to Corrigan had been risky enough.

So he said simply, "I don't make much of it. It would be natural for Rebecca and Zweig to talk in Boston."

"Maybe so," said Fitzgerald softly. "But what does it connote that she should tell him that *they*, presumably *you*, or maybe *Cowan*, have discovered nothing of importance?"

"I don't know," Reynolds replied thoughtfully, very thoughtfully.

Fitzgerald was not through. He reached into his attaché case and extracted another letter, an original, addressed to Zweig, from the Air Force Office of Scientific Research. It announced the award of a research grant to Harvard, with Zweig as principal investigator. The grant was for a modest twenty-five thousand dollars and was entitled "Gas flow around condensed objects." Reynolds smiled to himself, thinking of the similarity to his own grant from AFOSR and wondering if General Hughes had been involved in this one, too. It seemed likely, inasmuch as the grant date was June 1984, fully a year after the discovery of the short gamma-ray bursts from the asteroid belt. Interesting as the letter was, it was not as interesting as the material jotted in pencil along the bottom, clearly in Zweig's handwriting. First was a telephone number with the Washington, D.C., area code, which Reynolds recognized as General Hughes's number in the Pentagon.

"Is this telephone what I think it is?" Reynolds asked.

"Probably. It's General Hughes's FTS number at the Pentagon. I'm sure you must have seen it a few times by now," Fitzgerald replied. "But look at the two short items following it, numbered specifically (1) and (2), as if they were notes that Zweig had made in preparation to calling General Hughes. Read them aloud."

"OK, Boss," Reynolds said. "Here they are: (1) How did it get there? Capture impossible. There from the beginning! (2) Pioneer 11 infrared radiometer. Make a different explanation."

Reynolds sat without saying a word, although the two notes suggested quite a lot to him. The trouble was that he was not sure

131

what he could say to Fitzgerald, because the topic seemed to concern the top secret military consulting that Reynolds, and Zweig
before him, had done for General Hughes. Fitzgerald also said
not a word, as if he wanted to hear Reynolds's first words unprompted. The two sat looking eye-to-eye, both pretending to be
thinking about the letter, both actually thinking about what the
other might be thinking.

Finally, eyes twinkling, it was Reynolds who spoke: "Well,
Jimmy, I guess we'd better be going." He added a slow and theatrical reach for the check.

"Cut it out, George," Fitzgerald exclaimed, grabbing the
check. "What do you make of this letter?"

"I think you should ask General Hughes."

"I already have. Quit playing dumb. I want to know what *you*
think," Fitzgerald insisted.

Reynolds remained impassive. "I think the notes concern a
top secret military investigation. I can't talk about it."

"But I know about the topic of Zweig's consultancy," Fitzgerald
pleaded.

"Still, that doesn't empower me to discuss it with you, especially not on your word alone," Reynolds stated.

"Call General Hughes then. Ask him!" Fitzgerald retorted.

"It's Sunday. He won't be in his office," Reynolds said.

Fitzgerald reached again into his attaché case for a small address book. He flipped through it, then wrote a number on a piece
of paper. "Here's his home phone. He already told me we could
call him. Do it. I noticed that there's a public phone outside by the
filling station."

"Do you always notice such things, Jimmy?" Reynolds teased,
actually amazed that Fitzgerald seemed always on top of everything.

"It's my business," Fitzgerald boasted, sensing that his plan
was going well.

"OK. Have another beer. And order one for me," Reynolds
said.

Reynolds slipped out of their red leatherette booth halfway
along the row that lined the wooden walls of the cafe, and made
his way through the tables toward the door. He nodded and waved
at a tennis-playing acquaintance seated in the adjacent room, and
left. As waitresses will do when someone walks out, theirs glanced
back toward the booth, where Fitzgerald, all smiles now, held up
two fingers and an empty Lone Star bottle. The waitress herself
was the typical Texas middle-aged combination of bouffant hair,
horn-rimmed glasses with a hint of wings, a Hill Country red
cotton dirndl, and friendly, talkative efficiency. Fitzgerald won-

dered why she and all the others were so different from waitresses in Washington, D.C. His good humor reflected his assurance of elevating his status in the CIA if he could fit the international pieces together. The strategy, the beer, the steak, and the good rapport he was building with Reynolds made him downright mellow. In this mood he leaned back and began to pay attention to the sounds around him.

"I think we'll have more bucks out around Ozona than we'll have near Fredericksburg," came a voice from the booth behind him. "The ones near here don't live long enough before someone shoots 'em. The good racks will be pulled in near Ozona, during the rut."

Hearing this, Fitzgerald glanced at the deer trophies on the wall, interspersed with photos of happy hunters with their prizes. The waitress set the Lone Stars down with a "Here ya go," and a smile, and departed breezily. The continuing deer-hunting conversation was interesting, but Fitzgerald suddenly realized how easy it was to overhear.

Outside in the telephone booth Reynolds was listening to General Hughes's reply: "Yes, it is true that Fitzgerald knows about our evidence that a black hole is orbiting the sun. We discussed that finding with him because we had to."

"What do you mean, you *had* to?" Reynolds asked.

"I was *ordered* to by the secretary of defense!" Hughes replied. "Apparently Fitzgerald convinced the CIA director that he had to know what we and Zweig were working on. The director convinced the secretary of defense, and he gave me my orders. I really resented it a little, but you know how it is in the military. When the men upstairs give the orders, we carry them out."

"Does that mean that I can discuss it with him without violating security?" Reynolds asked.

"Yes, Fitzgerald has been placed in the Need-to-Know category. The only thing he can't know is anything about military applications," Hughes responded. "But you don't know any of that, either."

"Military applications?" Reynolds asked.

"Well, it *is* our job to consider any," Hughes replied.

"I really want to repeat what I told you in Houston," Reynolds said. "I would welcome, even urge, your office to use my consultancy on any such idea. The whole situation is so fantastic that it would be hard for any one person to consider all the consequences."

"We appreciate your willingness, Dr. Reynolds," Hughes went on. "Just stay away from such lines when you talk to Fitzgerald. Keep it to what's known physically and there is no security problem as long as no one else is in on the conversation."

"All right," Reynolds replied. "Before I go back to Fitzgerald, I want to know something else. Did Zweig telephone you some time ago to ask you about the infrared radiometer on Pioneer 11?"

"Why do you ask?"

"Because Fitzgerald has a letter from AFOSR to Zweig announcing his grant, and on the bottom Zweig has scribbled two notes beside your telephone number. The second said 'Pioneer 11 radiometer. Make a different explanation.'"

"I hope you're better at security than Zweig," Hughes said, remembering having said it before.

"And I hope you're telling me all I need to know to help you understand him," Reynolds responded.

"Zweig had been very concerned about the sensitivity of the infrared radiometer on Pioneer 11. The reason was that when Pioneer 10 passed Jupiter, it showed that Jupiter was radiating heat," Hughes said.

"I didn't know that," Reynolds said.

"It's published knowledge," Hughes replied. "The discovery was published in *Science* magazine, the special issue on the Pioneer 10 visit to Jupiter."

"I'll look it up," Reynolds said. "How much power does it radiate?"

"About three times more than the power in the sunlight falling on Jupiter," Hughes answered.

Reynolds whistled. "I guess I just paid no attention, or missed the announcement, because it's not my specialty."

"So Zweig was adamant that the sister ship, Pioneer 11, should carry an improved radiometer. It took some doing, but we managed to get one on board," Hughes said.

"What do you mean?" Reynolds asked.

"We had to channel some money into NASA to allow them to take a more expensive instrument than the one they had planned on. They were happy to accept it, because it did fit their scientific priorities. It was just sticky working it out," Hughes answered.

"Why in hell didn't you tell me this when you told me about getting the camera for the gamma-ray source?"

"Is it that important?"

"I don't know, but you're keeping secrets from me on a job where you want my help," Reynolds said, a little hotly.

"That really wasn't my intent," Hughes said. "I just wasn't sure we ought to get into the Jupiter radiometer stuff. At least not at the beginning."

"What I cannot fathom is that David Zweig gave a hoot and a holler about that radiometer," Reynolds said. "He never had any interest in solar system physics."

"He was absolutely adamant. Said he would not remain our consultant unless we tried to get it done. He said we needed it for the other project," Hughes said somewhat guardedly.

"Are you telling me that Zweig as much as demanded this because of the gamma-ray burst stuff?" Reynolds asked. "I don't get the connection."

"Neither do we," Hughes answered. "Zweig said he would explain it when the answer from Jupiter was better established. But then when the observation confirmed the Jupiter radiation beyond doubt, he gave us instead a rather unrelated analysis. Then before long, poof, he's gone. So I still don't know what his initial speculation was."

"It makes no sense to me, either," Reynolds said. "We'd better discuss this more fully when I next come up there. But when we do, I want to know all that you know about Zweig and this whole damn business. Frankly, I'm a little pissed that I have to dig up things that you already know from scribbled notes on letters that Fitzgerald extracted from Zweig's files."

"We have no obligation to tell you everything; you are . . ."

"And I have no obligation to continue consulting for you, either. Especially if you don't tell me freely what you know about the matter you hire me to consult on. If I have to squeeze info about Zweig out of you, forget it!"

"Im sorry, Dr. Reynolds," Hughes replied. "I can see how you might feel that way. There really isn't anything more except some details. But I definitely want you to continue as our consultant. I'll show you everything of relevance when you want to see it."

"OK. I've got to get back to Fitzgerald. He'll think I've been kidnapped."

"Glad you called," Hughes said, "and that we could straighten out this little misunderstanding."

As he returned to the restaurant, Reynolds's thoughts flew. The infrared radiation from Jupiter is such a specialized topic that it was staggering to imagine a specialist in esoteric particle theory involved in it. What made Zweig care? How did he ever get involved? It was certainly similar to his puzzling connection to the solar neutrino experiment and to the black hole among the asteroids. And how could Zweig have enough influence with the military to get them to fund an experiment that not even NASA could plead sufficient funds for—and all this in secret? Scientists do not normally have that much influence.

"Well, Jimmy. I talked to the man and he gave you a clean bill of health," Reynolds said as he slid back into the booth. "He said we could talk about black holes if we can think of anything to say about them!"

"Shh," said Fitzgerald holding a finger to his lips and casting his eyes jumpily around the room, as if to urge secrecy.

Reynolds could not believe his eyes: "What! You think this collection of deer hunters and churchgoers want to hear about Schwarzschild singularities?"

"We ought to be circumspect, just on principle," Fitzgerald said. "You never know who might be watching us here, or even listening."

Just then a platinum blonde woman, early thirties, in tight cream-colored designer slacks, pearl necklace dangling from an open white silk shirt collar underneath a deep-V light wool pullover with sleeves half pushed up into a cocky position, headed toward Reynolds's table with an equally cocky stride.

"Why George Reynolds!" she exclaimed. "Whatever are you doin' here?"

"Hi, Roberta, just lunching with my friend Jimmy Fitz," Reynolds answered, making the introduction with a sweeping gesture and trying not to count the number of different colors of makeup on eyes, cheeks, and lips.

"Pleased to meet ya, Jimmy," said the blue-red lips. "Are y'all gonna play tennis?"

"Jimmy only plays chess," Reynolds answered with a straight face, before Fitzgerald could more than smile.

The pink fingernails fondled the string of pearls while the blue-red lips continued, "I've just been to church with Mama and Daddy."

"It's about time," Reynolds suggested.

"Oh, George, don't be nasty. Can I join y'all? Mama and Daddy would gladly see me with y'all."

"Sorry, Roberta," Reynolds answered, "but this is a business lunch. Jimmy wants to know if I can put his moves on a computer."

"We could set it aside for a while, George," Fitzgerald interjected, also noticing the pale green eyeshadow.

"Not really, Jimmy. I've got to run soon," Reynolds said. "Thanks for dropping by, Roberta. Maybe some other time."

"Do give me a ring, George. We haven't talked in such a long while," she said, the attempted coquettishness not coming off quite right. A smile, then a little wave as she walked away.

"Oh, come on, George, who was that?" Fitzgerald said. "Think of me. I don't know anyone here."

"I figured you'd be getting back to D.C. when we're through," Reynolds said.

When Fitzgerald sighed, and nodded, Reynolds continued, "She's Roberta Howard, spelled with dollar signs. She's been trying for years to become a good tennis player. I gave her some lessons a couple of years ago."

"I thought as much," Fitzgerald said grinning. Then after a short pause, and a good-natured sip of beer, he continued, "But you're right that I want to stick to business, because I really do need your ideas on these Zweig letters. My instinct is that there is something in them. The remarks are cryptic, intriguing. Specifically these notes of Zweig's on the bottom of this letter. What ideas come into your head about the first one?"

"That's easy," Reynolds responded. "The minute I read the words (capture impossible) I thought of the small black hole that the Air Force surveillance satellites have found in the asteroid belt."

"General Hughes told me that this thing is orbiting the sun, like any of the planets," Fitzgerald said.

"That's right. It's in the asteroid belt, which is a ring of tiny planets in an orbit between those of Mars and Jupiter," Reynolds said.

"So why does Zweig's note make you think of it right away?"

"Because Zweig's consultancy with General Hughes was to study it."

"So (capture impossible) refers to our ability to capture it," Fitzgerald guessed.

"Maybe, but I don't think so. Zweig's note that it must have been there from the beginning suggests to me that he was thinking that the black hole must have been in the asteroid belt since the beginning of the solar system."

"Do you agree?"

"Yes. If a black hole out in interstellar space just drifted into our solar system, it would fall toward the Sun, gaining so much speed that it would simply sail past the Sun and drift back out of the solar system. It could not be captured into a nearly circular orbit around it."

"So that's what (capture) refers to? I had wondered what you meant by the sun *capturing* the black hole. You mean capturing it into an orbit rather than swallowing it up in the Sun?"

"Yep. And I'm pretty sure that's what Zweig would have meant, too. That's the way scientists use the word *capture*."

"So if I understand you," Fitzgerald broke in, "you think that Zweig is here concerned with how it came about that we have a black hole orbiting out there. He has concluded that it's always been there."

"Exactly. And I agree. But *always* is too extreme a word, because the sun has not always been there. Our sun was born out of interstellar gas about 4½ billion years ago. And the planetary system was formed along with it at that time. I guess that Zweig was puzzling about a sequence of events that could have caused the sun to form with a black hole already in orbit about it."

"Fascinating. What do you think?"

"Damned if I know. We have a real scientific puzzle on our hands."

The conversation paused quite naturally at that point. Each man took a moment to digest the information at his own level of understanding. Reynolds's mind was playing through his experience with ideas of star formation, trying to imagine how a large and distended cloud of interstellar gas with a small black hole within it could have collapsed and formed the sun so close to the position of that black hole. It made no sense to him, because the black hole would fall into the sun while it was growing, rather than circling it. The forming sun would have been so large initially as to engulf the black hole. Fitzgerald, on the other hand, was more concerned with trying to guess Zweig's overall purpose. Why should this admittedly astonishing scientific discovery be related, if it was, to Zweig's disappearance, to Cowan's murder, and to a scientific puzzle over solar neutrinos?

Finally it was Fitzgerald who spoke again. "The second of Zweig's notes is also tricky. I asked Hughes about it myself, and he told me an incredible tale about Jupiter radiating power in the form of heat. Zweig apparently convinced them to put a better heat detector on Pioneer 11."

"I know," Reynolds mused. "Hughes just now told me the bare bones of it. I was quite surprised to hear it."

"Why surprised?"

"Because it was the first I'd heard of it. The fact that Jupiter radiates heat had passed me by, even though it was published in *Science*."

"Why was Zweig involved with it?"

"That surprises me, too. The Zweig that I thought I knew seemed to have very little interest in planetary science. I knew him as a far-out theoretical physicist, interested only in elementary particles and black holes. I just can't picture him being so interested in Jupiter that he would muck around with the military and try to get them to put a complicated experiment on a NASA deep-space probe."

"I'm convinced there's some military application, George!" Fitzgerald interjected. "Why else would Zweig be consulting for the military? And why else would he be so chummy with Elias Hirschberg, who is the top Israeli scientific consultant to their military? What I've got to do is figure out what the military application of a black hole is." Fitzgerald leaned so excitedly into his point that he almost knocked his beer over, catching it just in time.

"It seems simpler than that to me," Reynolds responded in measured tones. "Zweig is interested because it's a black hole.

Nothing more; nothing less. He's a leading theorist of black holes, and that's why Hughes contacted him. I'm excited by a real live black hole, too, so it's easy to imagine how excited Zweig would be. And anyhow, I don't think there is any military use for a black hole in the asteroid belt."

"I may quote you on that someday," Fitzgerald said sarcastically.

"Look, Jimmy, don't preach to me about the value of pure knowledge! I'm already a believer. I'm trying to leave political stance out of this. I don't see any possible way in this century for someone to use that black hole. And as for Elias Hirschberg, for Christ's sake, you've got to remember that he is also a leading theoretical physicist, not some technical general. He and Zweig began writing papers about black holes immediately after Zweig's Ph.D. thesis, when he first went to Tel Aviv as a postdoc. Their relationship is based on a love that is profound, a love of knowledge and of the excitement of truth. Why look for a military plot in it?"

"I have my own reasons for suspecting one, and I'll not be getting into them with you. But Hughes is tight-lipped on the subject. He contends that it's their business, not mine. Anyhow, I do appreciate your forthrightness on this point. I would just like to encourage you to think about it. Let your imagination run freely. Let me know if you think of any military angle that might have occurred to Zweig. Don't be blind to the fact that he was consulting, *top secret*, for our military."

"Sure, I'll do that. But you do something for me. To understand Zweig, and also Hirschberg, and even me, you've got to understand that you're talking about people who get their main thrill from new knowledge. People like Zweig are literally one in a million. He should be likened more to Mozart, or to Picasso, than to a gentleman soldier. Of that I am sure."

"All right then. What about J. Robert Oppenheimer? What about Edward Teller? What about the entire Manhattan Project? Were those great scientists involved in a military operation or not?"

"Sure. I'll concede that that was military. And I see what you're driving at—that they were also top scientists motivated by their love of science. They were also mature men, and part of a national project. But Zweig is young, naïve, maybe even a little fragile emotionally. He has no obvious wheeler-dealer side to his personality. That Hirschberg is a military consultant, even a top one, is only circumstantial evidence, a coincidence. You'll need more to go on than that," Reynolds stated.

"What about Rebecca, then?"

"What about her? I suppose she's a four-star general!"

"No, but her father was. And our CIA files are rather thick on

Rebecca. You might like to read them. They tell a fifteen-year record of a girl caught up in patriotic security. They tell of her personal friendship, through her late father, with people who are today the elite of Israeli military. Her whole life drips of military. Do you know about her father?"

"Yes, Rebecca talked about him. He was a military hero. She admired and loved him. I'd say that's fairly normal. What kind of crappy argument are you onto, Jimmy? She didn't choose to be the daughter of a military hero! You're fooling around with a fabric of coincidences."

"And you sound defensive about her, George. Are you maybe so smitten that you don't care to see very clearly?"

Realizing his edginess, Reynolds relaxed his upper body with a deep breath and a shift of position. He never had known what to make of Rebecca's departing letter, a letter that he feared revealing, both for her sake and for his. "So, what else about Rebecca?" he asked.

"For one thing she vanished after Cowan's murder. For another thing, she was recommended to you by David Zweig, which I have learned is rather uncommon for scientists of different nationalities and different scientific specialities."

"But Zweig got to know her while he was in Tel Aviv. That's natural, to seek help from a famous acquaintance who knows you when you're looking for a job in the U.S."

"And for another thing," Fitzgerald continued, "we just read that she talked to Zweig at that Boston meeting without telling you about it."

"OK, Jimmy. I can see that you're in your element. But I don't see anything I can add to clarify your line of thinking."

"You could tell me what she was working on. Isn't there anything about that black hole and some way to use it?"

"Not a thing. She was working on models of the Sun. We were simply continuing a ten-year program of mine to try to understand the solar neutrino situation. That's it, everything. Maybe you suspect *me* of some military complicity!"

"I would suspect you if I saw some evidence," Fitzgerald said stonily. "Look, George," he continued, "I believe you when you say you see only a dead end here. I just want you to share some of my skepticism when you think about her."

"I do," Reynolds said quietly, "but I just make no sense of the whole thing. If I do, we'll talk about it, OK?"

"OK, let's shift gears one more time," Fitzgerald said, reaching once again into his attaché case. "I have one more letter. This one is addressed to Zweig from Dr. Allan Hale, an astronomer at the Lick Observatory in Santa Cruz, California. Here, read it."

Reynolds accepted the letter, this one from a well-known observational astronomer. It read:

Dear Professor Zweig,

Thank you very much for the preprint of your paper on eruptive phenomena in early stellar evolution. It is an extremely interesting idea and I think you should definitely publish it. I myself am a conservative thinker, so I find your model to be rather exotic. However, it does seem to offer hope of fitting the facts, for which there presently exists no known explanation. I urge you to publish these ideas and to interest someone currently constructing stellar models to check those ideas with numerical models of such stars. Your case will be much stronger if these computer models confirm your analytical conclusions.

In answer to the query in your letter, I find that you have treated the statistical occurrence of such stars correctly. The number of known cases is, as you assumed, three, the first having been discovered by Wachmann in 1939, and your treatment of the number of visible young stars of differing ages is also consistent with the facts. Your arguments on these matters can therefore stand as they are.

I will, as you have requested, not discuss this idea with anyone until you have submitted it for publication.

Sincerely yours,
Allan Hale
Professor of Astronomy

Reynolds handed the letter back to Fitzgerald. He could not but admire Fitzgerald's instinct for pinpointing puzzling things.

"Can you help me understand this one?" Fitzgerald asked. "What, for example, is Zweig's exotic model?"

"I know I must sound like a broken record, Jimmy, but I really don't know what this letter is about. My astronomy grapevine never included any gossip about Zweig having discussions with Allan Hale. The only thing I can do is telephone Hale to see if I can learn something. But not now. I'm bushed."

"Fine with me, George. I actually want to make the 3:00 P.M. departure to Dallas, so I can get to Washington tonight. There's a marvelous woman there who hopes I can get back tonight."

"Who's that, your mother?"

"Oh, come on, George. Just because you think you've had the best export Israel has to offer, and one that was shipped to you prepaid at that, don't assume that the rest of us must be hurting,"

Fitzgerald replied, trying to appear to be tougher at give and take than he was, trying to not show a small hurt at Reynolds's possibly thinking that he might be ineffective with women, and trying to not feel somehow inferior to this tennis playing Texas astrophysicist with just those qualities that his own life strategies did not encompass.

"I see Roberta Howard is still here," Reynolds replied, "but if you're determined to leave . . ."

"Very funny," Fitzgerald droned, reaching for their lunch check.

"Wait a minute, Jimmy," Reynolds said, grabbing Fitzgerald's arm. "I'll let you get the tab, but I would like you to do me a different favor, a real favor."

"What's that?"

"Can you find Rebecca?" Reynolds asked quietly.

"She's one of several people that we're trying to locate."

"But could you do more than you're doing? Is there any part of your grapevine that you could pick more vigorously? I need to know what's happened to her."

"Why is that, George?"

"I'm in love with her, Jimmy. I've fallen really hard. I can't imagine myself interested in another woman, and yet I have all this uncertainty about her. I don't know what she's involved with. I don't know where she is. I don't even know if she's alive."

"Well, George, it sounds as if you're admitting that there are things about Rebecca that you don't understand. It's about time."

Reynolds seethed. "Goddam it, Fitzgerald, what I know about Rebecca would fill volumes. But words will not capture her. So give 'em a rest, will you? What I have is a feeling based on my love of her. And just now I'm hurting. And I'll appreciate it if you wouldn't sound so prig-ass over it."

"I'm sorry, George. I don't berate love because, frankly, I've not been very successful at it. Would you marry her?"

"In a minute. But I'm not even able to think about things like that. I just need to know where she is. That's why I'm asking your help. I've not heard a single word from her, and I don't understand why. It's almost like someone you love dying. Six weeks ago we lived for the next day with one another, and since then she has existed only in my memory. I want very much to know where she is."

"Suppose the truth would kill your love? Suppose you saw her wrong?"

"Everything in me denies that possibility. But, of course, that's one reason I want to know."

Fitzgerald eyed Reynolds very carefully as he prepared the

lines that might teach him something about the man. It was by no means clear that Reynolds was being truthful and aboveboard; in fact, Fitzgerald held evidence to the contrary.

"I can't see how a man can feel so deeply confident about love when his lover just up and vanishes without even a simple *Auf Wiedersehen*," he said.

Reynolds paused, clearly searching for words. Fitzgerald noticed each blink of the eye, as if tuning in to Reynolds's brain, but at the same time did not seem too eager for the reply.

"I can't understand why she's disappeared," Reynolds said. "I'm afraid something may have happened to her."

"Like what, George?" Fitzgerald fixed his gaze.

"Hell! Maybe she was kidnapped. A girl like Rebecca draws a lot of stares. Even Austin isn't safe for a girl who insists on riding her bike around at all hours of the night."

"But don't you think she disappeared because of the Cowan murder?"

"So what are you saying, Jimmy, that she did it? How in hell would I know why she left?"

"From the letter she left you," Fitzgerald said without blinking.

Reynolds's mind raced. Maybe Fitzgerald had something to do with it. Maybe those were CIA men in the Big Bend. Maybe the whole damn thing was some big CIA scheme. The ground felt shaky, and his reply was a feeble, "What letter?"

"The letter she left telling you not to reveal her letter. The letter she left telling you to pretend that it was *you* who told the *Austin American-Statesman* that you thought the data tape was faked by a sick colleague. The letter that warned you that both of you were in danger."

Fitzgerald sat back and waited, but not for long until Reynolds burst out, "Have your men got her, Fitzgerald? What in the hell are you up to?"

"No. We don't know where she is."

"Well, how do you know about that letter?"

"I'm going to level with you, George, because I want you to know that we're on the same team. I got the letter from Corrigan."

"I might have known," Reynolds said, resignedly. "You guys are like cockroaches. You get into everything."

"Take it easy. That's my business. We have leverage over Corrigan. He had no choice."

"But suppose what she said is true. Suppose I am in danger over that letter."

"We've considered that. We're treating it as a high confidence. But I want to tell you something right now. There *is* something

143

dangerous in this. I can sense it. There is something big in it, and you will be doing yourself a favor if you tell me everything you know. How about it?"

Reynolds seemed to hold a bust hand. "OK. I will. The disappointment for you will be that I don't know anything more." Nonetheless, the two men spent another half hour, and another beer, going over the murder, the data tape, and the departure letter. When it was finally clear that there were to be no more insights, not even any more surprises, they quit just in time for Fitzgerald to make his plane.

"Will you try to find her for me?" Reynolds asked again as Fitzgerald got into his rented car.

"We've been trying, and we'll not quit," Fitzgerald replied. "I hope you can go on with business as usual. I need to keep after Zweig's purpose. When we find that, I think we'll find Rebecca. Just be patient, and help us all you can."

Sixteen

The gentle but incessant beep of James Fitzgerald's quartz alarm was a bit slow to rouse him. He should have known better than to go to Elan after his late arrival from Austin via Dallas and Atlanta, even if it did have a big reputation among with-it singles. Surely he was one of them; at least he had felt so until striking out again, this time with a rather beautiful professional woman from D.C. Now he cursed the wasted time and too many drinks before she had disappeared with someone else. But there was so much to be done today, starting with his confidential notes on his visit to Austin, so he dragged himself to the shower of his Arlington townhome, hoping to reawaken with hot water his momentum from the day before. Then he would have his morning tea, feed his cat, and select the correct clothes from his wardrobe. His morning ritual would put him back on the track of his rising status within the CIA.

Fitzgerald drove quickly to the CIA headquarters in Langley, Virginia, where about ten thousand employees of a much vaster world network were stationed. He stood impatiently in line at the security check and took the exit stairs to his floor to avoid the wait at the elevators. He waved hello to several acquaintances and, passing his secretary's desk, snatched his phone messages.

Fitzgerald was a busy man, particularly now that his investigation was acquiring new dimensions. He had to make every minute count. Fortunately, he had begun to write the notes on his meeting with Reynolds during the plane trip back to Washington. He unpacked his briefcase immediately, slapping notes and files into his correspondence box. Then he began returning telephone calls with perfunctory requests that the conversations be kept short.

Among the message slips was a note about a call from a Senator Larabee. The name was familiar, but he called his secretary and asked her to quickly compile some information about him. "Get me a rundown of his committee appointments and personal background." Fitzgerald liked to know to whom he was talking. It was meticulousness in his professional habits and in his powers of observation that usually made an immediate impression on his contacts.

Fitzgerald made another call, standing at the window, looking across the treetops bridging the considerable distance between the CIA building and the Mall in downtown Washington. The weekend trip had broken his stride with his number-one woman friend. He was anxious to restore the situation immediately, and although lunch with Laura usually meant meeting at the museum where she worked, which required two hours counting the driving time, she was important. She was a fabulous, beautiful, bright woman, and a tremendous contact. When she accepted the invitation Fitzgerald wrote across his calendar, "lunch with L. L." He had found himself thinking about her a lot lately, and when his secretary entered with the information about Senator Larabee, he was turning the pages of his calendar assessing his progress.

Senator Larabee was a Republican from Pennsylvania, serving as vice-chairman of the Emergency Military Appropriations Committee, a subpanel of the Senate Budget Committee. He had been referred to Fitzgerald by some CIA higher-ups cognizant of Fitzgerald's reports of Israeli acquisition irregularities. Fitzgerald hadn't been able to construct much of a big picture from his information, but he had continued his dogged surveillance of everything from purchasing to personnel reorganizations within their military. It was beginning to build up as a strategy. What had begun as a hunch about David Zweig had enlarged to encompass the recent subtle but curious behavior of many of the Israeli government departments. The parameters just kept expanding, and Fitzgerald marveled at the way information rolled his way once he had become more confident and aggressive in reporting on "new Israeli priorities."

In a brief call to the senator's office, Fitzgerald agreed to an afternoon appointment. By then he would have his most recent information. The senator gave him a preview of his concerns. Apparently, Israel had requested a massive emergency appropriation of tanks. It was a startling request, documented with some shocking intelligence, according to the senator. Fitzgerald was shifted into high gear by this news and by the attention his reports were commanding. It was a chancy business. He was reporting what he was required to report and what would be needed to gain attention, but he was also holding back. He was gambling that the irregularities he observed would add up convincingly enough to enable him to reveal a comprehensive Israeli strategy. He was playing his cards close to his chest, hoping that he could play his hand in a way that would initiate a great breakthrough in his career. At the moment the pieces of the puzzle didn't add up, but he had a superstitious confidence that he was on the verge of new understanding.

He would meet with Senator Larabee at 3:00. That would give him five hours to coordinate his people. Usually he would have to go to the Senate Office Building; but in this case the senator was coming to him, considering the security arrangements. That felt good. He instructed his secretary to gather his staff into the conference room immediately.

"Yes, Mr. Fitzgerald," she snapped to attention, or so he imagined. He believed in the psychology of the pecking order. He knew that when new staff came to him, they were told somewhere along the indoctrination route that he liked to be called Mr. Fitzgerald. The mystique was endemic. He put on his suit jacket, straightened his tie, and checked his hair before joining the hastily assembled group.

He outlined his problem. He would need all of their work updated by two o'clock, so that he could review it before the visit by, no less, a member of the Senate Budget Committee. Each staff member scribbled a few notes on his or her pad.

"Do any of you have significant new information that we should hear now?" Fitzgerald asked.

After a moment's silence, a young woman spoke up nervously: "I don't know how *significant* this is, but their military has ordered a huge quantity of ultraviolet eyeglasses from manufacturers in three countries. I've had some trouble tracing the exact order."

"Do you mean *sunglasses*?" Fitzgerald interrupted, laughing.

"No. I mean mountain-climbing goggles, like you'd wear on Everest, real high-tech eyewear. This is specialty equipment. Expensive. They've tried to order half a million pairs! One manufacturer in Sheboygan, Wisconsin, is working day and night to fill about a third of the order. There's another company in France and one in Germany with similar commitments. They were not eager to disclose the orders, but they did express off-the-record concern that they might be unable to fill the order by the requested date . . . July 1."

Fitzgerald recognized this as yet another strange requisition for midsummer.

"What do they want with these?"

"I have no idea. I did check with our military purchasing here, and they say that they stock not more than a few thousand pairs, mostly for rescue operations. These are not the extra-opaque ones envisioned for nuclear maneuvers. You'd use these to avoid white-out in high altitude snow. I don't think the mountains in Israel are even high enough to warrant such equipment."

"Perhaps they plan to visit the burning bush," Fitzgerald quipped. After fielding a few more suggestions but coming up with no serious insights into the reasons for the requisition, he concluded with a commanding, "Keep after it."

Another remarkable observation surfaced during the subsequent discussion. David Zweig had been found. It was certain. Agent Wolfe had positively identified him on two occasions entering his building in the company of Aaron Rabin or Elias Hirschberg. Fitzgerald was ecstatic. Locating Zweig might signal a turning point in the whole business. After all, Zweig was the key. Supposing he held Israel at his mercy, sort of a mad-scientist notion. That might be a crazy assumption, but it certainly would explain a lot, since Zweig was implicated in everything.

Reluctantly, Fitzgerald placed another call, setting his social life further in arrears.

"Laura, darling, Senator Larabee has buttonholed me for a meeting after lunch. Yes, Senator Larabee himself, and it's very important, but it interrupts our plans. I've got to see you, so could we make it dinner tonight? That's wonderful. I'll pick you up at seven . . . Can't wait."

On his calendar Fitzgerald crossed out "lunch with L. L." and wrote "dinner" in the margin. "We really would make a stunning couple," he thought to himself. "If I could ever get to it."

Senator Larabee exuded such a huge presence within Fitzgerald's office that Fitzgerald felt that they might as well be in the Senate Office Building. Its high ceilings were more in key with the senator's flowing hair and radio-announcer intonation. It did not suit Fitzgerald's self-image to not be in the position of dominance. Hoping to maneuver into a chummier equality, he oriented the beginnings of their conversation.

"By the way, Senator, it's an honor to talk to such a distinguished oarsman," he said.

The senator was surprised. "Who told you that?"

"No one had to tell me. I myself was rowing in the eights at Exeter the year of your great race at Penn against Yale. In my scrapbook at my mother's house I still have a photo of the finish, with you pulling third oar."

Senator Larabee was impressed. It had been in his senior year at Penn, a veteran back from the Vietnam War. "Which year were you in at Exeter?"

"Eleventh grade. I didn't earn my cap until the next year. And

148

it was your great race that inspired me to train harder. To help me along, my grandmother gave my family her Eakins watercolor of a rowing team. It hangs in our home. Would you like a glass of sherry?"

With the sherries in hand, the conversation was more free and Fitzgerald sensed with satisfaction the more confidential tone.

"The thing that really puzzles us about their request for fifty M−60 tanks is that they want them before August," Senator Larabee resumed. "I'm wondering if you can help me with their rationale."

"I'll try," Fitzgerald replied, pleased at being asked rather than ordered.

"It's important to the Budget Committee. The president is against more arms requests until they're totally out of Lebanon. On the other hand, we're committed to keeping them secure. So we need some intelligence information to justify their embarrassingly timed request."

"You might be surprised to know that we know nothing about this request. It surprises me, because we usually uncover things early on."

"I think it's because it was very sudden," the senator responded. "They came straight to us, without the usual prolonged discussion."

"What is the rationale for such a large number of tanks?"

"Hold on. Here's where it's very sensitive. They say that their military security has uncovered plans by Libya and Syria for a joint invasion of Israel in August. They say they're so sure of it that they need tanks before then, almost at once."

"We haven't heard a thing from our men planted in their military security. I find this hard to believe."

"That's what I wanted to know. Do you have any suspicions of such an attack?"

"No, although we have a lot of troop movements in those countries."

"Well, I've got here an AWACs photo that they gave me as partial proof. And they claim to have a lot more. Here. Look at this. This is southeast Libya, near the Egyptian border. Here are convoys, tanks, jeeps, guns."

"Well, we have some similar photos by satellite. But we think Khaddafi is just stirring things up again. He seems to be threatening Chad. We have a lot on that."

"I know, but look at this photo again. The convoys are assembling to the right of the border hills. If they were threatening to go into Chad, they would be on the left. Israeli military claim that the buildup could only be for moving through Egypt."

149

Fitzgerald was indeed amazed. It was exactly as the senator said, and quite unlike what his men were making out from satellite photos. "Could you leave this photo with me?"

"That was my intent. We need to know, for military appropriations in the new budget, if their request is reasonable."

"Another thing," Fitzgerald added. "Tell them you'll need a few more examples of evidence before you can consider such a large, ill-timed request. Then let me see what they give you."

Fitzgerald was willing to share some of his knowledge of other large pre-summer purchases of less obviously military items. Taken together, they implied that Israeli planners were anxious about preparations for summer. But Fitzgerald was selective in what he told the senator, and even as they spoke he became suddenly excited at his own powerful hunch. *Israel was preparing for sudden war.* But he would take time to build his case, so that it would be more impressive to his superiors. The next step would be to ask his lab to get new aerial views of the southeast Libyan border and a photo analysis to ascertain whether the Israeli AWACs photo in his hand was legitimate. What he had not revealed to the senator was the recent CIA information showing that Israel was under-representing its armaments while asking for more. How unusual to discover them exaggerating losses incurred during the invasion of Lebanon, as well as losses owing to age and attrition. Very unusual indeed.

Although the meeting with Senator Larabee had been somewhat exhausting, it was not thirty minutes before Fitzgerald decided to call General Hughes about another hunch.

"I want to ask about this deal to sell American components for a new fighter aircraft to be built in Israel," Fitzgerald told Hughes. "Did they indicate any rush on that, anything needed before next summer?"

"Oh, no," Hughes replied. "Those parts are for the new Lavie fighter, which they don't hope to even flight test before 1987. Its production is important for the 1990s."

"Oh, I had no idea; but that does make sense. Is there any other rush order for aircraft?"

"As you know, that has been impossible as long as they occupy Lebanon. But a very curious thing was relayed to me a few days ago from the secretary of defense. Confidential assurance has just been given by the Israeli ambassador that if we will sell them seventy-five F-16s at once, they will pull out of Lebanon immediately."

"Wouldn't that be a huge transaction at one time?"

"Well, they've been asking for seventy-five F-16s for a long time, but over a more extended delivery rate."

"What schedule do they project for this agreement?"

"If we can provide delivery of the F-16s by next summer, they will withdraw totally from Lebanon within two weeks."

"I thought so. It sounds as if they're trying to bargain a political peace against a prompt delivery."

"Exactly. They made no bones about it. The secretary of defense said that the Security Council found such a bribe, you might say, distasteful; but they didn't want to reject it, because the president and secretary of state are very eager to get Israel out of Lebanon."

"And how important was the condition on delivery next summer?"

"Essential. They said delivery by July, or no deal."

Fitzgerald had heard all he needed to hear. From here on he was to build his case that Israel expected war in August, whether attacked or attacking. The real coup for his career would be if he could link that plan to a new scientific discovery, or to the perplexing case of David Zweig and Elias Hirschberg. Fantastic that Zweig had been found!

"General Hughes, I have some news that concerns you. I've just found out today that David Zweig has been found. Our men have seen him with Elias Hirschberg in Tel Aviv."

"Incredible. I wish I knew what it means," General Hughes replied.

"Well, let's think about it. Isn't it true that his consultancy with you was for a single purpose?"

"True. He was hired to advise us on the black hole in the asteroid belt."

"And, by implication, on its possible military uses," Fitzgerald interjected.

"That *is* our business here in DOD," Hughes acknowledged. "I realize that it makes his sudden disappearance seem to point that way. It concerns me very much."

"Did you discuss a military application with him?"

"Only in general terms, brainstorming, I guess you'd say. We needed some understanding in order to decide whether this should be classified as a secret discovery or whether it should be opened up to the world."

"Yes, I understand that. But what is your intuitive reaction to Zweig's opinions?"

"He seemed very open-minded. But, after much discussion, he assured us that no military application would be possible. Then, two days later, he vanished."

"It's uncomfortable, wouldn't you say?"

"Very uncomfortable," Hughes admitted.

Even before hanging up, Fitzgerald's mind was made up. The potential for a military plan involving David Zweig was connected with that black hole among the asteroids. Everything pointed to it. One task now confronting him was that of motivating George Reynolds toward that idea. He was so caught up with the neutrino counts that it would be hard to redirect him toward the black hole. Fitzgerald thought a new consultant might be needed if Reynolds could not be made to cooperate.

Collecting his briefcase, Fitzgerald headed for his car. For tonight at least he could forget about it all.

Seventeen

George Reynolds walked purposefully out the front door of the National Academy of Science building in Washington. The panel meeting on the Earth's stratospheric ozone layer had been a bore. It was a vexation of scientific panels that they devolve too easily into report writing and general paper shuffling. Some of the more politically minded scientists seemed to like that aspect, but not Reynolds. Reaching the base of the steps on Constitution Avenue, Reynolds began the task of trying to snare an empty taxi. With so many new ideas swimming in his head, he wished he had not accepted the appointment to this particular panel. The stability of the Earth's ozone layer as a shield against dangerous ultraviolet radiation from the sun had become an important social problem in the last few years, however, and it had certainly been necessary for the Academy to carry out the commissioned study. Reynolds had accepted the appointment nine months ago because he felt that it helped him repay his obligation to society. After all, he was allowed to lead a life of intellectual freedom, one that he would choose even if he were wealthy. Reynolds never forgot that it is the collective toil of human society that makes possible the life of an intellectual, just as it does that of the artist or the professional athlete. He knew he was lucky. But this meeting had been neither productive nor interesting, so that Reynolds's attention had repeatedly wandered to his upcoming meeting with General Hughes. At least both meetings could be accomplished with one trip to Washington.

The taxi turned off Constitution Avenue to make its way back toward Memorial Bridge. Reynolds stared in admiration at the exquisite beauty of the cherry blossoms lining Ohio Drive toward the Tidal Basin. They were still in bloom owing to the coldness of this spring. Passing around the Lincoln Memorial, glimpsing that inspired statue of the seated Abraham Lincoln, Reynolds's thoughts momentarily drifted back to the Wichita Falls schoolboy of fifteen reciting the Gettysburg Address to his high school history class. How clear its issues had seemed then.

At the Pentagon it took half an hour to pass through the security checks. The memo from General Hughes easing Reynolds's entry had been mislaid but relocated following brief telephone exchanges between reception and Hughes's secretary. Then Reynolds was led to the offices of the Air Force chief of staff. There, two offices from the chief of staff himself, was General Hughes's glass-windowed doorway. Reynolds waited five minutes with the secretary before Hughes called him in.

In contrast to the unsympathetic austerity of the building, Hughes appeared to be comfortable and at ease on his home turf. He directed Reynolds to a somewhat worn army-issue armchair in a modest-sized office crowded with bookshelves and file cabinets. "Damned offices get smaller every year," joked Hughes, "because the machine just keeps getting bigger."

Sitting at his desk Hughes looked genuinely grandfatherly. His blue eyes had the same friendly twinkle that Reynolds had noticed in Houston. On a shelf behind him stood the neatly framed school portraits of his thirteen grandchildren. Each seemed to be the kid next door. But that image contrasted sharply with the grouping of professional photos hanging on the opposite wall. Reynolds turned in his chair to view the record of Hughes's service: the young man receiving his diploma and officer's commission from West Point; young Lieutenant Hughes standing beside General Omar Bradley in East Anglia in 1944; Hughes shaking hands with President Dwight D. Eisenhower upon Hughes's promotion to general; and Hughes receiving the National Medal of Honor from President Lyndon Johnson. Other photographs showed scenes from war in the Pacific, Korea, and Vietnam.

"Quite a record," said Reynolds, genuinely impressed.

"It's what you get if you try hard for forty years," Hughes replied, "but damned if some two-bit lock washer isn't about to ruin it. Oh, not literally, Dr. Reynolds, don't look so startled. I'm still smarting from this Zweig business in ways you can't imagine. It's caused me a lot of worry, and that's why I didn't tell you about it immediately. But since you dressed me down so severely during our last telephone coversation I've decided to level with you about this Jupiter radiometer business."

"I certainly hope so . . . ," Reynolds began, somewhat uneasily.

"Now don't get all excited, Dr. Reynolds. It's not intelligence

I'm talking about. It's not the black hole, either. The whole thing is embarrassing. I didn't say anything about it in Houston in front of Lieutenant Baker, because I don't want this getting around. I know you'll observe the confidence, but I don't want that kid at the CIA to know. Fitzgerald may look like a clean-cut fraternity brother, but he's a bit overzealous. I think you know what I mean. He's always prying into things. He's too studied, and he plays hardball. I've already been strong-armed enough by Zweig over this radiometer business. I don't want to get into it with Fitzgerald."

"I'm afraid you're losing me, General," said Reynolds.

"I may be a general," Hughes continued, "but if I pay $100 for a lock washer I'm in as much trouble as the next fellow these days. The problem is that Zweig's little thermometer cost $150,000 and I don't have so much as a report to show for it. I can't even explain to auditors why I ordered the thing!"

"But can't you say it's secret?" Reynold asked.

"I do. I stonewall," Hughes twinkled, "but that's not really enough. Even for secret expenditures we have a system of top-security auditors that keep us all in line."

"But Pioneer 11 to Jupiter was a NASA mission. It was a line item in the NASA budget," Reynolds protested.

"It was all a bit complicated," Hughes responded. "As I tried to hint on the telephone, we augmented the NASA budget by $150,000 in order to place a much-improved infrared radiometer on Pioneer 11. NASA didn't object, because it only improved their space probe to Jupiter, and we didn't demand control over the mission. Zweig assured me that they would observe what we wanted, and it would have been hopelessly awkward to have established formal conditions with NASA."

"So why did you do it?" Reynolds asked.

"That's the embarrassing part, Dr. Reynolds. I never really got a clear idea myself. I really was somewhat derelict in my duty. But as it happened, Zweig told me we could learn more about the black hole by measuring its emission of radiant heat. He was so adamant that he threatened to terminate his consultancy if I didn't support it. At the time I was so excited about the black hole discovery that I didn't even ask how the radiometer would give us more information. I was, I must admit, thinking about bigger issues. But I assumed that the radiometer would look at the black hole as we flew by, and that we'd learn a lot more directly."

"You sound as if you assumed incorrectly," Reynolds observed.

"Exactly. The trajectory of Pioneer 11 passed nowhere near the black hole. We never even got a look at it! The instrument was not even turned on until the craft neared Jupiter, and then it

155

spent the entire time measuring the heat flowing out of Jupiter. I was appalled."

"And how about Zweig?" Reynolds wondered.

"The rascal never batted an eye," Hughes replied. "He said only that I had misunderstood his intent. He said we had just the information we were looking for. He promised to explain as soon as he finished his calculations. But he never did."

"So you have no idea."

"Only a clue. I was not totally remiss, Dr. Reynolds. I repeatedly demanded an explanation from Zweig, and I had the feeling he was stalling for time. He kept on saying things like, 'I'm too busy with all the pieces. Let me call you next week,' and so on. He's a civilian, so there was really nothing I could do. But our auditors were breathing down my neck. They didn't care about the science, Dr. Reynolds, but they did care about getting some paperwork to cover their asses. They demanded a rationale, which could, of course, be secret, in the form of a purchase order backup. Without it, they should not have let go of the money, which we had arranged very rapidly, on my credit you might say. So I made the firmest demand possible to Zweig, telling him that I needed a scientific rationale, even if only a couple of pages, and that I needed it even if his conclusions were not yet secure."

"And did you get it?" Reynolds asked.

"Yes, I did," Hughes replied, "three days before Zweig disappeared. And I have the feeling I would have nothing if I had not been so insistent. I really think Zweig intended to vanish, Dr. Reynolds, and that worries me, too."

"Why?"

"Fitzgerald at the CIA pounced on me about it. He claims evidence that Zweig was some part of Israel intelligence. I went over to see the evidence."

"And how did it look?" Reynolds asked.

"There was quite a lot. It was mostly circumstantial, but rather impressive. You'd have to ask Fitzgerald. Unfortunately, I can't tell you about it. The trouble for me is that Fitzgerald will not get off my back about it. And it was a normal oversight, Dr. Reynolds. We've made such mistakes before, and found them to be not serious. But Fitzgerald is treating it like the biggest spy case of the decade. And I'm afraid I'm his scapegoat," Hughes concluded with a despairing look.

Reynolds was beginning to get the picture. Hughes was over a barrel, a double barrel. "You seem a bit annoyed at Fitzgerald," he observed.

"Damned right, I am," Hughes burst out. "You never know what people in the CIA are up to. They seem to make their own

156

rules. We in the military have a clear responsibility, and we have an organization to make sure that things are properly done. But I think that kid over there has some big bee in his bonnet. He think's he's going after something big, and I don't want to be it. Ever since he took that job monitoring Israeli military he's been calling me with questions about our military sales."

"Why you?" Reynolds asked.

"God only knows, but I think it's because my office handles their requests for purchase of fighter planes, especially F-16's. That I could handle. But now with this Zweig business I can't get rid of him. He tries to persuade me to tell him everything we're doing that Zweig had any knowledge of. It's too much. He went over my head through his boss to the secretary of defense to force me to tell him about the black hole. And now he's after me about our intentions over the black hole, when we haven't even had time to think it through yet. And finally, on top of that, I have no scientific justification for the radiometer funds from the air force. The fact that Zweig prevailed personally upon me to do that only makes Fitzgerald more suspicious. So he's got a bad case of Zweig-on-the-brain!"

"I know he does," Reynolds concurred, "because he's after me rather vigorously to come up with something."

"That's another thing that irritates me," General Hughes broke in. "We disclosed our intent to hire you as our air force consultant, hoping to replace Zweig with you, you might say. So what does Fitzgerald do but snatch you to help him think about Zweig. I really resented that, not on your account, Dr. Reynolds, because there's nothing wrong with the situation legally, but because I thought Fitzgerald should leave my consultant alone. I told him so. But again I got orders from upstairs to go along with it. But I tell you, Dr. Reynolds, we have no way of knowing what they're up to over there at CIA. At least in the air force we know the chain of command. None of us makes any plan that is not approved by someone up the line, all the way to the president, if it's important enough. But they have all these independent entrepreneurs. So you can understand, now that I'm in a little hot water, why I don't want that kid to be told that I'm lacking my scientific rationale for the radiometer."

"Don't worry," Reynolds replied, "that's totally between you and Fitzgerald. I'll not say a thing. But what can I do to be of help to you?"

"I can think of only two things," Hughes said. "One is to help me understand some ideas about military possibilities for a black hole—even far out ideas. I'll have no trouble covering myself here if I can show some thinking about military possibilities. Of course,

I could do that alone, but I would profit from someone to talk to who understands the physics of the situation."

"I certainly will do that," Reynolds offered, remembering that it was just exactly that opportunity that he had hoped for. The situation was too scary to be left alone. "But what's the second thing?"

"You might help me with the scientific rationale for the Jupiter observation. You can begin with these three handwritten pages from Zweig. He gave me this when I demanded something for our auditors. But I don't understand it." Hughes reached for the manila folder on his desk and extracted three sheets of lined notepad paper. They contained, in David Zweig's immaculate handwriting, a few paragraphs, with a dozen or so equations interspersed, under the title "Thermonuclear Power within Jupiter."

The title of this brief report immediately raised Reynolds's interest, because a decade ago he had published a paper showing that a gas sphere cannot be hot enough within to sustain thermonuclear fusion reactions unless that sphere is at least 8 percent as massive as the Sun. But Jupiter's mass, though large by human standards, is only 1/1000th the mass of the Sun. And yet Zweig's first paragraph made it clear that he was proposing to interpret the heat source within Jupiter as being thermonuclear fusion.

"Let me order you some coffee while you read this thing," General Hughes offered.

Reynolds accepted the offer gratefully and began to read Zweig's explanation of the rate at which Jupiter radiates heat. The infrared radiometer had measured it accurately as four million billion kilowatts, enough power in a single second to equal the power usage in the United States for an entire month. That was a large power, but still much less than that coming out of the Sun and, according to Reynolds's old calculations, still not enough to demand a hot Jupiter interior. As he read on, Reynolds caught some subtly misstated assumptions. With growing puzzlement he read a theoretical treatment that was, though mathematically elegant, almost certainly false. Almost every advanced concept in quantum mechanics was applied in a scholarly appearance to argue that thermonuclear reactions could indeed happen within Jupiter's interior. Physics was misapplied in ingenious ways, showing that the writer, who certainly must have been Zweig, understood it well but assumed that his readers would not.

"I hate to tell you this, General Hughes," Reynolds said twenty minutes later, as he laid the three sheets down, "but Zweig is pulling your leg."

"What do you mean?" answered a startled Hughes.

"I mean that Zweig cannot be serious with this report," Rey-

158

nolds clarified. "It is written with a kind of brilliance, but a brilliance of deception. My overall impression is that Zweig was having a good time creating a spoof. He must have been smiling to himself as he imagined staff-level technicians trying to comprehend this. I'm sure it's wrong, however."

"How can you be sure so quickly?"

"Only because I've spent fifteen years on the outskirts of this question," Reynolds replied. "If it had been any other area of science it would have fooled me, too. I'll wager that if you give this to one of your staff physicists as a memo from David Zweig, he'll treat it like a Dead Sea scroll. He'll mistakenly think this is great stuff. It's very clever."

Now it was General Hughes's turn to be dumbfounded.

"Surely he would realize that we would eventually expose it," Hughes said in a subdued voice.

"Eventually, sure," Reynolds agreed. "He must not have cared."

"In other words," Hughes rejoined, "he wasn't planning to be around. He already knew that he would be disappearing."

"It does fit," Reynolds agreed.

"God forbid that Fitzgerald should hear about this!" General Hughes said with a despairing laugh.

"But I think he must be told," Reynolds shot back.

"Tell me you're joking."

"I'm afraid not. This is the first thing that has been uncovered about Zweig's scientific life that's as suspicious as his other behavior. It must have a very significant meaning. I don't think that only you or I should consider it. We know that Zweig may actually be a part of Israeli intelligence, so there may be some unforeseen national risk in this. If we suppressed it we would in reality be guilty of something, wouldn't we?"

"I suppose you're right," Hughes said with obvious resignation. "But don't say I didn't warn you. You'll never get that guy out of your hair now! The only question is which one of us should tell him. I'd rather you did it, since it's your opinion. Just tell him that I openly urged you to disclose this peculiarity to him."

In the remaining half hour before Reynolds's flight to Houston, the two men speculated on possible military uses for the black hole. Reynolds was relieved to discover that Hughes was himself skeptical of any such use. Reynolds strengthened that skepticism with cogent arguments, so that when they parted Hughes said that the discovery could probably be declassified within several months.

Twilight was just beginning to dim the view of the ground below as the jetliner reduced its altitude and speed, just one hundred miles north of Houston. Reynolds put the copy of the Zweig report into his attaché case and viewed the expanse of the Crockett National Forest. How varied Texas is and how marvelously its beauties flow into one another. Directly beneath and to both sides lay thousands of square miles of magnificent pine trees, blending far to the east into the famed Big Thicket, an ecological treasure. Nearer lay giant Lake Livingston and the lackadaisical Trinity River, slumbering its way through the forest lowlands. The treetops obscured the more barren ground beneath. Their rich spread of cholorophyll-laden needles hungered for the bright light of the sun and for the chemical power that had made plant life one of the miracles of the earth. And far above, the ozone of the upper atmosphere absorbed the harsh ultraviolet sunlight that would be deadly were it to reach the ground.

Sometimes, especially while looking at the land as he now did, Reynolds wondered what a primitive life, a life with little or no human society, would have been like. What did people of high and sensitive intelligence do within primitive prehistoric tribes? The human brain has presumably evolved over a very long time, so there might have been an Einstein among Peking Man, or a Mozart among Australopithicus. They would have had no chance. Social evolution had made Reynolds's life possible, and he knew it.

Eighteen

The following morning in his office, Reynolds checked the numerical aspects of Zweig's explanation once again on his office computer. The result was the same. Nonsense. He was just working up his resolve to call Fitzgerald about it when his secretary buzzed.

"There's another newspaper reporter on the line who wants to talk to you."

Reynolds hesitated briefly, then said, "Tell him I'm not in."

Reynolds had been continuously uncomfortable at the hints of high-level intrigue that surrounded him. He had been uncomfortable in maintaining his public statement that Cowan's murder was the hideous act of a sick and jealous colleague. He suspected that he was closely watched, and he sporadically received telephone calls from the world press asking if he still believed the tape of the neutrino experiment to be a fraud. Reynolds maintained that position with special care following a return call to the *San Francisco Chronicle* two weeks previously. He had been shocked to find that their reporters had not telephoned him the day before. Reynolds had noticed other evidence that he was being watched, and he could not forget the alarming urgency of Rebecca's final plea for his welfare. The situation was worse than uncomfortable; it was frightening, and Reynolds did not know what he could or should reveal to whom, so multifaceted was the maze around him. It was just this insecurity that dampened his enthusiasm for talking with Fitzgerald. Reynolds sometimes entertained the thought that it might be the CIA watching him, and that Fitzgerald himself might be dangerous. He had certainly had enough of anonymous calls from reporters.

Nevertheless, Fitzgerald would have to be informed of Zweig's spoof, so Reynolds punched his phone for an outside line and dialed the number directly. Following the usual courtesies, Reynolds came to the point: "Well, I've finally found something really strange in Zweig's science. For reasons that I cannot fathom, Zweig concocted a complicated piece of nonsense to explain the excess heat radiation from Jupiter. In Washington yesterday General Hughes handed me a copy of the report that Zweig had prepared for him, and it's a stunner. It contains mathematical deception by Zweig to mislead people about his true belief about Jupiter's power."

"Am I to understand that you were in Washington yesterday?"

Reynolds thought to himself, "He probably already knew. What a weasel!"

"Yes. I had a morning meeting at the National Academy and an afternoon meeting with General Hughes," Reynolds replied.

Fitzgerald was piqued. "And you didn't come to see me."

"We talked just last week in Austin," Reynolds replied, "and I had a very busy schedule."

"Perhaps you should have stayed another day."

"Look, Jimmy. I didn't want to spend the night. I wanted to study Zweig's report in peace, on a quiet plane to Houston. I needed the time to be sure of my conclusions."

"You don't realize how important the case we're working on might be. I deserve to be fully informed."

"That's why I'm calling now. Don't forget, I did go see General Hughes; and it is he who has hired me as a consultant."

"But that's the air force, George. We're dealing with major suspicions of Israel's strategy. I feel that you should report to me."

"Look, Jimmy. I've already found that you two cooperate with each other. That's not my business. I don't make much of a distinction between talking to Hughes and talking to you."

"Well, perhaps you should!"

Reynolds paused, increasingly annoyed. "Do you want to hear what I've found, or shall we continue this debate?" In a flash of anger Reynolds wanted to hang up, then realized that that could be a dangerously intemperate act.

Fitzgerald paused, too, suddenly realizing that his ambition was causing him to act inappropriately. Lowering his voice to a conciliatory, if somewhat condescending, tone, he continued, "Of course I'm very grateful for the information. Please excuse my impatience with the sequence. Why has Zweig attempted to misrepresent his ideas about Jupiter's power source?"

"I don't know. I've never even been able to understand why Zweig was interested in Jupiter's radiation in the first place; so I could hardly be expected to understand why he tried to distort it. I cannot fathom why he was so interested that he actively persuaded the Air Force to put a better radiometer on Pioneer 11. Zweig's motive for caring about that puzzles me a lot. It's just not his area of science."

"Isn't it likely that Zweig's real interest was in the black hole orbiting with the asteroids? Maybe the radiometer was really for that."

"General Hughes had expected that, too, but it appears not to have been the case. The infrared radiometers didn't even attempt to see the black hole. The initial radiometer was intended for Jupiter; and the Air Force's improved one looked only at Jupiter. So Jupiter seems to have been the only target. But I don't see why Zweig cared about it so much. All I'm sure of is that he has created an elaborate deception. It must contain some clue to Zweig's motivation; but it stumps me. Just as much as the solar neutrino puzzle stumps me."

"Look, George, don't you think we're wasting our time with the solar neutrinos?"

"It's not a waste of my time. It's a fascinating puzzle."

"But don't you agree that it's the black hole that would be the center of any military application?"

"How can I say? I see no military application at all for a remote black hole in orbit about the sun. I said the same thing to General Hughes yesterday."

"But that *is* what General Hughes is interested in, is it not?"

"Sure, he's a military man. But I'm not. I have no thoughts of any military plan. I'm just trying to help understand the science."

"But it's also my position here at CIA to gather information about possible Israeli strategy. And Zweig did disappear with top secret military information about that black hole. That's what I want you to pursue, not your interest in solar neutrinos."

"But I don't know how to pursue it," Reynolds responded. The entire tone was uncomfortable.

"Just concentrate on this speculation," Fitzgerald gambled. "Suppose Zweig were a part of an unforeseen plan to use a new scientific discovery to start a war. I know that seems incredible to you; but just imagine it. What might that discovery be, and how might it be used?"

Reynolds's mind reeled. He could hardly believe his ears. He immediately recalled General Hughes's initial question about pulling the asteroidal black hole toward the Earth. But he could see no military way in which it might be used; and, in any case, it was too massive to have its orbit changed with today's supply of expendable rockets. Was Fitzgerald mad? Reynolds felt uncomfortable with the incredible question.

What Fitzgerald chose not to reveal was that the CIA had found Zweig.

Eight days later, on May 7, a manila envelope arrived from Corrigan out of FBI headquarters in Washington. As Reynolds returned to his desk to open it, he could not help but notice that it had been franked with common twenty-two-cent commemorative stamps. Two previous routine items of correspondence had come with metered postage. Something else was unusual. The address label was a plain stick-on label, and the FBI return address had been typed on it. The return address had been printed on the two previous envelopes. "Maybe I'm getting so nervous that I'm seeing things," Reynolds thought as he opened the envelope. He extracted a letter attached to a photocopy of a typewritten manuscript:

> Dear George:
> Here is a copy of the typed manuscript that Zweig mailed to Dr. Hale at Lick Observatory. We obtained it from him without difficulty, going there with a warrant. He said he even expected us, based on a conversation he had had with you. Let me know if you find anything in it for the Cowan case. We still have no more leads.
> Yours truly,
> Edward G. Corrigan,
> Investigator

The official FBI letterhead made the envelope look all the more amateurish. It was postmarked two days previously, in Washington; but Corrigan's letter was dated six days earlier. Resolutely Reynolds picked up his telephone, coded the outside line, and dialed Corrigan's office. Following a small wait for his secretary to drag him from the coffee room, Corrigan came finally to the phone.

"Hiya, Georgie. Didya get my package?" he asked, clearly in high spirits.

"Hi, Ed. Yeah, I got the letter and Zweig's manuscript all right. Did you mail it yourself?" Reynolds asked.

"Well, sure. I sealed it and gave it to my secretary to mail. Why?"

"It just came today, for one thing," Reynolds said. "And for another thing, the envelope and address label have no printed FBI return address. It's just typed on."

"Sounds strange all right. I gave it to my secretary a week ago Hold the line while I ask her about it."

Reynolds was sure what the answer would be. The mail had been tampered with. Indeed, Reynolds was being shadowed in so many strange ways, but by whom? There were the nameless people responsible for Cowan's murder, presumably the same people that Rebecca had warned him about. There was also the CIA, and Fitzgerald's insistent prodding. Reynolds was much less comfortable with them than with the FBI, which seemed in comparison as American as apple pie.

"George, it's been tampered with," Corrigan confirmed. "My secretary mailed it six days ago in our usual envelope."

"Shall I send you the envelope?"

"Sure. Send it. But drop it in the mailbox yourself. Wait, better yet, take it to our office in the Federal Building there in Austin. You know, near the main post office. Take it to Sam Esposito. I'll call him now so he'll know what to do. It'll be faster that way. When they've analyzed it, they'll call me and I'll call you," Corrigan concluded.

"OK," Reynolds replied. "Meanwhile check to make sure that none of your own thugs did it."

Corrigan laughed and assured Reynolds that they had not. Finally, he listened to Reynolds's recapitulation of the telephone calls from the so-called reporters. It seemed best, they decided, simply to maintain the story of the fake tape just as Reynolds had been doing. Corrigan could do no more than begin to trace calls coming to Reynolds. Both believed the calls to be related to the murder and to Rebecca's warning, so the situation looked dangerous.

In the wake of the tension over the Zweig report for General Hughes, Reynolds was not, he assured himself, in the mood to read something else of Zweig's. He reached instead for the new issue of the *Astrophysical Journal,* which he had laid out on his desk for perusal. After glancing through the table of contents, he opened the journal and began to read an article. But for only two minutes. "What's the use," he thought, slamming it down and picking up Zweig's manuscript, which was entitled "Eruptive Phenomena Due to Black Holes in Stars." It began:

> In this paper I wish to consider additional consequences of the prediction (Zweig 1968) that the early universe was left filled with black holes having a wide spectrum of masses. I have recently shown that due to quantum effects (Zweig 1974) all such black holes must be more massive than a million tons; otherwise they would have early radiated away their mass in quantum fluctuations. All black hole masses greater than this minimum are ex-

pected to persist, roughly in such a way that the number N(m) of black holes having mass m should be a decreasing function of mass (Zweig 1968). I have previously conjectured (Zweig 1970) that very large such black holes, about a million times more massive than the sun, reside at the centers of Seyfert galaxies, causing their intense luminosity, and that black holes of stellar mass in binary orbits around normal stars account for the binary x-ray sources. In this paper I propose a consequence of primitive black holes having masses comparable to those of planets; namely the gravitational attraction of those planetary masses to the surrounding gas within dense gas clouds like those in Orion has caused the gas to assemble into stars having black holes at their centers. These black holes are a partial cause of the formation of stars and, as I will also show, provide a natural explanation for the mysterious flare stars, which have been reviewed by Hale (1970).

At this moment Reynolds was hit by an idea that had been vaguely bothering him. How could there be a black hole in the asteroid belt if, as Zweig concluded, it must have been there from the beginnings of the Sun? About what would it have been orbiting before the Sun was condensed, that is, while the Sun was still spread out in a big cloud of gas very much larger than the entire solar system? Surely, he thought, it is too much to expect that by coincidence the final center of this huge contracting cloud, the newly born Sun, would lie *by chance* very near to a black hole, which would thereafter be trapped in an asteroidal orbit about it. That would be a huge coincidence. No, there must have been a reason why today's asteroidal black hole was already hovering about the center of the solar system before the Sun had even formed. The black hole in the asteroid belt must have been orbiting the Sun's position before there was a Sun. The relevance of Zweig's idea was clear: there must initially have been a pair of black holes! The larger black hole attracted the gases of today's Sun, and the present asteroidal black hole could have been in orbit about the larger one now lying at the center of the Sun! Perhaps here was the crucial connection to the Sun. Reynolds again felt the excitement of Zweig's thoughts, but managed to subdue his own long enough to read on:

The first flare star, FU Orionis, was discovered in 1939 by Wachmann. It was a normal-looking young star whose luminosity suddenly increased by a factor 100 in the short time of 50 days. Since that time two other well-documented cases have been discovered (Hale 1970). These changes are not at all understood, because the apparently stable main-sequence stars are believed to be very simple and well-understood gaseous structures, as explained for example in standard books by Schwarzschild (1958) or by Clayton (1968). Their great stability against fluctuations of all types does not admit any theoretical explanation of these sudden outbursts. In this paper, however, I will show that the structure induced by a black hole at the stellar center alters this impasse, making sudden rapid rises of the luminosity not only understandable, but probably inevitable.

Reynolds again set the paper down to lean back and recall the many times he had computed the structure of an ordinary star, which is believed to be nothing more than a huge ball of gas, predominantly hydrogen, and held together by gravity. He had published a thought experiment with a star. He had demonstrated that if one tries to make the center of such a star hotter, say, by imagining a large quantity of heat to be suddenly injected into its core, the nuclear reactions do momentarily burn faster, but the star quickly expands because the center then has too much pressure, and the resulting structure after the expansion is inevitably cooler than before the heat was injected. It was a cute paradox. Extra heat in the center of a star causes it to expand and become cooler. Ten years previously Reynolds had made a very thorough study of that phenomenon to prove that the centers of such stars can never experience a thermonuclear runaway. It is the ability of the star to expand quickly—letting off steam by puffing up, so to speak—that prevents an explosion. Reynolds's paper became a classic of the astronomical literature, so he quickly appreciated how correct Zweig was in saying that the young flare stars are an unintelligible mystery if the structure of the stars is in fact as simple as all of mankind's models of those stars. Reynolds had himself tried a few new ideas to produce young flare stars, all with dismal lack of success. Even so, he was a part of one of the strangest and most exciting adventures being acted out in the universe . . . an animal species on a planet orbiting a small star developing to the point of making model calculations in the attempt to comprehend the twinkling lights in the night sky.

Reynolds returned to the paper and read its technical arguments from beginning to end. It was in fact a rather brief paper for one with so much content. Zweig's main proposition was that having a black hole at the stellar center produced a model having significantly different properties than one that is a simple gas throughout. He first showed that the black hole would not swallow the star quickly. A black hole with a mass equal to that of the earth has a radius of only a few millimeters, about one sixteenth of an inch. Its size is proportional to its mass. The rate at which stellar particles hit such a small black hole is too low to consume the star quickly. Only slowly would stellar particles fall into the hole, never to be seen again, while the mass of the hole would gradually grow as it accumulated the stellar material. The star itself could live billions of years, depending on the size of the central black hole.

Zweig had next considered the effects of the gravitational attraction of the hole on the hot gas surrounding it. The forces were considerable, because an object weighing one pound on the surface of the Earth would be attracted by a weight of two million tons at a distance of one hundred meters from a black hole having the mass of the Earth. Although an Earth mass is only a millionth part of the total mass of the Sun, its gravitational effects as a black hole would clearly be profound at a stellar center. Matter would attempt to rush toward the small hole, blindly trying to fall into it.

Zweig had made explicit use of the fact that young stars, only recently born, rotate rather rapidly—approximately daily. This rapid rotation produces a centrifugal force that inhibits matter from falling into the hole. It is the same as twirling a rock at the end of a long string and then trying to reel it in. So strong can the centrifugal force become that it can snap the string. Zweig argued that the hot gas near the stellar center could be compressed toward the equatorial plane, flattened, but that this rotating plane could only slowly contract toward the hole. The structure assumed would be pancakelike—a massive disk rotating around the black hole at its center, somewhat as Saturn's rings orbit Saturn, or as all of the planetary system would have once orbited the Sun as a disk before it accumulated into planets. Matter in the disk could, on the other hand, only spiral slowly in toward the black hole, requiring frictional energy loss to get ever nearer the hole.

The key parts of Zweig's argument came next. He argued that a massive disk surrounding the black hole could not be established immediately within the stellar centers. It would take time for stellar gas to change its circulation patterns as it rapidly rotated about the center, so that material of low angular momentum could sink in to join the disk while matter of high angular momentum drifted outward from the center. Zweig had calculated that about ten million years would be required in a newly formed star until the central disk had grown sufficiently thick to become explosively unstable. The possibility of the central explosion was the key contribution of Zweig's paper.

Reynolds laid the paper aside while his mind drifted into a brief reverie, remembrances of his childhood. He had been seven years old, shooting down Messerschmitts in their daily dogfights with his model Mustangs, when his father, an Army Air Force captain, had returned to Wichita Falls from the Korean War. How exciting it had been to welcome back that beloved hero, who had served on an aircraft carrier supporting General Douglas MacArthur's dramatic landing at Inch'on, cutting the North Korean forces in two just one hundred miles south of the thirty-eighth parallel. Young Reynolds, excited, proud, tearful, had heard MacArthur's famous "Home by Christmas" speech on the radio with his mother. But that was before 180,000 Chinese soldiers entered the contest. Nonetheless, war had been exciting, even fun, a realization that was later to shock the grown man. In the tales of war from his father he learned that he had been born in the very month that the nucear bombs had been dropped on Japan, vastly shortening the Pacific campaign of World War II and bringing his father back home. As a boy he had sensed only that these bombs were quite unlike those he had imagined his model bombers dropping onto German industries, that they were instead a totally new weapon for use against our enemies. Reynolds remembered how his boyhood joy in this experience had in later years soured as he learned by means of photographs and readings of the mindless, brutal death of war, and of how the world went on with only vague recollections of the victims' dying screams.

He recalled once again when he began his studies of thermonuclear explosions in stars. How strange that he should find that the nuclei of the very atoms of our own bodies were born long ago as the cosmic fallout of this stellar thermonuclear debris. Death and birth from the same physical concepts. Drawn to it, Reynolds had studied it ever more deeply, and in more ways. He had become a consultant at Los Alamos for the underground tests, and later a consultant to the Arms Control and Disarmament Agency, where he tried to help with the technical requirements of surveillance of nuclear tests. It seemed as if thermonuclear explosions had become a theme of his conscious life—a fascination with their capabilities and role in astronomy and a puzzled dread of those mysterious emotional forces that could cause man to use them against himself. And now, as if by fate, here it came again, in a new form in this unpublished paper by Zweig.

The reverie ended suddenly, and Reynolds's eyes again concentrated on the manuscript in his hands.

Zweig estimated the ten million years of ripening required before the central explosion would occur for a black hole having a mass nearly equal to that of the Earth. He argued that if the black hole mass had been much larger—say, as large as Jupiter's mass—a star could never have formed around it in the first place, owing to the intense X-ray emission that would have heated and dispersed the original gas cloud. On the other hand, if the initial black hole had been much smaller than the mass of the Earth, it would have had no effect on the star for many billions of years. Inasmuch as the known cases of flare stars involved young stars, stars that Allan Hale had shown to be about ten million years old, Zweig assumed that the black hole masses nearly equal to the Earth's mass were the ones responsible for their observed eruptions of luminosity. He therefore concentrated on those cases.

Zweig's description of the instability leading to the explosion itself was fascinating. Although the black hole is only a few millimeters in radius, the disk gathered around it by its strong gravitational attraction was envisioned as extending outward for thousands of miles before fading into the ambient gaseous environment farther away from the stellar center. The disk itself would be expected to be significantly denser and hotter than the surroundings, so that the carbon-nitrogen cycle of nuclear fusion converting hydrogen into helium would always be occurring within it. Then had come the decisive points of Zweig's paper. (1) The disk would not for millions of years be able to grow appreciably hotter, because the thin, pancakelike shape would allow the nuclear energy to escape from its surface area. (2) The disk would grow in thickness as new matter slowly settled onto it, until a critical moment would be reached after about ten million years when the disk would be so thick that the excess heat could not escape. In the language of thermonuclear devices, the critical mass would have been reached. (3) After that critical moment, the temperature within the disk would begin to rise, causing the nuclear reactor to burn faster, causing the temperature in turn to rise even more, causing the nuclear power to rise even faster yet in an explosive runaway that could stop only when each carbon, nitrogen, and oxygen nucleus within the disk had captured all of the protons it could. By this time the temperature within the disk would have soared to 200 million degrees and would have developed a severe overpressure. The rise from 80 million to 200 million degrees would require only ten seconds for Zweig's disk, requiring only a single second to go from 120 million to 200 million degrees. It would happen so fast, as in a thermonuclear bomb, that the disk would not have the time to fly apart before all of its thermonuclear energy would have been liberated. (4) At the conclusion of that violent event, the disk would expand with enormous impact into the surrounding stellar center, generating a severe pressure wave moving outward from the center of the star. As that shock wave moved outward from the center it would leave matter compressed to temperatures of 100 million degrees as it passed by. At that temperature, the carbon and nitrogen nuclei there would also capture protons rapidly, generating more heat and pressure in the wake of the shock wave. That extra heat would strengthen the wave on its outward journey through the star. (5) The nuclear reactions triggered by the heat of the shock wave should liberate an incredible 10^{44} ergs of thermonuclear energy—as much energy as the sun radiates in a thousand years! (6) About ten minutes after it was first triggered at the center, that shock wave would break through to the stellar surface, causing an intense brightening and leaving the outer layers of the star almost completely ionized. (7) The ionized surface would be less opaque, allowing radiant energy to escape more easily from the star, so that it should remain much brighter than it had been previously. Finally, (8) The higher luminosity would likely continue for ten to one hundred years, until the overheated star will have been able to expand sufficiently to become cooler and more opaque once again.

It was a breathtaking scenario. Reynolds had the feeling of having peaked into the mind of a genius. The whirlwind cogency of Zweig's arguments was dazzling. For a full fifteen minutes Reynolds stared at his blackboard and retraced each step of the argument in his mind. Not only was the basic argument brilliant, but Zweig had outlined at one stroke the major impediments to the scheme and had presented a verbal solution to each. Reynolds ticked off in his mind the many calculations needed to see if Zweig's description would stand the test of computer models.

Reynolds finally got up and was plugging in his water heater for tea when the next question hit him. What would the neutrino flux from the star be doing throughout this sequence of events? Could the Sun also do something like that? Might this be the scientific link between Cowan's discovery of increasing neutrino counts and his murder by Zweig. Even if the possibility of these ideas for the Sun were so remote as to verge on science fiction, at least the ideas could have been very real within Zweig's mind. His fanatic preoccupation with black holes could have caused him to imagine such a fate for the Sun and perhaps have prompted a fanatic murder, although a rational motive was nowhere to be found in this line of thought.

When Reynolds turned to his teapot, his eyes fell as they so often did on his photograph of Rebecca. Her beautiful dark eyes seemed to stare at him with a new intensity. Why had she found it necessary to leave? What could possibly be so important and so dangerous that she could not have confided it? For what must have been the hundredth time, Reynolds wondered what would happen if he were to publicly expose the truth of the tape. He was committed to the idea of public exposure of the truth, but fear and contrary advice from both Corrigan and Fitzgerald inhibited him from doing so. Rebecca's eyes looked now so gentle and truthful that Reynolds could not but believe that she had advised him of a truly dangerous situation.

Nineteen

A small drama being staged in Morocco was typical of those that were erupting inside and outside of mosques scattered throughout Islam. It was part of what seemed to its instigators to be a drama of great significance to mankind.

The cedars of Marrakech swayed in the gentle breeze under the brilliant blue Moroccan sky on a day so serene that it was difficult for even the staunchest militant to pursue the struggle to bring Israel to its knees. Israeli counterintelligence had been resurrecting interest in the locally emotional issue of the Spanish Sahara. An Israeli agent had cautiously presented a bribe to the local imam. He was made to believe that the agent wanted only that public attention be shifted away from Israel to domestic pro-Moroccan issues. The real purpose of the request lay hidden behind the dramatic trappings. There was a point to be made to the people in this sparse Moroccan campaign: Libya had sinned against Allah.

Situated among the cedars was the beautiful Minaret-of-Kutubiyya Mosque, which had stood there since the twelfth century, when it was built of large reddish clay bricks from a plan by the great architect Guever of Seville. Dressed as a local Arab, the Israeli agent with the money listened within the mosque as the imam spoke to the worshippers there.

"I had a dream," he was saying, "in which I saw the archangel Djibrit appear in a burning bush, just as Muhammad met him long ago when he wrote our precious Koran. But the archangel was worried and distraught in my dream. He spoke to me saying, 'Have the hearts of my people turned to hate, that they so waste their energies against Israel that they no longer care for their own estate?' His meaning is that we Moroccans should concentrate on

173

seeking the return of our own lands in the Spanish Sahara. Allah himself will settle Israel in His own way in His own time. It is up to us to purify the heart of Morocco, not to purge evil elsewhere in Allah's kingdom.

"The archangel also seemed to me to speak a warning. Shall we be as the Libyans, spreading more hate than love? They so intensify their support of terrorism that they exceed Allah's desires for His people, yet they give us insufficient support for reunion with our Spanish Sahara. Indeed, Djibrit's vision expressed a warning that something terrible will befall Libya for its transgressions. We too will receive a warning at the same time, which he described to me, saying, 'Behold, I will show you a miraculous sign. Before summer's end, bushes will be in flame in Morocco, and the skin of sinning men will burn as if on fire. Heat will swallow up our land. When you see these things, which will soon come to pass, throw down your arms, remembering this warning, and pray that your sins will be cleansed.'"

Long after the sermon had concluded, the Israeli agent lifted himself from prayer in the mosque and took the purse of money to a small room where he left it with the imam for his good words, promising more if he could spread the warning to even larger crowds.

Two thousand miles to the east, on the Libyan Mediterranean, a related scene occurred in a park outside a mosque in the seaport of Tobruk, where oil tankers pulled in and out carrying away the high-grade sulphur-free oil arriving by pipeline from the rich oil fields of the Sarir. Here Israeli Intelligence had bribed one of the many religious fanatics preaching in the market square. He stood outside the mosque like a desert prophet, saying, "Take warning, sons of Allah and Muhammad! Allah spoke to me in a dream in the desert. He showed me a sign of a plague that is coming soon, a great heat, and skins that burn like fire. Remember this warning when it comes. Allah is grieved that we sin against our brothers. Our own leader is said to sponsor terrorism in Lebanon—brother turned against brother because of a cancerous hate of Israel. 'We shall be punished!' Allah has said to me. 'When these signs come, turn your faces to the sun and pray. Pray for forgiveness until your skins burn no more.'"

Omnipresent troops were standing nearby. They listened nervously to the insinuations against Colonel Khaddafi, but let the fanatic have his day, in fact, many such days. Modern-day prophets were considered harmless. After each speech the Israeli agent paid off according to how well his man had issued the warning. Hundreds of such speeches were suddenly occurring daily throughout Libya, which was, along with Egypt and Syria, a primary target of a campaign to promote hysteria.

In Libya and Egypt a primary thrust of this campaign was directed at the armed forces. Mailing addresses of government troops were purchased under false pretenses from Libyan agents, so that a brief circular from a fanatic religious organization could be mailed to each soldier. It claimed that Allah was revealing a coming miracle to their religious leaders throughout Libya. There would come in late summer an intense heat, and the soldiers' skins would burn with the heat, which itself expressed Allah's anger at Libya's continuing warfare. The soldiers were warned to greet the miracle by throwing down their arms, facing the sun and praying; otherwise Allah would strike down Libya and the oil wells would dry up. The circulars were instantly denounced by Colonel Khaddafi's government, which was unable to locate the self-proclaimed religious group.

In Cairo the action was taking yet another form. In the circular plaza outside the Medrese Mosque of Sultan Hassan, beneath the highest minarets in Cairo, a dozen agents quickly passed out handbills for ten minutes and then dispersed to reassemble for the next action, each too brief and too small to be worth serious suppression. Although President Mubarak was cracking down on Muslim fanaticism in an attempt to preserve the secular nature of the Egyptian state, he found no effective way to suppress the many independent fanatics that are a part of the fundamentalist tidal wave. Cries for a national return to the Sharia, the strict thirteen hundred-year-old Islamic legal code governing Muslim life, had become a modern Egyptian problem. Operating under the umbrella of Muslim fundamentalism, the Israeli agents scattered their own message. Slowly the prediction of an approaching miraculous sign of Allah's anger spread through the disbelieving land. The prediction erupted in northern Africa like mold on bread, spotty, nastily visible to all, but, it was hoped, not dangerous.

In a large hall in the offices of the Ministry of Defense in Tel Aviv, nine men sat around a long table reviewing the progress of Jericho. Aaron Rabin was addressing the progress of the psychological preparations.

"The efficiency of this kind of fanatical warning lies in the fact that it can be effective even if no one believes in the prediction," he was saying. "It is sufficient merely that they be aware of it. That it appears to come from a fanatic group, bordering on the occult and on religious mystique, is to our advantage, because we wish their eventual reaction to be similar—fanatic, religious, occult, irrational. A rational warning would stimulate a rational response, which is not what is needed in this case. We hope for a collective irrationality, a mass behavior fashioned by a dark fear shared by an entire people. Terror within a population can be augmented when they share awareness of the thing feared. And the worst fears involve those that are not understood, the irrational fixations that give rise to the rampant mysticism and fanaticism that abound in the world today. A thing greatly feared among their people would be an angry reprimand from Allah, delivered as a terrible natural catastrophe to punish their sins. This thought, although admittedly discarded by educated men as the ravings of lunatics, is now being implanted throughout Libya and Egypt, and is also being disseminated in Syria, Lebanon, Jordan, Algeria, and Morocco. As you've seen on the sheets before you, we have only two thousand men and a twenty million-dollar budget, so we must pace ourselves."

"How effectively has this warning reached the people?" Elias Hirschberg inquired.

"We have made random tests," Rabin answered. "In Libya the awareness percentage is already 47 percent; in Cairo it is 29 percent; in smaller cities along the Egyptian Mediterranean the awareness varies from 63 percent in Rosette, where we have bribed a religious leader, to only 10 percent in Fuka, where we have been able only to hire a nomadic fanatic. South of Cairo along the Nile we have not been able to make any substantial headway, but it is my understanding that the military operation will be confined to the north."

"But haven't there been slipups?" Hirschberg continued. "What has their effect been?"

"Amazingly, the problems may even have helped!" Rabin exclaimed. "Two churchmen in Libya reported the bribe to the police. In those cities the handbills were immediately described as one of our plots. The net effect was increased exposure, so that, in those cities, almost 60 percent of the people now know of its strange warning. Of them, only 30 percent actually believe the police accusation of an Israeli plot. We were helped in the same way by the scandal over the mailings to Libyan soldiers. Their incensed reaction only increased public awareness. I have discovered that the best help we could get would be if the large newspapers would describe this prediction as harassment by Israel, because they cannot prove it and because it can only bring the fanatic prediction to public attention. We have in fact now launched Phase 2, which is just such a plan. Newspapers in Damascus are being fed such a story 'from reliable sources.' We know from experience that most people will instead suspect a religious fringe and that they will quietly wonder at the strange prediction. With luck, we will greatly solidify our coverage by getting their news media to play into our hands. We are even contemplating a few sensational stories to ensure fuller coverage."

"What sort of sensational stories?" the defense minister wondered.

"I envision spreading rumors of sex orgies with religious cult leaders and young girls. We can stage photos for popular magazines and newspapers. That would get everyone's attention."

"I would think that one through carefully," Hirschberg remarked, with a noticeable lack of enthusiasm. At the other end of the table the commander of the air force leaned back laughing after the defense minister whispered something in his ear.

At this moment the prime minister, who had been silent, asked a question: "I want to know, Dr. Rabin, what you see as the psychological effect of the U.N. censure of Israel? I am really quite worried about this. It seems clear that most of our enemies will use our continuing involvement in Lebanon and the tragedy of the 1984 massacre as a moral excuse to continue, and even accelerate, their brutal harassments. I fear the censure will accelerate military mobilization on their part just now, at a time when we want their mutual preparedness to sag."

"Not necessarily," Rabin replied. "These things can often have just the opposite effect. Our enemies have clearly won a victory with this new censure. It was a victory of words and of paper, but it was nonetheless a victory; and they may be momentarily quite content with it. The will to fight comes from frustration, from the feeling that one cannot win a victory in any other way. The irony of the tragedy in Lebanon is that it has left our enemies feeling morally superior and self-satisfied. No, for Jericho it may even be better that they have won this silly victory. I think it will have them thinking more of diplomatic victories than of military ones. Perhaps they will try again to expel us from the U.N."

"Our intelligence tends to confirm that," the chief of intelligence joined in. "The chiefs of state inform us that the current movements are clear, supporting a downplay of military strategy and plans merely to hold status quo while the diplomatic channels try for new victories. Even Arafat is being turned into a diplomat by that momentum. In particular they are turning attention to the secretary of state's upcoming visit to try to forge the peace agreement, and to our total withdrawal from Lebanon. The Lebanese invasion has inadvertently formed a smokescreen for our present occupation with Jericho. In fact, the security of Jericho has been successfully maintained because we have been able to disguise our preparations as part of our activity there. We have also been exaggerating our equipment losses to the United States to support our requests for M–60 tanks and infantry weapons.

"Our one obstacle has been that public support in the United

States has eroded, and the president is sensitive to the pressure. We haven't had a decision about the M–60's yet, but we are hoping to secure some concessions. Still, we can manage without this equipment. Our armaments requests are based upon forecasts of the worst possible case. Without knowing the strength of the Joshua Factor, we can't know how much military resistance to expect.

"The beauty of Jericho as a military strategy is that it only has to work once. We are not cutting our throats by engaging in a protracted military prospect. And we will not need to rely upon the United States after the event. If the Joshua Factor works, Jericho will work."

"But are we agreed that our continued bombing of the Palestinian guerrilla bases in the Bekaa Valley is useful?" the prime minister continued. "The peacekeeping mandate of the Arab League has that part of eastern Lebanon under the control of Syrian forces. Yesterday's air strike was our eighth of the year, and we staged it one day after the inspection tour by the Syrian defense minister. It is too early to say whether the reaction will be the one we want."

"I believe it will be," the defense minister responded. "They surely believe our objective to be the continued destruction of Libyan-backed factions there. Their response will almost certainly be to keep a high level of foot soldiers there in an attempt to police the area themselves, according to the mandate. That's what we want, because those soldiers will be useless within hours after the Joshua Factor comes on line. They will not have heavy equipment for such purposes, and they will not have good supply lines. But maybe this is getting a little ahead of our agenda for this meeting."

"Yes, I suppose we are a bit off our agenda," the prime minister continued, "but I am relieved, if we do agree, that this air strike was correct. I have in my office a continuing problem of separating my normal motives from those dictated by the Jericho plan. These sporadic air strikes are such a halfway measure between a real cleanup and a total pullout that I was needing reassurance. Remember, it is I that has to face the press at 4:00 today—that is, unless one of you wishes to stand in for me."

General laughter filled the room, bringing a smile of relief to the prime minister's face. He then returned to the agenda: "This brings me to the main point of this meeting today, to review the schedule for Jericho, which is, of course, set by the Joshua Factor. Dr. Hirschberg is prepared today to review the evidence briefly and to project an actual date. Dr. Hirschberg, would now be a good time?"

"Certainly," Elias Hirschberg responded with an air of calm

authority. As he pulled the appropriate sheets of notes from his attaché case, the group turned to him in silent, almost awed, expectation. To anyone watching the secret deliberations of the Jericho Planning Group over the past fifteen months it would have become obvious that this man, world-renowned theoretical physicist, decorated infantry soldier in his youth, brilliant military strategist during the 1967 war, when he had been adviser to Moshe Dayan, and since then director of technological development for the secret security, was the spirit of Jericho. It was he who had turned David Zweig's interests to general relativity during his postdoctoral appointment at Tel Aviv. It was he who recognized Zweig's incomparable brilliance in astrophysical problems, and it was he who recognized how the Joshua Factor, itself discovered innocently by Zweig, could become the secret military plan called Jericho. It was Hirschberg who had been able to persuade military leaders that they could formulate a plan based on a surprising scientific discovery and a brilliant astrophysical analysis. It was he who, at a crucial moment in a heated conference with the minister of defense and the prime minister, had so moved them with his simple timely biblical reference: Joshua, too, had prevailed in the battle of Jericho by his sympathetic comprehension of God's will, when all about him would rush forward with their inadequate weapons. So now all present turned in expectant admiration to the man who had so skillfully led them through the maze of their earlier meetings.

"The key information comes from our neutrino detector in the Negev," he began in deference to those military men present who had not been a party to earlier meetings. "There we have a hundred-ton detector whose key element is thirty tons of gallium. It has been detecting neutrinos from the sun for the past eighteen months, and it has the useful property of responding well to the neutrinos from radioactive beryllium-7 and from radioactive nitrogen-13. These radioactive nuclei are produced at the center of the Sun. About fifteen months ago Professor Jamil Koren of Ben Gurion University, who is directing the experiment, began to notice a steady increase in the rate of arrival of these neutrinos from the Sun. Professor David Zweig has determined that this rise is due to a rapid change at the center of the Sun. The neutrino count has risen fantastically in a way we call *exponential*. It continued to rise exponentially for fifteen months. Look at this first slide showing a graph of the counting rate. Each heavy dot shows the number of counts in that month." Hirschberg's aluminum pointer traced with slow drama the yearlong increase displayed on the graph projected onto the screen.

"Ten days ago, on May 24, the neutrino count slowed its

179

steady rate of increase, indicating the onset of saturation in the number of possible radioactive nuclei near a disk structure at the center of the Sun. Our computer calculations of this show convincingly that the solar disk will explode exactly two months after the deceleration from the exponential rise has grown to a factor of two. The deceleration will occur about two weeks from today. The key dates are indicated by the arrows on the slide. The disk will explode on or about August 20. From that time it will take exactly eighteen minutes for the shock wave to reach the solar surface. This will be the key moment. With another month of observation we will be able to say whether it will occur on August 19, 20, or 21. However, it will not be until the final week that we will be able to say whether the eruption will happen during our night or during our day. Right now there is a 50–50 chance of it happening at either time. Therefore we will need to formulate two strike plans, one for a nighttime eruption and one for a daytime eruption. I want to return to this point in a few minutes, because I think it constitutes a major strategical uncertainty at the moment.

"What we feared from the beginning of Jericho fifteen months ago, and still do today to some degree, is the discovery of the Joshua Factor by the scientific world. But I no longer see this as a problem. Without a functioning solar-neutrino experiment, the world cannot be convinced of what will happen. The data tape that Dr. Reynolds recovered from the U.S. experiment is not adequate, especially since they doubt its authenticity. Although we will continue to watch Dr. Reynolds's activities, I think we should simply press ahead with our planning. His isolated opinion could not influence political action. It is more important that we guard against leaks from within our organization."

Hirschberg paused and looked around the room, waiting for reactions.

Finally one of the members of the cabinet asked, "Do I understand that you believe that U.S. scientists cannot decipher the meaning of their experiment before the eruption comes? Suppose they do?"

"Not exactly," Hirschberg replied. "My point is that it probably makes no difference if they decipher it. A man like Dr. Reynolds might come to an understanding of what will happen. But what could he do? If he went straight to the president or to the newspapers with the prediction, the reaction would now be the same; total skepticism. He has only a single tape at the very beginning of the neutrino rise made by a scientist who is dead. Even with respect for scientific expertise, the U.S. society would not believe something they cannot understand and for which the evidence is so slim. And in the U.S., large collective activities just cannot be initiated quickly without massive popular support."

180

"The plan is not without risk," interrupted Aaron Rabin. "We have taken every precaution to maintain secrecy. But, I think that we must not lose sight of the immense vanity of our decision. We have miraculously identified an unexpected feature of the Sun in time to anticipate a natural disaster, and we have decided to utilize it to our advantage. We will invade Libya and capture Libyan oil fields and realign the balance of power in the Middle East. Under normal circumstances this action would be an atrocious violation of human rights and international law. But we are talking about a changed world. It changed the day that we were blessed with this privileged information. God has, for His own reasons, bestowed the secret on His people. Our concern is survival. We are no longer in the luxurious position of making political decisions, or moral decisions. We are making survival decisions. If the outburst is more severe than Dr. Hirschberg projects, even these decisions may become moot. But we are gambling that we have a chance, and we are behaving to improve the odds. Our behavior has been unscrupulous by normal standards. We have lied to our allies to obtain armaments; we have overextended our credit; we have denied the rest of humanity our knowledge, as a matter of tragic necessity. We have taken this miracle of understanding, and done everything in our power to administer God's gift of life to Israel. Beyond our best effort, what happens will be God's will, and our actions will be judged by Him."

Perhaps the silence that followed reflected the ambivalence around the table. Hard men shifted uncomfortably at such arguments. Some heads nodded affirmatively. Some looked questioningly at others. And some stared blankly at the notepads before them. All save Elias Hirschberg lacked the scientific certainty, the undeniable knowledge, that the Joshua Factor was inevitable. Others doubted that such momentous conclusions could be reliably drawn from invisible heavenly messengers that left no mark on a man's senses. Each struggled in his own way with a sense of unreality about this human dilemma.

"I for one appreciate your wisdom and guidance, Dr. Rabin, but I am nervous about the implementation of the invasion," suggested the minister of defense. "I think we should return to the strike plans. You say we should have two, depending on whether the outburst comes during our night or our day. I would like you to elaborate on this."

Elias Hirschberg rose again to field the question.

"The shock wave at the solar surface will be quite abrupt. The first effect will be that the daylight will be several times brighter than ordinary sunlight. We calculate two and a half times brighter, which will require all of our outdoor population to be equipped with special sunglasses. The unprepared enemy will be blinded by white-out. We will discuss our provisioning efforts later. Suffice it to say that everything is proceeding on schedule. The second effect will be the intensely hot daytime temperature. Our computer models of the Earth in such a situation suggest temperatures of 60°C, or about 140°F, throughout inland areas around the Mediterranean. We have a large variety of special clothing and troop-advance operations planned to allow us to function adequately in such an environment. For example, we have all-white, full-coverage uniforms with face-covering, nonglare visors. Our troop transports have been enclosed, and air-conditioning units have been installed in each one. Each vehicle carries large tanks of water. We plan a very rapid advance of troops behind the tanks and behind a heavy airstrike. We have planned parachute drops immediately behind the airstrikes. General Sharim will describe these details later. It will be over quickly. If the solar event happens during daytime, our air force and rockets will probably strike Libyan air bases and weapons compounds about an hour after the outburst, when panic and disarray will be high.

"The next effects will take about twenty-four hours. There will be a serious disruption of ordinary communications when the first blast waves of intense plasma reach the Earth's magnetosphere. The aurora will undoubtedly be the most spectacular that modern man has ever seen. It will be visible throughout Canada, North America, Northern Europe, and the U.S.S.R. All of our radio communications anticipate a highly disrupted ionosphere, so we are converting to high-frequency radio. These communications preparations are almost complete.

"The next effect is the most serious of all, and has required extensive planning by many segments of our society. For a lengthy but unpredictable duration, the Sun will emit ultraviolet radiation and soft X-rays at intensities millions of times greater than we live with today. The energetic turbulence and shock waves following the initial shock will render the entire solar surface like a solar flare. We have been studying the ultraviolet and X-ray emission from solar flares with considerable scientific manpower. They are our best examples of what the entire solar surface will soon be like. And it is not a pleasant picture. At its worst it could become very difficult to sustain life on Earth. Understand that clearly. Fortunately, we think the conditions will not be that bad. Most of the Sun's energy will still arrive as ordinary, harmless light, but the ultraviolet will be very damaging. The unaware enemy will be blinded without protective sunglasses. The sunburns of exposed skins will be terrible. We expect the radiation with a wavelength near two thousand nine hundred to three thousand angstroms to increase by factors of several hundred over normal sunlight. This will give a sunburn in one minute as severe as several hours of mountain-top exposure. I must warn you, gentlemen: millions will die of simple sunburn, and hundreds of millions will be sick indoors with severe burns. The arguments are very technical, but basically this will result from the severe destruction of the Earth's statospheric ozone layer coupled with the much increased radiation of solar ultraviolet. Life on Earth would not be possible without this protective layer of ozone. It absorbs radiation with wavelengths smaller than three thousand angstroms, and these are the deadly rays. They kill not only by burning, they kill by attacking DNA itself. Laboratory experiments on plants exposed to increased levels of this ultraviolet radiation show that they grow to a much smaller size with increasing numbers of mutations. At the radiation levels we expect, much plant life will in fact die. The situation is going to be a disaster for the world's crops. Many who do not die of sunburn or heat prostration will die of starvation."

"Dr. Hirschberg," the prime minister interrupted, "you paint such a bleak picture that one hardly knows where to begin asking questions."

"I appreciate that," Hirschberg replied cheerfully. "That's why I have asked you to schedule tomorrow's full-day meeting on this problem alone. The questions are: Can Israel and its citizens survive? What precautions must we now be taking to help us through the most violent time? Fortunately, our think tank studies affirm that we *can* survive, but only with careful planning. We do not expect an outburst so severe that civilization will be destroyed. What we recommend, as part of Jericho, is that Israel take all precautionary measures and let the rest of the world cope as best it can. We can and should protect our own. Naturally, if we lived in a better world, our recommendations would extend to all mankind. But you know better than I, sir, the merciless persecution that the world has inflicted on our people throughout history. You know as well as anyone the vicious plots that exist only to destroy us. I therefore strongly urge all of us to look upon the Joshua Factor as an Act of God. He has mercifully warned us in advance, just as He did when the angel of death passed over the Israelite families at the time of our bondage in Egypt."

"It's a staggering thought, however," the prime minister replied in subdued tones. "All those dead. It's as awful as nuclear war. But I take it we will discuss all of this tomorrow?"

"Right," Hirschberg replied. "We have a long list of scientific experiments on the effect of ultraviolet radiation on life forms of all kinds. We will review this evidence and present our analysis of what this will mean for the world. We have various plans already in motion to protect our own plant life and our animals. We need

183

to discuss carefully our plans for informing our own population. Rabin has been working hard on this. We have a multitiered plan that consists of involving the most essential and trustworthy people first and warning more and more of our people as the day comes nearer. The extensive ultraviolet shields now being prepared to shelter our crops are being described as a new research effort of the Department of Agriculture. Many farmers are being instructed to plant seeds in unshielded land at an unusual time, early August, because they will be safest beneath the ground in lands that we will continue irrigating. We anticipate that the high ultraviolet period will last about a month, but we have nothing to go on here except calculations and analogies with small solar eruptions. It could, at the opposite extreme, be over within a day, or, if lengthy readjustments in the solar interior are needed, continue throughout our lifetime. It is our major uncertainty. We just cannot be definite on this point, but our best calculations suggest that the major epoch of atmospheric turbulence will last about a month. After that, the ground temperatures will remain oppressive, but the ultraviolet excess will damp out and the stratospheric ozone layer will recover. As you can see, the problem is so complicated that it will take all of tomorrow simply to establish a common awareness of what we expect."

"This is the first time that I understand why I was instructed to purchase those fantastic shipments of French wheat," the finance minister interjected.

"I'm sorry about that, Chaim," responded the prime minister. "We had to order it long ago, and at the time we felt that Jericho could not be immediately shared throughout the cabinet. There were just too many things that needed rapid and calm analysis by our think tanks. You were right, however, to oppose that grain purchase at first."

"On economic grounds Israel is bankrupt," replied the finance minister. "We have twice again devalued the pound in the last two months, so that our people are unable to buy almost any imported item. Our financial commitments for arms, safety preparations, and food have exhausted our last plausible assets. To purchase the French wheat I had to lie about its payment. I grossly obscured our actual intentions with the promised loans from the World Bank and from the U.S. I had to hide our weapons purchases. If the world fully realized all we have contracted to purchase in the past six months, I doubt that we could buy another thing. We would be the paupers of the world, living on handouts!"

"You've done a great job, Chaim," the prime minister replied. "We all know it has been extremely difficult for you; but, fortunately, it will all be over soon. If the picture Dr. Hirschberg has painted is correct, there will be little concern about bank balances three months from now. Fortunately, the French grain shipments are continuing to arrive, and distribution to the new storage tanks has been proceeding smoothly. Almost everything has gone better than I could have expected."

After a brief silence, the commander of the air force leaned forward and said, "Since time is getting late today, I wonder if we could return to Dr. Hirschberg's attack strategies? Suppose the solar eruption happens during our night. Strong scientific programs in Japan, Australia, Hawaii, or the continental United States will then detect the outburst. What should we then do? Attack at dawn?"

"I would think so," Hirschberg replied. "What other countries will detect is primarily the optical brightness, but the intense heat and the ultraviolet will not yet be fully appreciated. By attacking at dawn we will cause the Libyan forces to be deployed with maximum haste and with minimum preparation for the severe day to come. I would recommend rocket and air strikes against military targets, with just enough troops fighting to force them to deploy theirs quickly. But I would then engage in token fighting until midday, when the intense heat and rising ultraviolet will begin to take their toll. By midafternoon our well-prepared invasion forces should be able to go through Egypt and Libya like a knife through butter. The skirmishes we undertake early in the day should force rapid deployment of their largest infantry formations. Naturally, we'll try to take as much of their air force as we can in the first strike. From then on, we need only be relentless and organized."

Aaron Rabin remained seated following the meeting, until the conference room had cleared, to speak privately with Hirschberg.

"Elias, now that we have a date for the event, we must announce a public holiday. I propose to designate August 20 Civil Defense Day, and prepare our citizens in advance to participate fully in state-organized civil defense preparations. Such a public holiday would provide a perfect ruse for disseminating information to the populace."

Hirschberg replied with a dash of sarcasm, "Couldn't we call it Passover instead?"

"Only between you, me, and God."

Twenty

In the Computation Center at the University of Texas, George Reynolds and a team of two research assistants and a postdoctoral research fellow were planning yet another day's calculations. Questions concerning black holes had haunted Reynolds since his reading of Zweig's paper on eruptive stars. It had taken two weeks to complete the first calculations of a model sun having a black hole at the center. He had first attempted the easiest problem by ignoring the rotation of the solar center, so that the center would be spherically symmetric. The hardest task was programming the effects of the black hole, about which nothing was known except that it would have a strong gravitational field. After much theoretical starting, stopping, and starting over again, Reynolds had formulated a working model: as particles attempt to fall into the hole, they are accelerated to high energy by the very strong gravity and collide at high speeds with other particles. Those collisions make gamma rays, which diffuse outward from the center, heating the surroundings. The key point was a plausible assumption, namely, that matter falls into the hole just fast enough to make enough heat radiation to balance the weight of the gas temporarily. Seen this way, the flow into the hole would be self-regulating. The numerical simplification attendant on this balance at least allowed Reynolds to go ahead with a calculation.

Having that prescription for the black hole, the CDC 6600 had computed the required models of the Sun at the satisfying rate of nine seconds per model. The results showed clearly that the neutrino flux was indeed affected by the presence of the black hole, depending on its actual mass. For a black hole mass as small as the Earth's mass, there was no easily observable effect; but for a mass as great as ten Earth masses, in which case the black hole radius was one inch, the detectable solar neutrino flux was reduced by a factor of ten!

Reynolds was so excited by this result that he had to leave the clamor of the Computation Center. It was the first solar model with a calculated neutrino emission that did not exceed the limits that Fred Cowan had established over ten years of observations. Reynolds sat on a bench overlooking the great fountain at the LBJ Library and retraced, slowly, the implications of his new calculation. A whole new set of connections suddenly seemed possible. Cowan's experiment to detect the solar neutrinos might indeed have given negative results all these years owing to the existence of a black hole at the solar center. Or at least Zweig could have thought so. The idea provided a plausible link between Zweig's preoccupation with black holes and his surprising interest in Cowan's experiment. It was crazy, but it fit. But what would, in that case, be the meaning to Zweig of the sudden increase in the neutrino counts, unless it had something to do with the rise in temperature, as discussed in his paper about flare stars, in the pancakelike disk about the central black hole. But could this actually be occurring in our own Sun?

Placing himself in Zweig's shoes, Reynolds could connect the previous absence of neutrinos with the beginnings, just detected by Cowan, of a forthcoming eruption of the Sun. But why the murder? What possible motive could lead to something as horrible as murder? As a scientist, Zweig would surely have been elated by his discovery of a wholly new phenomenon at the solar center. Of course, he would have been concerned about the future of the Sun, but he could hardly expect to control it by murdering its earthly discoverer. For some reason the usual scientific excitement over a great discovery had been replaced by a fanatic emotional response. Even a sick mind must have a motive. What Reynolds could not overlook was Fitzgerald's very pointed question: "What if Zweig planned to use some scientific discovery to start a war?" But that would have to wait. First priority would have to be more calculations of the Sun. Only they would offer valid grounds for scientific belief.

Within another week Reynolds fit Jupiter into the picture with the aid of a third black hole. At first he recoiled at such a proliferation of imagined black holes, but the idea quickly grew more plausible. If Nature were to have black holes left over from the beginnings of the universe, then why not have two smaller primitive black holes in orbit about the largest one. These black holes would have constituted an invisible primitive skeleton for the solar system. Within this context it made sense to have the two largest objects in the solar system, the Sun and Jupiter, form

188

about two separate black holes that were previously orbiting one another. Only the third black hole, the one just discovered in the asteroid belt, the smallest of the three, was still exposed today. A small black hole at the center of Jupiter could provide the power for Jupiter's infrared luminosity in just the same way it could provide the solar power. Jupiter's black hole would have to be much smaller than the Sun's, however, with a mass no larger than one of the small Martian moons, Deimos or Phobos.

It all fit. After a week's computer models of Jupiter, Reynolds decided that Jupiter was important to Zweig because its excess heat provided another example for the theory and allowed the heating rate of the central black hole to be compared against actual measurements. Zweig's instincts had convinced him that there was a black hole within Jupiter.

With considerable help from his postdoctoral assistant, Ralph Polkinghorn, who nursed the computer program through modifications day and night, Reynolds had grown more and more astonished at Jupiter's evident sensitivity to the rate at which the black hole swallowed its central gases. Only a very small range of possible values of black hole mass could give a correct model of Jupiter today, 4.6 billion years after it first formed. A black hole slightly too small gave no infrared luminosity from the giant planet, whereas one too large gave far too much luminosity and would not have allowed Jupiter to live to its present old age. The proper balance determined the mass of the black hole. Thus it must have been that Zweig had recognized Jupiter's luminosity as one of the keys to understanding the Sun. The tough task now would be to distinguish Zweig's beliefs in this scenario from the truth.

"The program has failed again, George," said a weary Ralph Polkinghorn. "Trying to make the core rotate has introduced some real problems. It's about to wear me out."

"It looks like the program ran for twenty time steps before it bombed," Reynolds replied, looking at the computer printouts in front of them. "It stopped just where it stopped before—just when the disk has grown thick enough to trap its own heat. That's when we expect the temperature rise to begin. We'll never get the damned thing to explode unless we can figure out what's wrong with our instructions."

"I've got an idea that it has something to do with the radiative transfer," Polkinghorn replied. "Up to this time we aren't having to do radiative transfer within the disk. So we have something wrong in our logical statements there. It may arise from the pancakelike geometry. I'll search through that part again, but I might as well go back to my office and do it in peace."

"Sounds sensible to me," Reynolds replied. "Don't rush. You'll waste more time hurrying than you will in going slowly at this point. I want you to concentrate on this problem. Do it as fast as you can and still do a careful job, because I think the answer may be very important."

"What a fascinating problem!" Polkinghorn said. "Why didn't Zweig carry on with these calculations himself?"

"I'll tell you all about it soon," Reynolds said with a faint smile, "but right now I'd rather not explain why I'm so eager. Just call me the minute you find the error."

Unlocking the bicycle that he kept for on-campus travel, Reynolds's mind turned to Fitzgerald. He should call him to warn him that he might, at last, have found the track. Reynolds decided on sudden impulse to call from someplace other than his office, so he stopped at the pay phone just inside the old physics building.

"Jimmy, hold onto your hat," Reynolds began. "I think Zweig believes the Sun is about to flare up and stay brighter for a long time. And I wonder if that might fit his behavior from your point of view?"

"I'll be damned!" Fitzgerald exclaimed. "It certainly might. Do you think he's correct, if that is what he thinks?"

"I'm sure that's what he's thinking. His own papers led me step by step to that conclusion. But it will be much harder to know if what he describes is actually happening," Reynolds replied. "We're calculating models of the Sun right now that could have this behavior, but the computer program still has a bug in it."

"Just what might the Sun do, and when?" Fitzgerald asked, impatiently jumping to the main point.

"It might brighten a lot—say, many times as bright—and do it suddenly," Reynolds answered. "I can't say when, because I'm not at all convinced that the ideas are correct. But if I think like Zweig seems to have been thinking, and if the rise in neutrino flux is due to what he apparently thinks it is due to, I would say it would happen this year."

"This year?" Fitzgerald asked.

"Right, just guessing. Look, I know it's strange," Reynolds added apologetically, "so I don't want you to put too much stock in such a wild idea. It's just that . . ."

"Good heavens no, man!" Fitzgerald exclaimed. "It sounds to me like you're right on! Where did you get the lead—from the air force, from Zweig's letter to Dr. Hale, from . . . ?"

"Who told you about a letter from Zweig to Hale?" Reynolds asked at once, his mind flashing to his opened and resealed mail containing Zweig's manuscript from Hale's office.

There was a noticeable silence at the other end of the line.

"Oh, I don't remember—I think Corrigan mentioned it, " Fitzgerald said offhandedly.

"Mentioned what?" Reynolds asked. If Corrigan had also mailed a manuscript copy to Fitzgerald, surely both would have said so. Perhaps a little sleuthing on his own could help him discover where his personal danger lay.

After another silence Fitzgerald continued, "Mentioned that Zweig's paper to Hale was about stellar eruptions, or something like that." Fitzgerald then exclaimed with what seemed to be feigned exasperation, "Look, George, I hope you haven't told your discovery to anyone."

"It's not really a discovery," Reynolds corrected. "It's just a lead into the way Zweig was thinking."

"Well, that's what I mean," Fitzgerald affirmed. "Don't tell anyone what you think Zweig was thinking."

"All right," Reynolds said, smiling at Fitzgerald's loss of veneer. Then probing deeper he asked, "Do you think this could relate to the war plan?"

"What war plan?" Fitzgerald blurted, immediately regretting his high volume.

"You told me Zweig might have been thinking of starting a war with a scientific discovery," Reynolds said. "You suggested that I search for such a dramatic discovery."

"Yes, but I was speaking figuratively, of course," Fitzgerald said. "There may be no real war plan. I was suggesting only that you might search for something that might have, to Zweig's twisted mind, seemed so all-important," Fitzgerald answered, refusing to share his personal suspicions about Israel's preparations.

"But why did you choose *war* as an example of Zweig's motivation?" Reynolds persisted.

"I really have no logical explanation," Fitzgerald replied. "I just wanted to suggest something dramatic, something emotional, something that might unbalance Zweig. It was just a manner of speaking . . . like bad poetry!" Fitzgerald finished with a forced chuckle.

"Well, I really have no opinion whether this wild idea about the Sun, this idea that I attribute to Zweig merely by circumstantial inference, could be correct or not. We're studying it here, and if I can get the computer program to work, I'll be able to say something much more definite—probably next week," Reynolds stated calmly.

"Just don't say anything about it . . . to anyone," Fitzgerald repeated. "I want to travel down there to let you explain the idea to me. I may even want to give you a couple of bodyguards, just in case you're in danger."

Reynolds remembered that he was, in fact, in danger. Rebecca's warning came back to him in full force. He was willing to bet that the CIA had intercepted the package from Corrigan. Fitzgerald seemed to have given that away. Maybe he should ask Fitzgerald outright. Perhaps the police imposters in the Big Bend had been CIA men. And the photographer at the La Quinta, too. Could the CIA even have been responsible for Cowan's murder and for Zweig's disappearance—and for Rebecca's, too? Reynolds could not resolve it, but murder and talk of war was an integral part of whatever was happening. Fear erupted at the tone of Fitzgerald's voice—at his urgent warnings not to disclose his interpretation of Zweig's ideas. It was the second time he had been urged to conceal the truth. He was no coward, but Reynolds could not help but realize that there existed one sure way for someone to be certain that he would never be able to tell what he knew. If he was in danger, though, he also had something that Fitzgerald obviously wanted badly to know. That knowledge could be his security. Feeling more cautious now, he spoke disarmingly,

"Look, Jimmy, it's Friday and I'm about burned out on this computer program. So don't come to Austin until next week at the earliest. I'm going away for the weekend to play in a tennis tournament in Corpus Christi. Great tennis town, despite the winds. Next week we'll have that computer program working, and by then we'll be able to tell if it makes sense. I'm not even telling my assistants why we're working on this problem. They think it's just another strange calculation in astrophysics. If Zweig's idea is right, we should even be able to predict roughly when a solar eruption might come. It'll just take time, so be patient."

"All right, but keep it very quiet. I'll call you Monday just to check progress. But please rush it. June is almost gone, and I'd like to know the answer before August. The government is counting on you. I think you're on the right track. I'll be talking to you Monday."

"Goodbye," Reynolds said, assaulted by more questions than ever. Why should he want to know before August? Probably that was a slip. Why the secrecy when, in fact, if Zweig's idea were right, the entire situation would be extremely urgent for mankind? In 1936 the star FU Orionis had increased its power output one hundred fold. Were the Sun to do that, life on Earth would be quickly extinguished by unbearable radiation. That much was certain. The only hope for continuing life would be if it were to do something less violent—if, in fact, it was going to do anything at all. Reynolds had only recently become aware that the Earth's atmospheric protection against normal solar ultraviolet was tenuous. The National Academy panel on which he served was finding that even supersonic aircraft might injure it. And what of Mars, Venus, and the Moon? Did he not remember evidence being presented at the committee meetings suggesting that both Venus and Mars must have received much stronger solar radiation in the past? He decided to talk to someone in planetary atmospheres, to refresh his mind on that. But right now, Reynolds decided he had something else to do—and it was *not* driving to Corpus for another tennis tournament.

It was 2:45 P.M. when Reynolds turned on the ignition of his Porsche in the parking lot. On the way home he stopped at the Outdoor Center to make a few purchases: several boxes of ammunition for his deer-hunting rifle, several gallons of fuel for his kerosene stove, boxes of matches, a new tent, and several cartons of vegetable seeds of various types. At his apartment he selected his lightweight hiking boots and one pair of tennis shoes, several pairs of heavy socks and underwear, and an assortment of varied outdoor clothing, which he packed into a medium-sized leather suitcase. As an afterthought, he inserted the photograph of Rebecca. On his way through Austin he stopped at a supermarket, where he bought cartons of dried fruit, two dozen two-pound cans of assorted nuts, two large bottles of aspirin, Band-Aids, eggs, bread, and two huge steaks. It was almost more than he could fit into the car, but it was only the first of what were to be three preparatory trips motivated by a sudden and instinctive fear for survival.

As he crossed the Colorado River in south Austin, the afternoon sun reflected brilliantly off its broad waters. Turning west on Texas Highway 71, Reynolds noticed the heavy weekend traffic already heading outward toward Lake Travis. With aggressive use of high r.p.m. in second gear, Reynolds advanced through the slow-moving traffic, until at Oak Hill he burst around the last vestiges of bumper-to-bumper traffic and set out toward the Sun. A sharp right just past Oak Hill took him onto the exclusive branch of 71 where it divided from the more heavily used U.S. 290. He hit 70 mph in third gear before dropping quietly into fourth as he settled into the drive toward Llano. The rear-view mirror confirmed again that no one was following him. By 4:30 he had passed the road to the dam for Lake LBJ and knew he would make it before sunset. In another thirty minutes he turned right on Texas 16 just south of Llano, then left again on Farm-to-Market 152. In just fifteen minutes he saw the water tank five miles ahead for the town of Castell shadowed against the setting Sun and knew that the dirt road lay just a few hundred yards ahead. Slowing now he turned right and followed that dirt road for two miles, past the Clinton Ranch to a dead end just before the banks of the Llano

River. Easing left, he followed the rough drive about two hundred yards to his own small ranch house. He had purchased it from the Clinton Ranch three years previously when they had decided to sell it to raise a little extra capital to send their only son to Rice University in Houston. Reynolds pulled the Porsche into the left half of the old barn that he had converted into a garage and workshop. He made a mental note to repair the broken siding on the other half of the barn.

After removing the goods from the car, Reynolds locked the padlock on the sliding door and walked toward the small house fifty yards to the north. It was a beautiful summer evening, and he suddenly felt much better. There was no sound but the murmur of the Llano flowing over its stony bed another three hundred yards to the north. The two-bedroom wooden frame house was nestled in the shade of two huge live oak trees growing on its southern and western flanks. Before entering the house, Reynolds opened the well cover and switched on the pump to pressurize and fill the steel water tank. It was a sweet well, bringing all the fresh underground water that he could want. He checked the manual pump and found that it would also work after he purchased replacement gaskets for it.

There was a musky but pleasant smell inside the house. Reynolds found everything in order, which was the usual situation, although from time to time drifters tried to break in and caused some damage. He found his goods and previous supplies all there and concluded that no one had broken in during the two months since his last visit. His transitorized portable radio was sitting out on the coffee table where he had left it, and he made a mental note to bring more batteries. Pulling out a sheet of paper, he began a list of things to do, items to purchase, repairs to make.

Reynolds dumped his clothes onto the bed in the east bedroom, where he preferred to sleep. It had the better bed and the cheerful morning light. As he did, he saw his other photograph of Rebecca on the bed stand, where he had placed it during their last visit almost four months ago. How ironic. During several peaceful weekends here, they had often jested that, if the world ever fell apart, they would simply retreat here to live. Now alone, Reynolds wondered if the world was indeed falling apart and what he could do if it were. He stared at Rebecca's photograph and looked at the bed where he had held her during those cold winter nights. Then he walked out to the kitchen, pulled his bottle of Old Grand-Dad from the kitchen shelf, poured himself an extraordinarily large drink of his favorite Bourbon whiskey, and took a long, full sip.

Relaxed almost at once by the warmth in his stomach, Reynolds pulled out his bag of charcoal. He opened one of the two

194

large T-bone steaks that he had purchased and carried it out to the small outdoor grill. The sun was already on the horizon as he got the fire started. Waiting for it to burn down, he took his drink, swallowed another large shot, and walked in a peaceful mood toward the river. How he loved this river. It was the main reason he had decided to buy this particular property. As he came to the top of the small rise leading down to the river, Reynolds stopped short at the sight of four beautiful white-tail deer drinking at its banks. A buck and three does. They saw him at once and leaped up the eastern hillside with a speed and grace that left Reynolds breathless. The last brilliant rays of that great fiery ball in the sky followed their exit, like spotlights in a Broadway show.

Twenty-One

David Zweig left the Physics Building of Tel Aviv University at about 5:00 P.M. on a hot midsummer evening. He had been involved in nothing less innocent than his usual interest, the theoretical physics of a black hole. Two research students and a postdoc at the university met with him to discuss ideas for new directions in research. For Zweig's creative genius, it was business as usual, amid the world's problems. He nimbly crossed a heavily trafficked street and made his way to the bus stop for the southbound buses. He had an appointment to keep.

While waiting Zweig glanced at the people around him. In the heat of early July, no one looked especially significant, least of all David Zweig, in his old sandals, khaki trousers, and open-necked short-sleeved shirt. He felt comfortable in casual surroundings with students, professionals, shopkeepers, and ordinary people simply trying to make the best of their lives. None of them owned very much. Their earnings were modest and heavily taxed to support Israel's overwhelming defense budget.

The bus was crowded and hot, and Zweig was barely able to squeeze between others standing near the door. As it pulled out and continued its way south toward the center of town, Zweig's thoughts turned to his upcoming meeting. He tried once again to analyze the urgent request he had received by telephone from Jerusalem. Jostling with every movement of the bus against the other passengers, Zweig was thankful that he would not be riding far. Three more stops and he got out, just before the bridge.

Four students also got out, Zweig noticed when he turned to look. He didn't know if he would be followed, but he doubted it. He had now been in Israel more than three months, and doubt about him had subsided. The students were walking the same direction, down the path at the right of the bridge toward the banks of the Yarcon River. Eventually they stopped at a bench amid some of the brush trees beside the small river. Zweig wandered on alone among the many people who were also enjoying the park. There were a lot of lovers. They sat on the riverbanks, on benches, or lay on blankets under the small trees. Quite a few people walked alone. Zweig saw several prostitutes loitering there and several homosexual men eyed him curiously as he walked by. Zweig found the general atmosphere of the park appealing. He passed several old men on their late afternoon strolls. Here many worlds co-existed, enjoyable to all for the contrast offered to the city streets. Zweig wondered what they would all be thinking and doing if they knew what lay slightly more than one month away. Glancing at the wrinkled face of a feeble old man lighting his pipe on a park bench, Zweig felt a sudden impulse to warn him. Then he realized immediately it would do no good. It was in the hands of God.

At a designated point along the riverbank, Zweig turned to the right and walked toward a cluster of shrub trees. There he saw her, sitting on a blanket, her braided black hair hanging down in front of her shoulders. Their eyes searched each other tentatively as Zweig approached.

"Hello, Rebecca," Zweig said. "How good it is to see you again. It's been a long time."

"Yes, it has," Rebecca replied. "Since Boston. Here . . . sit down with me on this old blanket."

Rebecca began immediately to ask how he had been enduring his fugitive months in Israel.

"I'm in good health and spirits," Zweig replied. "I've finally started to do a bit of relativity research at the university. Two students there have . . ."

"Did you kill him, David?" Rebecca interrupted.

Zweig's face flushed in pain, and he looked puzzled, as if he didn't, or wouldn't, understand. He had, after all, spent three months trying to forget.

"Did you kill Fred Cowan?" Rebecca repeated.

"Rebecca, you can't ask me such a question. It's indecent, who-ever did it. You know enough to know that I am not supposed to talk about that incident," Zweig said.

"I know that, David, but I hoped I might persuade you to talk to me. I myself feel very troubled, and since it seems clear that you did murder Cowan, I thought you might be in some misery over it," Rebecca said, looking gently into Zweig's averted eyes.

Zweig looked back, paused, and shuddered. "It has been a hard time for me. I haven't slept or worked very well at all. But you know that Cowan was eliminated by the organization. It wasn't me, Rebecca; it was a planning group on a matter of urgency for Israel. You are a part of it, too. You remember our first conversation in Hirschberg's office last year?"

"Yes. I remember it very well," Rebecca replied. "At the time I was thrilled to be part of something so important for us here. The danger for our small nation has always been so great. I was eager to actually do something. You remember how angry I had been. But now . . . I can't describe it, David. I just feel sick at heart."

"In what sense?" Zweig asked.

"It's just that the matters of nations and wars do not seem so important anymore. I feel depressed; and I long for a life of innocence. I don't even know what is happening. I only know that something terrible will occur next month, because I am still being used as part of Domestic Preparations. But I don't know what to expect. What *is* the Joshua Factor, David?"

"I am not supposed to reveal that even to members of Jericho," Zweig answered. "And even though I feel a bit disillusioned myself, I still see a clear need for Jericho. The world will not let us be, Rebecca. Jericho can change the world. It will be terrible, but it will not be our fault; and we can hope to help our people survive and to make a better world afterwards."

"You say that you've felt disillusioned, too?" Rebecca queried.

"At times," Zweig replied. "I have only recently learned that the situation here in Palestine and in Lebanon is more complicated than I had thought. We have here a world of religious fervor, shared by Christian, Moslem, and Jew alike, and a common need for the traditions of a homeland. This is a different world than the ghettos of pre–World War II Europe, Rebecca, and that was the world I inherited from my father, from family photographs, from an agonizing education into the origins of myself. But here all people fight for a homeland. There is a need for all of us to maintain the brotherhood of man, rather than just our nation. The Arab nations seem eager to find a lasting peace, and it would be difficult for me to prosecute our plan. Fortunately, it is in the hands of harder heads, like Elias. He has no doubts, and he can argue the need for Jericho. He too fears the untold suffering that is about to occur, but he views it as an act of God, like the destruction of Sodom and Gomorrah. He argues that the disaster is inevitable, and that our challenge is to guarantee the best possible world afterwards. I can't really disagree when he puts it that way."

"How bad is it going to be, David, and will the disaster be worldwide?" Rebecca asked.

"Do you mean, will it also occur in Texas?"

Rebecca stared at Zweig, saying nothing as tears began to well in her eyes. Then slowly they overflowed, trickling slowly down her nose and cheeks. She made no attempt to brush them away. At last she said, "Yes. That's what I really mean. I became a different person in Texas when I fell in love with George. I laughed at such sentiments before I felt them myself. But since I have been back in Jerusalem, my heart has not been in my work. I'm afraid I left it in Texas!" Trying to laugh, the tears flowed faster, and little sobs punctuated the attempted laughter. Zweig could say nothing.

"I'm not naïve, David," she went on, "but loving George has been so different for me. My interests shifted outside of myself—outside of my background, outside of my people. Perhaps being away from this land actually liberated me. Being finally free of myself made our love so intimate and new. I had feelings and thoughts with a man I had never known before. David, do you understand me?"

"I think I do," Zweig replied, "but I have to confess what you probably suspect, that your experience in these matters greatly exceeds my own. I have never experienced the kind of love you feel, Rebecca, and sometimes I despair that I never will. Please don't be offended, but what you have just said makes me feel as if I could love you."

Rebecca sympathized with the admission of emotional inadequacy. "You will certainly find love if you will just open yourself like this to others. It's a wonderful and complete feeling. In the three months I have been back in Jerusalem I have felt empty and unhappy. So, here I am, working on a plan I do not understand for the future welfare of Israel while my heart remains in Texas. Oh, David, sympathize with me."

"I do, Rebecca," Zweig replied. "I have only my parents in Louisiana. They are, and always have been, full of love for me. Now they have no knowledge of what is coming, and I dare not warn them."

"That frightens me, David," Rebecca carried on. "What will happen to the people of Texas? To George? Will the Joshua Factor be crucial to him, too?"

"Yes, it will," Zweig replied, "and we do not quite know enough to foresee how bad it will be. But for sure, it will be very rough in Texas. At the best, the present way of life there will screech to a halt and many will die. At the worst, all will die, including us, despite our preparations. But you should not try to give warning, except perhaps by a personal letter scheduled to arrive at most a few days in advance. Please don't try to give any warning now. A warning will do very little good to anyone, and it could upset the entire plan."

"David. Listen to me," Rebecca said urgently. "I want to go

back to Texas. I want to be there when it happens. I have changed, and I don't belong here any longer. I want to be with George when it happens. Please help me."

"I don't see what I can do to help," Zweig said.

"Help me get back to Texas. I can't leave the country without good reason," Rebecca explained. "They will not allow anyone within Jericho to leave the country without a special pass showing that their mission has relevance and urgency."

"But what would I have to do?"

"I've been thinking about it for weeks, David, and I have what seems to me a sure way," Rebecca replied eagerly. "Do you know of the European Space Research Organization?"

"Yes, but not much."

"They have an office in Geneva that is concerned with global environment. They are especially concerned with weather satellites and with the earth's atmosphere—also with stratospheric chemistry. That's where Nicolet is, the Frenchman who has published all those papers about chemical effects on the stratospheric ozone layer."

"Oh, yes," Zweig said. "I know the group you mean now."

"Well, you could get me a pass to visit them to discuss models of the ozone layer. We are doing a lot of that work in Jerusalem as part of Domestic Preparations."

"Why not ask them to send you then?" Zweig asked.

"There are two reasons, David. In the first place, they have developed their own pecking order in Domestic Preparations, and I am just not important enough to be sent. They would have to discuss the reason for my going, and so on. The second reason is that I dare not enter the U.S. on my passport. The CIA and FBI will both be watching for any sign of me, just as they would for any sign of you."

"Yes. I've thought of that many times," Zweig admitted.

"David, I need a fake passport. I've brought some passport photos with me. You can get a forged passport made as a member of Jericho. I'm sure you could do it. I've decided to use the name Ruth . . . Ruth Weissmann. Please try to get one prepared for me. I would use my real passport to go to Geneva on official Jericho business. But once there, I would use my forged passport to catch plane from Geneva to New York. There is a good Swissair flight daily, and one to Chicago, too. Israeli Security would never see my forged passport, which I would use only in Geneva and in New York."

Zweig thought about it a while. "It sounds very possible. I've been to so many top meetings now that all of the military men know me They've been using a lot of forged passports, and I'll talk to someone I know well to see if he can provide me with a passport for an agent to get from Geneva to the U.S. I'll tell him we need it for a quiet scientific reconnaisance. He is so busy with so many things that I feel certain he'll get it for me with no questions. He'll probably even regard it as a request from Elias Hirschberg. There is so little time left that everyone is worrying less and less about security and more and more about the practical preparations still to be finished. I'll try it, Rebecca."

"Oh, David! Thank you so much. It will mean so much to me. I just want to be in Texas when my fate is determined. My only other wish would be for more knowledge about what to do there to help us survive. Could you give me any advice?" Rebecca said.

"Yes, I can," Zweig replied, "but you must in return promise to do something important for me."

"What is it, David?"

"I will give you a full set of instructions when we meet for the last time, at least if I can get the passport," Zweig explained. "With it I will give you the telephone number of my parents in Baton Rouge. When you get to Austin, you must promise to telephone them and give them the warning. Tell them how to make as many preparations as possible to try to outlast the worst part. They are so old I fear they will not make it. Also, I want you to tell them that I am well and that I hold them close to my heart." At the sudden thought, Zweig's chin quivered. His face fell and his reddened eyes stared blankly at the ground.

"Of course I will," Rebecca promised, moved by the visible waves of emotion that Zweig was trying to hold back. She threw her arms about him and hugged him to give comfort and to express her gratitude. Slowly, uncertainly, he held her, too.

To the strollers along the Yarcon, David Zweig and Rebecca Yahil looked for a moment like many other pairs of lovers exchanging embraces. Very much relaxed by the catharsis of having made their emotional requests, they sat and talked for two hours more. They were the best two hours either had experienced since returning to Israel. They both loved Israel, but each had also found that the joy of life depends on the loved ones who make it meaningful.

Twenty-Two

The pursuit of Zweig's ideas so gripped Reynolds that, when National Academy secretary Chuck Stevens telephoned him about another meeting of the ad hoc Committee on Atmospheric Pollutants, Reynolds had wanted to beg off. It had seemed a poor time to waste three days and a lot of energy on a committee meeting. What changed his mind was concern with the Earth's atmosphere itself. Because it is the buffer between Sun and life, it would moderate any solar change. There could be no better time than this committee meeting to talk to people who knew more about it. Barry Dunn, who had recently published models not only of the Earth's atmosphere but also of all the planets, would be at the meeting. Why not confide in him? The more he thought about it, the more Reynolds found new reasons to attend a meeting he would otherwise have skipped.

Dunn's office in the theoretical division at NASA's Goddard Space Flight Center in Greenbelt, Maryland, had, at least, a nice view of the surrounding trees. Following the two-day committee meeting at the National Academy, Reynolds was pacing the floor of that office pointing to some chemical equations they had written on Dunn's blackboard.

"Damn it, Barry," Reynolds said with uncharacteristic impatience, "I know that your models show that *modest* increases of solar output will not greatly disturb the ozone layer. But isn't that because those models assume that the nitrogen in the atmosphere cannot be broken up? Aren't your calculations restricted to the near ultraviolet, where it would affect only the oxygen?"

"Sure, that's so," Dunn replied. "But we know that the Sun emits very little *hard* ultraviolet. The solar ultraviolet light is incapable of disrupting the nitrogen molecule."

"OK. But consider a very violent event that would raise the Sun's hard ultraviolet radiation by a big factor, perhaps a million times. I am talking about a big burst of photons having energies higher than ten electron volts. These photons would disrupt a lot of N_2 molecules," Reynolds added, pointing to two processes he had written on the blackboard. "Either one of these processes would set loose nitrogen ions," Reynolds went on, "and those ions should be destructive to ozone. Either one might rather quickly deplete the ozone layer."

"Maybe," Dunn agreed. "In fact the nitrogen monoxide molecule will also destroy ozone by this reaction." He carefully wrote the chemical equation, $NO + O_3 \rightarrow NO_2 + O_2$, on the blackboard underneath Reynolds's suggestion.

"What I would suggest doing," Dunn went on, "would be to run my atmospheric computer program with abnormal solar conditions. The nitrogen-destroying reactions are in the program. They have just never been important. A much higher flux of ultraviolet photons could have so many other effects that I would rather just run the program, which has the physics already built into it, and see what it says would happen."

"That would be perfect," Reynolds said. "Will you call me in Austin as soon as you've been able to do it?"

"Sure," Dunn replied, "but why wait? The program is ready to go. I can submit the job right now. It will take me ten minutes to punch a few cards changing the input data to the larger ultraviolet flux. Then we'll go have lunch and it will be done when we get back."

"Great!" Reynolds agreed. "Then I should change to the 6 o'clock flight to Dallas out of Baltimore. Can I use your phone to make a reservation?"

"Sure," Dunn said, "just give me some idea of what to put in for the solar ultraviolet. I need that before I can punch the cards."

"I have a guess at it here in my briefcase," Reynolds said. "It's based on a model of what will happen to the solar photosphere when a strong shock wave hits it. Here's my graph of the flux I would expect. Instead of trying to incorporate it in full detail, however, I think we can approximate with this portion here." Reynolds pointed to the key portion of his graph.

"For God's sake, George," Dunn exclaimed, "that's about a million times its normal level. Solar flares are not that strong. I wouldn't want to be around if that were to happen!"

"That's something else I want to talk to you about over lunch," Reynolds responded grimly to Dunn's good-natured remark. "For now, just plug in the numbers and let's see what comes out."

Half an hour later the computer was working on Dunn's program while the two men were sitting in the Goddard cafeteria having lunch. Dunn was astounded to see that Reynolds was serious about the possibility he had described. Dunn had supposed it to be just another academic exercise by a free-thinking astrophysicist, whereas Reynolds talked as if this sudden outburst were actually about to occur.

Reynolds was deadly serious. Before their meeting he had been to Fitzgerald's office, and the pressure there had left him worried. Fitzgerald had been so agitated by Reynolds's speculation about a solar outburst that he had again recommended bodyguards. That was a strange suggestion considering that he could not explain why they might be needed. Fitzgerald's lack of candor so disturbed Reynolds that he had resolved to fill in the blanks in his own understanding as best he could. There seemed no choice but to confide in Dunn.

"Listen, Barry," Reynolds said, "there are many aspects to this thing that are classified by the Defense Department. But I think I have to level with you on my seriousness about such a solar outburst. Do you remember the murder of Fred Cowan about four months ago?"

"Sure. That was a shock!" Dunn replied.

"Well, the data tape that we found was genuine," Reynolds said. "On it was a sure sign of an exponential growth of the solar neutrinos. The FBI asked me to create the story, which you no doubt heard, that I thought the tape was a fake prepared by the murderer. Don't ask me why. They're stumped by the case. Anyhow, I stood by that story for the press, but in the meantime I have been wondering what could cause a sudden rise of neutrinos. What I have come across is a thermonuclear instability that should happen every million years or so within the Sun. A consequence of each instability would be a sudden luminosity rise for the Sun and a sudden outburst of hard ultraviolet. I want you to keep this to yourself, since it's only speculation, but I also want to tap your experience with such matters in planetary atmospheres. Do you think there is evidence for a periodic destruction of the ozone layer and of life forms on Earth?"

"I'm positive of it," Dunn replied, much to Reynolds's surprise. "I normally wouldn't be aware of some of these things, but I happen to have been working with Sol Spiegelman, a biologist at Johns Hopkins, about the extinction patterns of floral and faunal species. You've probably heard, for example, that about one-third of all living species on Earth became extinct at the end of the Cretaceous Period."

"Yeah. I've heard of it, but I don't see what you can make out of that," Reynolds replied.

"Well, something very severe must have happened. One idea that we've been exploring is periodic reversals of the Earth's magnetic field. While it's reversing poles, the magnetosphere cannot shield the Earth from cosmic rays, so the Earth's radiation level could go way up at such times," Dunn carried on. "But let me tell you the more astonishing fact that Spiegelman has come up with. Microorganisms that live in water are very intolerant of ultraviolet radiation. Some of them live on the edge of death even in normal times. By using deep-sea cores obtained from various places in the ocean bed, Spiegelman was able to correlate the fossils of these dead organisms with the epoch in which they died. In a nutshell, there are eight species of these fossils that are now extinct. They died off in huge numbers at six different times within the past four million years. These times of extinction seem to be evenly spaced, moreover, and they occur at intervals of about seven hundred thousand years. Every seven hundred thousand years or so, something happens to extinguish whole species of these marine organisms. It is almost surely ultraviolet, since they are quite hardy except for a low tolerance to sunburn. His conclusion is that something happens to the Earth's ozone layer every seven hundred thousand years."

Reynolds was stunned. "Good God! The mechanism I'm working on should be repetitive, every million years or so. It's quite a coincidence. I can't calculate exactly how often it should occur, because I don't know enough about a very peculiar structure at the solar center that causes it. So my calculation is not accurate enough to tell the difference between a million years and seven hundred thousand years. All I know is that it should repeat about that often."

"Maybe you're on to something, then," Dunn said, warming to Reynolds's enthusiasm. "What else do you know about your mechanism?"

"Well, frankly, Barry, it should be getting stronger," Reynolds replied. "I might as well tell you that my model has a black hole at the center of the Sun. Don't laugh—it's not as crazy as it sounds. And the black hole is slowly growing more massive as more and more of the solar center falls into it. Because the black hole is growing more massive, it makes each subsequent outburst more violent."

"Oh, I get the idea," Dunn said with noticeable sarcasm. " A black hole, huh? I was having a hard time imagining big changes in the sun. You've made it all so clear."

"Damn it, Barry, I do mean it!" Reynolds said, for once in his life too stressed for jokes. "I know it sounds crazy. That's why I ask you to keep quiet about it. I'll disclose it soon enough. I just don't want to sound like a fool. No one else will believe it, either. So for the time being, will you keep it to yourself?"

"Sure I will," Dunn replied, "unless you tell me it's going to happen again this week! Ha!"

"Very funny," Reynolds acknowledged. "Tell me, when did this last extinction of marine fossils occur?"

"That *is* a coincidence," Dunn said, looking a little more serious. "As near as Spiegelman can tell, it happened about seven hundred thousand years ago."

Both men laughed; but the laugh didn't last very long. Instead, they both sat silently, thinking. Maybe it was an accident that the evidence of the fossil extinctions indicated that the world was due for another one. But Cowan's tape of the rising neutrino counts convinced Reynolds that something was happening *now*. The big, tantalizing coincidence would be for a new instability to have arisen in just that decade in the long and unrecorded history of man when his technological capabilities had risen to the point of being able to detect the telltale neutrinos. It would be a staggering coincidence, but not a scientific reason to rule it out.

"You know, George," Barry Dunn finally said, more serious now, "there are two things about Venus and Mars that come to mind, and that I now see in a new light."

"What's that?" Reynolds asked.

"It's the hydrogen in Venus's upper atmosphere and the eroded canyons on Mars. Venus is closer to the Sun than the Earth is, so it's much hotter. In fact, as you know, Venus's atmosphere is very thick and very hot. But it seems to me that all of its atmospheric hydrogen should have evaporated into space if that atmosphere is as old as the solar system. The presence of hydrogen suggests that the atmosphere is much younger than Venus itself. Only a few million years old. It is as if something in the last several million years has heated Venus and caused its atmosphere to suddenly become so enormous—by vaporizing its oceans and the CO_2 trapped in carbonate rocks."

"Maybe I have a reason for that," Reynolds interrupted. "My model suggests that this thing can happen to the Sun only about one hundred times or so. Here's why. For most of the lifetime of the Sun the black hole is too small to cause the thermonuclear runaway to grow to critical size. During that long history the Sun shines peacefully. But the black hole keeps slowly growing by swallowing solar gas. Once it does grow to critical size, the thermonuclear explosion at the center can only happen about one hundred times before it becomes so energetic that it will disrupt the entire Sun. But one hundred million years is much less than the age of Venus. All such outbursts should be relatively recent.

Therefore Venus's atmosphere should be recent. How many layers of these fossils can Spiegelman find?"

"Only six," Dunn answered. "He and I have assumed that this is because of motions of the ocean floors. The problem with that explanation is that the geologic evidence shows that the new ocean floors are being created much more slowly than we require. We don't really know why there are no fossil extinctions older than four million years."

"Maybe it really has happened only six times," Reynolds suggested. "In that case the first solar outburst would have occurred only four million years ago. If the Venus atmosphere was outgassed at that time, it would explain why it's only four million years old."

"That's brilliant! It really fits, George," Dunn exclaimed. "It could even provide a natural explanation for Mars. I can't believe it!"

"What about Mars?" Reynolds asked, eager to understand that problem, too.

"I reckon that Mars is now in an ice age," Dunn replied. "There's almost no water in its atmosphere, but its canyons look like they were eroded by flowing water. It could be that these flare-ups of the sun have melted the ice frozen in the Martian surface, and that the resulting flowing water made the canyons."

"Fascinating," Reynolds said. "Let's see. How much more solar heat would Mars need to melt the water frozen there?"

"I couldn't say exactly without a calculation," Dunn replied, "but I think the Sun would have to get about twice as bright."

"That fits," Reynolds observed. "That would have been enough to have made life tenuous on Earth without eliminating it entirely.

"You're making me nervous, George," Dunn exclaimed. "Let's go back and see what the computer has to say about the ozone."

The computer news about the ozone was unmistakably bad. The ozone layer would be almost totally eradicated by the solar flux that Reynolds had predicted.

Throughout the return flight to Dallas, Reynolds pondered the problem. Could the whole horrible picture be true, or was he being carried away into a scientific wonderland? According to the computer the dosages of lethal ultraviolet at the Earth would exceed the normal levels by a factor of about one thousand. Reynolds did not know how severe that would be, but it seemed likely to him that most outdoor species would simply not survive. He would just have to take the matter up with biologists at the University of Texas.

The key question remained whether the event was really happening. The bizarre business of the false policemen in the Big Bend and Rebecca's warning to disavow the tape publicly could suggest that *someone* believed that the tape was significant. Reynolds felt that Fitzgerald must know something more. The CIA might be responsible for the sordid events. No wonder, then, that he had constantly pestered Reynolds seeking his views on what might be going on. The hardest thing was deciding what to tell Fitzgerald now. How much should he trust him? Maybe he should say no more unless his computer models of the Sun actually reproduced explosions. Without such results the idea would be hard to believe. Or maybe he should blow it all to the newpapers. Maybe that wouldn't be so dangerous. It would at least get all ideas out into the open. It was another Friday, and tomorrow was to be the first of August, the target deadline that Fitzgerald had set for the results of Reynolds's models of the sun; but when Reynolds had left on Wednesday for Washington, he and Polkinghorn had still not been able to get the computer program to work completely.

Reynolds had been thinking more and more about ways to determine whether a thermonuclear runaway of the Zweig type could actually be occurring, and, if so, exactly when it would happen. He had been able to think of only one way to find out for sure—through data from a functioning solar-neutrino experiment. The neutrino evidence remained the most puzzling thing about the Cowan murder. He had for that reason discussed with Argonne National Lab the possibility of getting their neutrino experiment running again. He had been disappointed to find that they had very little enthusiasm for restarting an expensive experiment that had achieved only negative results. Reynolds had not at that time told them the truth about the data on the tape, but he had ascertained that it would take a year or more to get the Big Bend experiment refurbished.

He could think of only one other possibility for getting the needed scientific facts—the Israeli experiment in the Negev. He had never been sure what had happened to the plans for that experiment, but he could contact Jamil Koren to see if, by any chance, they had a working experiment that could shed some light on the mystery. They had once built and tested a downsized pilot experiment with an inadequate amount of gallium. If the runaway at the solar center was actually beginning, the neutrino flux would now have to be rising at an astonishing rate. According to Cowan's tape, the flux had been doubling every two weeks in January. If Reynolds's hand calculations were correct, the flux should now be doubling almost daily, and it would be so large that even a modest experiment would detect it. It was frustrating to realize that there existed adequate techniques for finding the answers, but no operating experiment to measure them. Furthermore, the neutrinos seemed to provide the only way to get the answer in advance. All the other effects would come mixed together as one sudden and unexpected shock.

Of one thing Reynolds was certain. It would be 11:00 P.M. by the time he got to Austin. He would go straight to bed, but tomorrow morning he would do another round of heavy shopping for survival supplies, and then he would go to his ranch house near the Llano River to spend the rest of the weekend. There at least he could prepare, like some insane visionary, for an unpredictable outburst of the Sun and he could think in peace about what to do. For the first time in his life, Reynolds wondered if he were behaving rationally. How had the world's crazy prophets felt as, throughout history, they had predicted doomsday just around the corner? Reynolds seemed to himself to be in control of his thoughts. He did not imagine that his mind controlled the universe, or that he had a privileged communication from one that did. He was, he reassured himself, simply confronted by a barrage of mysterious and perhaps coincidental facts that all happened to fit an unsuspected scientific drama. At such times the bright 6:30 A.M. sunrise over the hills, the quiet nights, the deer, the cacti, the spiders, the plants, and the river were just the companions Reynolds wanted.

Twenty-Three

At about 11:00 on Wednesday morning, August 5, Ralph Polkinghorn burst into Reynolds's office.

"It's working, George! The program works," he said. "I submitted another revised program last night, and when I went by this morning I found out that it had run for twelve minutes calculating the explosion."

"Great news!" Reynolds said, rising to clear his desk for the computer printouts that Polkinghorn was carrying. "Have you looked over the results?"

"Sure have," Polkinghorn replied, then quicky unfolded the CDC printer paper to the main results. "The explosion looks about as we expected, with a few refinements we didn't think of. It really starts when the temperature reaches 100 million degrees near the black hole. It takes only another second for it to run up to the peak value, which was 183 million degrees for this model. The detonation wave then moves outward in the disk faster than it moves outward in other directions. We hadn't thought of that. It makes a kind of explosive doughnut—one that is traveling outward to larger sizes. This sets up a shock front whose leading edge is traveling outward along the solar equator. I drew a figure of it at three seconds after the detonation wave begins to roll. Here it is. You can see that the shape's about elliptical at this time and, at the equator, has reached a radius of about ten thousand kilometers." Polkinghorn placed the figure in front of Reynolds.

"What are these? Contours of equal temperature?" Reynolds asked, pointing to the concentric ellipses.

"That's right," Polkinghorn replied. "You can see how they bunch together at this boundary between high temperatures and normal temperatures. That's where the outward moving shock

211

wave is at this moment in the calculation."

"If the postshock temperature is ninety-five million degrees, the shock must be quite strong. Does the thermonuclear runaway go fast enough at that temperature to keep it hot even while the center expands?" Reynolds asked.

"It looks marginal," Polkinghorn said. "The cooling due to expansion will occur almost as fast as the heat liberation from the thermonuclear reactions. So I can't yet tell if there will be significant nuclear burning throughout the sun after the shock wave has heated it. I had instructed the computer to stop when the shock wave reached ten thousand kilometers in radius only to save computing time. We can run it again and let it go all the way."

"This is good, Ralph," Reynolds said admiringly, "but why wasn't the code working previously? What change did you make last night that enabled it to finally work?"

"It was in the radiative transfer, as I suspected," Polkinghorn replied, "but it just took me longer to find it than I expected. I'm not accustomed to thinking of the logical operations except in spherical symmetry. But at a fixed distance from the black hole it's hotter in the disk than it is above the disk. As a result the iterations on temperature were being mixed with the iterations on radius. It was a mess."

"What did you do to fix it?" Reynolds asked.

"I set the problem up in terms of surfaces of constant temperature instead of surfaces of constant radius. Then everything worked."

After a moment's thought, Reynolds switched gears: "I just thought of something that will make the detonation continue to lower temperature. So far we have only proton captures by carbon in the calculation. But when we get below fifty million degrees the reaction of ^{3}He will still give a lot more heat."

"That's right! I didn't put the helium-3 into the calculation because I couldn't get the basic disk explosion to work. But now that it works, I'll put it in. It should give almost 10^{14} ergs of energy per gram of matter! That will keep the interior hot and keep the wave rolling toward the surface," Polkinghorn said.

"I think we've got it, Ralph!" Reynolds exclaimed. "Here's what I want to do next. First put the helium-3 in to see how much difference that makes. Next, change the black hole mass and see how much difference that makes to the explosion. What black hole mass are you using, anyhow?"

"It's ten times the mass of the earth—about ten-millionths of the sun's mass," Polkinghorn replied. "That's how massive it needs to be to have caused the neutrino flux to have been too small all these years."

"Oh, yeah. I remember choosing that mass from our experience with the spherical nonrotating models," Reynolds said thoughtfully. "Now we should calculate the neutrino flux in this rotating model just before it explodes so that . . ."

"I already did that," Polkinghorn interrupted. "Cowan's experiment could never have detected the neutrinos until the buildup to the explosion was well under way. Just roughly it looks to me as if Cowan's detection of the rising neutrino flux would have corresponded to the time when the disk temperature had grown to forty million degrees."

"Fantastic, Ralph! How long would it take for the disk temperature to rise from forty million degrees to the full explosion?"

"Several months, maybe half a year. In other words, just about now!" Polkinghorn said with amusement, still not knowing that this was more than just another calculation.

"I'd like to see how tightly we can pin that down, Ralph. Let's try to reproduce the rate of growth of Cowan's counts. We have about five months of old data while the neutrino flux was growing monthly. Suppose we identify those data with the neutrinos from the disk as it gets hotter, and just see if any of our models can reproduce its growth. Unfortunately, we don't know what black hole mass to take, because we've only looked at the effect of its mass on the spherical solar models. About ten Earth masses seems right, but I want you to run the program with one Earth mass, five Earth masses, thirty Earth masses, and one hundred Earth masses. Then, at least we can see what the size of the black hole mass has to do with the thermonuclear runaway. I suspect that in the past, when the mass was only one Earth mass, the disk would not have been big enough to cause the thermonuclear runaway. Let's see what we can find out about these things," Reynolds concluded.

Polkinghorn, who had been watching Reynolds intently, was suddenly silent. Then he asked, "George, are you thinking that Cowan's observations could actually be due to a heating central disk? I thought the data were faked. Are you thinking there may actually be a black hole in the sun?"

"Look, Ralph, I know it sounds far out," Reynolds replied, "but I *do* think it's possible. We have to at least admit it as a possibility if it explains the facts. Cowan's data are genuine. It was my rejection of it that was faked. There is even more to it, stuff that I don't want to get into right now. Paleontology, evolution, etc. Let's just make the calculations."

"But if that's the correct explanation," Polkinghorn persisted, "we would expect some sudden changes in the Sun before long. This could be of tremendous importance to mankind and to all life on Earth."

"I know that, Ralph," Reynolds replied slowly and calmly. His eyes fixed on Polkinghorn's in total honesty. "That's why I want to get those calculations done immediately. We need to be sure that the model fits the facts. So let's get back to the computer, OK?"

"OK. But if this thing shapes up, we had better warn people," Polkinghorn said.

"Right," Reynolds added, "but we don't want to make fools of ourselves. Think how difficult it would be to convince anyone. Let's talk it over after we have more of the pieces of the puzzle in place."

"That makes sense," Polkinghorn agreed. "I'm off to the computer then. There's a lot that needs doing."

"That's the idea, Ralph. I'll be in my office the rest of the day, so call me or come back with each new result. I'd rather know the result of each calculation as you get it than wait for them all at once. So keep bothering me, will you! Oh, and one more thing—don't tell anyone yet about the tape. The FBI told me to give a false opinion. I'll explain that some other time."

When Polkinghorn left, Reynolds sat thinking for quite a long while. He realized now that he did believe that it was happening. Years of experience in such astrophysical problems and the intensity with which this one had dominated his thoughts made him certain of the outcome of Polkinghorn's calculations before they were even done. For a fleeting second it seemed that the whole scientific history of civilization had been nothing but a preparation for this moment. Quickly Reynolds blinked aside the mystic impulse. There were still some uncertainties. Which black hole mass would work best in reproducing Cowan's data? When would the outburst be expected to occur? It would likely be soon, unless he was completely mistaken.

Fitzgerald's insistence that he know by the beginning of August kept coming back to Reynolds. It was as if Fitzgerald had independent evidence that something terrible, or at least important, was going to happen in August. The coincidence was, as Polkinghorn himself had observed, that August was also indicated by the neutrino counts.

What could Fitzgerald possibly know? Only a highly trained scientist could put together the scenario that Reynolds had uncovered. Cowan might have understood the significance of the neutrino flux, Reynolds speculated, and maybe overzealous CIA schemers had silenced him for some reason. Perhaps Cowan and Zweig had predicted this thing together and had both been silenced. The only evidence Reynolds had that Zweig was still alive came from the photographic identification by Avis Car Rental in Midland. But why would Zweig have rented the car in the name of

Davidson unless he had wanted to be untraced? And if he had planned the murder, surely it would not have been so primitively done. That made no sense at all. It seemed that Zweig had planned to sneak away, perhaps hiding the fact that he had ever been at the mine, but that the murder had been sudden and unpremeditated. How could Zweig have had a fake Swiss passport ready? That sounded like CIA work. Fitzgerald had probably gotten the pass for Zweig, who had then surprised Fitzgerald by leaving without fully explaining what he thought was happening. Or perhaps, Reynolds thought on, Zweig had not actually made the numerical calculations. Computer work was not his style. No, that made no sense either. If the CIA wanted solar models computed with black holes at the center, they would have simply done it. They could hire a scientist and persuade him to work in secret. That they had approached Reynolds for a thematic study of Zweig's work confirmed that they didn't know what they were looking for. They may have been responsible in some way for the murder, but they were still in the dark about the scientific possibilities. That much seemed clear.

Despite his growing mistrust of Fitzgerald, Reynolds was certain that the next thing to do was to talk to him. The best thing seemed to be to tell him the truth, that their computer program was now working and that they were seeking the answers to many of the obvious questions. Since Fitzgerald so clearly wanted to know the answer, Reynolds had nothing to fear from him by revealing that the answers lay just around the corner. He called Fitzgerald immediately.

Fitzgerald was noticeably excited at hearing that the computer models now generated exploding objects at the solar center. He was, as usual, impatient to have a full explanation of all of the implications, expressed as certainties rather than as scientific probabilities. In this, Fitzgerald was typical of the political personalities of Reynolds's experience, demanding the certain meanings, the sure implications, the undeniable consequences, and the simple solutions. He wasn't interested in the caveats, the reservations, the reminders of facts still unknown, and the caution that not enough measurements exist to be certain of the answers. This state of affairs was, in the present case, exactly as Reynolds wanted it. It seemed safest for Fitzgerald to expect more answers to be forthcoming, but on a schedule that Reynolds could give only as he himself found his own way.

"Well, when do you expect to be able to estimate the time of the outburst more accurately?" Fitzgerald asked.

"We still have to see how the sun behaves with black holes of differing masses at its center. This will take several days. We have

215

to see how strong the outgoing pressure wave will be when it hits the surface. This means we have to put more nuclear reactions into the program and we have to examine the hydrodynamics of the shock wave. The many questions concerning the response of the outer layers of the Sun would take years to answer. But we will try to have a simple-minded estimate in another week or so," Reynolds replied.

"Can't you be more definite about when this eruption will happen?" Fitzgerald asked.

"Sure. If I had a functioning solar neutrino experiment," Reynolds replied. "How many times do I have to explain it! If we had reports of the rate of arrival of solar neutrinos from the time of Cowan's murder up until today, I think I could tell you exactly when, and if, the outburst would occur. I have been thinking of telephoning a Dr. Koren in Israel. He was starting a new neutrino observatory a few years ago, and I just don't know if they ever got that experiment to work at all or if they gave up on it. The talk was that they had to discontinue their efforts because they couldn't afford to buy the quantity of gallium that they thought they would need."

"How much gallium would they have needed?" Fitzgerald continued.

"About thirty tons," Reynolds replied.

"Thirty tons! That sounds like a lot."

"About half of the world's annual production," Reynolds confirmed.

"Maybe I can check for that in the past reports of the gallium markets," Fitzgerald offered. "But please do not call Koren yourself!"

"But we've got to find out if he has any data," Reynolds insisted. "Even an experiment of much lower sensitivity than Cowan's could detect the much higher rate that would be arriving today if this model is correct. Why not phone him?"

Fitzgerald was silent a moment, clearly thinking again. Reynolds was alert to his hesitations, and to indirectness in his answers.

"No. Don't," Fitzgerald came back. "I think it might be dangerous for you, at least if Israeli Security is involved with Cowan's murder. These things are better left to the CIA. Let me try to find out with our agents there. In the meantime, keep all of this to yourself, and call me as you learn more."

"Look, Jimmy. I've been thinking of the danger we're all in if my computer models are correct. Have you thought that this might be quite serious to the entire world?"

"No, I really had not, because I have had no reason to think so until now; but, sure, what you're describing could affect the entire world. This possibility comes as a shock to me. When you're more sure about what's happening, we must decide what to do. If there seems a real threat to human welfare, perhaps the CIA should invest money to get Cowan's experiment repaired. It's not our usual line of work, but we could justify it. Call me immediately when you know anything more. Just say nothing to anyone else."

"All right, Jimmy," Reynolds reassured him, being made aware once again that Fitzgerald was indeed a worried man.

As he placed the receiver on its cradle, Fitzgerald admitted to himself that he was bewildered. He reconsidered the latest reports. The Knesset had just declared August 20 National Civil Defense Day in Israel, urging citizens to prepare supplies for it as they would for a sustained siege. The photos that they had provided of troop movements in Libya were almost surely fraudulent. U.S. spy satellites did not confirm them, but they did reveal massive covert Israeli military mobilization. He could find no explanations of the surprising rate of massive purchases of odd items. Now he should check on gallium purchases. He could not identify the mysterious Joshua Factor, referred to several times in key CIA reports, or even if it was related to David Zweig, to the Cowan murder, or to solar neutrinos. Although Fitzgerald had been exploring the inference that Zweig's science had something to do with the Joshua Factor, he had found no clue that decisively related the two. He had imagined the Joshua Factor to be a new weapons system, or a tactical surprise, probably based on black holes. And now, just when it seemed that he might be about to expose such a weapon, Reynolds had confronted him with a problem bigger than politics. It could be a problem for all mankind. This was decidedly not what Fitzgerald had been hoping for.

Fitzgerald's nerve was deteriorating. Perhaps he should go at once to the president. The CIA chief would have no tolerance for complicated rumors. But he still feared damaging his credibility in top Washington circles. Reynolds's models would seem to be only the harebrained cries of some far-out academic scientist. You could no more take that kind of warning to the president of the United States than you could take him a prediction of the Second Coming. What Reynolds had said of the need for a solar-neutrino experiment made sense. It seemed the only way to know if something was happening inside the Sun. Fitzgerald immediately ordered a check for any massive purchases of gallium during the last five years.

He spent the rest of the day in worried indecision. It carried on into an evening of too many martinis and a final exhausted stumble into bed. He had been able to make only a single decision that he would stick by. Tomorrow he would work through CIA agents in Israel to see if they could determine whether they actually had a functioning solar-neutrino experiment. Fitzgerald made one shrewd conclusion from what Reynolds had told him: if the Israelis also did not have a working experiment, then the target date, perhaps the August 20 National Civil Defense Day, could have nothing to do with anything as wild as an eruption of the Sun. They simply could not pinpoint the date without that knowledge. In that case he would just forget Reynolds's calculations. The thought that made sleep difficult was the alternative: what should he do if Israel did have an operating solar-neutrino experiment?

It was late on Monday, August 10, when a message from Robert Parker, CIA agent in Jerusalem, arrived from a CIA front, an air cargo business in Athens: "High security gates exist around laboratory of Dr. J. Koren in Negev Desert. Failure at seeking purpose; tentatively suspect nuclear weapons except for lack of shipments in and out and lack of obvious industrial capability. Birds see nothing. Local security have refused any explanation. Sorry. R. P."

On August 11 Fitzgerald revealed this brief report to Reynolds. Reynolds expressed increased urgency, because he knew that Koren's planned neutrino observatory was to have been constructed in the Negev. At the same time Reynolds related the results of his latest calculations. The black hole mass should lie somewhere in the range of five to ten times the mass of the Earth. There would have been only about five previous eruptions in the entire history of the Sun, because a black hole of the required size today would have grown massive enough only about four million years ago to be able to cause a thermonuclear runaway at the center. And finally, the rate of increase in Cowan's counts before the murder, coupled with a black hole mass of ten Earth masses, suggested that an eruption would happen sometime between July and September. It would be impossible to be more precise without experimental data. So that was where the matter still stood, only slightly better defined than it had been previously. There seemed no way of rendering the uncertain more certain. So Reynolds, without telling Fitzgerald so, decided to telephone Dr. Jamil Koren himself.

During these days the entire state of Israel was being prepared for the weeks to come. The M−60 tanks were moved by night to camouflaged sites near the Sinai, from where they could strike swiftly at the Suez. Peace-keeping U.N. observing teams were temporarily denied access on grounds that, no matter how feeble, had to be negotiated. Special storage tanks of gasoline were deployed, and a fleet of military gasoline trucks was filled and moved into position. The most advanced air-to-ground rockets available from the U.S. weapons empire were loaded onto the jet fighters, all made combat ready. Guided-missile launching sites were programmed for the attacks on Egyptian, Libyan, and Syrian air bases. Suitable food and water were distributed and stored in every home in preparation for National Civil Defense Day. On the assumption that the outburst would not be too severe, new seeds were ordered planted under tinted glass shields with special irrigating provisions. A whole host of small but well-planned survival strategies were deployed by a well-disciplined citizenry. It was very obvious to all informed observers that many things were happening at once, and foreign military security men were openly alarmed. Reports poured in at the CIA. On the other hand, Israel was always sharpening its defenses, so in these matters of degree it was hard to be sure what was happening. In a surprise move, the government dramatically announced a plan for a total withdrawal from Lebanon, with details to be agreed to during the U.S. secretary of state's next visit.

On the fifteenth of August two cautious persons met again on the banks of the Yarcon River in Tel Aviv. David Zweig carried with him an Argentine passport in the name of Ruth Weissmann. A photograph of Rebecca Yahil was affixed beneath the Argentine seal. He also had the letter from Jericho authorizing her mission to the European Space Research Organization in Geneva, where she was needed to consult on the ozone problem. Rebecca herself had been able to obtain five thousand Swiss francs from Jericho Jerusalem with a carefully trumped-up expense statement for the emergency studies in Geneva; and she had telephoned Swissair in Tel Aviv to reserve a seat for Ruth Weissmann on SA 111 from Geneva to New York. As they exchanged the necessary papers, Zweig told Rebecca that Reynolds had disappeared.

"But how can you be certain?" Rebecca asked. "Perhaps he is just out of contact for a day."

"We don't think so. Here is what happened," Zweig explained. "Yesterday morning Reynolds telephoned Jamil Koren about the solar neutrinos. He may have figured out what is going on in the Sun. Koren, of course, said that we have no experiment working, but he tried to ascertain why Reynolds was so interested. I fear that Reynolds tricked Jamil by making his answers just provocative enough that he gave away his anxiety by further pointed questions. Jamil is a dedicated scientist, and not well suited to matters of guile. Naturally he informed Jericho of Reynolds's inquiry and added his opinion that Reynolds intentionally provoked him with statements about military interest in neutrinos. Hirschberg instructed our men in Austin to pick Reynolds up, but when they arrived at his home on Friday evening Reynolds was gone. An open can of beer was sitting, still cool, by the sofa and the radio was playing, but Reynolds had vanished. We have looked all around Austin and he is nowhere. Our only clue is that his car is also gone. We called Dr. Polkinghorn, with whom he has been working, but he said he knew nothing of his whereabouts."

To Rebecca, this was unsettling news. But she had an idea where she could find him. So she said, "David, it does not change my plan at all. George is there somewhere, and maybe he will appear by the time I can get to Austin."

"Are you sure, Rebecca?" Zweig asked. "Shouldn't you just stay here with us? You may end up alone in Texas at a time when each of us will need all the support available."

"I'm going, David. It's all I care about. I feel that my entire life has been but preparation for this moment. And don't forget that your parents need help, too," Rebecca said.

"I had not forgotten," Zweig said. "God be with you, Rebecca." He embraced her, hiding as best he could the tears welling in his eyes.

The call to Jamil Koren had confirmed Reynolds's suspicions, despite Koren's disclaimer. For about ten minutes they had discussed the scientific problems confronting a gallium solar-neutrino experiment. Following Reynolds's provocative statement that the U.S. military had asked him to find out whether Koren's experiment was working, Koren had become suspiciously obsessed with ascertaining why it was that they wanted to know. Hanging up, Reynolds had decided immediately to act. He would warn people of the danger. But he must also guard himself against the group responsible for Cowan's murder. Unquestionably, someone would soon be after him.

He had put a note in Polkinghorn's mailbox and had told him by telephone to pick it up before going home that afternoon. He had then typed a short letter to the president of the United States, including a careful handwritten explanation of what he expected from the sun. Following that Reynolds had hurried home to pack the Porsche for a getaway to his ranch house. About 5:00 P.M. two CIA men had come to Reynolds's townhome, identified themselves, and explained that he would have to come with them to preserve security on his life. Reynolds, suspicious and not a little frightened, had agreed calmly, but when he went to his bedroom to pick up a clean shirt, he had quickly lowered himself from his bedroom balcony and raced to the Porsche. The CIA men had slowly moved in to keep an eye on him and realized what had happened only in time to hear the car racing out of the parking garage. They saw the speeding Porsche approach the end of the block, but they never stood a chance of catching it. The State Highway Patrol could eventually have picked up Reynolds's car, but the CIA had no ready access to state agencies. They thought they would find him later.

At about the same time, Ralph Polkinghorn was reading an astonishing note from Reynolds:

Dear Ralph:

You may never see me again, because my life, like all life, is in danger. I am convinced that our models of the Sun are correct. There will actually be an outburst of the Sun, perhaps even next week. Other evidence confirms it. It will be very severe and the people must be warned. Forget about trying to warn the whole world. That's impossible for a scientist. Instead call Bill Roberts at the *Austin American-Statesman*. He did the story on the Cowan murder and the tapes. I have the true story written out on the enclosed sheet. Give it to him. Urge him to warn the people of Texas particularly to prepare as best they can for the dangerous times to come. I've given survival suggestions on another enclosed sheet. It is urgent that the *American-Statesman* publish these survival instructions. Other papers will pick it up. Don't look for me. No one knows where to find me. Make your own family ready. Best of luck to you,

George

P.S. Attached is a copy of my letter to the president.

Reynolds had made copies of his explanation and survival hints and put them in an envelope addressed to the president and marked "Urgent!" He had smiled even as he wrote the word. He had also made another copy for the president's science adviser. He had marked it "Special Delivery" and stuck four 22-cent stamps on each, being unsure of the correct postage. He had prefaced this information with a letter:

Dear Mr. President:

Do not fail to give this handwritten note immediate and full attention. Attached is a brief account of a world-wide natural disaster to occur within two weeks. Quick references to my credentials are obtainable through the National Academy of Sciences and through General Hughes of the Air Force. Scientific clarification may be obtained through my colleague here, Dr. Ralph Polkinghorn, who should be contacted by your office only. I myself have fled because my life is in danger from men I cannot identify. James Fitzgerald III of the CIA knows the most about whatever is going on.

Respectfully yours,
George Reynolds
(Professor of Astronomy)

As he sealed the letter, Reynolds had felt a momentary remorse that he could not take more direct action. His technique for communicating seemed almost comic. But he knew well that making believers of government would be a lengthy, frustrating business. From the telephone conversations with Koren and Fitzgerald, he could see that unwelcome people might soon be looking for him, and he had made up his mind, for better or for worse, not to be found for a while. Finally, as a diversionary tactic, he had left a note on his office door saying simply that he had gone to Houston to play in a tennis tournament and would return on Monday or Tuesday. Following the subsequent CIA encounter in his townhouse, he decided to wait it out in his ranch house.

Reynolds had in fact done almost all he could have done. Neither he nor anyone else could have convinced the world to prepare for a catastrophe. Without the solar neutrino experiment, the warning would appear to be only a personal prediction of a bizarre doomsday by a specialist member of society. It was a warning that the world had heard too many times, from visionaries having no scientific grounds at all. For Reynolds it had been a long and increasingly frightening problem, one in which the sum total of the circumstantial evidence had left him a believer. But he had had the advantage of knowing from the beginning that Cowan's tape was authentic and that unprecedented events in the Sun would be necessary to explain the curious history of the neutrino counts up to the time of Cowan's death. So the body of circumstantial evidence had meant more to Reynolds than it could have meant to an impartial and rational committee of scientific laymen. Perhaps the sum total of Reynolds's efforts would be only that they had led him to his small Hill Country shelter, where he waited to learn Nature's reply to the most interesting problem of his life.

On Sunday, August 16, the *Austin American-Statesman* published Reynolds's warnings, along with an interview with Ralph Polkinghorn in which their revolutionary model of the Sun was explained in as much detail as possible for a daily newspaper. It aroused high local interest, but understandable skepticism. In Austin only an occasional person took Reynolds's warning seriously enough to make any preparations. Still, it was a far higher percentage than in Libya, where local news agencies also picked up the story. After all, they had been listening to fanatic predictions all summer, and they were hardly newsworthy any longer.

Reynolds was able to enjoy a quiet weekend at his ranch house. He worked hard on a variety of small repairs and amused himself with trying to invent ways to make the building a better survival station. The manual tasks were soothing. It was clear to him that he would not be going back to Austin any time soon, and he was relieved that he had not shared the knowledge of this place with colleagues at the university. Of course his bank knew, but the CIA wasn't likely to pursue him that thoroughly, especially with the outburst imminent. On Monday, August 17, Reynolds did venture into the little town of Castell to buy an assortment of tools, hardware, and dried and canned foods. For delivery the next day he ordered new strips of highly reflective roofing, four large containers of water, which he reasoned he could easily refill at night from the good well in the yard, and, as a devil-may-care afterthought, twenty cases of beer. Pearl beer from San Antonio was not his favorite, but it was the only one he could get in quantity in Castell, and it was as good as most. He bought several boxes of ammunition for his rifle, a dozen boxes of matches, and last, a copy of the Sunday *American-Statesman*, where he read his story. He was at first relieved to see it, but later much amused at the thought of going back to the university if his prediction proved incorrect. He could not but think of the great eighteenth-century Swiss astronomer Loys de Cheseaux, who had eaten crow after predicting Christ's Second Coming for the year 1749. Reynolds was, in reality, as calmly in control of himself as he was in the middle of a big tennis match. He appreciated in good spirits the fantasylike nature of his actions, and felt an amused kinship with Alice falling down that dark tunnel. At least the timing was right, because it was his usual vacation period from now until mid-September and, if nothing happened, he would slink back into Austin with his tail between his legs.

On the very same day, Rebecca Yahil arrived on a Continental flight from Dallas to Austin. She still had eight hundred dollars in her pocket from the remaining Swiss francs exchanged in New York. She took a taxi to Reynolds's street and got out half a block from the townhouse. Her heart thumped wildly as she looked down the street to the bedroom window she knew so well. Home! After paying the fare, she walked slowly along the street carrying the modest suitcase full of special survival apparel. Her first thought was for her own safety and she looked for signs of men watching the house. How beautiful the street looked to her! The huge pecan trees were heavy in their August fullness, and the late

223

afternoon sun of the blue Hill Country skies caressed her face. At the house she walked nonchalantly into the garage, where she placed her suitcase on a small rack above the place where Reynolds's car was usually parked. Tears welled in her eyes as she saw something she had never expected to see again—her bicycle. It leaned against the wall where she always left it, locked with a chain and combination lock. George had left it there, next to his own. She walked to it and tested the tires as if squeezing a long-lost loved one. The pressure was low, so, sobbing like a fool, she pumped both tires with a small hand pump attached to the frame. Much relieved by her outburst, she looked calmly around the building. She saw no one. She looked intently at Reynolds's window and saw no sign of activity. Clearly, Reynolds would not be there, since his car was gone, but still she stuck to her planned routine.

She walked briskly to the corner, where she knew there was a telephone booth.

"Dr. Reynolds's office," came the secretary's reply.

"This is Janet Jones, one of the summer school astronomy students. I've been wanting to talk to Dr. Reynolds. Is he there?" Rebecca asked, her heart thumping.

"No, he's not here today," came the reply.

"I just can't find him at all," Rebecca said. "I went by his office twice yesterday, but he's never in."

"We haven't seen Dr. Reynolds this week," the secretary answered.

"I need to ask him about his course this fall," Rebecca persisted. "Can I reach him somewhere?"

"No. I really don't know where he is," was the exhausted reply, as if she was repeating something for the hundredth time. "All kinds of people have been looking for him, and no one knows where he is. But I have information about his course here in the office."

"Thanks, I'll come by." Rebecca said, and hung up.

Then she dialed Reynolds's home number. It rang two minutes before she hung up. She walked to the Texaco station and asked the attendant, "Do you know how I could get to Llano?"

"You don't have a car?" the attendant asked, and when Rebecca nodded, said, "Why don't you rent one?"

"I don't have a driver's license," Rebecca said.

The man eyed Rebecca with interest. "I'll be through with work at 7:00 p.m. I could drive you out there."

"My God!" Rebecca thought, then said, "No, thanks, I need to arrive tomorrow. Is there any way to get there?"

"Well, sure," he said. "You could catch a bus at Continental Trailways, over on I-35. They stop at Llano on the way to Abilene."

"Thanks very much," Rebecca said, walking quickly away.

She telephoned the Trailways office and found that they did have a bus at 9:00 A.M. the next morning that would stop at Llano on its way to Abilene. She found that she could even take her bicycle along if she paid an extra baggage fee. Much relieved, and with her plan fully in mind, she returned to the townhouse. Finally, after looking around, she went up to the door. After a moment of listening, she knocked. Surprisingly, she heard someone coming to the door. Suddenly she wanted to run, but she had to wait to see.

"Yes?" said the swarthy young man who answered the door.

"Oh," Rebecca said, looking surprised. "I wanted to see Dr. Reynolds. Is he in?"

"No. He is not here just now. He may be back soon. If you will tell me what you want from him, I will try to telephone him to let him know."

Rebecca thought feverishly. "My name is Ruth Jones, and we're supposed to be doubles partners in a tennis tournament this weekend. Will you tell him I came by? He knows my number."

The man looked at her thoughtfully. Rebecca turned, walked briskly down the steps, waving a friendly goodbye. Slowly the man closed the door. Knocking at the door had been a foolish curiosity, and Rebecca escaped unrecognized only because Reynolds had taken the photograph of her to the ranch.

Resolving to fool around no longer, Rebecca quietly eased her bike out of the garage and rode quickly away to the Trailways Bus Station. Later that night she went back to get her small suitcase, and the next day, August 18, she traveled with bike and suitcase to Llano.

From Llano she would pedal all the way to the ranch house near Castell. He had to be there. She was certain.

Twenty-Four

Fitzgerald calculated that he hadn't had a day off in months. It hardly mattered, since he was too geared up to think about relaxing. Work would always find an avenue into his free weekends. It was his style. He played golf with politicians and squash with government bureaucrats, so business always slipped into the locker room talk. Laura was his only frequent nongovernment companion, but with the escalation of the Joshua Factor crisis their schedules had become hopelessly askew, and he had hardly seen her.

Just four days after Reynolds's disappearance, and in the thick of Capitol Hill concern about Fitzgerald's suspicions about Israel, he rose early one morning to drive neither to the office nor to Washington for appointments. He wheeled his three-year-old Datsun instead into an auto dealership in north Washington, where he made an instant transaction and drove away in a BMW 528i.

From there he drove to Laura's apartment building near Georgetown and whisked the astonished woman away in the new car. "Like it?" he asked, as they whizzed toward the Maryland coast.

For Fitzgerald the day was half inspiration, half apprehension. Laura was to be inspiration, the new car was to be inspiration, the beach was to be inspiration. He needed to talk, and he hoped the inspirations would balance the apprehension. Today he couldn't face the investigators of Israeli foreign policy, or the Defense Department chiefs, or the National Academy of Science consultants, or the secretary of state, or even the president. Fitzgerald had become a hot commodity in Washington lately. Everyone was clamoring after him. So, it was in an uncharacteristic act of bravado and self-interest that he had scheduled himself away from the office for the entire day. If the president wanted to talk, he would have to wait. Fitzgerald was escaping for a consultation that he hoped would yield some clarity, some good sense, and some peace of mind. Speeding along the interstate, he could converse with one of the two people he needed to talk to. George Reynolds, the other, was nowhere to be found. His only regret was the need to sacrifice Laura's impartial insulation from his work.

Laura was a calm, clear-thinking, energetic modern woman. Her style contrasted with Fitzgerald's. She often took days off during the summer. She called them "sanity days," and the spark of spontaneity in Fitzgerald's suggestion appealed to her. It was a lovely hot Wednesday, and although Fitzgerald took a roundabout route, savoring the new car longer, the interstate melted before them and they were soon basking in sun and neutrinos.

Slender, tan, bikini-clad Laura lying beside pale Fitzgerald on a beach towel had no idea that she had been whisked midweek to a beach retreat to play confidante and conscience. But Fitzgerald had lost the practice of recreation, and the conversation drifted almost immediately back to business like the tide sneaking back across the shore. In the current flood of uncertainties, he needed to check his assumptions. Fitzgerald always guarded CIA confidences carefully, and Laura never asked questions about CIA business. So, it was a double irony to be lying in the sun, describing Reynolds's model of the impending solar outburst, and telling Laura secrets that no one now wanted to hear.

"It breaks down this way," he said taking her hand. "I have spent months deciphering the existence of rapid military preparations in Israel. Each day additional intelligence confirms that my theory is correct. Israel plans action on a big scale, probably timed to take military advantage of a natural occurrence. But the event Reynolds predicts would be more than disastrous weather. It would be a complete catastrophe."

Laura was unconcerned. That was reassuring. An enthusiastic swimmer, she interrupted his narrative several times, running into the water to cool off. Returning this time, shaking water all over him, she asked in mocking disinterest, "Weren't you telling me something about the end of the world?" She was refreshing.

There hadn't been much humor in recent government consultations. Far from it. But Fitzgerald's own themes found little space for humor, either. He told Laura one by one about the events that had been dominating his life—the Cowan murder, Zweig's disappearance, the Israeli strategy, and now Reynolds's prediction and disappearance.

"Laura, I'm deflated," he said. "I could prove my point independently of Reynolds. If I had gone to the secretary of state two months ago with a bold argument, I would have walked away with credit for my work, for exposing a mixed scientific and military strategy of significant proportions. But no, I pushed and pushed to understand the entire plot before playing my hand, and what Reynolds has come up with is so radical that it overshadows my entire argument. No one in Washington wants to believe it, or even that the Israelis believe it. They all look at me as if they wish that I would just go away. We could have really twisted arms in Israel. If I had Reynolds now to convincingly explain the Israeli scientific assumption, I could still press my case. Instead, my hands are tied. So here I am at the beach begging for commiseration."

Laura teased him about his internal struggle. "Reynolds jumps out of a window and runs away, and your reaction is to run out and buy a new BMW. Selfish, isn't it? What about the rest of the world?"

"No, no, when I heard the news about Reynolds I went out and got very drunk. I had a terrible hangover the next day. The BMW came later," he protested, but she wouldn't let up.

"You only bought the BMW as a hedge against the possibility that Reynolds's prediction is true. It's like a last request, I know it. I suppose you'll trade it in for a station wagon if nothing happens."

"Nothing is going to happen," he snapped, his pride wounded. "If you like I'll hammer our initials on the fender. JF loves LL, so the car can never belong to anyone else."

"Is that what you believe? That nothing is going to happen?" she insisted seriously, brushing aside the romantic overture.

"Yes," Fitzgerald answered, but his reply was a policy decision. He had brought Laura to the beach to explain his quandary and to hear her instinctive reaction. He needed an objective voice to balance the scales of his uncertainty. "Reynolds left me with a terrible predicament," he explained, "with not enough evidence to believe his prediction but just enough to suspect it. I am not *all* government department. I am anxious about the human aspects of this thing. You're a voice of humanity for me. What do you think? Should I be warning people?"

"James," she answered seriously, "I have never wanted to know CIA business, and I didn't want to learn this. I'm not comfortable influencing a decision that might affect so many lives. Still, I'll give you my opinion. When the blades of grass become conspirators, it means that you're working too hard. Reynolds's prediction is one man's guess, and an inconclusive one at that. Its a chimera, paranoia with an astrophysical twist. You told me that he himself was uncertain during your last conversation. His disappearance doesn't change anything but the circumstantial evidence.

"I don't believe the prediction. Nuts are always predicting catastrophes. Look at this beautiful sun. Do you really think it will be

229

a raging explosion next week? Who is George Reynolds, anyway? I think you have a soft spot for him because he taunts you, he calls you "Jimmy," he's cavalier, and you admire it. I think he's got your number. How can you be sure of him? After all, he was involved with an Israeli agent, and the ideas that are the basis of his doomsaying are the ideas of a murderer.

"Leave it, James. There is no torch to carry. If Reynolds is so sure of himself, let him warn the world. What could you do, anyway? Stand on a street corner wearing a sandwich board printed with a warning?"

"There are some things," he began.

"Well, what have you done so far" she asked, "and what have other people said? Is there a consensus among your government cohorts?"

"There is. They dismiss the prediction as inconclusive; but no one in government is ever interested in preventing an implausible tragedy. I want your view, as a humanist, as someone who can listen to the facts and formulate an answer that is not a political decision. I've taken the case to every responsible agency that I can think of. They all wait for someone else to abandon ship first. The days are ticking past now like a rocket countdown. There isn't much time to get going, if any."

Fitzgerald concluded his dismayed narrative by revealing to Laura what had transpired since Reynolds's disappearance. His men had brought a nervous and uncertain Ralph Polkinghorn to Washington as a scientific stand-in for Reynolds. Although he certainly understood the computer model of the solar outburst, he had not worked with Reynolds through any of Zweig's papers, or through the classified material about a black hole in the solar system, so he couldn't be an effective spokesman. He wasn't even convinced himself. He had been in a great state of anxiety, however, and kept insisting on his concern for his wife and daughter. Fitzgerald had finally sent him home as useless.

The National Academy of Sciences had received copies of the urgent communiqué dispatched by Reynolds as he fled, but time scales meant nothing to them. They were forming an ad hoc committee to study the problem scientifically, but even their preliminary conclusions would be months away. From them Fitzgerald heard once again the phrase that had become etched on his brain, "Without a functioning solar neutrino experiment . . ." So he exerted some lively pressure for funds to reopen the experiment. It would be well beyond the crisis period before it would function again, but everything was a long shot now.

The greatest obstacle to his efforts was the State Department. The secretary of state had just finished organizing the terms of agreement for a complete withdrawal of Israeli troops from Lebanon. He would not hear Fitzgerald's suggestion that the Joshua Factor reduced his tremendous personal political success to an irrelevance. He patently rejected Reynolds's solar analysis as unsubstantiated.

"It's a big government, and it moves slowly," Fitzgerald remarked with resignation.

"But what does it matter," Laura asked excitedly. "If there is no outburst, maybe there will be no military action."

Fitzgerald nodded. The connection between the two ideas was purely circumstantial. "Unless their military plan is based on something else. But I'm a cautious person!" he said. "In fact, my brother has a vacation house upstate. We could go there for a few days next week, as a precaution. If anything did happen, I'd like to be with you."

She smiled, "No thanks, it's not personal, but my life is in Washington; it's the museum, it's the history of art, it's my social world. I am a creature of culture, not a pioneer. If this life goes, I guess I go, too."

They were both silent for a moment, enjoying the ocean, the clouds gathered on the horizon.

"It's the same for me," Fitzgerald answered at last. "No job, no joy."

Laura was gathering the beach things. "I'm starving," she said plaintively. "And it seems to me that after chewing my ear all day about your troubles, you owe me a good dinner."

"Sure," said Fitzgerald, "it's part of my plan. Try to not get sand all over my new car, will you?"

Twenty-Five

On August 21, the morning sunrise was clear and cool as Japan rotated eastward into its rays. Near Osaka, at the solar observatory, a visiting Israeli team of scientists was exercising its grant of observing time on that day. When it was certain that the rising sun was still normal, they reported that fact by telephone to Tel Aviv. They knew what to expect and of the need for secrecy. Their constant vigil awaited a signal that would change the world. The computer predictions, based on Jamil Koren's up-to-date neutrino counts, estimated that the fireball would occur shortly after sunrise in Tel Aviv, but when that time arrived, near midday in Osaka, no sign had yet been seen.

The solar observing teams around the world were an important part of the coming attack. Israel's troops slept with the assurance that they would be warned immediately if the outburst occurred during the night. To a person they sensed the strangeness, the poetry, of awaiting a sign from heaven, of replaying the legends of their history. Beneath the normally rising Sun, they calmly breakfasted and moved to battle-ready stations. There was no rush, because the tactical plan called for the strike to begin one hour after the outburst.

Two hours later it happened. Giora Kozkov was watching the solar image, one meter in diameter, reflected onto the viewing plate in the observation room, when flashes of light appeared, first at the north pole of the Sun and only a few seconds later at the south pole. There were irregular flashes that seemed to spread from the pole to the equator, leaving behind two brightly glowing caps that grew in size until they merged to cover the entire Sun. At the first sighting he alerted his colleague at the color photometer, who quickly confirmed that the Sun was growing rapidly brighter in blue light. After the shock wave dissipated itself over the entire surface, it left behind a solar surface of about 10,000°C, in contrast to the normal 6000°C. Kozkov quickly entered these measurements into the computer and started the programs for the photospheric properties. Another colleague communicated these findings over the open telephone line to Tel Aviv, where the defense minister confirmed that the sighting had just been made there, too. It was 8:45 A.M. Tel Aviv time, perfect timing from a military point of view. Thousands of small computer programs were instructed, "Run."

Early-morning scouting aircraft had hardly had the time to have reported the considerably larger than usual number of tanks and trucks amassed toward Suez, so well hidden were most of them. Nor was it obvious why all of Israel's fighter-bombers were lined up at airports waiting to taxi into takeoff positions. But at 9:45 they all began to move. Planes swept off low toward targets in Egypt and Syria, carrying full loads of rockets and bombs, and the tanks and troops moved vigorously toward the Suez Canal. Missiles shot out of their silos on radar-guided paths toward the large air bases, where they would scream in with the first devastating strikes a bare minute in advance of the Israeli bombers.

On the ground an excited Middle East watched the Sun, half in awe and half in terror, as it momentarily shot to ten times its normal brightness, then within ten minutes settled back to a luminosity about three times the normal value. Routine life came to a fascinated halt. Unalerted troops in Libya became quite hot by 9:30, beginning to feel the extra warmth of the special morning. Egyptian troops milled about excitedly, shedding apparel to keep cool, joking nervously, unaware that death was speeding in several guises through the morning air. The Israeli troops tightened up their protective covering and calmly endured the rising heat, which already exceeded that of an ordinary midafternoon. By 10:00 the rocket and air strikes began to pummel their targets in northern Egypt and, within another half hour, zeroed in on surprised air bases in Libya. Quickly, the defensive troops positioned themselves as best they could, but in their routine summer clothing. Those planes that could get aloft went up, but the airborne glare on clouds and sand was too bright for the normal jet-fighter goggles. Few ground soldiers had sunglasses, and none were prepared for the deadly solar ultraviolet rays, which were, from the outset, ten times their usual intensity, and worsened as the ozone layer began to be eroded by the disrupted nitrogen molecules. By afternoon, the sun was severe. Its normally friendly glow was now a fierce torch.

The world wanted to object to Israel's attack but could not do so effectively. In Moscow and in Washington attention quickly turned to the severe dangers to the populace and sounded domestic alarms. The Russians threatened on the first morning to intervene; the Americans called for an immediate stop to fighting, and warned the Soviets that the U.S. would not tolerate outside intervention. By afternoon, however, a scant five hours later, the entire world had all but forgotten about this latest Mid East war, and by the next day civil defense teams around the world were busy everywhere trying to alleviate the effects of the catastrophe.

The Israeli troops cut through Egypt with frightening ease. The skins of the defending soldiers burned ferociously, and many were practically blinded by white-out. The will to resist was, over the next three days, reduced to zero by sunburns, the intolerable bright light, and the intense heat. Through careful planning and determination, the Israelis maintained the assault. Planes were kept in the air, attacking and refueling in waves, while the advancing military in white uniforms and protective helmets moved steadily in their wake, seizing or destroying supplies. By the third day the remaining defense troops deserted their stations and weapons, seeking only relief from the sun and treatment for their burning skins. For most it was too late, and severe burns, heat prostration, and dehydration began to take lives, first in the thousands, but soon in the millions. Food and water lines broke down, as Israeli troops quickly seized all such survival necessities.

For Israel, the war was a carefully computed operation. Its biggest military problem was simply the small size of its armed forces. They took over all manner of weaponry in their advance, either securing arsenals or destroying them. They worked continuously on the distribution of water and food to the fronts, much of it obtained from the lands they raced through. On the sixth day the ground troops reached Libya, where they joined paratroopers established the first day in front-line positions. There was no longer any organized Libyan resistance. Central military planning was impossible with soldiers dying of heat and the population in panic. Syria could not organize retaliation on the eastern front. Israel took the lands it wanted without the need to fight, realizing that the hardest part would be to hold them when the sun returned to normal.

Death overwhelmed the world's populations in savage and unpredictable ways. In Los Angeles, seven million people were without emergency preparations. Grocery stores tried to close when food distribution began immediately to break down, so panicking people invaded and looted them. Within five days the food supply of Los Angeles was exhausted. Any shipments of food were ambushed by snipers who stopped trucks to make off with what they could. Vegetables and fruit rotted at their sources, and cattle died in the fields. Chaos and terror strode the city like new angels of death. Gangs roving the streets at night robbed those who still had supplies. People desperately defended their own, and the millions of privately owned guns came into use in a world gone mad. Water supplies failed and thirst stalked the dying and the sick. Disease spread rapidly from corpses rotting where they fell. By the beginning of September, there were two million dead in Los Angeles alone, and four million sick, starving, and thirsty. Cannibalism began as the first brave few dared to eat those struck down by bullets. People attempted to escape in cars, but there was no place to go, and most were intercepted by desperate snipers. All of society, so carefully constructed on the premises of law-fulness and altruism, fell victim to its own genetic weakness.

What happened in Los Angeles happened in Boston, Chicago, Baltimore, Detroit, Houston, Dallas, Atlanta, San Francisco, Phoenix, Cleveland, and Washington, D.C. The American city was, like the dinosaur, huge, successful, and dramatic, but vulnerable. And like the dinosaur, the structure of society in the modern American megalopolis never stood a chance. It fell victim to its own inflexibilities as the sudden pressures of rapid evolution found it wanting. Food supplies and distribution centers were too far from the people. Electricity supplies failed within the first week in all of the big cities of the United States, and the huge air-conditioned towers became decaying skeletons. The evolution of society had taken man far from his origins as a beast of the prairie. Instincts told him to seek food, water, and shade, but there was none. The New York Stock Exchange was silent. There were no buyers for grain futures, no profit takings on 20 percent capital gains, no speculation on world gold markets, no run on the British pound sterling. All fell together into a scorching hell.

In northern Europe the catastrophe was the same, except that there the people died with less violence. Scandinavia and the U.S.S.R. were the hardest hit, because the long midsummer days began when the Sun rose at 3:00 A.M. and did not set until midnight. Rich surface vegetation wilted and died. The highest survival rates during the first months were in South Africa, South America, New Zealand, Australia's agricultural areas, and Malaysia. The winter days there were mercifully short due to the tilted axis of the earth, and the simpler societies in many of these places met the initial crisis more easily. But even for them it was only a matter of time until, four months later, they would face their longest midsummer day.

Pockets of people survived, however. They were mostly close to the land and had dependable water supplies. George Reynolds and Rebecca Yahil were among them. They had enough food, shelter, and water to survive the late August exposure in the Texas Hill Country. The daytime temperatures rose to 130°F while they rested in their small house and bathed each other with towels soaked with water from the well outside. Their food supplies alone would last for three months, and after the adjustment of the first month they immediately began finding other live food. All of their activities took place at night, when the warm evening air felt, by contrast to day, as cool as an autumn north wind. Even so, nightly temperatures hovered near 110°F for almost a month. After four weeks, the beginning of cloud cover mercifully lowered the daytime temperatures to near 115°F, and the nights dipped below 100°F for the first time in Texas, as the days grew shorter. But the severe ultraviolet remained a daily plague.

Amazingly enough, nocturnal deer still came to the Llano River to drink, though their numbers also dwindled. The shrubs on which they grazed were badly parched and vanishing, so their population was weak and starving. Only the insects were little disturbed. They died by the hundreds of billions, to be sure, but as always they gave birth to hundreds of billions and reasserted their claim as natural heirs to the earth.

Twenty-six

*For yet seven days, and I will cause it
to rain upon the Earth forty days and forty
nights; and every living thing that I have
made will I destroy from the face of the
Earth*

Genesis, 7, 4

Of the world's history of wars, few remembered and most
long forgotten, some have been well calculated and precisely exe-
cuted, whereas others have simply boiled. This strike by Israel had
been in the first category, but the bitter fruit of meaninglessness
soon choked it. The scientific brilliance of Israel's culture could
not surmount the curse of the still unknown—how hot northern
Africa would become and how long it would remain so. How
simple a thing, our Sun, and yet how incomprehensible without
the benefit of hindsight. For all of science's success in explaining
the well studied, it remained primitively weak at predicting the
unknowns of a great event that happens, seemingly, only once. It
was not enough to conclude that the Sun's surface would be severely overheated owing to the vast energy deposited in its interior by the thermonuclear runaway. Its recovery, like that of a patient with a stroke, hinged on unknown recovery capabilities. The
dense central regions would remain inflated and would require
thousands of years to fully settle, releasing large supplies of power
in the process of gravitational settling. But the hope was that this
power would be absorbed in structural changes in the outer layers
of the Sun, allowing its surface luminosity to be more benign during the succeeding human generations of readjustment. But it was
not to be, due to the devastating strength of the shock wave that
had blasted its way through the Sun. It had left the outer layers so
hot that most of the atoms had been broken up into ions, with the
result that their opacity was reduced too much. Because of that,
convection could no longer play the role hoped for in the readjustment. There was nothing to be done but await the day when

the ions could recombine with their electrons and the Sun would cool once more.

The Israeli soldiers had lost their resolve to hold the oil fields after a month. When no sign of the Sun's readjustment was detected, scientific hopefulness could no longer support flagging spirits. David Zweig himself was stationed at the solar observatory near Beersheba, in the desert hills just a few miles from where Jamil Koren's neutrino observatory had monitored the impending outburst with such accuracy. At the optical observatory he had followed with sinking heart the postoutburst observations of the surface of the Sun. These confirmed within two weeks that the pessimism of the soldiers was well founded. The surface was just not cooling at all. At the time of the outburst, he had been tremendously excited by the rate of neutrino detections in Koren's laboratory. Before the first optical indications appeared, the neutrino flux had risen rapidly to a billion times the normal level. This rise had matched his calculations exactly, and he had understood that the abundant radioactivity was being created by the rapid capture of protons in the expoding disk at the solar center. He had been able to comprehend why the flux of neutrinos decreased by a factor of two every ten minutes after the outburst, in exact accord with the half-life of radioactive nitrogen-13, which was, by its decay, the major source of neutrinos for the entire day after the outburst. In the following days, the remaining neutrinos were due mainly to longer-lived radioactive beryllium-7, which had also been synthesized in the wake of the shock wave. Their intensity, too, matched Zweig's elaborate expectations and, despite the heat, he had been carried away by the familiar scientific joy of simply understanding what was happening.

Throughout his life Zweig had been motivated by that simple joy. As a gifted and sensitive child he had learned that reasoned understanding was the particularly human gift that had allowed him to reduce the chaos and anxiety that lies at the core of the human experience. It had become a joy to learn each new thing, thereby reducing it to the friendly world of the understood. Fastening on that primitive joy, Zweig had been able to construct an internal world that in part replaced the real external world. That is what the artist, the musician, and the chess player also achieve, each in his own way, an inner world more important than the real world. This inner importance gives to each artist the daily motivation that fuels the genius of creativity. It is a trademark of the human species that had emerged along with his brain in some long-forgotten past. So it had been that Zweig had experienced this addictive joy even in seeing the understood eruption burst forth from the sun as surely as it had from the computer. But something in that world of inner expectations failed, because understanding the outburst in no way ameliorated the daily hell of fire that it imposed on mankind.

It was the optical and ultraviolet observations that precipitated Zweig down his final path of depression. The luminous output of the Sun held steady at two and a half times its preoutburst value for a solid month, following a brief decline in the first twenty-four hours that had been due simply to the initial radiative cooling of the shock-heated surface. Zweig had grown more despondent each day as the solar telescope continued to show intense solar flares that maintained the dangerously high ultraviolet flux, now only slightly impeded by the emaciated ozone layer. As each day destroyed his hope that the solar output might relax to a more gentle level, his emotions ate at him like a dark disease of the spirit. His inner world was failing. At night he repeatedly dreamed of his uncle, whom he knew only by photograph, being burned in some Nazi oven in Poland. During the first week in September he awoke screaming from a dream when he recognized the face in the fire as that of his father, Jakob. A telephone call to the United States never got through. The world had lost its technical organization. It was obvious to all about him that David Zweig was quickly losing his mind. But no one cared. Many seemed even to blame him.

Exactly four weeks after the outburst, David Zweig lost his will to live. Outside the hilltop observatory, he walked off toward the neighboring hill, the highest near Beersheba. Sweating profusely up the hill, he began removing his protective clothing. Finally, stripped to his shorts, exhausted, and with quickly reddening skin, he reached the top. He had no recollection of why it was that he had come, or if there had even been a reason. Squinting into the distant brightness he saw Gaza to the west. How inviting it looked against the sparkling Mediterranean. "I must later go down there and get a drink," he thought. To the north, past the Carmel Hills and Hebron, he dimly recognized parts of Jerusalem. The Holy City! Childhood Bible stories raced through his brain for the final time. To the south and west lay the wilderness through which Moses had led his people. "Like Moses, I must tap a stone and have water! Where is a stick? I must pray for a stick," he thought, falling to his knees and gazing toward the Sun unaware of his hopeless burns. His eyes were so nearly blind that he saw only the Sun. Like Job, he wondered what he had done to offend God, and like Job, dreadful sores came out on his body and he sat in great pain in the ashes of the world. He never moved from the spot, as death came quickly.

At the end of September the rains began. There had been in northern Africa only a hint in the days before, when great clouds had obscured the sunset, and at night when sudden strong winds had raged across the land. In October it rained every night—huge, torrential downpours from a sky laden with water. But, during the day, the bright and deadly Sun scorched the ground again, evaporating the moisture from the parched land. Nightly the rains became more severe, and the Nile valley flooded, drowning the few million who still clung to life there.

In the Hill Country of Texas the October rains were at first a relief, and later a problem of their own. Fierce nighttime storms blew down trees and old barns, and by late October nighttime hail often pelted the land with marble-sized balls of ice. They were formed high in a chilled and water-saturated atmosphere. But still the days were unsafe with intense heat and sunlight, although increasing cloud cover began to make occasional days more livable.

No planner had foreseen this effect of the intense Sun on the oceans of the Earth. The heat evaporated huge amounts of water. Cyclonic winds and new atmospheric turbulence moved these moist air masses around the globe. In Canada and the northern United States, nighttime snow fell heavily in October, at first melting before it hit the hot ground. But as the Earth continued in its perpetual orbit of the Sun, the north pole tilted increasingly farther away from the Sun with the approach of winter. The nights grew longer and the heavy snow no longer melted. Like a white mirror, it began to reflect the still-intense daily sunlight. The heat absorption in the north fell catastrophically as snow and cloud cover reflected so much solar light back into space. Quickly an icy chill spread south through Canada, even while the temperate zones still suffered exhausting heat daily. The atmospheric water was such an efficient radiator of its warmth that it chilled quickly each night, then drifted back to Earth as ever deeper snows that packed across the surface of the land. The northern regions were simply not absorbing heat, but shielding and reflecting it away. And the fantastic tonnage of water vapor moving poleward from evaporating oceans was unparalleled in recorded history—though, unknown to most, it had happened seven hundred thousand years before.

The reflecting snow drifts built up with incredible rapidity. The Johansen family on their farm in northern Minnesota watched the snow for two weeks before it would stay on the ground in the intense daylight. On October 7, it survived the daylight hours for the first time. On October 8, a deep field of snow surrounded them. On the morning of October 9, the Johansens could not see out of their ground-floor windows because the snowdrifts had covered them. On October 10, snow covered the entire farm-house, and what began as a joyful respite became a new night-mare as the snows became increasingly intense. On October 11, the windows of the house broke and snow pressed into the dark interior. Another five feet of snow fell that night, and the family was hopelessly trapped by the now heavily compressed snow. Two nights later, the walls of the house caved in under the pressure, and none of the family could long resist the avalanchelike crush of their icy grave.

By mid-October, the levels of the Earth's oceans were lower by about a foot than they were before the outburst, and that huge mass was compacted as thick sheets of ice over the northern conti-nents. The process continued unmercifully, and by late Novem-ber, all of Canada and Russia lay under a sheet of ice about twenty feet thick. Large glaciers from even thicker layers of ice in the north slid south over the snow-covered land, so that the process of deposition was greatly accelerated. By November, Chicago was frozen in a shallow sea of ice, and on January 7, a huge glacier toppled buildings as it slid into that area from the northeast. Be-fore spring would arrive, Chicago would have practically disap-peared amid a jumble of sliding ice. It was the rapidity and scope of it all that defied imagination.

When spring finally turned to summer, the ice receded rap-idly in the intense heat along its southern borders, where the fierce sunlight was absorbed and converted to heat once again. But so good are the reflecting properties of snow that the north-ern regions never did thaw, despite the solar intensity. The thaw line receded only as far north as central Canada, exposing a dev-astating two hundred million dead in North America alone. The same scenario was then beginning near the south pole, where giant glaciers connected Antarctica with South America and Aus-tralia. The following winter the ice growth in North America was even more extensive, having a head start from the surviving ice.

And so it was to continue for several thousand years. During that time the poles of the Earth were encased in huge sheets of ice that penetrated in winter as far south as Oklahoma. At the same time the lands between the tropics suffered from the severe heat, day in and day out, with only the occasional nighttime rains to break the scorching drought. The Earth's atmospheric circula-tions were such that the atmosphere moved toward the poles, cooling and making clouds as it went. There was to be, for the mil-lennium, no place on Earth truly hospitable to life. The vast ma-jority of the human race, 3.4 billion of them, perished, leaving a mere 100,000 humans to await the day when the Sun would return to normal. In those hundreds of dark generations, civilization could not be maintained. Mankind regressed to a stone age, amid the haunting rubble of a glory that was no longer remembered.

In the abnormally hot September two years after the outburst, Rebecca lay delirious on their bed in the small ranch house. Beads of sweat appeared spontaneously on her agonized brow and ran down her cheeks and through her matted black curls. Reynolds wiped her face and shoulders once again with the damp towel, and between cries of pain lifted her head for short sips of water. He could not lose her or the life would go out of him. George felt her hot forehead and knew that fever racked her even as her now ripe belly contracted and groaned, and he cursed the two weeks of bacterial illness that had left them both almost lifeless. For the second time Reynolds stumbled to their old chest of drawers and took two aspirin from the bottle, cursing himself for not having gotten more of such a simple thing, and with a glass of water coaxed them down Rebecca's throat. She lay almost unrecognizing with 105°F fever in the 125°F afternoon. Then he toweled her again and took a drink himself before stumbling to the well to pump some badly needed water. Two hours later, in a gasp of conscious pain, a tiny head of wet dark curls burst out, and, with her whole strength, Rebecca expelled her heritage. The infant cried weakly, but clearly alive, and Reynolds placed him still with placenta into the arms of his unbelieving mother. Slowly, he washed the baby with a wet towel and cut away the afterbirth, while Rebecca, her fever down, fell into exhausted sleep. The child cried weakly and sucked its tiny fist, finding no milk in Rebecca's sick body. Reynolds mixed a little sugar into some water and fed the infant drops from a spoon. Then near exhaustion himself, he returned to fanning their dampened bodies.

Two days later, Rebecca's fever was gone. She was safe. She gnawed on a piece of the deer that Reynolds had shot and smoked the month before. Crying louder now, the infant drew increasingly more milk from Rebecca's breast. He had survived a hellish birth, and George and Rebecca named him Jakob, because he had wrestled with God and won.

In the years of bare survival to come, George and Rebecca had two more sons, one of whom did not survive, and two daughters. In their home, unlike most other small pockets of survivors, they spoke with reasoned understanding of the world about them . . . two Ph.D. scientists in a world where school no longer existed. They entertained each other with their intellect and love and wrote out many things on the dozens of tablets of paper that Reynolds had stored in the house. They lovingly nursed their babies through the hard years of infancy that were fatal to so many others. They spoke, ever hopeful, of a new life to come when the Sun would be cooler. They didn't live to see the day, but their children, and their children's children somehow passed on the same hopeful respect for knowledge and literacy that they had inherited from George and Rebecca. After one hundred years, their descendants in the Texas Hill Country constituted the nearest thing to a culture that still remained on the Earth. After two hundred years, only a select few still learned to read, but all knew that the strange markings on paper carried valuable information from those who had gone before. Their descendants shared a special sense of brotherhood and regarded themselves as tribes chosen by God to inherit the Promised Land in that distant day when the Earth would be a garden, as the legend said it once was. It was to take six thousand years.

Slowly then, civilization would begin again. At least this time mankind could discover what had happened. During the remaining thirty-eight years of his life, George Reynolds found the time and energy to write out a full description of what seemed to have happened. He and Rebecca educated their children, and they grew to understand the importance of the Joshua Papers, which, after Reynolds's death, were stored in a tight wooden chest, which became a kind of shrine. Generations would worship at that shrine, even when its meaning had been long forgotten. People in Texas would become scarce and primitive, but much knowledge was nonetheless passed on by a special few. Ultimately, when civilization had the chance to grow again, scholars of prehistory would ask what had happened. Anthropologists would decipher and study these supposedly "obscure and primitive papers" and find instead a shockingly brilliant account by an unknown patriarch and his wife . . . George and Rebecca.

Epilogue
The Missing Link

Although George and Rebecca survived in the Hill Country of Texas, the remainder of their lives and the lives of their descendants were not the idyllic adventure one might have wished for them. They were spent in unrelenting combat with elements far more severe than in the preoutburst era. They suffered through summer heat that kept them on the edge of death. They escaped only because of their intelligent life-style, evolved as a compromise with the Earth's inhospitality. Texas was only a little better off than the equatorial regions, where lack of rain-bearing cloud cover left the surface exposed to rays so intense that little life above the insect and plant world could survive without great intelligence. Fortunately, the high clouds reflected enough ultraviolet rays for plant life to survive.

Winter months were unbelievably severe at the opposite extreme. Fierce northern winds, driven by circulating currents much stronger than in the preoutburst era, drove south each winter from the ice cap, which reached in winter as far south as northern Oklahoma. Even in the preoutburst days, the changeable temperatures in northern Texas had often fallen by 40°F inside twenty-four hours in the face of a wintry Canadian high-pressure blast, but in the new winters there was no relief from the freezing sleet that beat with intensity across the land.

Four of the five children of George and Rebecca also lived full lives. This record much beat the odds of average humanity, in part because of good genetic luck, but also because of the outstanding intelligence, dedication, and love that they managed somehow to bring to their thankless task of surviving. Most newly born children died either in the fierce summertime heat or in the winter freeze.

The pattern did not relent for six thousand years, but finally opacity changes in the outer Sun began leading it slowly back to its normal benevolent output. Roughly three hundred generations of infants of *Homo sapiens sapiens* were consigned to life in a ruthless heat that was almost too severe for survival. It was, unknown to all, the same struggle in which mankind had first emerged following the previous outburst seven hundred thousand years before. The sudden forces that killed more than three billion humans were the same forces that had stimulated man into existence. Here, then, is the true tale of the data tape.

At the time of the previous outburst, seven hundred thousand years earlier, man had arisen from the animal kingdom, and his own special breath of life was breathed into him. It had happened in three major geographical pockets, in China, in India, and in central Africa, where there were simultaneously large populations of very similar offspring of the hominoid *Ramapithecus*. These descendants of *Ramapithecus* were the most humanlike of all species on Earth, because they had already been refined by the five previous outbursts of the sun into an evolutionary experiment that only they were following. But it had been the sixth and most severe outburst seven hundred thousand years ago that had almost extinguished our own ancestors. Several near kin did not survive. And it had been that last, most awful, fire that had quickly tempered man, by a miraculous selective breeding, into the grandest of all of life's experiments. It was the suddenness of this evolution and its extreme sweep that already inspired Alfred Russell Wallace, co-inventor with Charles Darwin of the theory of evolution, to suspect that some divine act had touched mankind at just that special moment of history. It will suffice, in concluding this tale, to reveal how these events had worked during the sixth outburst to bring about the very features that so puzzled Wallace and anthropologists since his time.

The migrations around the earth had been very limited seven hundred thousand years ago, so that the only sizeable pockets of this nameless pre-man were in temperate zones where the sixth outburst was much more severe than the previous five. Most of the race was wiped out, but for several thousand years new infants were born into the furnace. Most of them died in infancy. Only the luckiest survived because of a very peculiar marginal adaptability. The body temperature remained low enough only in those with the least hair, so that perspiration and evaporation could be effective. About one thousand generations of this selection resulted in smooth-skinned and sweaty man, with his superior thermostatic system. This rapid evolution was nothing more than a very severe filter for gene types already prevalent in pre-man.

Even more important was the high fatality rate among the most active infants. In the hostile environment infants were too weak to survive without a slow maturation during a year or more of quiet rest, so that a peculiar reversal of the common principles of selection happened quickly. The most active and rapidly maturing ones died subsequently of infant heat prostration, whereas the slower and more sedentary survived better, specifically because they had to be cared for by parents. Once again, one thousand generations had been sufficient to intensify greatly a genetic disposition toward a lengthy and helpless infancy. This most vulnerable characteristic of *Homo sapiens* was in fact the one that allowed him to survive.

Along with this extended infancy went a surprising correlation locked into the mysteries of DNA. Due to some ancient chance, implanted long before man, it happens that brain growth in animal species terminates substantially when infancy terminates. Sudden maturity demanded dominance of raw instincts of survival and self-sufficiency, whereas lengthened infancy allowed and even required the suppression of these instincts. For unknown reasons, rapid brain growth in all species is concentrated into a period that precedes the assertion of instincts. So, miraculously, almost by chance, the lengthening infancies were accompanied by lengthy postnatal brain growth. The new human brain grew quickly to three times its birth size, unlike the gorilla's, which grows hardly at all as he quickly matures into near self-sufficiency. Here lies the key to the puzzle of man's brain—that he needed to lie helplessly through the heat of a lengthened infancy while his parents carefully nursed his survival with techniques that they gradually came to discover and understand. In helplessness lay his strength.

It should not be thought that man appeared full blown in only a few thousand years. However, the evolutionary filtering had succeeded to a sufficient degree that the next step of the story happened with irreversible assurance over the next half million years. Saddled with weak and slowly maturing instincts, it was necessary that the small pockets develop new social structures to care for them. The strong family bond happened then, so that the infant brains could mature in safety. The adult brains, though not yet fully man, saw ever new and better ways of social organization. The families sought food together and worked together in new ways. The Sun had returned to its former gentle state, but mankind would never turn back to his previous blissful ignorance. He came truly from a Garden of Eden, and the emotions of guilt, loyalty, pride, shame, and altruism joined him for the first time. The best family units were found to be about ten to twenty in number.

Man became a social animal. His great discovery was that his most valuable resource was the knowledge shared by his family. Men taught men for the first time not merely what leaf or animal to eat, but increasingly abstract thoughts. Language was needed to convey them.

One other ingredient was needed to complete the evolution of man—routine incest. In the families of ten to twenty, sexual relations between all mature members were common. The families clung together; therefore they bred together. This form of life lasted half a million years, and the close breeding greatly amplified the selective breeding that had been begun by that great solar outburst. The skin turned ever smoother, the facial bones continued to reinforce those characteristics supporting greater brain weight, the upper cranium continued to enlarge, and postnatal brain growth accelerated. The families of man followed exceedingly similar evolutions, even as interfamilial breeding also distributed man's genes. The new gift of intelligence brought the advent of weapons and the resultant extinction of all close relatives of *Homo sapiens*, who then stood alone a great distance from the animal world from which he had exploded in the pain of a fiery birth. Indeed, the incest-dominated reproductions resulted in many bad experiments, but they mostly died out. Evolution cared not for the bad ideas. It was the single great new idea of Nature, conceived in agony, that grew ever stronger as it produced ever more dominant man. The day would even come when man would forget that he grew out of nature's pot, and he would believe that a mysterious force had placed him here with instructions to take dominion over nature.

Thus it is that the Joshua Factor might in reality be called Genesis, a great and unremembered event that drove man from the Garden of Eden and placed him forever in conflict with his own new brain. That brain grew so successfully that it possessed everywhere great powers, even in primitive tribes that hardly communicate or otherwise utilize its potential. It was this observation, that even the most primitive savage had mental powers that he had never been called upon to use in his present society, that had led A. R. Wallace to suspect that our race had been touched by the Deity. But it was not so. The missing link that Victorian biologists had already spoken of lay not in God, as Wallace supposed, but in an incredible fiery furnace around a black hole at the solar center, where matter of this universe is even now falling into new but unobservable realms from where it can never return.